ADAMS Free Library

92 Park Street · Adams, MA 01220
phone · 413 743-8345

** DID I READ THIS ALREADY? **

Place your initials or unique symbol in a
square as a reminder to you that you have
read this title.

MW					
R. M					

D1300095

WEATHERED TOO YOUNG

Center Point
Large Print

Also by Marcia Lynn McClure and available from
Center Point Large Print:

Dusty Britches

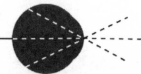

**This Large Print Book carries the
Seal of Approval of N.A.V.H.**

WEATHERED TOO YOUNG

Marcia Lynn McClure

CENTER POINT LARGE PRINT
THORNDIKE, MAINE

This Center Point Large Print edition
is published in the year 2015 by arrangement with
Distractions Ink.

The text of this Large Print edition is unabridged.
In other aspects, this book may vary
from the original edition.
Printed in the United States of America
on permanent paper.
Set in 16-point Times New Roman type.

ISBN: 978-1-62899-766-8

Library of Congress Cataloging-in-Publication Data

McClure, Marcia Lynn.
  Weathered too young / Marcia Lynn McClure. — Center Point Large
Print edition.
  pages cm
  Summary: "When a destitute Lark Lawrence appeared on his porch,
Tom Evans hired her to keep house and cook for himself and his
cantankerous elder brother, Slater. Although Tom had befriended Lark
first, it would be Slater Evans—handsome, brooding and twelve years
Lark's senior—who would unknowingly abduct her heart"
  —Provided by publisher.
  ISBN 978-1-62899-766-8 (hardcover : alk. paper)
  I. Title.
  PS3613.C36W43 2015
  813′.6—dc23
                                                      2015032384

To Sandy,
Here's to twenty-six years
of "bosom" friendship,
Treasured memories of love and laughter.
To you . . . my cherished, beloved,
forever friend.

• • •

My everlasting admiration,
gratitude, and love . . .
To my husband, Kevin . . .
Proof that heroes really *do* exist!
I Love You!

Chapter One

"I sure could use the help," the rather frail-looking, elderly woman began, "but I'm afraid I just can't afford to pay ya . . . not just now with summer endin' and winter just around the corner. Things slow to a crawl in my shop in winter."

Lark couldn't keep the breathy sigh of disappointment from escaping her lungs.

"I'm sorry, honey," the woman said. "Truly."

"Oh . . . no worries," Lark said—though, in truth, her own worries were profound.

Still, she studied the older woman a moment—her silvery hair, the deep wrinkles life had carved upon her pretty face. She was a kind woman—Lark was certain she was. Kind and truthful.

The bell hanging on the door of the quaint little seamstress shop jingled, and the woman glanced up.

"Hey there, Hadley," she greeted, smiling.

Lark turned to see a dusty cowboy remove his hat. She'd seen him before—earlier that morning when she'd been in the general store inquiring about the possibility of working there. He was young—perhaps only a year or two older than Lark—with light brown hair and blue eyes. Handsome too.

"Mornin', Mrs. Jenkins," the cowboy said. "I'm in need of a new Sunday shirt. Mrs. Jones says I ain't fit to step one foot before the Lord in the one I been wearin'. And all us boys runnin' cattle for Mr. Jones . . . well, Mrs. Jones insists on Sunday church-goin'."

"Of course, Hadley," Mrs. Jenkins giggled, her blue eyes transforming into half-moons as she smiled. "I'll be right with ya."

"Thank you for your time, Mrs. Jenkins," Lark said, forcing a grateful smile. "I'll let you help this young man. We certainly can't have him missing services."

"Certainly not," Mrs. Jenkins said, still smiling. "I really am sorry, honey," she added.

"Oh, it's nothing to concern yourself over," Lark assured her, even despite the growing sense of panic that was rising within her.

"I've got a shirt in the back that'll suit you just fine, Hadley," Mrs. Jenkins said then. "You hold on there. I'll just be a minute."

As Mrs. Jenkins disappeared into the back room of her small seamstress shop, Lark exhaled a heavy sigh of discouragement. Time was running short. Summer was waning, and though the weather was still kind and the nights yet warm, autumn and winter were not far away. She had to find some means of earning a wage—had to find some place to wait out the winter.

Tucking a tired strand of chestnut hair behind

her ear, she tried to remain calm. Yet the growling hunger in the pit of her stomach only added to her anxiety.

"Excuse me, miss," the young cowboy said, startling her from her worrisome thoughts.

"Yes?" she asked, again forcing a smile.

"I . . . I couldn't help but notice that yer lookin' for work over at the general store . . . and I'm guessin' here too," he began. "And I wouldn't want to stick my nose in where I shouldn't, but . . . are ya only lookin' for sewin' and mendin' and such? Or might somethin' else do for ya?"

"I'm willing to do anything," Lark answered. When she saw the young cowboy's eyebrows rise in astonishment, however, she blushed, adding, "Anything honorable, that is."

"Cookin'? Cleanin' and warshin'?" the man asked.

"Of course," Lark assured him, the tiny flicker of hope within fanning to a flame.

"Well," the man began, glancing to the door through which Mrs. Jenkins had exited the room, "I might know of somethin' . . . though I doubt Mrs. Jenkins would approve. Otherwise she mighta mentioned it herself."

But Lark was beyond worrying about what a woman she'd only just met might think. If the cowboy knew of work that might suit her, Lark was determined to consider it.

Lowering his voice, the young man said,

"Well, ol' Mrs. Simpson died and got planted last month . . . and I know them Evans brothers have been lookin' for someone to come in and take her place. Ya know, do the warsh, the cookin', and such."

Lark felt a smile spread across her face. Hope! She was very adept at keeping house and cooking—at looking after others. Why, hadn't she been doing it for near to four years now?

"That sounds perfect!" she exclaimed in a whisper.

"They're hard-workin' ol' fellers," the cowboy explained. "And . . . and not married . . . neither one of 'em." He glanced up, obviously worried Mrs. Jenkins would return and hear him suggesting that a young, unmarried woman might find employment in the company of two unmarried men.

Lark likewise understood his concern—and the danger. "Are they good men?" she asked. "I mean . . . I mean, are their reputations sound?"

"They ain't womanizers, if that's what you mean," he said in an even lower voice. "They run cattle on their ranch out west of town." He shrugged and continued, "They keep maybe three or four hands out there. But the cowboys all live in the bunkhouse and do their own cookin' and all, so Mrs. Simpson only took care of the Evans brothers. They're hard-workin' men, and I know they could use the help."

Lark smiled and bit her lip with hopeful delight. "Where do I find them?" she asked. "Can you tell me how to find their property?"

The cowboy smiled. "Yes, ma'am," he answered. "In fact, I got the wagon in town with me today. I could take ya out there myself. It's on my way back." He nodded and added, "I'm Hadley, by the way . . . Hadley Jacobson. And I'm no rounder, miss. You can trust me."

He offered her a rough, callused hand, and Lark gladly accepted it.

"Lark Lawrence," she told him.

"Here ya go, Hadley," Mrs. Jenkins said, entering from the back room. "Do ya think this will do?"

Lark watched as the older woman held up a new, pristinely white shirt. She wondered how long it would remain so pristinely white. Even if Hadley did only wear it on Sunday, Lark knew how hard cowboys were on clothes.

"I imagine that'll be just fine, Mrs. Jenkins," Hadley said. "Just fine. How much do I owe ya then?"

"Don't ya wanna try it on and make sure it fits ya all right?" Mrs. Jenkins asked.

"No, ma'am. Everyone says you can fit anybody by just lookin'."

Mrs. Jenkins smiled. "Well, then . . . I'll take two of your hard-earned dollars for the shirt, Hadley." Retrieving a length of brown paper from beneath a counter, Mrs. Jenkins began to carefully wrap the shirt in it.

Hadley smiled. He shoved a hand into the front right pocket of his well-worn trousers and retrieved two silver dollars. He placed them on the counter as Mrs. Jenkins tied the parcel with twine and handed it to him.

"Thank ya, Mrs. Jenkins," Hadley said. He plopped his hat back on his head and smiled. "You have a good day now."

"You too, Hadley. I'll see ya on Sunday," the woman giggled.

"Thank you again, Mrs. Jenkins," Lark said as Hadley opened the shop door, causing the bell to jingle again.

"Don't you worry, honey," Mrs. Jenkins said. "Somethin' will turn up for ya."

"Yes, ma'am."

Lark picked up the old carpetbag protecting the few things she owned. Smiling at Hadley, she passed him, exiting the store as he held the door for her.

"Mrs. Jenkins," Hadley said, touching the brim of his hat and nodding to the seamstress.

As Hadley helped Lark up onto the wagon seat, she glanced into the seamstress shop. Sure enough, Mrs. Jenkins stood at the window—a scowl of concern on her already wrinkled brow.

Lark knew the woman was disapproving of her riding off in a wagon with a cowboy she'd only

12

just met. Therefore, she could just imagine what the sweet old seamstress would think if she knew Lark's intention of seeking out the possibility of working for two unmarried men. Still, the ox was in the mire; the toe was in the trap. Lark needed work and shelter for the coming months, and every other venue she'd tried offered nothing.

So she simply straightened her posture as she settled next to Hadley on the seat of the wagon—simply did not glance back at the disapproving gaze of Mrs. Jenkins as Hadley slapped the lines at the back of the team of horses.

"Is it far?" Lark asked as Hadley drove the wagon out of town.

"Nope. About five miles is all," he said.

The cowboy seemed nice enough—trustworthy. After all, hadn't he just purchased a new shirt for Sunday church meetings? Still, as ever, Lark was wary. It was a difficult thing—to always be in the company of strangers—to try to sift out the ones that could be trusted from the ones that couldn't. Still, Hadley seemed nice, and he was a church-going man. Therefore, Lark attempted to remain calm where Hadley Jacobson was concerned—tried not to worry about the fact she was about to ask two solitary men for employment.

The sky was beautiful in its cloudless blue. Lark inhaled, relishing the clean scent of dry air, High Plains grasses, and wildflowers. She felt a sharp pang pinch her heart—disappointment in knowing that soon the green and colorful things of summer would be gone. Autumn held its own unequaled beauty, and winter snow often glistened like stars. Yet summer was warm, warm enough to allow a traveler to sleep comfortably under a midnight sky.

Lark smiled as she gazed out across the plains, over the endless sea of prairie grass and flaming Indian paintbrush. She could hear the meadow-lark's echo, the music of lines and traces as the team pulled the wagon, the low rumble of the wagon wheels over the dusty road, and it soothed her.

"It's beautiful out here," she said.

"Yeah," Hadley agreed, smiling. "It lets yer soul rest a bit."

Lark inhaled once more. It was a beautiful day—a beautiful road to follow.

"I hear the Evans brothers have been pretty ornery to work for since Mrs. Simpson passed," Hadley said. He shook his head and chuckled. "At least, I hear ol' Slater's been ornery. Ol' Tom, he's a good ol' boy . . . always smilin'. But I seen Eldon Pickering in town last week—he cowboys for the Evanses—and he told me that if it weren't for the time o' year, he'd be movin' on . . . lookin' to ride for another brand. I guess ol' Mrs. Simpson dyin' tossed them Evans brothers right into a twister."

Lark frowned. "Are . . . are you trying to

encourage me . . . or discourage me?" she asked.

Hadley chuckled and shook his head. "Just thinkin' out loud, I suppose. Mrs. Simpson, she was like a mama to them ol' boys. I think she'd been with them for near to ten years. May be that they just miss her. Maybe that's what's makin' 'em so ornery."

Lark giggled. "Again . . . I can't decide if you're trying to give me hope or scare me."

Hadley smiled. "Oh, they need the help. I just talk my thoughts too much. My mama always said I did." He paused a moment and then asked, "Anyway . . . where ya from?"

"East," Lark answered.

"East?"

Lark nodded.

"East where?"

Lark shrugged. "Just east."

She was grateful Hadley didn't press her further—that he accepted her simple response—accepted it or understood she did not want to offer him any further details.

Lark looked to the horizon—to the blue sky, green pastures, and approaching end of summer.

Ornery or not—bachelors or not—she needed to find some kind of employment. What choice did she have? She needed shelter, even more than she needed wages. Sleeping under trees and bathing in creeks was fine in summer. Even food could be scrounged for in winter—enough to exist, at least.

15

But shelter—shelter was absolutely necessary, especially on the southeastern plains of Colorado. As the wagon rumbled along, Lark admitted it was shelter she needed most.

"Now, when we get to the Evanses' place, don't you let ol' Slater scare ya off. He's just a moth-eaten old bear hide. It's his brother ya wanna be speakin' with . . . Tom. He's the younger of the two and a heap more friendly." Hadley chuckled. "I doubt he'd have the heart to say no to ya, even if they were gettin' along on their own . . . which they ain't. So you talk with Tom. Ask for him if Slater gets to ya first. Tom will do right by ya. I'm sure of it."

"Thank you for your help, Mr. Jacobson. I do so appreciate it," Lark said. She frowned and looked to the carpetbag she held in her lap. "You've been so kind . . . and to a stranger." She smiled up at him, and he winked at her.

"Plenty are the times I've been a stranger, ma'am," he said. "You know how us cowboys are. One brand quits suitin' us . . . then we're a stranger once more lookin' for another brand to ride for."

Lark smiled and nodded. It was true. In the towns Lark had known since traveling out west, it was often she would see cowboys doing exactly what she was doing—looking for work and a place to winter. Hadley smiled at her, his blue eyes bright with compassion. She fancied his eyes were

16

the color of the sky—wished hers were such a color.

Still, in that moment, her mother's voice echoed in her mind. *Your eyes are as green as the summer grass,* Lark's mother had always told her. She liked to think it was true—though she knew it had simply been her mother's love that thought her eyes so beautiful. The thought of her mother caused her to wince. She glanced down at the carpetbag, protectively squeezing it tighter still.

"Mind if'n I ask what yer doin' out west, travelin' all alone, ma'am? It's a might unusual to see it—a woman by herself and all. 'Specially a young one . . . from the east." He winked, unwilling to abandon his curiosity altogether.

Lark giggled. She bit her lip, considering whether she should reveal anything to him. Still, he'd been kind to her—helped her—cared for her in a manner.

"You don't have to tell me nothin'," he sighed. "I shouldn't have asked. Ain't my place."

"It's not that," Lark began, "It's just that I'm a very private person. Will you be satisfied with knowing I just ended up here . . . life just led me here . . . and you've helped me?"

The cowboy chuckled. "I guess I will be . . . since you ain't givin' me a choice."

Lark smiled. He was a kind cowboy. She liked him.

As the wagon rumbled along, Hadley ceased in

trying to coax Lark into revealing the details of her life or how she'd come to be where she was. Simply he told her about the town, the people, the weather. Lark found his conversation easy and interesting, and hope continued to burn in her heart. If Hadley Jacobson was so kind and help- ful, perhaps there were others nearby who were as well.

As Hadley talked and drove the team, Lark listened. His voice was comforting—so com- forting that she was almost sad when he pulled the team in before a sturdy-looking, two-story ranch house. There was a barn a short distance off and another building beyond that—perhaps the bunkhouse.

"Here we are. That there's the Evanses' place," Hadley said, nodding toward the ranch house. He turned to Lark and grinned. The sudden frown of panic that Lark felt puckering her brow caused Hadley to chuckle. "Don't worry," he said, hopping down from the wagon. "I know Tom Evans. He couldn't turn away a stray three-legged dog . . . let alone a purty little filly like yerself."

Lark smoothed her worn skirt and gripped the weathered handle of the carpetbag. Hadley offered a hand and assisted her to climb down as well.

"Now, you just run on up there to that house and ask to talk to Tom. I'll wait here for ya," he said, "in case ya need a ride somewheres else."

He took the carpetbag from her, adding, "I'll keep this safe for ya 'til yer sure you'll be stayin'."

Gulping down the large lump of trepidation in her throat, Lark nodded to Hadley and started toward the house. The nervous quivering in her stomach was almost unbearable! Still, she somehow managed to climb the squeaky steps leading to the porch and front door.

Lark drew a deep breath, tucked a limp strand of hair behind her ear, smoothed her skirt once more, and puffed out a frightened sigh. Raising a trembling hand, she knocked on the door. When no one opened the door or called to her from behind it, she glanced back to Hadley.

The handsome young cowboy stood leaning up against the wagon that had carried her to the place. He smiled and nodded to her. "Go on," he mouthed, motioning for her to try again.

Biting her lip, Lark knocked again. She wasn't at first certain whether to be relieved or terrified when she then heard heavy footsteps approaching from the other side of the door. The pace of her already rapidly beating heart quickened. As the door swung open, a low, irritated grumble resonated out onto the soft late-summer breeze. Lark gulped again as she lifted her gaze to see a scowling, very angry-looking man glaring down at her. Obviously annoyed, the large man pulled up one suspender strap that had been hanging loosely from his waist, pushing it into place over a broad shoulder and bare torso. He repeated the action with his other suspender strap—all the while still glaring at Lark.

Lark was so stunned by his appearance, any words or utterance were momentarily lost to her. The man was several days unshaven yet clean. He was tall with hair that appeared fair at first glance. Yet Lark quickly realized his hair only appeared fair, for his whisker growth was dark. In addition, as he tipped his head to further consider her, his hair moved, revealing that it was indeed brown beneath the top sun-bleached layer. His eyes were a deep, dark, rather dusky shade of brown that pierced with clear disapproval. He clenched a firm, square jaw tightly, and there was a rather weathered look about him—as if the sun had parched his spirit or sleep had thoroughly abandoned him. Still, even with the deep frown puckering his brow, Lark was stuck by his being so handsome. He was older than she—much older—and this only served to further intimidate her.

She swallowed, still unable to speak.

"Who in the hell are you?" he growled, clearly having lost patience with waiting for her to explain herself.

"I-I'm sorry to disturb you, sir. I was hoping to speak with Tom Evans. Is . . . is he at home?" she choked at last, trying to portray some sort of confidence.

The man's frown intensified, and he rolled his eyes in a gesture of annoyance. "Tom. Tom! Get your lily-white . . . get in here! There's a . . . someone askin' after ya."

The man turned, leaving Lark standing in the open doorway, trembling with intimidation.

Lark exhaled a breath of relief. Glancing over her shoulder to Hadley, she saw him smile.

Slater Evans? she mouthed to him.

Hadley chuckled and nodded emphatically.

Lark shook her head with near disbelief. No wonder Hadley had directed her to ask to speak to Tom. Slater Evans seemed as mean as the day was long.

Straightening her posture once more—for Slater Evans had managed to whip her courage down like a stray dog—she quickly pinched her cheeks to rosy them up and forced a smile.

A second man, looking quite similar to the first, only with a welcoming grin and overall pleasant countenance, came to the door. The man's smile broadened as he came to stand in the doorway, and Lark felt a wave of relief wash through her.

"Well, howdy there, miss," the man greeted.

Lark sighed, delighted by his friendly, easy manner.

"And what is it has me so lucky as to find you on my porch?" he asked.

"Are you . . . are you Mr. Tom Evans?" Lark ventured.

"Yes, ma'am. Handsome feller . . . ain't I?" he teased.

"Yes . . . well . . . um . . ."

Tom Evans chuckled, his radiant smile out-shining the sun. "What can I do for ya, honey?" he asked then.

Lark was grateful he'd chosen not to tease her any further. She thought she might not be able to endure any more—not with being so tired and hungry—so desperate to find some position that would see her through until spring.

"I'm Lark," she began, "Lark Lawrence." She cleared her throat. It suddenly felt very dry. "I've heard that you've recently lost your housekeeper . . . and I am so sorry to hear that, by the way."

"Thank ya. We loved dear ol' Mrs. Simpson. She was near like our own mama."

"Yes. I'm sorry for your loss," Lark managed. "Well, someone in town thought you may be in need of an individual to keep house and cook for you . . . and suggested that I inquire as to whether or not you did."

Tom Evans's already wide smile broadened. "Why, we do indeed! We've been havin' us a downright awful mess of a time 'round here," he explained. "Me and ol' Slater—he's my charmin' brother—we've got too darn much to do with keepin' the cattle and crops in line. Don't leave much time for cookin' . . . even if we did know how. And between you and me, darlin', I'm plain sick and tired of eatin' jerky and hard biscuits every meal."

Lark smiled as hope bloomed within her bosom. She bit her lip a moment, attempting to rein in her sudden exuberance. "So you are in need of someone then?" she asked.

"You bet your sweet . . . ah course we are!" Tom exclaimed. "But you ain't quite what I was thinkin' our next mama would look like." He winked at her, and she couldn't stop the blush from rising to her cheeks.

"I'm more than capable, Mr. Evans. I assure you my youth does not denote incompetence," she assured him.

Tom paused a moment. His smiled faded a little. Yet even as he studied her from head to toe, the expression of casual amusement never left his face—even for the slight puzzling frown that puckered his brow.

"Honey, you talk like a schoolteacher. You can't be from 'round these parts. Where ya from?" he asked.

"East," Lark plainly answered.

Tom Evans nodded—did not press her for further information—simply nodded.

"Alrighty then," he said. He gestured toward Hadley. "You go on and tell ol' Hadley Jacobson to run along home now. We'll let ya give us a try for a while and see if you can tolerate two ol' bachelors."

Reaching out, she took hold of his hand, shaking it with relief, gratitude, and sheer delight. "Oh! Thank you, Mr. Evans! I promise you won't regret accepting me into your employ!"

He smiled at her and shook his head, chuckling. "Well, I'm sure I won't if'n I can get used to the way you talk."

Lark giggled as she ran back to the wagon. She nearly threw her arms around Hadley Jacobson's neck to thank him but caught herself a moment before performing such an impetuous and improper display. Instead, she took his hand and shook it as sincerely as she had Tom Evans's a moment before.

"Oh, thank you, Mr. Jacobson! Thank you!" she gushed. "He's offered me a chance. He's offered to see if I can do the job, and I can't thank you enough for your help!"

The young cowboy handed her the old carpetbag that hid her only possessions, touched the brim of his hat, and said, "Yer welcome, miss." He climbed up onto the wagon seat once more, gathering the lines to the team. "I hope I'll be seein' ya in town now and then," he said. "But not too soon."

"Thank you, Mr. Jacobson," Lark sighed.

Hadley nodded and slapped the lines at the backs of the team. The team lurched forward.

Lark didn't wait to watch him drive too far away. She wanted to make certain Tom Evans knew she was committed to working hard.

Therefore, she turned and hurried back to the house.

"Here I am!" she announced excitedly, running up the steps to the porch.

Tom Evans chuckled. "Here ya are indeed." He studied her for a moment and then stepped aside and gestured that she should enter the house.

"Well, let's get you settled in, Miss . . . um . . . Miss . . ."

Lark thought it was sweet—the way he'd already forgotten her name.

"Lawrence," she told him. "Lark Lawrence, Mr. Evans. But please call me Lark."

Tom nodded. "Lark it is then," he said as she stepped into the house.

She felt like jumping up and down with glee and utter elation. She'd prove her worth—yes, she would—and then she'd have a place to winter. Still, she concealed her delirium. She didn't want Tom Evans to think she was some sort of lunatic woman. No. She needed to remain calm—to move and act with the grace and composure of a refined woman. These Evans men were more mature, in their late twenties perhaps. They would respond more positively to the nature of a more mature woman. After all, she had the sense that their recently departed housekeeper had been quite maternal—an older woman. Thus, they were most likely used to less giddiness—a quieter sort of existence.

As she stepped into the front of the house, she looked about. It was a rather large house, larger than it appeared from the outside. There was a parlor to her right, a kitchen to her left, and a hallway and stairs before her. It was instantly obvious that the house was inhabited by men—solely men. The furniture was thick with dust—strewn with blankets, clothing, and other clutter, even in the parlor. The kitchen looked as if a small twister had blown through. Still, the furnishings were of quality and the general decor very tasteful. She credited this fact to the late Mrs. Simpson.

"Not much to look at," Tom began, "but we find it cozy enough."

"It's wonderful!" Lark exclaimed sincerely. "It's sturdy and temperate and ever so masculine," she commented.

"Temperate?" Tom chuckled.

Lark smiled and nodded. "Yes. It's very cool and comfortable inside," she explained. "And I've no doubt it's very warm in the winter." Warmth! The thought of being warm in winter purely breathed respite in her.

Tom chuckled again. "Well, we don't always leave it such a pigsty," he said, glancing around, "but we been bringin' in the crops the past few days and just ain't had a chance to tidy it up."

Lark bit her lip and stifled a giggle as he reached over, attempting to conceal a pair of red flannels strewn across a nearby chair. He was a delightful man! Yet the thought of how kind and lighthearted Tom Evans seemed led Lark's thoughts to his brother. At the sudden reminder that Slater Evans also lived in the house, Lark's joy was somewhat lessened.

"There's a room off the kitchen here that was Matilda's," Tom said, leading Lark to a door just at the foot of the stairs. "You'll like it, I think. It's more, ya know, all lacy and white . . . with a pink pitcher and basin for washin'. It's more . . . more . . ."

"Feminine?"

"Yeah! That's it! Couldn't quite think of the word," he mumbled, seeming thoughtful. "Anyway, it's right over here."

He opened the door and stepped aside for Lark to enter the room. Lark smiled, surprised and delighted by his awkward yet somehow well-groomed manners.

She gasped a little as she looked about the room. It was charming! Its small dimensions were perfectly cozy. A comfortable-looking bed covered with a bright white and pink quilt stood invitingly in the center of the wall to the right. Lace curtains hung at the window at the back, and above the washstand sitting next to the bed hung a lovely painting of an old southern mansion.

"What a beautiful scene," Lark said, going to stand before the painting.

"Matilda was from Richmond. I think she always hankered for the life she remembered before the war," Tom explained.

"It's a lovely painting," Lark breathed as she studied the tall pillars of the antebellum house—the lilac-colored wisteria blossoms engulfing them. Sighing with rare and pure contentment, Lark glanced around the room again. "This is the most wonderful room I have ever seen," she whispered. And it was true.

"Well, I don't know about that . . . but I hope it'll do." Tom nodded to the back wall. "There's a wardrobe just back here for your hangin'-up things. And, of course, that old trunk at the foot of the bed is yours as well. It's empty."

Lark looked around awkwardly and set her worn carpetbag on top of the old trunk. She certainly wouldn't need much space for the few things she had with her.

"Thank you, Mr. Evans," she said.

"Oh, help us all," resonated a growl from behind them.

Lark turned to see Tom Evans's brother standing in the doorway—scowling at her as if she were infected with some ghastly disease.

Chapter Two

"Don't tell me ya actually let her in, Tom," he grumbled. "Next I'll find ya out buryin' dead mice, savin' spiders, and nursin' stray pups."

"And this, Miss Lark," Tom began, "is my charmin' brother, Slater." Tom shook his head as he looked to his brother. He smiled and chuckled a bit.

Tom Evans chuckled more than any man Lark had ever met. Yet she saw nothing amusing in his brother's behavior. Feelings of intimidation and anxiety flooded her.

Still, Tom continued his introductions. "Slater . . . this is Lark. She's gonna cook me somethin' to eat for dinner 'sides yer leather-hard jerky and puny old biscuits."

"My jerky is fine," Slater grumbled. "And my biscuits."

Mustering every ounce of courage left in her, Lark offered a hand to the menacing man. "Hello," she greeted. At least he'd found the decency to put on a shirt. Lark was grateful for that. His previous state of undress had greatly unnerved her.

Slater Evans wiped his hand on his pant leg and dutifully accepted hers. He gripped her hand so tightly, Lark nearly winced. He was strong; the proof was in his grip. Furthermore, he labored hard; that evidence was also in his hand, for his palm was callused—and warm. His touch unsettled her. She had the sense he could strangle her with little effort. Yet she mused such a man could likewise complete any task necessary for survival.

"I hate rabbit stew," he stated. "Anything cooked with rabbit makes my stomach churn, and I won't eat it. We get up early 'round here . . . well before the sun. We like to eat before we get to work. We're ornery old men, set in our ways, and we don't take kindly to change."

Lark felt her eyebrows arch in surprise. Could it be he was actually going to accept her? "I-I've never made rabbit stew," she said. "Not in all my life."

Slater Evans nodded. "Good. It makes me sick."

"That's 'cause it's made outta cute little bunnies," Tom teased.

Lark quickly glanced to Tom. Was he truly going to tease his brother? She didn't think Slater Evans appeared the sort to tolerate teasing.

"We used to have some rabbits when we was boys," Tom explained. "We kept 'em for pets . . . or at least me and Slater thought that's what they was. But times got mighty desperate one winter, and Mama had to cook one up for supper. Ol' Slater won't eat rabbit since." Tom chuckled and patted his brother on the back. "He ain't never quite recovered from the shock. Have ya, Slater?"

Slater ignored his brother's teasing and continued to glare at Lark. "How old are ya, girl? Fifteen? Sixteen?" he asked.

"Twenty," Lark lied, feigning offense. Still, she'd be nineteen in three months. She assured herself that was close enough to twenty to justify her misleading response.

"You don't look no older than sixteen," Slater mumbled, his eyes narrowing as he studied her. "You ain't got no strange habits, do you?"

"Strange habits?"

"You know . . . strange things about ya. You ain't insane or got some crazy man chasin' ya all over creation, do you?"

"N-no, sir. No one's looking for me," Lark answered—and this was the truth.

Slater Evans reached up and rubbed his chiseled, whiskery chin with one callused hand. "Well, I guess if Tom's dead set on havin' a pet . . . I might as well enjoy a good meal myself now and again." His eyes narrowed, and she fancied a slight grin curved his rather well-shaped lips. "Leastwise we won't be eatin' you for supper if things get desperate come winter." With that, he turned, his long legs striding him away.

Tom chuckled, winking at Lark. "See . . . he ain't all thistles and thorns."

Lark was suddenly disturbed—for she found Slater Evans very intriguing. She fancied his

31

hostility and gruffness were exaggerated. Furthermore, the way his brother teased him—even his last remark before leaving—indicated Slater Evans had some breath of a sense of humor in him—somewhere.

"You just ignore ol' Slater, and you'll be just fine. He's full of beans and other stuff anyhow," Tom said. "And that there reminds me . . . let me show you where we keep the supplies and all. We usually like to eat our supper about sundown this time of year. That all right?"

"Oh yes. It sounds wonderful!" Lark exclaimed. And it did! Food aplenty? Shelter? A bed? The idea of one or the other was delicious—but all three? Divine! "I had better get started if dinner is to be served promptly."

As she followed Tom into the kitchen, Lark could hardly contain herself. Real food—perhaps even meat and sweets now and then! It had been so long since she had a good supper. Her mouth watered with anticipation as Tom showed her where the vegetables and meats were stored. The rich aroma of the smokehouse nearly swarmed her into a faint!

"I'll give you a hint 'bout Slater," Tom began as they returned to the house. "He loves baked things. Mainly sugar cookies . . . with sugar and butter frostin' on the top 'specially. If you wanna get on his good side, you get him some sweet thing baked tomorrow." Tom winked at Lark, and she nodded. "Now, I gotta be gettin' back to work. You go on ahead and fix whatever you've a mind to. We've been eatin' leather and dust for so long that anythin' would taste good by now. Except rabbit, of course."

"Of course," Lark giggled.

Tom smiled and began to leave, yet Lark caught his shirtsleeve to stay him. "Thank you, Mr. Evans," she humbly said. "You've no idea how much you've helped me."

Tom was touched—deeply moved by the girl's obvious gratitude. He smiled down into the lovely face of the very pretty young woman. It was obvious she didn't have much at all in the world—that life was treating her harshly. Her dress, though clean and fresh-looking, was very well worn. Tom figured it had once been red, but it was more a dull shade of brown now. Lark Lawrence looked a might too thin to him too. Still, she was mighty pretty! Her long chestnut hair was pinned up neatly, and her green eyes flashed with hope and enthusiasm. When she smiled, it made a body feel as if he'd stepped out the door in the middle of winter, only to find spring had snuck in and turned everything to blossoms. She was small but sturdy-looking, with a voice like music. He thought how much nicer it would be to hear her happy, light voice call him in for supper, instead of poor Matilda's. He'd begun to grow guilty every time he'd come in for one of Matilda's suppers. She'd grown so old—so tired and worn. Yet she'd insisted on mothering him and Slater until the day she died. He thought of the old woman now—missed her—hoped she was up in heaven doing nothing but her knitting.

"Well, Miss Lark . . . you don't have no idea yourself how much you're gonna help us out," he told her. "Now, you get to cookin', and I'll get to workin'." And with that, he left and followed his brother out the front door.

Lark listened and frowned as Slater Evans began to complain to his brother. Tom and Slater were still standing on the front porch. From her place in the kitchen, she could hear every word, being that the window was open.

"I cannot believe you, Tom," Slater growled. "What's got into you? Hirin' that little runt of a thing? We been doin' just fine on our own. Ain't nothin' wrong with hard jerky and biscuits. It puts hair on yer chest."

"I already got enough hair on my chest, Slater," Tom said. "Besides . . . she's mighty pretty. Even you gotta admit that," Tom chuckled lowly.

"She's a baby, Tom," Slater grumbled. "And it's all too plain what she's up to."

"And what's that?"

"She's runnin' from somethin'," Slater growled.

Lark gulped and continued to listen.

"Oh, come on now! You're always so suspicious of everybody," Tom argued.

"You just don't see women travelin' 'round the country by themselves. Somethin' ain't right about it. Besides . . . with a pretty little filly like that livin' under our roof, you and me's gonna get accused of all kinds of doin's. What'll folks think?"

"Now, Slater, you ain't never cared what other folks think . . . not in all yer life. You're just angered at me for not consultin' you about it first. That's all, and don't think I ain't wise to it. I've been yer younger brother for far too long not to be."

"I ain't just talkin' to the wind, Tom. She's hidin' somethin'. I know she is."

"Is that so? And what if she is? Ain't we all hidin' somethin', big brother? I woulda thought you'd know that better than just about anybody."

"Hmmf," Slater grumbled. "I'm tellin' you, Tom, I feel trouble simmerin'. You mark my words. Trouble . . . it's in the air."

"I know right well what ya feel simmerin', brother," Tom chuckled.

"She's your wounded sparrow, Tom . . . not mine. That's all I'm sayin'."

Lark heard heavy footsteps stomp across the porch—descend the porch steps. They were gone.

Lark exhaled the breath she'd been holding. She needed a place to winter—so very desperately!

But it was obvious that if Slater Evans had his way, she'd be sent packing. Frowning, she turned back to the sink and began the task of preparing an evening meal. Inhaling deeply to calm herself once more, she smiled as she gazed at the heap of carrots, potatoes, and herbs she'd gathered from the cellar. The sight of the slice of beef Tom had stolen from the smokehouse caused her mouth to water. She would thoroughly relish cooking that evening and prepare such a fine meal that Slater Evans would be purely bewitched into keeping her on.

As she began to slice the vegetables, Lark whispered a prayer. She was so thankful to have a place to spend the winter. The previous winter had been miserable. The Larsons were kind to let her sleep in the barn as payment for helping around the house and with meals. Mrs. Larson, being consumptive, wasn't able to carry out many of her duties as wife and mother. When she'd passed away early in the spring, Mr. Larson divided the children among his sisters and set out to find a new life somewhere else.

Thus, Lark had to leave the Larsons. Still, being a fine seamstress, she'd been able to find work with Mrs. Macy, the seamstress in town. However, Mrs. Macy was elderly and decided to close her doors. Mrs. Macy had begged Lark to stay with her, but Lark was unable to find work and knew the aged widow could not afford to have her living in her home. So with that chapter of her life at an end, she set out to find another position to sustain herself. It wasn't an unfamiliar way of life to Lark Lawrence. Indeed not. The truth was it had been nearly two years since she'd left—since she'd escaped—since she'd begun taking care of herself. So she'd left Mrs. Macy and set out to find a new place to winter—and it seemed as though she had been successful.

By the time the sky was pink and orange with a tranquil sunset, a hearty beef stew and freshly baked rolls were waiting, warm, scenting the kitchen with a soothing, beckoning aroma. Lark hoped the meal was as good as it smelled—hoped the other tasks she'd been about, like tidying and freshening the house, were noticeable.

As she placed a mason jar filled with wild-flowers in the center of the freshly polished kitchen table, she heard her new employers talking as they ascended the porch steps. She smiled, pleased by the sound of their low, masculine voices. It comforted her—caused her to feel safe—somehow protected.

As they entered, Tom drew a deep breath and smiled. "Mmm-mmm!" he hummed in exclama-tion. "Smell that, big brother? Heaven, that's what it is. That's the smell of heaven." Tom sighed a sigh of contentment, and Lark smiled. At least one of the Evans brothers was pleased.

Slater Evans remained silent and scowling.

"Smells good enough to eat, Miss Lark Lawrence," Tom said, stepping into the kitchen.

"Well, I hope it tastes good enough to eat," Lark said, nervously glancing to Slater.

Slater Evans's scowl softened some, and he nodded a greeting. Lark forced a friendly grin in return.

"Could be I'm a little tired of jerky and biscuits myself," the menacing man muttered as he sat down at the table.

Lark puffed a breath of relief. She'd been afraid Slater Evans would still overrule his younger brother and send her away.

As the two weary-looking men sat at the table, Lark began, "Mr. Jacobson said you employ cowboys . . . but that they see to themselves. I neglected to inquire after them before you left . . . so I went on Mr. Jacobson's word and prepared just what I thought you would need."

"We have four hands ridin' for us," Slater answered. His dark eyes met her gaze, and Lark struggled to keep from glancing away. After all, it was rude not to look at someone when they were addressing you—especially one's employer. "The boys see to themselves, and Eldon Pickering is a fine cook. He sees to their meals," he explained. He shrugged his very broad shoulders, adding, "Anyway, they're out roundin' up right now. They'll be gone a couple more days, I suspect."

"Oh, good," Lark sighed. "I was afraid I hadn't prepared enough."

Quickly, she went to the stove and ladled stew onto two plates. She'd placed a pat of butter on a roll—and then another—and added the warm bread to the plates.

"Here you go, gentlemen," she said, placing the plates on the table—one in front of Tom and one before his brother. "I hope it appeals to you."

She smiled, feeling more hopeful as the faces of both men brightened. The stew would be good— she knew it would—and both Tom and Slater would want nothing more to do with jerky and hard biscuits once they'd tasted the stew and soft, warm rolls.

Tom glanced up to her as she stood beside the table. Smiling, he said, "Sit down, Miss Lark. You must be starvin' to death."

Lark shook her head. "Oh no, I couldn't. I'll wait until you've both finished."

Both men looked to one another and then to her with sincerely bewildered expressions.

"You're funnin' with us," Slater said, glaring at her with doubt.

"Well, no. I thought I should wait until you've finished and clear things away before . . ." she began.

"Oh, for cryin' in the bucket," Slater said, shaking his head. "Where you from, girl?" Slater chuckled.

"East," Lark answered.

"East?" Slater asked. "Well, don't folks east sit down to their supper all at once?" He shook his head once more and said, "Now, get yerself a plate and sit down with us, girl. We're just two ol' cowboys. And we don't have the patience to be treated no different."

Lark looked to Tom for reassurance. He smiled.

"What are you lookin' at him for?" Slater asked, however. "I live here as much as Tom does. Ya don't have to look to him for everything."

"Well, ya scared her clean outta her corset, Slater," Tom scolded, grinning. "Ya make out you're such an ol' grump."

"I am an old grump," Slater said. He looked to Lark again. "I said to get yerself a plate and sit down with us, girl," Slater reminded.

"Don't mind Slater, honey," Tom said, yet he nodded at her to do as Slater instructed. "He's a might better with cattle and horses than he is with people these days."

Lark nodded and turned to retrieve another plate from the cupboard.

"Honey?" she heard Slater ask his brother. "She ain't even been here a day, and already you're callin' her honey?"

"What of it?" Tom asked.

"Well, I never heard ya call Matilda 'honey,'" Slater said.

Lark ladled stew onto a plate for herself. She

placed a pat of butter on a roll and returned to the table. When she looked at him, Slater nodded his approval, even for the lingering scowl on his handsome brow.

"I think you oughta be the one to give thanks this evenin', Slater," Tom said.

Slater scowled at his brother. He looked to Lark and mumbled, "Tom always thinks I'm more in need of talkin' to the Lord than him. Thinks he's already got his place in heaven and that I'm still a long way off from earnin' mine."

"You said it . . . not me," Tom said as he offered a hand to Lark.

Lark placed her right hand in Tom's palm, smiling as she saw him reach across the table and take Slater's hand. She startled, however, when she felt Slater take her left hand. Tom let her hand lay easily in his palm. Yet Slater's grip was firm.

As Tom and Slater closed their eyes, Lark closed hers, bowing her head with respect.

"Dear Lord," Slater began, "thank ya for this fine day . . . for the hard work me and Tom done. Thank ya for talkin' Clifford Herschel into sellin' me his little bull . . ."

Lark nearly giggled out loud. She couldn't help opening her eyes just a bit to glance to Slater. He wore a frown, as usual, and seemed sincere in his prayer. She looked to Tom, however, to see him grinning, as usual—his shoulders bouncing with a barely withheld chuckle.

Slater continued, "Thank ya, Lord, for this house and ranch . . . for the good boys me and Tom got cowboyin' for us. Thank ya for this food . . . and it does smell good, Lord . . . so I suppose I oughta be thankin' ya for the girl too. Thank you for dumpin' this little wounded sparrow on Tom's side of the porch so that he can have somebody to call honey and so I don't have to keep makin' biscuits."

Lark heard a low chuckle escape Tom and bit her own lip to keep from laughing—for she had the feeling that Slater Evans was entirely sincere in his offered prayer—at least, mostly.

"Thank ya for the good earth, the sun, the moon, and the stars, Lord," Slater continued. "And for them lilacs we had last spring. They sure were nice. Amen."

"Amen," Lark managed, though Tom chuckled the closing word.

As the men released her hands, Lark opened her eyes.

"I forgot to mention," Tom began, winking at Lark, "that ya might want to keep yer distance when Slater's prayin'. Ya never know when he might be struck by lightning . . . and ya don't want it to swallow you up when it does."

"I pray just fine," Slater said.

Lark held her breath as she watched him pick up the spoon she'd previously set on the table and tentatively tasted the stew. Already she knew the

Evans brothers well enough that her stew could taste like mud and Tom wouldn't say a word. But she wasn't so certain it would be easy to please Slater.

"Mmm!" Slater said, however, his frown finally fading. "It's good," he added, nodding to Lark and smiling.

It was the first time Lark had seen a smile break his face, and it was fascinating! At first sight, she'd thought him a very handsome man—even for his scowling and grumbling. But with a smile donning his face, he was truly extraordinary!

Lark sighed, relieved, and watched as Tom plunged his own spoon into the stew.

He too nodded and smiled, pleased with the flavors of the meal placed before him. "Matilda never done stew this good," Tom said.

"No indeed," Slater agreed. He looked to Lark and smiled once more. "It's a fine meal, girl. A fine meal."

"Thank you, Mr. Evans," she said. "I'm glad you're pleased."

"My name's Slater," he said, pulling apart the buttered roll and biting into one half.

"Yes, sir," Lark said, nodding.

"Sir?" He was frowning at her again. "How old do think I am, girl?"

"Well, yer actin' like you're old enough to be her granddaddy," Tom teased.

"Well, I am old. I'm at least old enough to be her daddy," Slater grumbled.

"Slater, you're thirty . . . and that ain't old. And it certainly ain't old enough to be her daddy," Tom chuckled. He turned to Lark. "Thirty . . . that ain't old, is it, honey?"

Slater answered for her. "Shoot, Tom . . . twenty-five is old to a young thing like her. Ain't that right, baby?"

It was the way he'd said the word *baby,* not as if he meant to point out her youth but rather as an endearment—similar to his brother referring to her as honey. It made Lark uncomfortable— because she liked it!

"I have to agree with your brother, Mr. Evans," she somehow managed to answer. "Thirty isn't old." He grinned at her as he chewed his bite of bread, and it gave her courage. In that moment, she began to understand, and she would let him know that she did. "You're not fooling me with your decrepit old-man behavior, sir."

Tom chuckled and broke full into laughter. "She's got you spiked, brother Slater," he laughed. "Tarred, feathered, and nailed to the barn door!"

Though he still wore a slight grin on his handsome face as he studied her, Slater mumbled, "Leastways I'm outta diapers."

Lark felt her own smile broaden. She liked the two men—the Evans brothers. They were kind, and she sensed they would prove to be very entertaining. Furthermore, it seemed as if her stew had ensured that she would be sleeping in a nice warm bed all winter. That in itself was worth smiling about.

The two men ate several helpings of stew and rolls, all the while complimenting Lark on having prepared such a fine meal. They talked of other things as well—the new bull Slater had managed to purchase from a man named Clifford Herschel, the south fence that needed mending. Tom even mentioned a girl named Ella May. Apparently she was growing up. He'd seen her out at her daddy's place, and she was turning into a fine-looking young woman. Both men talked about remem-bering when she'd been born—thus mused over their own aging awhile.

When supper was finished, Lark was surprised when neither man left the table. Simply, they stretched back in their chairs, continuing their conversation as Lark cleared the dishes from the table.

"Ol' man Brown's sellin' that colt Montana sired," Slater said, yawning.

"The bay?" Tom yawned the question.

Both men were tired—it was sorely obvious. Lark's heart pinched a little, imagining how difficult it would be to maintain such a ranch as she understood theirs to be.

"Yep. I'd like to have him," Slater said, nodding. "He's a good-lookin' colt. I think we'd be smart to buy him."

"I think yer right. How much is ol' Brown askin'?"

"Too much. But I'll talk him down."

"You always do," Tom chuckled.

As Lark stacked the washed and dried dishes in the cupboard, the long, laborious day began to make itself known on her body and in her mind. She managed to stifle a yawn—but just barely. Suddenly, she felt as if she couldn't take another step, hear another word, or keep her eyes open a moment longer.

"Gentlemen?" she began, folding her hands neatly at her waist as she stood at the head of the table. Both Slater and Tom looked weary—worn to the quick.

"I-I think I'm finished here," she ventured. "Would it be all right if I retired for the evening?" She was nervous—afraid she would cause offense or had perhaps forgotten some task.

"Of course, honey," Tom answered. "I'm sure you're plum wrung out. Though I can't imagine you needin' any beauty sleep." He winked at her, and she smiled, delighted by his compliment—and kindness. "Still, tomorrow does come early . . . so you just go on to bed whenever the notion takes hold of ya. All right?"

"Thank you," Lark said, nodding. She felt a slight blush rise to her cheeks as Slater's attention lingered on her a moment. "Thank you for allowing me to work for you both."

"Thank you for savin' me from another meal of leather and flour paste," Tom said.

"Oh, you just go on and keep that up, little brother," Slater growled. "Go on . . . if ya dare."

Tom chuckled and nodded to Lark.

"Good night, Lark," he said.

"Good night," Lark told him.

Slater only nodded to her, but she said, "Good night, Mr. Evans," all the same.

She dropped a mild curtsy and left the kitchen.

Once inside the cozy room with the pretty painting, lace curtains, and welcoming bed, Lark shut the door behind her, exhaling a heavy breath of fatigue and relief.

Oh, she was tired! More tired than she'd been in a long time. Yet she knew a measure of comfort, for the Evans brothers had liked her meal. They even seemed to like her—though it was obvious Tom was still more accepting of her existence than Slater. She hoped she would begin to feel more at ease in Slater's presence. Something about him greatly unsettled her, and she couldn't imagine living months and months with such unsettling feelings—though she'd rather live with them than shelter in a cave all winter long.

Opening her worn carpetbag, Lark withdrew her very tattered nightdress. As she changed her dress for her nightdress, she began to notice the throbbing in her feet. They were sore, worn from walking so far. It would be heavenly to sleep in a bed—to remove her shoes and simply rest well-sheltered. In truth, Lark didn't mind so much sleeping under the summer moon and stars. Still, there was much to be said for resting on a mattress instead of the hard ground.

With a sigh of weariness of mind and soreness of body, Lark offered her prayers and snuggled beneath the clean, beckoning softness of the sheets and quilt. She fancied a moment she was resting on a cloud—swaddled in the linens of heaven. She smiled as she closed her eyes, for if the soft bed were a cloud made of heavenly linens, then the two men for whom she would now cook and clean must indeed be no less than guardian angels. She mused that it had been a long, long time since she'd slept in such a haven of safety. With two such capable men as the Evans brothers so close at hand, Lark knew she would sleep well. Not only had she found a means of earning wages, food, and shelter for the winter, she'd happened upon a sense of sanctuary she'd not experienced for many years—ever so many.

Chapter Three

"Good morning," Lark cheerily greeted as Slater entered the kitchen the next morning.

He looked startled and quickly adjusted his suspenders. "I didn't think you'd be up and about yet, girl."

She smiled. Indeed, the sun had not yet risen,

though a warm orange glow peered over the horizon. "Why ever not? Those were your instructions. You said you and Mr. Evans rise before sunup." She arched an eyebrow, proud of herself for having surprised him. "Now, if you'll sit down . . . I have hotcakes and bacon ready."

Slater shrugged broad shoulders, his face marked by an expression of indifferent surrender. He pulled a chair out from the table, depositing himself in its seat. Lark set a plate of hotcakes and bacon on the table before him, smiling as a grin curved his handsome lips.

Slater picked up a slice of bacon, mumbling, "Where is Tom? That ol' . . . he better think 'bout gettin' himself outta bed. We gotta lot to do today."

He was silent for a long space of time as he ate and seemed to enjoy the food. Lark owned a sense of pride, for it was obvious her cooking pleased him.

Suddenly, however, he scowled. Lark held her breath, worried that perhaps Slater had bitten into a hard lump of flour or salt in the hotcakes—that he'd found a flaw in her efforts.

"He better get his fanny out here," he grumbled, however. "Maybe I oughta send you upstairs to look in on him. That would sure enough get him movin'. Don't ya think?"

Lark felt her eyes widen at the suggestion.

"Matilda was always havin' to drag Tom outta

bed," he continued, still eating. "That boy couldn't get himself up on time if the house was fallin' down."

"Now, that ain't true at all, Slater," Tom said, yawning as he entered the kitchen. He grinned at Lark, running fingers through pillow-tousled hair. "If the house was fallin' down, I'd wake . . . sure enough."

Lark couldn't help but giggle. Yet she bit her lip when Slater glared up at her.

"Don't go encouragin' him to smartin' off, girl," he scolded. "I have a hard enough time lightin' a fire under him without him havin' any conspirators nearby to herd him on."

"Yes, sir," Lark mumbled. She was nervous, anxious over having vexed him—that is, until he winked at her, implying he was only teasing her. He didn't smile at her, but she read his implication all the same. Could it be that Slater Evans was as much a teasing trifler as his brother?

Tom sat down in a chair across the table from Slater. As Lark placed a plate of food before him, he scowled, studying his brother for a moment.

"You done combed yer hair already?" Tom asked then.

"Maybe I run my fingers through it before I come down," Slater answered, placing his fork on his plate and stretching back in his chair.

Tom smiled and shook his head. "You never run yer fingers through it when I cook breakfast."

"You don't ever cook breakfast, boy," Slater said.

"All the same . . . ya even put a shirt on before comin' down," Tom continued, shoving a slice of bacon into his mouth. "I think havin' Lark around just might civilize ya a might."

"I'm plenty civilized," Slater said to Lark as she sat down next to Tom. She'd had her own breakfast already, but she didn't see the harm in sitting a moment before moving onto the rest of her daily chores.

"Civilized enough to know it's gonna take us all day to fix that length of fence that needs fixin'," Slater continued. "And then I gotta ride over to Clifford's place and get that bull. We'll need to brand him soon. I don't want to wake up one mornin' and find he's found its way onto somebody else's pasture."

"Well, let me eat my breakfast in peace . . . before ya go plannin' my whole life out," Tom grumbled.

Lark smiled, amused by the fact Slater had finally gotten the best of his brother's good mood.

She glanced to Slater to see him grinning at his brother. He nodded and winked at her again.

Lark's smile broadened. She was beginning to understand—Slater was nearly as playful as Tom was! He simply came about it from a different point of view. Where Tom was always smiling,

51

teasing, his mood always discernible, Slater was measured, guarded—a rascal.

"Well, while you're eatin' yer breakfast in peace," Slater teased, "I'll get busy. Finish up and meet me in the barn. I'll show you how a man shoes a horse."

"Oh. You plannin' on watchin' me shoe, Slater?" Tom countered.

Slater smiled and stood, saying, "Just get yer fanny out there. The mornin's half wasted already."

"The sun ain't even up yet, Slater," Tom grumbled.

Slater chuckled, and the sound caused an odd sort of thrill to run through Lark's limbs. "That was a right fine way to start the mornin', girl," he said, nodding at her with approval. "Thank ya kindly for breakfast."

"You're welcome. Thank you, Mr. Evans," Lark said.

"We'll be seein' you about noon then . . . for some lunch. All right?" he asked.

"Yes, sir," Lark agreed. She knew the heavy sigh he exhaled was due to the fact she'd addressed him so properly. Still, he didn't scold her—simply took a weathered hat from its place on the chair by the front door and left.

"See . . . he ain't all that bad once you get to know him, is he?" Tom asked once the front door had shut.

Lark shook her head and smiled. "No . . . I suppose not. He just makes me a bit nervous somehow."

"That's 'cause he's so good-lookin'," Tom chuckled. "All women everywhere in the world get a little jittery when ol' Slater's lingerin'. The amusin' thing is . . . he don't even know it. He just believes anything feminine in nature thinks he's mean and worn out. Ain't that somethin'?"

Lark smiled. "Why would he think that?"

Tom shrugged broad shoulders. "He's got some strange kind of humility, I guess. Like a disease or somethin'. Whatever the reason, he thinks he's on the finishin'-up side of life instead of the startin'-out side."

Lark frowned. Slater Evans was thirty—that's what she remembered hearing the day before. Thirty wasn't old. Why, most great men didn't even begin greatness until far into their thirties. She thought it sad—that Slater Evans would go about his days and nights thinking the best part of his life was behind him.

"I expect it's 'cause he's been livin' a man's life for so long," Tom continued. "He left home to cowboy when he was fourteen, you know. That there's sixteen years of man life. That's about ten years ahead of the rest of us."

"Fourteen?" Lark breathed, astonished. "Why ever did he leave home so early?"

Tom finished and placed his fork on his empty

plate. He sighed, leaning back in his chair the way Slater had done earlier—as if he'd eaten too fast and his stomach was too full.

"Slater was restless," he explained. "He fought with our pa somethin' awful. They was too much alike, Ma always said. He couldn't wait to be his own man. Now, me . . . I was content to help Pa run the ranch." He smiled at her and continued, "I didn't see no reason to make life harder than it had to be before its time."

Lark nodded. She understood. How wonderful it would have been to have a home—linger in comfort, security, and routine until she'd been of an age to leave along a more natural course.

"Slater . . . he came home two years ago after . . . when he was ready to. He's content here now, I think, but he woulda never been happy if he hadn'ta left first. Matilda always said he finally run his oats out. Banged himself up a piece doin' it too."

Lark shook her head. "I would have loved to have grown up here," she wistfully mumbled. "I can't imagine wanting to leave."

Instantly, she scolded herself for having spoken her thoughts aloud. She blushed a little, horrified that she'd revealed so much longing in her intonation.

Still, Tom seemed unaware of it. "Where did you grow up, honey?" he asked.

"East," she answered.

Slater frowned. He'd paused on the front porch and lingered near the open kitchen window. Why was it that Tom found it necessary to tell the girl Slater's personal business? Why did he find it necessary to spin such a piece of nonsense as telling her Slater made women jittery? He swore under his breath as he stepped down off the side of the porch. It seemed Tom's gums were always flapping about things that were none of his business—and certainly nobody else's. Slater didn't want the girl knowing anything about himself—not his past, his manners, or his ways of thinking. He'd have it out with Tom about his flapping gums later, for there was something else gnawing at his mind—something far more intriguing than the life and times of Slater Evans. Yep! Slater found the mystery of little Lark Lawrence far more interesting than his own.

His experience had taught him well, and he knew when someone was running. Oh, maybe his brother had a blind eye to anything unusual or suspicious in nature—but he didn't. The pretty little filly his brother had hired on to keep house and cook—she was running.

"East," he mumbled to himself. It was all the girl would give them of her origins. "East," he mumbled again, frowning as he considered her answer. It was obvious by her tone, her speech, even her mannerisms that she'd had a proper upbringing. Why then was she wandering the world on her own? What was chasing her? What would drive her to enough desperation that she would seek employment from two unmarried men—two unmarried men who lived on an isolated ranch with four other unmarried men?

Slater frowned. He wasn't worried about Tom mistreating her—or himself. They were both gentlemen of sorts—rough gentlemen maybe, but gentlemen respecting of women all the same. Still, a rather unsettled sensation rose in him whenever he considered the cowboys working the ranch. There was Eldon Pickering—even older than Slater and a good man. Slater's concerns over whether Eldon would find Lark's presence a little too distracting to keep his mind where it should be weren't too awful thick. Still, Ralston Bell, Grady James, and Chet Leigh—the other cowboys working the ranch—they were younger, a little more inclined toward occasional bad behavior. Lark was pretty—very pretty. Slater knew the cowboys could hardly ignore her.

His frown deepened. What in tarnation had Tom been thinking? He was always dragging home some crippled dog or wounded sparrow—literally. Still, Slater knew Lark was different. Crippled dogs and wounded sparrows didn't inspire lustful thoughts in cowhands. After all, though he was weathered and old and possessed an unusual amount of self-control, even Slater had been aware of her—allowed his gaze to linger on her soft lips, to wonder how her hair would feel slipping between his fingers. Nope, having such a pretty thing on the ranch wasn't good—or safe—for anybody.

Slater exhaled a heavy sigh. He shook his head, discouraged. He'd have to protect her—sure enough he would—and he'd grown weary of protecting folks. Slater Evans simply wanted to run cattle, repair fence, shoe horses, and linger under a bright blue sky—that's all. He didn't want to have to worry about his cowboys saying something improper to a young girl—or worse, doing something improper. Nope. In that moment, he simply wanted to saddle his horse, ride out to the canyon rim, stretch out in the grass, and watch the clouds drift.

Suddenly, he felt tired—as if the small amount of sleep he'd managed to find the night before just hadn't been enough. His shoulder ached, and he reached across his broad chest and squeezed it, willing the soreness to go away. He didn't have time for a sore shoulder. There was work to be done and a wounded sparrow to keep an eye on—rather, a fleeing lark.

After breakfast, she'd given the Evans brothers' house a good looking over before beginning the daunting task of putting things back in order. Having been awash with a sense of overwhelming tasks at hand, Lark had decided to start with the front rooms. Her thinking was that the front rooms were the rooms first viewed by the Evans brothers upon returning home each evening and therefore, once tidied, would offer a good example of how having a housekeeper might benefit. It was plain they were both satisfied with her cooking. Yet she felt the need to prove that a tidy house would also be worth paying a wage. Thus, Lark washed the kitchen windows, dusted furniture, and swept. After she'd tidied the parlor (for clothing, books, hats, socks, and even a length of barbed wire were strewn here and there throughout), she took the parlor rugs out and gave them a good beating. She hung them over the hitching post to one side of the house to allow them to breathe some fresh air too. If there was one thing Lark didn't like, it was the smell of dusty rugs. She wasn't sure why, but she just didn't like it.

As she continued to labor, Lark found a great sense of satisfaction and comfort in her work. It was obvious that the Evans brothers' house had once even been a family home, for there were photographs in frames sitting atop a bookcase in the parlor and near every other surface through-out the residence. A basket filled with yarn and knitting needles sat next to one worn armchair, and Lark wondered if it had belonged to Slater and Tom's beloved Matilda—or had it belonged to their mother? An old desk, dusty and cluttered with papers, stood in one corner. Lark had begun to tidy it but paused when she noted that the documents and letters scattered across its surface were dated nearly five years before—and many bearing the signature of "Vernon J. Evans." It seemed the Evans brothers had left things just as they had stood when their parents had gone. She knew both their mother and father must've passed, for Tom spoke of them both in the past tense. Thus, as she tidied, she wondered when they had died—and how.

It was nearly noon when Lark finally paused in tidying to quickly make a batch of cornbread and pan gravy. She was not surprised when Slater Evans proved to be as prompt in arriving for his midday meal as he had been for breakfast. Tom arrived a few minutes later and joined his brother and Lark at the table.

"Mmm!" Tom moaned with satisfaction at the first taste of the cornbread and gravy. "Lark . . . this gravy is good!"

"I'm glad you like it," Lark said. She was glad—glad and very relieved. She wasn't sure how the men would take to gravy made with bacon drippings after only just having had bacon for breakfast.

"Mighty fine cornbread too," Slater mumbled. In truth, Slater's compliment meant more to Lark even than Tom's. She knew Tom Evans would've told her the meal was fine even if it tasted like tree bark. She wasn't so certain Slater would've offered a compliment had he not sincerely meant it.

"Thank you," she told him.

"You've been busy this mornin'," Tom said. "Them rugs in the parlor needed a good shake."

"Yes, they did," she admitted. "And I wanted to make certain . . . the clothing that was here and there in the parlor . . . I had planned to wash it all. I'm assuming it needs washing?"

Tom chuckled, shaking his head. "I wouldn't rightly know, honey," he said. "I don't string my shirts and drawers all over creation the way Slater does."

"Oh, you got yer own bad habits, Tom," Slater said.

"Matilda nagged him about it. I swear she near wore a hole in his head with naggin' him . . . but it didn't do a lick of good," Tom explained. "Slater still walks in the house every evenin' and strips himself down to nothin' first thing. Usually there's a trail of clothes leadin' up the stairs too."

Lark looked to Slater—waiting for his retort—but none came. He simply continued to eat his lunch, pausing only to say, "Them clothes in the parlor was dirty. Just heap 'em up in the basket in the back of the house, and I'll get to 'em eventually."

"But I'm here now," Lark reminded him. She

60

must be allowed to work, to prove to the Evans brothers that they needed her now that Matilda had passed—or they might not think they did! "I'll take care of the laundry."

Slater ceased in eating—looked to her scowling.

"The laundry? You mean the wash?" he asked.

"Yes," Lark answered. "Didn't your Mrs. Simpson take care of that for you?"

"Well . . . well, yes, she did," Slater admitted, still wearing an expression of concern, however. "But I don't know how I feel about you doin' it."

"What do you mean?" Lark was truly puzzled. She was their new housekeeper, wasn't she? Wasn't she supposed to take care of the house, the laundry, the cooking—everything Matilda had taken care of for them?

Tom chuckled. "He don't want you seein' what a downright hog he is when it comes to gettin' dirty."

"That ain't true," Slater defended himself. "I . . . I just don't know if it's right . . . expectin' a young girl to wash my drawers and all."

"Most times you don't even wear drawers, Slater," Tom teased.

Slater pointed a fork at his brother. "Now, that ain't true neither."

Lark couldn't suppress her giggles. They erupted suddenly, and she bit her bottom lip as she smiled, trying to stifle them. Joy—it seemed so unfamiliar suddenly—the joy nurtured by amusement. In that moment, Lark knew true happiness. She had shelter, food, protection, and companionship of sorts. Winter did not look so bleak now.

"I'm here to work for you, Mr. Evans," Lark reminded Slater, somehow managing not to burst into more giggles. "How am I to earn a proper wage if you don't feel comfortable allowing me to work for it? After all . . . it seems to me that I'm much younger than Mrs. Simpson was. Laundry won't exert me nearly as much as it must've her."

"We're talkin' about my drawers. That's all I'm worried about," Slater said.

"It's cause they're ratty," Tom chuckled. "Mama used to say Slater's drawers weren't fit for rags . . . let alone drawers."

Slater pointed his fork at Tom once more. "Tom, I'm gonna kick yer . . . yer backside all the way to town if ya don't stop talkin' about my unmention-ables that way."

"Unmentionables?" Tom teased, smiling.

Lark noted the way Slater's jaw clenched. He was not as amused as his brother.

"I've laundered men's underthings before, Mr. Evans," she offered, attempting to soothe the situation. "I'm not inexperienced or averse to it in any way."

He looked to her—still uncertain, still scowling.

"Please," she added, "if I'm to pull my weight

for wages . . . if I'm to take over all the responsibilities that were your dear Mrs. Simpson's . . ."

"All right," Slater grumbled, shoveling a bite of cornbread and gravy into his mouth with his fork. "I'll let ya wash my drawers." He paused, looked to his brother, grinned, and said, "And you better be careful, boy. You got yer own bad things about ya. Sooner or later this girl will learn them too."

"Maybe," Tom said, shrugging with indifference.

Slater chuckled, and Lark smiled at the sound. She'd never been privy to such delightful meal conversation. Again, the long-lost sensation of joy filled her bosom. She'd be warm when winter came—and entertained!

"I'll take Coaly to move them logs the boys been workin' on," Tom said. "We gotta get them poles sunk for that fence . . . and I don't want a cold spell comin' in to find us without the woodpile ready."

"You best take Dolly too," Slater said. "She don't like to be left out." Slater looked to Lark then. "Coaly and Dolly are a team of Clydes. They were our pa's pride and joy, and he spoiled 'em somethin' awful and never worked 'em as anything but a team. So they're a little temperamental . . . especially Dolly."

"I don't need 'em both, and I'd rather have Coaly along," Tom said. "She ain't so cantankerous as Dolly."

"Well, just don't blame me if Dolly kicks ya in the head for it," Slater warned.

"She'll be fine," Tom mumbled.

Lark said nothing. After all, who was she to have an opinion on a team of horses she didn't own, had never even seen? Who was she to have an opinion on the subject at all? Yet she loved horses; she always had. To Lark, horses were magnificent creatures—full of spirit and power. She thought there was nothing quite so wonderful in the world as a horse. Furthermore, she owned a deep sense of their nature—their dispositions. Therefore, Lark knew that a team of draft horses that had most likely been raised together, teamed together since they were young, no doubt would feel lost and afraid without the other. Thus, silently she agreed with Slater—that Tom should not take Coaly and leave Dolly behind. Still, she was the housekeeper—the cook—the hired girl. She said nothing.

Lunch was over nearly as quickly as it had begun. Lark felt an odd sense of abandon and loneliness when Slater and Tom left the house to resume their labors. Still, she found herself glancing out a window in one of the back rooms of the house, hoping to catch a glimpse of one of them—hoping a glimpse would somehow restore her sense of confidence. A large barn and two corrals were a ways off but close enough that she could easily see Slater and Tom as they worked. She'd watched Tom harness Coaly—watched Slater shaking his head as he spoke to his brother as he did so. No doubt Slater was again trying to convince his brother that taking only one member of the team might prove unwise. Dolly was indeed agitated. Lark could see the small corral from where the enormous Clydesdale watched her counterpart being harnessed—watched Coaly be led away, alone. Dolly reared and whinnied, stomping the ground in protest. Slater went to the corral and stepped up onto one fence rung. Lark could see he was speaking to her—guessed his voice was low and soothing—and the horse seemed to settle a bit. Eventually, Dolly seemed soothed, and Slater disappeared into the barn.

Lark's empathy for Dolly grew, even as she worked gathering laundry, dusting, and polishing furniture. Somehow the situation—trivial as it seemed—weighed heavy on her. She began to hope Tom would not keep Coaly away long. She found herself going to the window—peeking out toward the corral more often than was necessary. The horse was restless, shaking her head, snorting as she pressed against the corral fence with her haunches.

"Be patient, girl," Lark whispered. "It won't be long. You'll be fine."

She thought about going out to the corral herself to comfort the animal. Still, it wasn't her place, and therefore she paused—even knowing her own uncanny ability to soothe horses might assist Dolly in settling.

"Just clean the house and cook supper, Lark," she told herself as she went about straightening. "Remember your place."

Lark busied herself attending to a few details in the parlor. Soon, all that was left to do was to bring the rugs in and return them to their places on the floor.

She stepped out of the house, shading her eyes from the bright sunlight. The day was warm and still. Scents of pasture grasses, wildflowers, and hot soil soothed her, and she drew in a deep breath, determined to fill her lungs with the beauty of the late summer day. When winter came—when things were not so green and welcoming—she would draw upon the memory of that moment, knowing that winter would end and summer would come again.

Lark stepped down off of the front porch, turning toward the hitching post where she'd hung the rugs to air. However, she couldn't help but glance back toward the corral. Dolly was stomping there, stomping with agitation, even kicking at the corral gate with her front hooves. Concern overwhelmed her, and Lark passed the hitching post, slowly starting toward the corral. Dolly was indeed upset. Dolly whinnied and kicked, and Lark began to panic as she saw the horse break the gate's latch. In an instant, the large draft horse pushed its way through the gate, breaking into a lumbering gallop—headlong in the direction Tom had taken Coaly.

Instinctively, Lark shouted, "Slater! Stop her! Slater!"

As Lark hitched up her skirt and began running toward the barn, she gasped as she glanced in the direction the horse was running—for a fence strung of barbed wire was directly in her path.

"Slater!" she cried out again.

Slater stepped out of the barn, frowning in Lark's direction.

"She'll run right into the wire!" she called, pointing to Dolly.

Slater's gaze followed her gesture. Without pause, he sprinted after the horse, shouting, "Dolly! Whoa! Dolly!" But the horse did not heed its master's voice.

Lark slid to a stop, crying out and covering her mouth with her hands and as she heard Dolly whinny in pain. The beautiful horse crumpled to its front knees a moment. Lark could only watch as it struggled to stand.

"Get me a rope! There's rope in the barn!" Slater hollered.

Without further pause, Lark raced into the barn. She was momentarily confused, for it seemed there was rope hanging or lying everywhere! Still, her gaze fell to a length of sturdy rope hanging on a hook near one stall—a lasso. Quickly she took it down from the hook and hurried out of the barn.

Dolly was still near the fence, having stopped her attempt to escape for the pain of her wounds, no doubt. The animal was obviously frightened and hurt. Dolly slightly reared as Slater approached her.

"Dolly . . . whoa . . . whoa, Dolly," Slater said, his voice a low, calming intonation. "Just walk the rope over to me, girl," Slater said over his shoulder. "Slow . . . real slow."

Lark nodded, inhaled a calming breath, and started toward Slater and the horse. Dolly whinnied and took several steps backward. Lark paused in walking toward her, nodding at the horse.

"It's all right, Dolly," she said aloud. "It's all right now."

The horse shook its head, pounding the dirt with one hoof. Lark started toward Slater again, and this time the horse did not startle. She felt tears welling in her eyes, for the lacerations on the horse's chest and front legs were deep. Blood poured from the wound at her chest—streamed in crimson rivulets down her legs and over long white hair below her knees. The barbed wire had inflicted terrible damage. Lark knew the damage could well be extreme enough to force Slater into putting the horse down.

"Shhhh," Lark soothed as she approached. The horse nervously nodded but did not back away. "Shhh, Dolly," Lark said as she handed the rope to Slater.

"Stay back," Slater whispered. "She's fearful and hurt. She might—"

"She won't hurt me," Lark interrupted, however, taking several steps closer to the horse.

"Girl, you stay back!" Slater warned in a still lowered voice.

"I can help," Lark told him, however. "I'll soothe her while you rope her and inspect her injuries."

"No," Slater growled. At the sound of Slater's warning to Lark, Dolly stomped the ground, shaking her head with agitation.

"Shhh," Lark said to Slater. "I can help, I promise."

"You don't want to fool with an injured draft horse, girl," Slater told her. "You'll get us both killed."

"No, I won't," she told him, stepping toward the horse.

She paused when she felt Slater take hold of her arm. She looked over her shoulder to him as he said, "I'll rope you up and carry you back to the house if you don't stop right now."

He was angry with her—she knew he was. Yet she was certain he was only angry for the sake of worry—worry that she might be injured.

"Trust me," she whispered.

"No," he growled, glaring at her.

Lark smiled as she saw Slater's eyes widen. As he'd stood arguing with her, Lark had offered her hand to Dolly—and Dolly had accepted. Lark allowed Dolly to smell her a moment longer before gently placing her palm on the horse's velvet nose. She looked away from Slater then— away from Slater and to Dolly. For a moment, she was indeed frightened. The horse was so enormous! Its shoulder stood as tall as Lark, its neck and head giving it the appearance of a giant. Still, as Dolly pressed her nose against Lark's palm, Lark smiled.

"Dolly," Lark said, her voice tranquil—soft. "You're very hurt, Dolly," she cooed. "Slater has to tend to you. You won't fight him, will you? You'll trust him to help you. You'll trust me."

"Well, I'll be damned," Slater mumbled, frowning.

"I certainly hope not, Mr. Evans," she said, smiling as she glanced to him.

She could see the astonishment still vivid on his face. He was awed that she'd been able to so easily calm the horse.

He grinned and chuckled just a little. "I hope not too."

Lark's own smile broadened, for she was some-how delighted that she'd managed to amuse him.

Slater looked to Dolly then, slowly stroked her

70

neck as he said, "I'm gonna lead ya back toward the barn, Dolly. We gotta tend to these wounds. And once I've seen to you . . . I'm gonna ride out and find yer friend Tom . . . and see to him."

Dolly whinnied, stomping several times as Slater pulled the rope over her head and around her neck.

"Dolly," Lark whispered, "you can't hear my voice if you fuss that way."

Instantly, the horse settled, pressing its nose against Lark's shoulder.

Gently, Lark stroked the horse's head and whispered soothing words to it as Slater led it back toward the barn. "Will she be all right?" Lark asked as the horse nuzzled her shoulder.

"I don't know," Slater mumbled. "Depends on whether or not she'll let me tend to the damage. She'll need some stitchin' up . . . and then there's infection to worry about."

"She'll let you tend to her . . . won't you, Dolly?" Lark whispered. "I'll stay with you while Slater patches you up. You'll let him work on you, Dolly. You will."

Once they were closer to the barn, Slater tied the rope haltering Dolly to a post. He frowned as he looked to Lark, the intensity of his gaze causing her to feel uncomfortable. Lark could've sworn he could see right through her skin—right through to her very bones.

"I've gotta see to her wounds," he began, "and I

ain't too proud to say it'll take both of us. She might fight me a little, and if she does . . . you need to move fast. She'll break ya in two before ya know it if you're not careful."

Lark nodded and said, "I understand."

Slater reached up and patted Dolly on one shoulder. He removed his hat, tossing it onto a fencepost, and ran his fingers through his hair.

Lark smiled. She liked the way the gesture exposed the true color of his hair—the dark beneath the sun-bleached gold. He was a dangerously handsome man. And though it was an odd moment to wonder such a thing, she did wonder why he had never married. Tom too, for that matter. Surely there were women who would have the likes of Slater Evans for his appearance alone. Why then had he never settled in?

"I'll fetch a couple buckets of water. We'll have to clean her up good first," Slater said. He frowned, shaking his head. "I told Tom to take 'em both," he mumbled. He sighed and stroked Dolly's mane. "There now, Dolly," he whispered, his voice low and soothing like a summer's night. "You'll be fine. I'll see to that."

Lark wondered how it felt—to be held in Slater Evans's capable hands. She fancied Dolly was soothed by his touch—hopeful at his words.

"I will not put her down . . . not Dolly . . . not without tryin' everything else first," he muttered to himself. He glanced to Lark. "Let's get rid of the blood and see how bad she's hurt."

"Yes," Lark whispered.

"Stay here . . . but be careful," he ordered, wagging an index finger at her.

Lark nodded and smiled as Dolly nudged her arm. She watched Slater reach into the barn and pick up two buckets waiting just inside the door, and then he turned and sauntered away. She thought for a moment of how much she liked the way his shoulders swayed as he walked—liked the way his sun-bleached, brown hair feathered a moment as the breeze caught it.

"He'll take good care of you, Dolly," she whispered, tenderly stroking the horse's jaw. "I'm not sure there are many people or things he values . . . but I can see that he cares for you. You're a lucky girl."

Dolly puffed a heavy breath, nodding in seeming agreement.

Lark smiled and whispered, "Oh, I see. You are a woman, after all . . . and Mr. Slater Evans is handsome, isn't he?" Lark gently stroked Dolly's neck. "Handsome . . . and I think perhaps far more tenderhearted than he'd like us to know."

Chapter Four

"She healed up real good," Tom said as he currycombed Dolly, "no thanks to me."

"She sure has," Slater agreed as he hung the enormous harness on the barn wall. "And she don't seem to be holdin' a grudge neither." He smiled at Tom, a reassuring smile that he didn't hold a grudge either. Slater knew Tom would never have taken Coaly out alone if he'd known it would have distressed Dolly the way it did. Furthermore, he knew that, even though Dolly's wounds had healed nicely, Tom would never forgive himself.

Slater hunkered down, gently running a hand over the deep scar on Dolly's left leg. The wound at her chest had also healed, even better than he'd hoped. It pained him to see the scars on the beautiful animal, but she was alive and well, and that's what mattered. His mind lingered a moment on the day over a month before—the day Dolly had run headlong into the barbed wire fence north of the barn. In all his life he'd never seen a woman who had such a way with horses as Lark did. Fact was, Dolly should've been mad with fear and pain—could've nearly stomped either he or Lark to a paste of bones and blood—but she didn't. It hadn't been just luck that had found Lark able to calm the animal either. The young woman Tom had hired on as housekeeper and cook had since proven her gift with horses was a constant one. Not only had Lark calmed Dolly (and Dolly had grown quite attached to Lark because of it), but Slater's teeth had nearly dropped clean out of his head when his own horse, Smokey, had taken to her like a kitten to milk.

"She's lookin' good, boss," Eldon Pickering said as he approached. Eldon hunkered down to inspect Dolly's healed wounds. "You done some mighty nice stitchin' there."

Slater grinned with satisfaction. "Yep. She's healed real well."

Eldon nodded, patted the horse on the neck, and then asked, "Me and the boys was wonderin' if it's all right if we spend the evenin' in town." Slater looked to him as he continued, "We got the rest of the brandin' done . . . except for that new bull you come draggin' home from Pete Walker's place."

"I swear, Slater," Tom chuckled, shaking his head, "you already got that little bull from Clifford Herschel awhile back . . . and ol' Outlaw ain't none too happy about it. Why in tarnation did ya need this new one? An Angus at that?"

Slater shrugged. "I don't need him," he mumbled. "But you didn't need them new boots ya bought last week neither."

Tom chuckled, "Ya got me there, brother."

Truth was, Slater had an eye for cattle—especially bulls. He'd made a pretty penny by purchasing young bulls for a low price and then selling them as they matured, proving to be fine breeding stock. Tom was right—the Evans ranch's infamous sire bull Outlaw, a massive Hereford—more ornery than a cactus in summer—hadn't taken too kindly to the young bull, Little Joe, Slater had acquired from Clifford Herschel. Slater knew Outlaw was feeling his age, wary of any other young bull that might step too close to his territory. Still, Little Joe was already showing promise. Whether or not Slater chose to keep him, he knew Little Joe was worth three times what he'd laid down in purchase. He figured the same was true of Pete Walker's young Black Angus bull. Some ranchers were still wary of Scotland's Black Angus, yet Slater saw potential in the breed. His gut told him there would be wisdom in breeding them. Thus, he'd purchased the black bull from Pete Walker. His hopes were he'd manage to talk Pete into selling him a couple of Angus heifers. Then he could have a try at breeding Black Angus as well as Herefords.

"So . . . whatcha think, boss?" Eldon asked, rattling Slater from his thoughts on cattle breeds. "Is a night in town for the boys and me all right with you? It is Saturday."

"You know ya don't have to ask my permission, Eldon," Slater said. "If things are done 'round here, yer nights are yer own." He paused and glanced to Tom. "Just don't be bringin' no trouble home with ya."

"Oh, we won't," Eldon chuckled.

Still, Slater arched one eyebrow, remembering a Saturday night several months previous when the Evans ranch cowboys had gotten into a brawl over one of the girls at the saloon. Slater and Tom had had quite a time talking Sheriff Gale into letting the boys come home instead of spending the night in jail.

"No trouble, boss," Eldon assured him. "Honest." Tom chuckled, and Eldon added, "Why don't you boys come with us? You ain't seen a Saturday night in town in a month of Sundays."

"Ain't nothin' to interest me in town," Slater said, patting Dolly's neck as he stood. "But you oughta go, Tom. It'll do ya good."

"Ol' Tillman Pratt's got a new actress workin' at his drama house, Slater," Eldon said. "The boys over at the Herschel place say she's mighty purty. They say she's got a voice like a bird . . . and I know how ya like good singin'. Why don't you boys join us, boss?"

Slater did like a pretty voice and a sweet song now and then. He figured it was probably because his and Tom's mother had sung so pretty—and near to constantly. It seemed Ada Evans always had a song on her lips, as well as in her heart. Slater had a moment of mournful melancholy—of missing his mother.

Suddenly he was tired—tired of chopping wood, hauling hay and oats, mending fence—just plain tired. "What're you thinkin', Tom?" he asked his brother.

"I think I could use a little pretty singin' . . . and a few hours spent somewhere besides the ranch," Tom said. "And I know you could."

Slater nodded. He was weary of choring and could use a little distraction. He frowned, however, and asked, "What about Lark? Should we be leavin' her here alone?"

"Tillman Pratt's theatre ain't no place for a girl . . . but I ain't quite sure we oughta leave her either," Tom agreed.

"Ol' Mrs. Simpson used to stay home by her lonesome all the time," Eldon reminded. "Seems to me I remember she liked it that way. Women need time to themselves, after all."

"And yer such a wise man where women are concerned?" Tom teased. He chuckled a moment and then said, "I suppose we could ask her if she'd mind bein' here alone for a time."

"Oh, she'd never tell us the truth if she did. I have a hell of a time tryin' to figure what that girl is thinkin'," Slater mumbled. It was true too. More often than not, Lark Lawrence was determined not to let on what her thoughts were. Slater found the fact both intriguing and frustrating.

"I suppose that's what makes her so interestin'," Eldon said. "I swear ol' Chet's knees go to water whenever he gets sight of her."

"Well, if we're goin' . . . we probably oughta tell her before she starts supper," Slater said. "You go on in, Tom," he said, brushing his hands. "I'll get these horses stabled."

Lark lingered at the window in the small room at the back of the house. She'd been watching Slater and Tom curry Dolly and Coaly. She didn't quite know why she'd lingered in watching them, for she couldn't hear their conversation. Still, she often found comfort in just quietly observing them. Lark surmised that it gave her comfort to know they were nearby—that it instilled a long-absent sense of safety in her subconscious.

Eldon Pickering had joined them. He was a pleasant man. Tall, good-looking, with tawny hair and blue eyes—kind too. The other cowboys on the ranch were polite as well, though something about Chet Leigh unsettled Lark a bit—made her glad the cowboys ate, slept, and played cards in the bunkhouse behind the barn instead of in the ranch house with Slater and Tom.

Lark gasped as she saw Tom start toward the house. Dropping the curtain she'd been holding back as she'd watched them, she hurried to the kitchen. She was late with starting supper and worried that Tom was on his way in to inquire as to what she planned to prepare. Oh, Tom never got angry—not that Lark could see—but she didn't want to serve supper late all the same.

"Hey there, darlin'," Tom greeted as he entered the house. He was smiling—Tom was always smiling, and Lark loved him for it. Over the past few weeks, Lark had come to care very deeply for him. He was kind to her, his countenance always pleasant. She often thought she couldn't have loved a brother more than she loved Tom Evans, if she'd had a brother.

"Hello, Tom," she greeted in return, a smile of delight spreading across her face to accompany the instant sense of security washing over her. "I was just starting supper. I hope you're not too angry with me for not having it on the table yet."

Tom chuckled as he strode to her. "Not at all, honey," he said. "In fact, me and ol' Slater was thinkin' about goin' to town with the boys tonight. I guess ol' Tillman Pratt has a new actress singin' at the drama house. We'll just scrounge us up some stew or somethin' there . . . that way you don't have to cook for nobody but yourself." He smiled, his brown eyes rather merry with anticipation.

"So . . . a pretty actress, is it?" Lark teased. She felt little like teasing, in truth. The fact was that the idea of being at the ranch house alone troubled her. She inwardly scolded herself for such feminine weakness. After all, she'd been on her own for a long, long time—been alone for longer.

She also scolded herself for the thick lump of jealousy rising in her throat. A pretty actress? An unsettling thought crossed her mind—a thought that she didn't like the idea of Slater Evans being in the company of a pretty actress. Still, she buried the ridiculous notion of jealousy where either of the Evans brothers was concerned.

"That's what Eldon says," Tom answered. "She's supposed to be right pretty and sings like a bird. You know how Slater likes nice singin'."

"No . . . I didn't know that he did," Lark admitted, the anxious, albeit ridiculous heat of jealousy rising in her again.

"Yep. Our mama was a singer . . . had the voice of an angel," Tom explained. "I suppose that's why Slater has always been partial to fillies who can sing a pretty song."

"Oh. Well . . . well then, I'm sure the two of you are bound to enjoy your evening," Lark said.

Tom's eyes narrowed with sudden suspicion. Ah ha! At last! He and Slater had both been downright frustrated at their inability to read the thoughts and feelings of their little housekeeper, but the fog was lifting, and Tom was watchful. Lark was uncomfortable. He could see it in her eyes—the way the sparkle in them dimmed suddenly. He also read it in the way she cast her gaze from him momentarily and by the sudden deepening of the pink in her pretty cheeks.

"If ya don't want to be here alone, then one of us would be more than willin' to stay home with ya, honey," he offered—for at first he thought she was simply uncomfortable about being left behind.

"Oh no! No, no, no," she assured him, smiling and tucking a loose strand of hair behind one ear. "You all go on . . . have fun. I could use an evening by myself. I've so been wanting some quiet moments to read . . . if that's all right with you, I mean. Would it be all right if I read one of the books from the shelves in the parlor?"

"Of course, darlin'," Tom chuckled. "You can read anything you want in there."

"Well, then . . . I'll delight in an evening by myself," she said, smiling.

Tom studied her a moment, however. She was rattled—indeed she was.

"You and Slater go on and have a lovely time," she added. "Maybe the two of you will even get to meet that pretty actress. Oh, you two certainly deserve an evening of entertainment and respite. And what could be more entertaining than a pretty actress with the voice of bird? I'm sure Slater's bound to be smitten with her."

Tom grinned as full understanding washed over him. She was jealous! Lark was jealous of the actress in town—jealous of the possibility that the actress might win Slater's admiration.

"Smitten?" he asked, having decided to further

press Lark into revealing her feelings. "Slater don't get smitten with nobody."

"Oh, everybody is smitten at one time or another," Lark said, waving a hand in a gesture of indifference. "Even Slater."

"Nope," Tom said as the imp in his playful nature perked. "Slater gets to wantin' after a woman somethin' powerful now and then . . . but he never gets smitten." It was all he could do to keep from bursting into laughter, for instantly Lark's eyes widened.

"Well . . . well, I . . ." Lark stammered. "I . . . I wouldn't know about such things as wanting after a woman, as you phrase it."

Immediately, Tom was guilt-ridden. He shouldn't tease her about such things—not when it was apparent Slater had somehow managed to unknowingly weasel his way into her heart. Tom wasn't at all surprised, however. He'd always suspected Lark's discomfort in his brother's presence had more to do with the strange ability Slater had to attract women than it did with his often brooding and cantankerous demeanor. Tom knew he likewise owned a certain something that drew women to him. Yet it seemed where Lark Lawrence was concerned, Slater had prevailed.

"Oh, I'm just teasin' ya, honey," he said, taking one of her hands in his and kissing the back repentantly. "I'm sure ol' Slater gets as smitten as every other feller." The imp in his nature was not yet squelched, however, and he added, "Could be you're right and the pretty little songbird at Pratt's will be the one to do it."

"It could be," she mumbled, and he didn't miss the worry on her brow.

"But more than likely . . . it'll be me that finds himself smitten," he added in an effort to comfort her where Slater was concerned. "Actresses are more my type of women then Slater's, I would think."

Lark seemed somewhat encouraged and smiled at him. "Well, whether or not one of you is smitten with Mr. Pratt's pretty new songbird . . . I hope you enjoy your evening," she told him.

He guessed her friendly smile was a little more forced than usual and silently scolded himself for teasing her.

"Goodness knows the two of you deserve some relaxation."

"Oh, you're far too good to us, Lark," Tom told her. "You just be sure and enjoy yer time to yerself."

"I will," she said. "I'll just read a book . . . and be warm."

Tom felt his brow pucker a little, for it seemed an odd thing to say.

"Now you better change your shirt if you're going to town," Lark told him. She reached up, brushing a smudge of dirt from his forehead.

"You'll want to look your best for Mr. Pratt's new actress."

As Tom nodded and headed up the stairs to his bedroom, Lark tried to swallow the lump of insecurity and jealousy settling in her throat. The Evans brothers did deserve a night of entertainment and distraction. Furthermore, if she regarded it from another perspective, she probably would enjoy an evening of reading by the fire.

It was true, Lark liked to keep busy. Keeping busy kept her tired out—kept her mind from wandering to ridiculous musings. It kept her from worrying about the fact that the weather was cooling—that winter was on its way. So, since arriving at the Evans ranch more than a month before, she had kept busy—as busy as she possibly could. The truth was she'd nearly worn her fingers to the bone with keeping busy. Consequently, she was almost afraid to be left alone in the ranch house. Not because she was fearful of anything about the house—just that she knew her irrational inner fears would attempt to surface and try to whisper doubt and uncertainty to her mind.

Still, she wouldn't let it—no! She would build a nice fire in the parlor hearth, choose a book from the shelves, settle in the comfortable chair nearby, and read. She'd read all night if she chose to! It had been so long since she'd had time to read— since she'd had a book available to read from.

Truly it would be a wonderful evening—or so her mind tried to convince her.

Lark startled as Slater entered through the front door.

"You'll be all right here alone?" he asked.

Lark forced a smile. "Of course," she told him, trying to stop the fluttering that began in her bosom at the sight of him. "It will be very soothing to have an evening of quiet."

As he strode nearer to her, however, she was unable to stop the wild fluttering that erupted in both her bosom and her stomach. Silently she scolded herself, disgusted with the reaction her body experienced each time Slater was near. She'd thought surely by now he would cease in affecting her so. Over the past several weeks, Lark's attraction to Slater Evans had multiplied with each passing hour, it seemed. Still, she was far too practical a woman to pay heed to such things—or so she tried to convince herself. Furthermore, it rather vexed her at times that it should be Slater who caused her heart to beat so quickly, for Tom was the congenial one—the calm, charming, and friendly one. At times Slater seemed nearly as cold and unfeeling as an old river rock. Yet Lark had grown to suspect this was a mask he sometimes wore, for often she would enter a room to find him and Tom erupting with laughter or discussing some melancholy sentiment.

Yet the fact remained—Slater Evans was her employer. That was all. He had no interest in her beyond expecting her to keep house and cook meals, and this was as it should be. Thus, each time Slater's presence would cause Lark's innards to begin wildly trilling, she would simply remind herself of her position. Most times this worked in subduing any goose bumps threatening to erupt over her limbs at the sound of his voice. Most of the time this allowed her to hide her feelings, for she was nothing if not guarded in her thoughts.

"We oughta be back by midnight," he said.

She nodded. "Enjoy yourselves. You are very deserving of reprieve."

"So are you," he said. He smiled at her, and Lark fought to keep her sudden breathlessness hidden.

"Then, if you don't mind, I'll just be about my own business," Lark said. "Good night."

Slater couldn't help but smile as Lark began to struggle with the knot in her apron at her back. He'd not missed the fact that their little housekeeper had a tendency to grow frustrated with apron strings, tie them into a knot, and forget she had done so until the end of the day. More often than not, Lark found herself frustrated with the task of trying to remove her apron when the knot had grown so tight at her back.

She grumbled under her breath, already frustrated as her small fingers struggled with the ties.

"Here," he said, taking her by the shoulders and turning her away from him. "You best let me get you out of this apron . . . or else we're bound to come home in the dead of night to find you still tied up in it."

Lark couldn't move! She felt his hands at the small of her back—heard a mild, mumbled cuss escape him as he struggled with the knot in her apron strings. She had a sudden and nearly over-whelming desire to lean back—to rest her body against the strength of his and beg him to enfold her in his strong arms. But these were schoolgirl fancies, and she inwardly scolded herself—and harshly.

"There ya go," he said at last.

Lark exhaled the breath she'd been holding as she felt her apron go slack at her waist. "Thank you," she said, pulling the white ruffled bib apron up over her head. She'd braided her hair that morning instead of pulling it up into a more practical bun, and somehow her braid caught in the apron.

"Ow!" she exclaimed, pausing in removing the apron—for the motion had pulled her hair as it entangled it with the apron.

"Here," Slater said. "Hold on. You're all snarled up here . . ."

Lark felt his hand at the back of her neck—felt

the rough calluses of his palm against her flesh—and she could not will away the goose bumps erupting over her arms. She could feel his hands working to separate her hair from the apron, and simply the knowledge he was touching her caused her to slightly tremble.

"There ya go," he said, pulling the apron off over her head and handing it to her.

"Thank you," she said, draping the apron over her arm and pulling her long braid to lie over one shoulder. "Enjoy your evening, Slater."

"I will," he said.

She watched him take the stairs two at a time —heard him begin to whistle. She couldn't help but smile, for it was a rare thing to see Slater Evans experiencing a moment of lightheartedness.

Lark sighed. There was no reason to cook supper now. She'd satisfy her hunger with some bread and butter, perhaps a strip of Slater's special peppered jerky. Then she'd choose a book from the shelves in the parlor and do nothing—nothing at all.

Suddenly, an evening alone began to appeal to her, and Lark smiled and began to hum as she rather strolled into the kitchen to tuck her apron away in the pantry. She giggled a moment later when she realized she'd been humming the same tune Slater had been whistling—"Little Lucy Sparrow." A vision of her mother sitting next to her bed, darning stockings, and singing "Little

Lucy Sparrow" wafted through her mind, causing her heart to ache a moment. She wondered if Slater's mother had once sung the song to him.

"Little Lucy Sparrow, perching on a limb so narrow . . . oh, won't you trill a love song for me?" Lark began to sing. She smiled, remembering how dear the song was to her—how dear were the memories of her sweet mother. *"A handsome caballero that wears a wide sombrero . . . is only what I wish for, you see."* Lark giggled, suddenly delighted by the melody and clever words of the song. *"Please, Lucy, trill him to me, as a blossom bee to honey. A handsome caballero he'll be. And as I perch on his knee, just as you there perch in your tree . . . Oh, Lucy, trill a love song for me."*

Lark paused and frowned, momentarily unable to remember the next trail of lyrics. "Little Lucy Sparrow, perching on a limb so narrow . . . oh, won't you trill a love song for me?" she mumbled, closing the pantry door behind her. "La la la la . . ." Lark shook her head, frustrated at being unable to remember the next line of the song.

"A pretty senorita, perhaps named Rosalita . . . for that is what I wish for, from thee," Slater sang in a low, masculine voice as he descended the stairs, a clean white shirt in hand.

"That's it!" Lark smiled.

"Oh, Lucy trill her to me," she sang in unison with Slater—awed by the dazzling smile on his

face. *"We'll kiss beneath the plum tree,"* they continued. *"Oh, won't you trill a love song for me?"*

Lark giggled and clapped her hands with delight.

"My mother used to sing that to us when we were boys," Slater said, smiling. Lark watched as he slipped muscular arms into white shirtsleeves.

"My mother sang it too," Lark said. "When I was very little, before . . ."

"Before she passed?" he asked.

"Yes," she answered.

He didn't press her for further information as she feared he would. Simply he nodded and began buttoning his shirt.

Tom descended the stairs then, smiling as always.

"You must be in a good humor, Slater," he began, slapping his brother soundly on the back. "Singin' sweet songs with Lark here. I ain't heard you sing somethin' like that since . . . well . . . I can't quite remember when."

"Fact is, I'm a might more pleased about gettin' into town than I thought I'd be," Slater said as he tucked his shirt into the waist of his trousers. "You sure you'll be all right here alone, baby?" Slater asked Lark.

Lark nodded, attempting to appear calm. It was true that the Evans brothers had taken to addressing Lark with rather endearing-sounding nicknames. Tom rarely called her by name—

choosing to address her as *darling* or *honey*. But it was Slater's habit of referring to her as *baby* that sent her nerves to nearly drowning her in delicious waves of delight. Oh, she knew it was just their way—their casual manner. Yet she liked to imagine that Slater's referencing her as such meant more—that he favored her somehow.

"I'll be fine," she managed to tell him.

"Then let's get," he said, nodding to Tom.

"You enjoy yourself, honey," Tom said, winking at her.

"You too," she said as she watched them snatch their best hats from the hat rack by the door.

"Good night," Slater said, nodding to her as he pressed his hat onto his head and left, closing the door behind them.

"Good night," Lark mumbled.

Almost instantly she felt alone—deeply alone. She felt chilled as well.

Hurrying into the parlor, she started a fire in the hearth, feeling even more alone as she heard the sound of horses breaking into gallops as the men left for town—all the men.

Forcing herself to an appearance of serenity for her own sake, she began to read the titles on the spines of the books gathered on the parlor bookshelf.

"Ah, there you are," she said as she carefully selected a book. "Mr. Twain's *Tom Sawyer*. I've heard you're a wonderful adventure."

Sighing, Lark snuggled down in the big, worn, and very comfortable armchair near the hearth. Opening the book, she began to read, attempting to ignore the feelings of loneliness and insecurity threatening to grip her. Slowly the story began to enthrall her—to distract her from any feelings of lonesomeness. Furthermore, the fire in the hearth was comforting, an ever-present reminder that she was warm—and would be warm—all through the cold winter.

Chapter Five

She was pretty, Tillman Pratt's new actress. Oh, not as pretty as some women Slater had known—not even as pretty as some women he currently was acquainted with. Yet she was pretty, and she sang well. He did marvel at her costume, it being hardly more than a glorified, embellished corset—marveled at the depth of confidence and wild abandon a woman would need to possess in order to appear so nearly bare in public. He smiled yet immediately scolded himself as a thought flitted through his mind—a wondering of how Lark Lawrence would look dressed in such a lack of dress.

Slater shook his head to dispel the inappropriate if not highly agreeable thought—tried to return his attention to Miss Josephine Glory and her rendition of a Stephen Foster melody.

"She's got a purty voice," Tom whispered.

"Yep," Slater agreed. He glanced to one side, curious as to what the other Evans ranch cowboys thought of Miss Josephine Glory and her black and pink corset. He smiled, amused as he saw Eldon Pickering's eyes were as wide as supper dishes. Ralston and Grady were mesmerized as well, grinning so wide that Slater wondered if their faces might crack clean in two. He leaned forward a bit, looking down the row of seats and tables to see if Chet were enjoying the performance of the scantily clad songbird. He frowned slightly when he saw that Chet no longer sat next to Grady. He glanced to his other side—to the chairs and tables beyond Tom. Chet was not there either.

"Where's Chet?" he whispered to Tom as a strange sense of unrest began to rise in him.

Tom looked from one side to the other, a frown furrowing his brow as well. "I don't see him," Tom whispered. He shook his head. "That boy has near to a barrel of whiskey in him . . . and we don't need no trouble."

"I'm tellin' ya . . . we shouldn't let our boys drink liquor," Slater mumbled.

"They're free men, Slater. Ain't much we can do when they ain't at the ranch."

"Maybe we oughta start hiring boys that don't take to whiskey then," Slater growled. "He'll get himself in trouble, sure enough."

"Well, you ain't his daddy," Tom reminded. "You can send him ridin' off if he gets into trouble . . . but you can't keep him from drinkin' if he has a mind to do it."

"You worried about Chet, boss?" Ralston asked in a whisper.

Slater nodded. "That boy favors hard liquor too much for his own good."

"Oh, don't worry none, Mr. Evans," Grady whispered, leaning forward and offering a reassuring nod to Slater. "Chet said he was headin' home. Said his thirst was too mighty powerful to quench at the bar . . . that he needed to get home and take care of it. I figure he'll just fall right into bed . . . if'n he makes it back to the bunkhouse, that is."

Ralston chuckled, but Slater did not. Tom and Eldon frowned as well.

"He wouldn't do nothin' to Miss Lark . . . would he, do ya think?" Eldon asked.

But Slater's instincts had already warned him that a drunken Chet Leigh should not be any-where near Lark. Chet Leigh had proved himself to be an ugly drunk once before. In that moment, Slater wished he and Tom would've let Sheriff Gale lock the boys up for a night the time before when the boys had gotten into trouble in town after drinking.

He was on his feet in an instant. He did not pause to see if Tom or anyone else would accompany him. Simply he strode from Tillman Pratt's drama house and across the street to where Smokey was tied to the hitching post.

"Slater!" Tom shouted as Slater rode off at a mad gallop.

He knew Tom would follow—Eldon too. Gritting his teeth with anger, he determined that if Ralston and Grady weren't back to the house near to as close as he was—well then, they could spend the winter somewhere else.

"Come on, Smoke," Slater growled, leaning forward in the saddle as the horse raced toward the ranch. He would beat them all home—he knew he would. Smokey was the fastest horse in three counties, with endurance the like he'd never seen. It was five miles back to the ranch, and he'd run Smokey all the way.

Slater didn't like Chet Leigh; he never had. He'd only hired him on at Ralston and Grady's assurance he was a good cowboy. Chet did prove to be a good ranch hand and cowboy, but Slater had never been convinced of his possessing a good character. Furthermore, he wasn't as blind to Chet's infatuation with Lark as Eldon might have thought. He'd seen the way Chet watched her—seen the smile spread across his face whenever he did watch her. He and Tom shouldn't have left Lark home alone. He shouldn't have left her home alone. After all, he knew far more about the likes of Chet

Leigh than Tom did. He should've known better.

He clenched his jaw tight, tried to concentrate on Smokey's pace—on the horse's breathing—on the sound of muscle and leather straining. There was a good rhythm to it. He'd be back at the ranch soon—but would it be soon enough?

The knock on the door startled Lark. She'd been reading for hours—reading about Injun Joe, about Tom and Becky trapped in a cave. Thus, she nearly jumped out of her skin when she heard the hammering at the door. At first she wasn't sure whether her heart was hammering so brutally in her chest that she'd imagined the beating on the door.

"Miss Lark?" came a man's voice from the other side of the door.

Lark sighed with relief, placing her hand on her bosom to try and settle the mad racing within. "Chet? Is that you?" she asked. She indeed recognized the cowboy's voice. Still, something told her to be wary.

"Yes, ma'am," came Chet's friendly assurance.

Breathing another calming sigh, Lark opened the door to find it was indeed Chet standing on the porch.

"Did you all have fun in town?" Lark asked, glancing past him to see if the other men were home as well.

Chet smiled a knowing, rather devilish smile

that did not comfort Lark in any regard. "No, ma'am," Chet said. "I figure on havin' my fun here . . . now."

"You're drunk," Lark said, noting the harsh scent of whiskey about him. "You better get to the bunkhouse and sleep that off before morning. I'm certain Slater and Tom don't have much tolerance for drunkenness."

A low, rather threatening chuckle emanated from Chet's throat as he pushed the door wide open, stepping into the house. Slamming the door closed behind him, he drew the small bolt. Suddenly, the Evanses' ranch house did not seem as safe as it had a moment before.

Though she'd hoped her instincts had been wrong, Lark knew they hadn't been. Chet meant her harm, of one sort or the other. She shouldn't have opened the door—but it was too late now.

"If your intentions are not honorable—" she began.

"I ain't had an honorable intention in my life, girl!" he growled, reaching out and taking her face between his hands.

But Lark was not without experience where the vile intentions of some men were concerned—nor was she without a sense of self-preservation. She stomped on Chet's foot with the heel of her boot and drew her knee up to hit him below the waist where she knew it would cause the most pain. Chet doubled over, but only slightly.

No doubt the whiskey Lark could smell on his breath had somewhat numbed his sense of pain.

She cried out as he reached out, taking hold of her arm in a firm grip. Still, she was not so easily assaulted. She raised a foot, kicking him in the stomach. This time when he doubled over, Lark turned and bolted toward the back of the house. Chet was quick, however, and Lark gasped as she felt him take hold of her hair at the back of her head. He pulled hard on her braid, and she crumbled to the floor.

"Let go of me!" she shouted. "Don't you dare touch me!"

"You've got spirit, girl!" Chet chuckled as he took hold of her shoulders and pushed her back to the floor. "I'll give ya that."

Lark fisted one hand, hitting him square in the jaw with as much force as she could muster. Chet shouted, letting go of her as he put a hand to his chin.

Frantically, Lark scrambled away from him, but she was not quick enough, and his grip on her ankle found her facedown on the floor once more.

"You best quit fightin' me, girl," Chet growled. "You'll have more fun if ya just give up."

"I'll die first," Lark cried, tears escaping her eyes to stream down her face.

"No," Chet chuckled. "No . . . you won't."

Easily he flipped her over to her back on the

floor. Lark beat at his chest, his arms, his face, but he was unaffected.

"Shut your mouth," Chet growled, clamping a whiskey-scented hand over Lark's tender mouth. "What do you think, girl? You think us boys are just gonna sit by and watch them Evans brothers have all the fun?" He chuckled, maneuvering her body so that he was soon sitting down hard on her legs, hovering over her like some wretched disease. "No, siree. I figure it's time Slater and Tom Evans learned to share a little of the goods they got."

Desperately, Lark struggled and slapped Chet Leigh hard across the face—attempting to pull out a handful of his hair. She was startled into stillness when the back of his hand brutally met one side of her face. Again he hit her, sending her senses reeling with explosive pain and dizziness. She tasted the blood as it entered her mouth by way of her damaged lip.

Summoning every ounce of courage and life-saving determination she could, she said, "You hit me again, Chet Leigh . . . and I swear . . . I swear to you I'll gouge out your eyes."

"Don't you make to threaten me, girl," he breathed, chuckling as he bent and kissed her cheek. "Don't you dare . . . or I might have to knock you out cold and then have my fun."

Again he hit her, and Lark's consciousness reeled. She felt his mouth on her neck, but her arms were too weak with the pain at her face and the whirling in her head to return the abuse.

"What?" the drunk breathed, suddenly.

Lark blinked—thought she'd heard something too—a loud thud, as if something had been hurled against the back door.

"Who's that?" Chet shouted. "Is that you, Ralston?"

The sound of shattered glass hitting the floor helped draw Lark from the painful stupor Chet's beating had cast over her. She heard Chet swear —saw an arm reach through the now broken window next to the back door and pull the bolt. A moment later, Slater burst into the house.

"Why you filthy son of a . . ." he growled, taking hold of Chet by the back of his shirt collar and pulling his body from Lark's.

Slater didn't pause, and Lark winced as she saw his fist meet directly with Chet's jaw. The loathsome cowboy reeled—stumbled—but he didn't fall.

"Get on yer horse, boy!" Slater shouted. "Get on yer horse and ride outta here!"

"What?" Chet said, wiping the blood from his nose. "You're sending me off? Just for havin' a little fun with yer girl here? I ain't done nothin' that you ain't done a hundred times!"

Lark gasped as the brutal power of Slater Evans's fist met with Chet's jaw again. This blow sent the man to his knees and his mouth to bleeding too.

Chet chuckled and spit blood and saliva from his mouth as he shook his head. "You're a tough old dog, Slater Evans. I'll give ya that."

Lark rose to her feet, wiping tears from her face as she watched Chet struggle to stand. Yet stand he did, spitting once more, this time on Slater's boot.

"And you're a sturdy drunk. That's all I'll give ya," Slater growled. He looked to the blood and saliva Chet had spit on his boot. "But ya know what?" he asked.

Chet's eyes narrowed. "What's that?"

"These are my good boots," Slater growled an instant before his fist sent Chet sprawling to the floor a third time.

Slater didn't pause for Chet to regain his senses. Instead, Lark watched in horror as Slater fisted Chet's hair in one hand, delivering another brutal blow to his face—and another. He released the cowboy then, and Chet's head hit the floor. The man was still conscious, however, as Slater began to pace back and forth in front of him—fury causing his powerful body to tremble.

"You dared to come into my house?" Slater growled as he paced. Lark thought he looked more like a mountain lion stalking his prey than a man. "You dared to come into my house . . . and lay yer hands on that girl?" he shouted, pointing to Lark. Instantly, he quit his pacing and hunkered down before Chet, taking hold of the front of his shirt. "I'd as soon kill ya as look at you, boy!"

"You wait, Evans," Chet growled. "You wait 'til I'm sobered up. We'll see if you can knock me down when I ain't drunk."

"I could kill ya easy," Slater threatened. "Drunk or not."

Lark cried out as Slater delivered another powerful blow to Chet's face. "If you're wantin' me to prove it . . ."

"Slater!"

Lark sobbed as she turned to see Tom step through the back door. Eldon was with him, Ralston and Grady looking on from behind.

"Let him go, Slater," Tom said. "Just let him go. He can ride out, and we'll be done with him."

"You don't know what his intentions were here," Slater said, wagging a finger at Tom with one hand as his other held tight to the front of Chet's shirt.

"I'm sure I do know," Tom said. "But ya gotta let him go. Let's just tie him to his horse and send him off."

Lark watched Slater's eyes narrow as he looked to his brother. He nodded.

"You're right, Tom," Slater said then. "I oughta let him go."

Lark cried out, however, as Slater delivered one last powerful blow to Chet's face. Angrily he shoved the man backward as he released his hold on the front of his shirt. Chet fell, sprawled on the floor—unconscious.

Standing, Slater wiped the blood and saliva from his boot on Chet's trouser leg. "He spit on my good boot," he said to Tom.

"He shouldn't have done that," Tom said, shaking his head. "But he's out cold now. So let's just move on."

"Matilda gave me these boots . . . last Christmas," Slater said.

"I know she did," Tom said. "It was a right thoughtful gift too."

"Damn right it was," Slater mumbled, nodding emphatically.

Lark was trembling. It was obvious Slater was infuriated. She knew the meaningless banter between the brothers was their way of settling themselves. She watched as Slater's broad chest and shoulders rose and fell with the labored breathing of restrained fury.

His eyes narrowed, and he pointed to Eldon and then to Ralston and Grady, who stepped into the house, mouths gaping open in astonishment as they stared down at their unconscious friend. "None of you other boys . . . none of you got any ideas where Miss Lawrence is concerned . . . now do ya?" Slater asked.

"No, sir," Ralston breathed, shaking his head, nearly quaking with fear.

"Grady?" Slater asked.

"No, sir," Grady assured his boss. "Not me, sir."

"Eldon?"

"I ain't that sort," Eldon said. "You know that."

"All right then," Slater sighed. "Drag him outta here. Make sure he's gone before I wake up in the mornin'. If he wakes up in the night . . . you best see him on his way, boys."

"Yes, sir, Mr. Evans," Grady said as Ralston and Eldon nodded.

With trembling hands, Lark brushed the tears from her cheeks as the three conscious cowboys dragged Chet's limp body from the house.

"The minute he's awake . . . you boys send him off," Tom reminded them as they left the house.

"Yes, sir," Grady said, closing the door behind them.

"Let me see this," Slater demanded, striding to Lark and gently taking her chin in one strong hand.

Instantly, she began to tremble—wildly affected not only by residual anxiety but also by his touch. He frowned as he studied her. She could see his strong jaw clenching as he did so.

"I shoulda killed him," Slater mumbled as he pressed his fingers against the soreness already beginning to throb at Lark's cheek. "I shoulda killed that son of—"

"No. Now, Slater . . . no," Tom said.

Lark was momentarily mesmerized by the emotions apparent in Slater's smoldering eyes—anger and guilt. She watched as he quickly licked his thumb, wiping at the blood on her lip. At this, the entire surface of her body broke into involuntary goose bumps. His touch was overpowering to her senses!

"You're bleedin' here," he mumbled, licking the appendage again and stroking her tender lip a second time. The repeated action caused moisture to flood Lark's mouth, for she knew it was as close as she might ever come to knowing affection from him.

"I-I'm sorry," Lark heard herself apologize in a whisper. "I'm sorry for this . . . for the broken window glass . . . for the . . . the mess."

Slater's frown deepened. "You ain't got nothin' to apologize for, baby," he said. "This ain't yer fault. Not a bit of it. It's mine. None but mine. This is my fault . . . for hirin'—"

"Me?" Lark interrupted as pain pierced her heart. He regretted hiring her—she knew he must. She was certain nothing the likes of what had just transpired ever happened when Mrs. Simpson had been alive.

"For hirin' Chet," Slater said. "It's my fault . . . for hiring that no-good cowboy."

A wave of relief washed over Lark—such a great wave that she began to weep once more. She tried to restrain her tears, for she didn't want to appear any weaker before him than she already did.

"Let me see that," Tom said, taking her chin in his hand. Tom clicked his tongue as he shook his head. "That's gonna be awful sore and swollen come mornin'."

"Maybe we oughta let Chet stay a day or two," Slater suggested. "You know, heal up a bit . . . so I can horsewhip him before he goes."

"Come here, darlin'," Tom said, gathering Lark into the warm protection of his arms. Instantly, Lark's emotions were weakened, and she clung to him, soaking his shirt with her tears.

"Thank you," she whispered, at once overwhelmed with gratitude. Yet she was grateful not only for the protection afforded by Slater and Tom Evans but also for the fact they'd taken her in at all. "Thank you."

"Oh, ain't that always the way," she heard Slater grumble. As Tom held her, she looked to Slater to see the frown on his face had softened a little. "Seems I always do the fightin' . . . but Tom's the one who always gets the sugar."

Though the thought caused her to tremble—to shiver with anxious delight—Lark knew she must somehow find the courage to thank Slater as well—to thank him as she'd thanked his brother. Tom had been the one to hire her, it was true. But Slater had saved her virtue—perhaps her life.

Quivering with trepidation, she stepped out of Tom's embrace as he released her and looked to Slater. Still, her courage was spent. She couldn't embrace him—she just couldn't! Surely if she allowed herself to be enfolded in his strong, capable arms—even for a moment—surely then he'd be able to know the depth of her true feelings for him. And it was carefully, near desperately, that she guarded the truth of them. Slater Evans could never know that his orphaned, penniless cook and housekeeper was in love with him.

Tentatively, Lark offered her hand to Slater Evans—offered her hand in order to shake his in showing her gratitude.

Slater smiled, obviously amused—the enraged fury gone from him. "You're gonna shake my hand?" he chuckled.

Lark could only nod, otherwise frozen with battling her desire to be in his arms.

"Alrighty then," Slater said, taking her hand in his.

At once the warmth of his grip traveled through her hand enveloping her arm to fan out to her bosom, her stomach, and her face.

A low chuckle rumbled in his throat, and Lark gasped as he pulled her to him, wrapping her in powerful arms, drawing her snuggly against his strong body.

Lark could not resist him—could not keep her wits steady in that moment. Allowing her arms to travel around him, she fisted the fabric at the back of his shirt in her hands—sobbed against the solid contours of his chest—nearly swooned when she felt him press his face to the top of her head. He hadn't really kissed her; it was his cheek that pressed against her hair. Still, she allowed herself to pretend he'd kissed her. She clung to him a moment longer as she whispered, "Thank you," into the soft folds of his shirt. He smelled like warm sunshine, saddle leather, and green pasture grass. She imagined he wanted her there—there in his arms—imagined he wanted her there as desperately as she wanted to linger there—forever. He was warm, strong—and he would protect her. For all the horror of Chet's attacking her, Lark could not remember the last time she'd felt so safe. In that moment, she knew nothing could harm her. And he was so warm. She imagined how warm a winter would be spent in Slater Evans's arms.

"So the next time me and Tom head to town to watch some red-haired robin singing while wearin' nothin' but her drawers . . . maybe you oughta come along. Whatcha think?" Slater asked.

Lark was disappointed when she felt his embrace slacken. Yet she smiled, even breathed a giggle and nodded as she stepped back away from him.

"Maybe I should," she whispered, wiping more tears from her cheeks.

"Why don't you find yer bed, darlin'?" Tom suggested, reaching out to tuck a strand of hair behind her ear. "It's late . . . and them bruises are gonna pain you somethin' terrible come mornin'. Just rest in. We'll take care of ourselves for breakfast."

"Oh no!" Lark began to argue. "No . . . I'll be fine. I'll be up and ready as usual."

"No," Slater said. "If you're up before sunrise . . . I'll put you back to bed myself."

Lark tried to ignore the mad fluttering erupting in her stomach as she gazed up at him a moment. His hair was tousled—windblown—and she wondered if he'd ridden hard to get back to the ranch. She wanted to reach up—to run her fingers through the brown and tawny layers of his hair. Instead, she nodded.

"All right," she whispered. "As long as you're both going too."

"We got a few things to finish up . . . but then we'll settle in," Tom assured her. "Don't you worry none about us."

Lark nodded and felt tears welling in her eyes once more. "Thank you," she managed to squeak. "Thank you both . . . for everything."

Slater nodded, as did Tom.

"Good night, honey," Tom said. "Sleep sound. Ain't nothin' gonna harm you."

Lark nodded, knowing nothing would. "Good night, Slater," she managed.

He nodded, and Lark resisted the urge to run to him—to throw her arms around him and beg him to hold her.

Lark's body ached as she crawled beneath the covers of her bed. The house was cool, and she knew that, even for the sore throbbing at her cheek, she would sleep deeply.

As she closed her eyes, she thought of Chet Leigh—of what his intentions had been. She frowned a moment, even though it had not been the first time a man had harbored such intentions toward her. It had, however, been the first time she had not been able to escape. She inhaled a deep, calming breath, thinking that it had also been the first time a man had fought to protect her—and this was both a soothing knowledge and a delightful one. Of course, it was not so soothing to think on the brutal blows he had delivered to Chet Leigh's person—or the blood he'd spilled. But even so, it was comforting to know that Slater had come to her rescue. In truth, Lark was secretly delighted by the fact.

Sometime later she heard heavy footsteps ascending the stairs—heard one boot hit the floor overhead and then the other. The boards in her ceiling (which were likewise the boards in Slater Evans's bedroom floor) creaked as he walked. Soon all was quiet, and she knew both men were settled for the night.

Swaddled in the comfort of knowing she was safe, Lark at last drifted into deep slumber. Her last thought was of warmth, of the warm fire she'd enjoyed in the parlor while reading and of the even better warmth—the warmth of being held in Slater Evans's arms.

Chapter Six

Chet Leigh was gone by morning, all right. Slater had half expected to wake up and find the man still passed out cold somewhere, but he hadn't. Instead, he awakened to find Chet Leigh had indeed ridden away. However, Chet had apparently opened the east fences and scattered cattle as he went—the idiot. Slater nearly rode out after him, intent on giving him a beating that would make the one he'd given him the night before look like a waltz. Still, he hadn't. He knew the best thing to do was just to let the dirty dog go.

Slater swore under his breath as he spotted the young Black Angus bull off in the distance. Sure enough, the little cuss had headed straight back to Pete Walker's place. He scolded himself for not having branded the bull the day before. Slater knew Pete Walker well—not the most honest man in the world. If the young bull made it back to Pete's herd, no doubt Walker would try to pass it off as a different bull entirely.

"Go on, Smoke," Slater said, spurring his horse.

As Smokey galloped toward the bull, Slater readied his lasso. It would be easier to herd the bull home once a rope was round him. He'd rope that bull and haul him back to the ranch—brand him right then and there—before he helped Tom and the other boys to round up the scattered herd. He wouldn't have Pete Walker claiming the young bull was still his.

Slater easily roped the little Angus. He wound the lead around his saddle horn and turned Smokey back toward the ranch. "Come on, you sorry little devil," he said. "I got enough to worry about without you causin' me any trouble."

Soon the bull was headed back home, and Slater's mind wandered to other things—things he'd been attempting to keep it from wandering to.

The fury that rose within him every time he thought of Chet Leigh laying a hand on Lark was almost irrepressible. Several times during the night, he'd thought about heading outside, finding where the boys had tossed Chet for the night, and getting in a couple more good punches. He stretched his right hand and then made a fist. It was sore—indeed it was—but he'd like to have let go a few more on Chet, even though his bloody knuckles had stained up the sheets of his bed pretty good already.

Slater ground his teeth, stiffened his posture, and inhaled a deep breath in trying to calm himself. Chet Leigh had touched her—the dirty drunk had dared to touch Lark! What if he hadn't ridden back in time after finding out Chet had left the drama house? What if he'd paused one more moment in doing so? Still, Slater's daddy had always told him and Tom not to dwell on what might have been—good or bad. Thus, Slater decided to just be glad he'd ridden out when he had.

Still, he'd never forget the sight of it—of breaking the window with his elbow and opening the door to see Chet Leigh about to have his way with Lark. Slater Evans had seen some mighty terrible things in his thirty years, but in that moment he silently admitted to himself that nothing—nothing—had ever scared him more or provoked him to such rage as the sight of Chet Leigh abusing Lark.

He reached up and lifted his hat, wiping the sweat from his forehead. He looked up to the sun, which lingered behind a cloud. It wasn't even warm out. Fact was, he was wearing his slicker and still felt the cold on his face. Why then was he perspiring?

It was Lark. She had a way of warming up his blood. Anytime he was near to her, he nearly thought he might fire up to such a boil that he'd need to run off and dip himself in the creek. At first, he'd thought it was just the scorching heat of summer, for it had still been summer when she'd come to him—when she'd come to him and Tom. Yet it hadn't taken Slater long to realize it wasn't the heat of the day causing him to feel restless and warm: it was Lark.

Oh, certainly he could never say a word to

Tom—or anybody else, for that matter. He was Slater Evans—hard-hearted, hard-working, cattle-driving Slater Evans. Some little wounded sparrow wasn't about to get under his skin—at least, he'd never let on.

A vision of her beautiful green eyes leapt to his mind. The way her dark eyelashes shaded them— the way the tiny, light freckles scattered across her nose caused him to chuckle and smile with delight sometimes. He wondered how it would feel to bury his hands in the soft silk of her hair.

Again he cussed a breath—shook his head in an effort to dispel such adolescent musings. He didn't have time for a woman. He had cattle to herd, a ranch to run, endless work to do. Anyway, Lark was young and vibrant. The evidence of the fight she'd put up where Chet was concerned was proof of that. Slater winced as he thought of her pretty face—imagined how bruised it would be by the time she climbed out of bed. Still, she was vibrant, and he had no doubt she would recover and move on. Yep, young and vibrant— and he was old and weathered. Lark was like a daffodil in springtime, and he was like a worn-out old boot.

Slater rubbed at his eyes, trying to keep his mind from lingering on the memory of holding Lark in his arms the night before. He'd nearly been driven mad with wanting to keep her there— with pure wanting her altogether. He growled, thinking himself no better than Chet Leigh at having such thoughts.

She's a good cook, Slater thought, attempting to steer his ponderings to simpler, more suitable trails. *And she keeps a fine house too.* Still, the truth was Slater Evans didn't care too awful much for such things. What he liked was the sparkle in Lark's eyes first thing in the morning —the way the evening sky lit up her face with a pretty smile—the way her pretty smile lit up his soul.

The Angus bull tugged on the rope, and Smokey whinnied his complaint, breaking the smooth rhythm of his step.

"I had me enough trouble to last quite a spell already, boy," Slater called to the bull. "You simmer down. We're almost home."

Slater could see the house and barn in the distance. He could see Tom was bringing in a few heifers. No doubt he'd corral them until the other boys rounded up the rest. In that moment, he hoped Chet Leigh was long gone. It wouldn't do a bit of good to have the herd scattered again. Cold weather was moving in. The cattle needed to be close.

Slowly, Lark opened her eyes. The painful throbbing of her cheek and lip had caused her a fitful sleep. Soft sunlight streamed through the lace curtains, painting the opposing wall with lovely designs born of shadow and radiance. Lark smiled, for it was a beautiful sight to wake up to. She could hear birds just outside her window—fancied the scents of grass and dust, of the fading wildflowers of autumn were nature's perfume in that moment.

She sat upright in bed, however, as she heard the drumming of horse hooves thundering past her window.

"We need to brand him right now," she heard Slater shout. "So get that fire stoked, Tom."

Leaping from her bed, Lark drew back the drapes. She unlatched the window and opened it, tenderly pressing a warm palm to her sore and swollen cheek.

"Yer gonna have a time bringin' him down, Slater," Tom chuckled as he hurried from the barn carrying a branding iron. "We'll see if you still think that polled breed is worth raisin' after you try and bring down a hornless bull."

"Oh, he's plum tuckered by now," Slater said. "Surely he ain't got much fight left in him."

Lark shaded her eyes from the morning sun and looked to the small corral to the left of the barn. Slater's newest bull, the young Black Angus he'd acquired the day before, was there.

Astride Smokey, Slater rode past the window once more, and Lark marveled at how well-matched the horse and rider seemed to be. A large tan-colored horse with black mane and tail,

Smokey boasted the opposition of Slater's hair—Slater's sun-bleached hair being fair on top and dark beneath.

"But is he tuckered enough to let you take him down easy?" Tom asked. He laughed and added, "I don't think so."

"Even so, we gotta brand him," Slater said. "You know we can't trust Pete Walker any more than we can Lucifer himself."

Guilt washed over Lark as she realized Slater and Tom had most likely been up for several hours. They should've had a good breakfast—and it was her fault they hadn't. Remembering that they had both insisted she sleep longer than usual, she thought it no excuse for laziness. She was certain they'd ridden out with little more than jerky to start their day.

Tom glanced over, smiling and tossing a wave. "Ya think you could help us a minute here, honey?" he asked.

Lark raised her eyebrows and pointed to herself with one index finger. "Me?" she asked.

Tom nodded, still smiling. "Yep. The other boys are off herdin' up, and we gotta get this little bull branded before Slater has hisself a fit of apoplexy." Tom frowned and grimaced. "If ya feel up to it, that is. That's an awful sore-lookin' cheek you're wearin' there, darlin'."

"I'm fine," Lark fibbed as the pain of deep bruising on her face increased when she smiled.

"Then come on out," Tom said. "It'll only take a minute."

Lark nodded, fastened the window latch, and pulled the drapes. Hurriedly, she dressed and pulled her hair back into a braid. She gasped when she saw her reflection in the small mirror hung above the pitcher and washbasin table. Her right cheek was swollen and purple, her lower lip likewise puffed with a dark scab down its center. For a moment, she considered not leaving the house—for any reason—even if Tom and Slater did need her assistance. Still, inhaling a deep breath of determination, she nodded. After all, her face would heal, and she knew that if Slater had not ridden to her rescue when he did, Chet Leigh might have caused her pain and damage that would not have.

As she opened the front door, the frigid morning air sent a shiver through her. It was colder than she'd expected. Still, she hurried to the small fire where Tom and Slater were waiting. The branding fire was warm, and she rubbed her hands together before it, soothed by its heat.

Still mounted on Smokey, Slater frowned at her. Removing the black slicker he wore, he held it out toward her.

Lark smiled and shook her head, however. "Oh no. I'll be fine," she said, even as a visible shiver quivered her.

"I can't wrastle that bull to the ground with it

on anyhow . . . and you'll catch yer death out here in this cold." He tossed the coat to her, and she caught it, awkwardly slipping her arms through the sleeves and bunching them up to her elbows. The slicker was blissfully warm—warm from Slater's having worn it, from the heat of his body. It smelled heavenly—of jerky and leather and wind.

"Slater's gonna rope him and wrastle him down. I'll help hold him, and you put the brand to him. All right?" Tom asked as Slater rode toward the corral fencing in the young bull.

"What?" Lark exclaimed. "Surely . . . surely you're only teasing me. Aren't you?"

Tom laughed and removed his gloves.

"Here," he began, helping her to pull the gloves on. "It ain't hard. See . . . the gloves will protect yer hands. You just take hold of the iron by the stick end. See how the brand end is gettin' hot there in the fire?"

Lark nodded, though still uncertain she could actually perform the task. She'd seen the men brand cattle before. It wasn't that it looked difficult—at least putting the brand to the animal's hindquarters. It was that she knew it must hurt the beast more than she cared to fathom.

"Just lift the iron out of the fire, get a good stomp on him, and push it hard to the bull's hind end there," Tom explained, misunderstanding Lark's trepidation. "Me and Slater will keep him still for ya . . . but ya need to be quick in doin' it. All right?"

"But . . . but it has to hurt," Lark said.

Tom chuckled, nodding. "I'm sure it does, darlin' . . . but it's necessary. Now, you just brand him right on his left hindquarter. It'll be over before ya know it."

Lark shook her head, but Tom only chuckled as he picked up a nearby rope and began to wheel a small lasso over his head.

There was no more time to consider. Lark turned to see the young bull bolt out of the corral and charge straight for them. Slater and Smokey were a length behind, and Lark's heart began to hammer as she saw Slater wheel his lasso and spring it, roping the bull's head.

Slater pulled the rope to tighten it around the bull's neck as he wrapped the lead end around his saddle horn, and Tom sprung his lasso, roping the animal's back feet. In an instant, Slater slid from his saddle, taking hold of the bull's head and twisting its neck sharply. The bull rather toppled over, and Slater kept his neck twisted while Tom wrapped his rope around the animal's feet, rendering it helpless to escape.

"Now, Lark! Now!" Slater shouted.

Gasping a deep breath, Lark took hold of the branding iron. Awkwardly she wielded the heavy iron implement, placing one foot on the bull's rear end to ensure her balance and then firmly pressing the red-hot brand to the left hind-quarter. The bitter stench of singed hair and smoldering flesh stung her lungs.

"Hold it . . . hold it. Press it hard, Lark," Slater instructed.

Lark grimaced at the increasing stench and winced as the bull made a guttural sound in his throat. "Now?" Lark asked, desperate for the branding to cease.

"A little longer. You gotta burn it through to the skin and then some," Slater said.

Lark swallowed and applied more pressure on the branding iron.

"All right . . . all right. That's good," Tom said at last.

Lark sighed as she lifted the iron from the animal's flesh and set it aside. She winced, grimacing as she saw the smoking wound on the beast. She understood the need for branding cattle, but it didn't mean she enjoyed having to do it herself.

A moment later the bull was on his feet, Tom wrapping his rope through his palm, around his elbow and back. The young bull charged Tom, but a sharp whistle from Slater put Smokey between them.

"Oh, he's mad now," Tom chuckled as Lark removed his gloves she'd been wearing and returned them to him.

Lark tried to draw a regular breath, placing a

hand to her bosom to calm the hammering inside. She looked up to Slater and saw him smile as he studied the young bull. She frowned, however, puzzled when he began to chuckle.

"Well, he oughta be," Slater said.

Suddenly, and without apparent provocation, Slater and Tom erupted into laughter—hard laughter—nearly uncontrollable laughter.

"What's so amusing?" she asked. She'd missed something—she must have—for both Slater and Tom were so overcome with amusement they could neither draw breath nor offer a response to her question. Slater pointed to the recently branded bull as Tom wiped moisture from his eyes.

"He'll never forgive you, baby," Slater managed to choke out. "I know I never would."

"Forgive me?" Lark asked, utterly confused. "Who won't forgive me . . . and for what?"

"Wait. Wait," Tom gasped. "I can't hardly catch my breath."

"One thing's for sure," Slater said, trying to settle the mirthful convulsions racking his body. "Ol' Pete won't want that bull runnin' with his herd now!"

Both brothers exploded with amusement again. Lark sighed with exasperation. There was nothing she could do—no more she could understand until they were settled. Still, she couldn't help but smile. She was used to Tom's jovial manner—to his near constant state of amusement. But Slater was not normally so unguarded. The sound of his laughter was delightful—wonderful—and she giggled with the pleasure it invoked in her.

"What is so funny?" she demanded at last, however, stomping one foot on the ground. She placed her hands on her hips as she studied the fire, the branding iron, the bull, the laughing men. "Didn't I do it right?" she asked, stamping her foot once more.

"Oh! You did a fine job, honey! Just dandy!" Tom breathed, putting his hand to his chest.

At that moment, the bull turned, heading away from the corral. All became clear then—the reason for Slater and Tom's mirthful amusement. For the first time since putting the brand to the animal, Lark could see the brand clearly. She gasped, covering her mouth with one hand. In her haste to brand the animal, she had failed to pay attention to the position of the iron before pressing it against the animal's flesh. Ordinarily, the Evanses' brand, "Lazy Luck Five" or "LazE-luck-5," was read as a backward E and an upside-down horseshoe, followed by the number five. However, Lark had held the branding iron itself upside down. Thus, the upside-down brand on the young Black Angus bull read simply ꙅUE—"SUE."

"Sue?" Lark exclaimed, mortified. "Oh no! I'm so sorry! I-I apologize. Oh no!" She struggled to calm herself as Slater and Tom both sighed with amusement. "Can you . . . can you fix it?" she asked.

Instantly, Slater and Tom's laughter erupted once more. Tom bent over, resting his hands on his knees as he struggled to breathe. Slater dismounted and assumed the same position. He wiped the moisture from his eyes with the back of one gloved hand, sighed a moment, but was near instantly wracked by another riddling of amusement.

Lark, however, was not as amused as were the men. She knew that bulls were valuable to a herd—valuable in any circumstance. "I do not see why you two find this so amusing," she scolded. "I've ruined him, haven't I? He'll be worthless now . . . won't he?"

Slater drew a deep breath and sighed as his irrepressible laughter finally subsided. Nodding, he answered, "Maybe I couldn't sell him for much now . . . but I wasn't plannin' on sellin' him anyway. I plan on usin' him to sire me a nice herd of Black Angus." He smiled and added, "And besides . . . Sue . . . it's priceless in itself." He smiled at Lark and chuckled once more. "That there brandin' job . . . that is priceless!"

As Tom laughed a little longer, Slater chuckled and wiped more moisture from his eyes. "He can still grow up to do the job I bought him from Pete Walker to do . . . even if his name is Sue."

Tom nodded. "What'll we call him for the papers . . . Little Sue?"

"Naw, we already got us a Little Joe," Slater said, still smiling at Lark.

Lark fidgeted uncomfortably, for the approval apparent in Slater's expression was somehow disconcerting. Again she was deliciously affected by the scent of his slicker as it warmed her—wind, leather, Slater Evans.

"Well, he's black . . . and already a strange breed to see . . . with no horns and such," Tom said.

"How about Black-Eyed Sue?" Lark suggested. "After all . . . black-eyed Susans are one of my favorite flowers."

Roaring laughter commenced. The Evans brothers were overcome with mirth once more, and this time Lark couldn't help but laugh too. Slater wasn't angry with her for the mistake—far from it, though she was rather astonished by the fact. The truth was she'd never seen him enjoy himself so thoroughly before. If Slater and Tom were enjoying the branding mistake, she might as well too.

"It'll take quite a bull to live down a name like Black-Eyed Sue," Tom chuckled, putting a strong arm around Lark's shoulders. "Ol' Sue will probably end up bein' the orneriest bull in the county for the sake of tryin' to prove himself a man," he said, smiling at her.

Slater still smiled. "I knew a feller over in Arkansas like that once. His name was LaVern . . .

and he spent every wakin' minute tryin' to prove to everyone he was as tough as they come."

Tom nodded. "You might well have you quite a herd of Angus in a few years, Slater," he began, "if ol' Sue gets it into his mind that he's got somethin' to prove." He tweaked Lark's nose and added, "You probably just accidentally done my big brother the best favor anybody ever did."

Lark giggled. Still, doubt entered her thoughts, and she looked to Slater for comfort. "Are you certain you're not angry with me?" she asked.

"That's the best laugh I've had in years, baby," Slater said. Lark quivered as he reached out, caressing her undamaged cheek with the back of his gloved hand. "How could I be angry?"

Tom's eyes narrowed as he tried to keep his smile from broadening. Old Slater Evans was falling fast—fast and hard. He wondered if his brother even realized he'd taken, quick as a rabbit, to calling Lark "baby." He wondered if Slater even realized the way he watched her almost constantly. Tom figured he hadn't. Slater wasn't aware of the trace signs he gave away himself; he was always too busy noticing other folks'.

Smokey approached and rather nudged Slater out of the way—nodding and shaking his head as he stood before Lark. She reached out, gently stroking Smokey's nose as he nudged her arm.

Tom shook his head. Even Slater's horse was dead gone on Lark.

Tom smiled. It would be mighty interesting to watch—mighty interesting indeed.

Lark smiled. "Thank you, Slater," she managed, though her entire being was quivering with the residual delight caused by his touch. "I was afraid you might send me away."

She was relieved when Slater shook his head and said, "I only send bad men away." Removing the glove from his right hand, he reached out and gently took hold of her chin, turning her face in order to inspect the damage to her cheek and lip. Lark was terribly self-conscious, knowing she must look frightful. And she didn't want to look frightful—not in front of Slater Evans.

"How's that feelin'?" he asked as his warm thumb tenderly traveled over her healing lip.

"Better," she lied.

"I'm sorry I didn't get back sooner," he mumbled, his handsome brow furrowing into a familiar frown. He gently pressed at the bruising on her cheek. "And I'm sorry I didn't beat that boy senseless."

Lark felt herself blush, for she was simultaneously delighted by his touch and heroic nature toward her but likewise humiliated by her no doubt ghastly appearance. As he started to put his hand into his glove again, Lark gasped as she caught sight of his bruised and bloodied knuckles. "Oh no!" she gasped, taking hold of his hand in order to study the damage done to him by his fighting with Chet Leigh. Carefully she ran her fingers over the already scabbing wounds on Slater's hands. "This is terrible!" she breathed.

Slater pulled his hand from hers, however, slipping it back into his glove. "It ain't nothin'," he mumbled.

But it was something; to Lark, it was an ultimate something. No man had ever championed her, not in all her life. Well, once—a long time ago, perhaps—in a manner. Still, no man had ever fought for her safety—protected her with such sacrifice as Slater Evans had. Before Slater had bested Chet Leigh and sent him away, Lark was certain she could not have loved him more than she already did—but she did. Even his patience and lack of temper where the bad branding of the little bull was concerned caused her love for him to grow. She silently prayed for the ability to love him less—for she knew loving such a man as Slater Evans could only lead to disaster and heartache.

"Well, I'd better see to the boys," Slater said. "We gotta get them cattle back to the fenced pastures before nightfall."

"Oh!" Lark said, realizing Slater would need his slicker if he planned to be out rounding up cattle. Quickly, yet rather unwillingly, she removed the coat and offered it to him. She was cold at once —lonely for the warmth of his body that lingered in the slicker.

She frowned as a puzzling thought entered her mind, however. "I thought the cattle were all in already," she said.

"We think Chet opened the fences and spooked 'em out when he left," Tom explained.

"I'm sorry," Lark apologized at once. "I'm . . . I'm . . ."

"It ain't none of it yer fault," Slater said, wagging a gloved index finger at her. He grinned, "But my bull bein' branded Sue . . . that is. So maybe you'll feel guilty enough about brandin' that poor feller with a girl's name . . . to make up a batch of them cookies I like so much. What do ya think?"

Smokey nudged Lark's shoulder, and she smiled, reaching up to tickle his velvet nose with her fingers. "I think I might be able to manage it," she said.

"Alrighty then," Slater said.

Lark smiled and watched him mount Smokey.

"I'm gonna run that Angus back to the pastures. You comin', Tom?"

"Yeah," Tom said. "I'll be right along."

Slater nodded, touched the brim of his hat to Lark, and rode away.

"He's really not angry with me for the bull . . . is he?" Lark asked Tom. She needed just one more moment of reassurance.

"Hell no!" Tom chuckled. "I swear, that's the hardest I've heard Slater laugh in years. It done him good."

Lark smiled and nodded with gratitude.

"Now, you run on in and get warmed up," he said. "Next time take a minute to fetch yer coat. All right?"

Lark nodded. She wondered if she'd be asked to do any other outdoor chores—for the truth was, she didn't own a coat. She wondered if she could make it through another winter with just her shawl for warmth.

"Well then, we may not be in for lunch today. Might take us 'til supper to get the herd back together . . . though they couldn't have gone far," Tom explained. He turned and headed for the barn. "I'll see ya later, honey."

"Bye-bye," Lark called after him.

She watched him disappear into the barn. In a few moments, Tom rode out on Willis, his bay mare.

"You have a good day now," he called as he rode past her.

Lark waved and watched him follow his brother—watched as they rode Black-Eyed Sue the Black Angus bull toward the fenced pasture.

Turning, she hurried back toward the house. The air was chilled, and she didn't want to linger. Furthermore, she had cookies to bake, and she wanted to have a nice supper waiting when Slater and Tom returned.

She smiled as she entered the kitchen. "Black-Eyed Sue," she giggled to herself. No doubt the other cowboys on the Evans ranch would hear the tale soon enough—or see the evidence for themselves. Everything was wonderful in that moment. Lark had a home—at least for the winter. Things had settled into a comfortable routine, and Chet Leigh hadn't ruined it either.

As she busied herself in the kitchen, Lark hoped the men could round up the cattle quickly. The weather was certainly turning colder. Slater had explained that the deep snows that buried the higher pastures each winter would soon descend from the darkening skies. The cattle needed to be close—to find protection in the windbreaks of the close pastures.

"Cookies," she breathed, smiling at the memory of the light that had flashed in Slater's eyes when he'd asked her to bake for him.

She thought of his touch, of the feel of his fingers on her cheek, of her chin being held in his hand. She allowed herself a moment of daydreaming—wondering what it would be like to have Slater Evans kiss her. Yet she did not linger too long in such fanciful musings. He was a man—an older man—and no doubt used to the company of more mature women. What would an orphaned girl such as herself have to offer? How could she ever endeavor to entertain him with her youthful conversation or flirting?

Sighing, she determined to keep busy. It was ever her way. Thus, humming a favorite melody, she set about ensuring the Evans men returned home to a warm and fragrant house—to a hearty meal—and the warmest, sweetest cookies they'd ever tasted.

Lark heard a gust of wind suddenly whip around the house, and she shivered in thinking of the men out in the weather. She hoped they would return soon. The sun had already set, and still Slater and Tom had not returned. She hadn't heard the rumble of the other cowboys' horses in bringing them back to the bunkhouse either—and she began to worry.

A loud banging arrested her attention. It sounded as if it had come from the barn. At once, she thought of Dolly and Coaly—hoped that Dolly was not having another moment of being frustrated with being kept in the stall in the barn. Pulling her thin shawl snugly about her shoulders, Lark left the house by way of the back door.

The wind was indeed chilly and rather fierce in nature, easily penetrating her slight shawl. Immediately, her teeth began to chatter. She could clearly see the barn door standing open. She knew the door must be kept bolted at night in order to keep coyotes from wandering in and startling or harming stock.

Quickly, she made her way to the barn and

struggled to close the heavy doors. She felt a hand on her shoulder suddenly, and Lark cried out—entirely startled. Spinning around, she found herself face-to-face with Slater.

"What're ya doin'?" he demanded, looking tired and somewhat irritated.

"The barn door was open. I-I was just bolting it," she stammered. She fancied his jovial, friendly mood of earlier in the day had been wrung from him by hard work.

"Why didn't you put your coat on?" he asked. "Do ya wanna catch yer death?"

"I-I'm sorry," she stammered as he took her hand and began dragging her back to the house.

"Don't apologize to me. Yer the one that'll freeze."

He pulled her along for a time and then stepped aside so that she might enter the house ahead of him. Instinctively—for she was far more chilled than she'd realized—she rushed to the fire in the parlor. Kneeling before it, she began rubbing her hands together to warm them.

"It's so cold!" she exclaimed. "I-I didn't think . . . well, the day wasn't so cold . . . I thought . . ." she rambled nervously as Slater stood staring at her, an expression of suspicion owning his handsome face.

"Go get your coat," he rather ordered. "I want ya to go out and help me slop the pigs before supper."

"Um . . . of course," she began, "though I do have a few things to finish up before I can get supper on the table. I would rather just stay in, if it's all the same."

"It's not," he grumbled. "Now go get yer coat."

Taking a deep breath, Lark stood and turned to face him. "The truth is . . . I don't really . . . I don't really have one."

His eyes narrowed, and he asked, "You don't?"

"No. But I do just fine without . . . most of the time."

Slater chuckled, and she could see disbelief in his eyes. "You don't own a coat?"

She shook her head proudly.

"It gets way below freezin' here, baby . . . and you can't be without one." He inhaled a long breath, and she could see the fatigue in his eyes. "I'm goin' into town tomorrow. I can pick one up for you . . . unless you wanna go yourself."

Lark swallowed hard. "Well, that would be fine, but . . . but . . ."

"But what?"

"Well, I-I don't really have the means to purchase one." She was humiliated! What would he think of her now? She was nearly destitute, and now he would know just how desperate she had been when she'd come to his door—how desperate she still was. "I really can do without."

His frown deepened, and she walked past him toward the kitchen. "Anyway, I better see to your supper. I'm sure you haven't had anything to—"

"Hold on there," Slater growled, catching hold of her arm. "You can't do without a coat here. And what do you mean you don't have the means for one? Ain't we payin' you enough to afford a coat?"

Lark tucked a loose strand of hair behind one ear. "Well . . . well," she stammered, "in truth, Tom and I have never actually discussed . . . wages." She was beginning to feel frantic. What would Slater think of a young woman who was willing to work as hard as Lark did for no compensation? Still, to Lark, shelter, food, comfort, and companionship were far more important than money.

"You never discussed wages?" he asked. All at once, Slater seemed to fly into a temper. "How old are you really, baby?" he growled at her. "I want to know . . . the truth . . . here and now . . . 'cause I know you lied to me when you first came here, and obviously you ain't even old enough to know how to dress right for the weather! I don't wanna be goin' to jail, accused of kidnappin' or somethin'! Now, you tell me, on the level, Lark Lawrence. How old are you, and where did you come from?"

Devastated by his sudden apparent disapproval, Lark sat down on a nearby chair. All the delight she'd known in daydreaming—in her imaginings that Slater Evans approved of her, even liked her—melted. He would loathe her now, just like everyone else who hated orphans—especially runaway orphans.

Turning from him, she spoke calmly, masking her emotion—for, after all, she had grown accustomed to doing so. "I'll be nineteen in two months," she confessed. She heard Slater sigh, but she dared not look at him in trying to interpret whether he sighed with relief that she was not younger or with disgust that she was not older.

"My father died when I was a child . . . and my mother when I was fifteen," Lark began. "I was sent to an orphanage in New York City, and I couldn't breathe there. It was always so dirty . . . and so cold in the winter. I imagine it was worse than prison. So almost two years ago . . . I ran away. I've been running ever since, working for seamstresses mostly. But the one here in town, Mrs. Jenkins, she doesn't need any help. I needed somewhere to sit out the winter." She shrugged. "That's no different than the cowboys who work for you and Tom, is it?" She didn't look up at him, only continued her confession. "Hadley Jacobson told me about your Mrs. Simpson having passed . . . and I came here . . . spoke with Tom . . . and he hired me."

She nearly sprang from her seat then, standing to face him as all her fears and frustrations erupted. "I've done a fine job here! You can't tell me any different! I've cooked and mended and cleaned, and I don't expect anything but shelter, food . . . a place to winter," she cried. "I'm no different than those cowboys out in the bunkhouse. I've worked hard for you . . . and . . . and with the exception of what happened last night with that horrible Chet Leigh . . . I've done nothing wrong!" She paused, and he said nothing, only continued to study her with narrowed eyes.

"You patronize me because you see yourself as better than me . . . older, more mature . . . a man. You think I'm just a child, but I'm not. I work hard. And now, just because I don't own a coat . . . you're ready to turn me out? Well, that's fine, Slater Evans!" she cried, though anger had joined fear and heartache in her bosom. "If you can't see past the nose on your face to the fact that I'm as much of a woman as you are a man, that I've worked hard for you, that I can take care of myself . . . well, then . . . fine! I'm sure I can find someone else who'll be willing to . . . to . . . !" Lark turned from him and stormed off toward her room. She would pack her shabby little carpetbag and be on her way. Tom would drive her into town; she was sure he would. She had enough money tucked away for a train ticket to—to somewhere.

Lark tried to break free when Slater caught up with her, taking hold of her arm. "Settle yourself down, Lark," he growled.

Lark sobbed once—knowing Slater Evans would never call her baby again.

"Settle down."

Unwillingly, Lark turned to face him, awash with humiliation—and anger.

"Why didn't you tell me this before?" he asked quietly.

Lark was awestruck by concern she saw in his expression. He was no longer angry—she was certain of it—only concerned. She swallowed the lump of fear and disappointment that had gathered in her throat—tried to choke back any more tears demanding escape. "People think badly of orphans . . . in case you weren't aware of it," she told him. "And besides, you and Tom needed a housekeeper and cook. I needed employment. What does it matter how old I am or if I ran away from an orphanage?"

Slater's eyes narrowed again. He said nothing for a moment—seemed to be pondering all she had revealed to him. Lark held her breath and tried not to think of the approach of winter, tried not to think of how her heart was aching at having disappointed him.

"You still need a coat," he said at last.

Lark frowned, bewildered by what he'd said. She'd confessed, told him everything—well, nearly everything. And yet his only response was that she still needed a coat?

"Like I said," he began, "I'm goin' into town tomorrow. I can pick one up for ya . . . or you can come with me and get one yourself." He raised a scolding index finger and added, "And I'll see to it you're paid up beforehand."

"You're letting me stay?" she asked in a whisper.

He frowned. "Of course," he growled as if she'd offended him somehow in asking. He seemed to force a smile, however, and added, "As long as you made them cookies I asked for earlier."

Lark nodded, still bewildered, still uncertain. "I-I did."

Slater grinned and unexpectedly slapped her on the back a little too soundly. "Good," he said. "I'll help Tom with the horses, and we'll be in for supper."

"Yes, sir," Lark mumbled.

Slater raised an eyebrow, however. "Oh, we're back to that, are we?" he asked. He feigned a thoughtful expression for a moment. "Hmm. Keep that up, baby . . . and I might have to think of somethin' that'll make us more . . . intimate acquaintances."

As Lark's eyes widened, Slater chuckled.

"A good game of poker might be just the thing," he said. "Always helps new cowboys to gettin' along better with the old ones."

"Oh! Oh . . . I'm certain of that," Lark stammered.

Slater nodded. "We'll be in shortly then."

"All right," Lark managed as he turned to go.

She watched him stride across the room and

exit the house through the back door. He hadn't sent her away! He hadn't! The truth of it was, he seemed little affected by her story—other than the fact she hadn't told him the truth before.

Lark glanced to the warm fire in the hearth in the parlor. She'd be warm for winter—all winter. Her body would be warm—as well as her heart.

"I told you she was hidin' somethin'. Didn't I?" Slater quietly mumbled to Tom as they sat in the parlor some time after supper.

Tom chuckled, amused by his brother's ability to determine a person's secrets. "Yes . . . you did," Tom said. "Still, it ain't no big deal. She didn't run away from a lunatic asylum or nothin' the like . . . and there ain't nobody lookin' for her. She's just an orphan. I guess me and you are orphans in a manner if ya think about it . . . and it don't matter with her bein' as old as she is anyway. "

"Still . . . I was right, all the same."

"Yes, you were right," Tom mumbled, rolling his eyes with exasperation. "You been readin' folks ever since I can remember. I'm a bit surprised about her age though. She looks a might older."

"Mm-hmm," Slater agreed. "I thought she was tellin' the truth 'bout her age at least." Slater shook his head, still disbelieving, and added, "Imagine . . . not even ownin' a coat. I wonder what she was plannin' on doin' to keep warm all winter."

Tom smiled as mischief entered his mind—and he couldn't help himself. "Maybe she was plannin' on wearing you," he chuckled.

Slater frowned and glared at Tom with his usual scolding expression, wagging a likewise scolding index finger at him. "That ain't funny, and you know it," Slater growled.

"But you wouldn't mind . . . now would ya, Slater?" Tom teased. "You wouldn't mind keepin' Lark warm all winter . . . now would ya?"

Tom chuckled as an impish smile spread over Slater's face.

"I wouldn't mind it in the least, brother," Slater chuckled. "But if you point me out a man who wouldn't want to warm that little wounded sparrow up a bit . . . I'll eat my hat."

"If it's all right, I think I'll retire for the evening," Lark said, stepping into the parlor unexpectedly.

Tom smiled, for Slater looked like he'd gotten caught stealing sugar from the sugar tin.

"That's fine," Slater said, nodding to Lark. "And that was a mighty fine supper. Mighty fine! I thank you for it."

Lark smiled at Slater, and Tom felt warmed and contented inside. He'd grown to understand how Lark treasured reassurance—reassurance that she was earning her keep.

"Yep," Tom said. "You're even better at fixin' vittles than ya are at brandin' bulls."

● ● ●

Lark sighed with exasperation as Slater chuckled. The Evans brothers had been merciless at supper, endlessly teasing her about the branding incident. Tom claimed Eldon Pickering had been forced to his knees with laughing so hard when he'd seen Black-Eyed Sue's new brand—Grady and Ralston too.

"You'll thank me one day," Lark sparred. "One day when Slater has the best Black Angus herd around . . . you'll both thank me."

"I don't doubt it a minute," Tom said, winking at her.

"You gonna be warm enough in your room, baby?" Slater asked.

Lark nodded. "I'm sure I will be."

" 'Cause we can stoke yer fire for ya a bit before ya turn in."

"Yes," Tom said. "We want to be sure yer comfortable." Tom's smile broadened as he added, "And ol' Slater here . . . he worries about ya bein' warm enough. Why, just a minute ago he offered to—"

"I'll come stoke that fire for ya," Slater interrupted, fairly pouncing from his chair.

Tom chuckled—but Tom always chuckled—so Lark shrugged and said, "Good night, Tom."

"Good night, honey," he said, still chuckling.

Slater had stoked the fire in Lark's room. He opened her window just a hair too, telling her the evening breeze would complement the warmth of the room and keep her comfortable through the night.

As Lark lay in her warm, cozy bed, she breathed the aromatic scent of burning cedar and early autumn air. She sighed as she closed her eyes—as Slater's image moved through her mind—his tall, muscular frame, his tawny and dark hair, his handsome face. The crackle of the fire mingled with the soothing noises of cattle lowing in the distance, and Lark fancied she'd never known a more tranquilly serene moment.

Chapter Seven

Even though she was very tired, even though the warmth of the room and the comfort of her bed were nearly intoxicating, Lark had neglected to change her day dress for her night one. With a heavy sigh, she tossed the blankets aside and stood. She'd never sleep well if she kept her day clothes on. They were dusted with flour from cooking—not to mention that her body was begging her to relieve it of her corset.

Standing before the fire, Lark began to fumble with the small buttons at the back of her shirt-waist collar, but her fingers were tired and would not cooperate.

"Oh, for pity's sake," she whined, frustrated,

pulling her hair aside in an endeavor to make the small buttons more manageable. Still, it was as if her fingers had forgotten how to accomplish the task, and she stomped her foot with annoyance.

"Here, baby . . . let me help ya," came a low whisper from behind her.

Startled, Lark spun around to see Slater was standing just inside her bedroom. He was bare from the waist up, wearing only his underwear. His hair was tousled in the manner Lark had come to prefer—for it fell over his forehead, lightly brushing his dark brows. His eyes were warm, a smoldering sort of brown, and the smile on his face was likewise the one she preferred—the one that hinted at mischief.

"Did you want something?" she asked in a whisper as he slowly strode toward her.

"Just turn around," he gently commanded.

Lark smiled as he reached out, taking her by the shoulders and turning her away from him. She felt his fingers at the back of her neck as he fumbled with her collar buttons. His touch sent a fiery excitement racing through her—sent her arms and legs to sprinkling with goose bumps. She felt her collar loosen, yet her eyes widened as she felt his hands at the middle of her back. She realized then that he hadn't unfastened simply the buttons at her collar but several more down her back!

Lark was unable to move—unable to speak. It was highly inappropriate that he should be taking such a liberty, yet the river of delight racing through her found her unable to react. She gasped then—held breathless as the warmth of his mouth softly pressed the flesh on her neck.

"S-Slater?" she stammered, knowing she should move away from him. Yet as she turned to face him, he caught her in his arms, drawing her body against his.

Slater Evans smiled, winked at Lark as his head descended—and she gasped once more as his mouth found her throat.

"Please . . . please don't tease me!" she cried in a whisper.

"I'm not," he said. He took hold of her hand, sliding it over the chiseled contours of his chest to rest just over his heart. His skin was smooth and hot, and Lark did not attempt to remove her hand from where he placed it.

"You want me to kiss you, don't you?" he asked, placing a light kiss to her bruised cheek.

Lark couldn't believe Slater was holding her— teasing her—asking her if she wanted his kiss! Of course she wanted it! She'd wanted Slater Evans to kiss her nearly from the moment she'd first seen him. Yet the moment was surreal— overwhelming—wonderful! She thought her heart might leap from her bosom—that her knees, gone so weak from his caressive attentions, might not continue to support the weight of her body.

Oh, she well knew he was taunting her. Yet as he

kissed her other cheek softly and then the corner of her mouth, she knew his next intention was her lips. She tried to draw a steady breath—swallowed the excess moisture of desire gathering in her mouth.

"Slater," she breathed as his head descended.

Lark gasped as her eyes immediately burst open. She held her breath a moment—clutched her quilt to her throat as the dream faded. It was always the same, her fancy's dream of Slater Evans. Always she awoke a breath before knowing his kiss to her lips. Always it was a dual disappointment—the fact that it was only a dream and the fact that the dream could never endure until he'd kissed her.

The room was chilled, the fire having burned out sometime during the night. Exhaling a heavy sigh of disappointment, Lark climbed out of her bed and tiptoed across the room to close the window. She paused in doing so, however, for the early autumn breeze was fresh and the sounds of morning on the Evans ranch enchanting.

Still, she did not wish to find herself catching a sniffle, so she closed the window and went about readying for the day.

Lark blushed when Slater entered the kitchen—her romantic dream of him still all too fresh in her mind. She feared that he might somehow know she'd been dreaming of him. Therefore, she found it difficult to meet his gaze.

"How's that cheek doin' this mornin'?" Tom asked as he entered the kitchen, adjusting his suspenders.

"Looks to me it's a little more yellow than purple," Slater said. "Swellin's down a bit too."

"Mm-hmm," Tom agreed, taking hold of Lark's chin and turning her face to study the damage more closely. "Is it feeling better?"

"Much better, thank you," Lark assured him.

Tom winked at her and took a seat at the table. As Lark set a plate of biscuits and ham before him, he looked to his brother and asked, "You still plannin' on goin' to town today?"

Slater nodded. "Yep. I wanna get them supplies laid in. It wouldn't be smart to wait much longer."

"You takin' the boys with you?"

"Yeah," Slater mumbled. "I figure I'll take both wagons . . . and I'll need some help loadin' 'em. You comin'?"

"Naw," Tom said. "I wanna get that woodpile heaped up a bit."

"How about you?" Slater asked Lark. "Do you wanna come to town with me and the boys? I mean . . . if you're not feelin' up to it yet," he said, gesturing to her sore cheek, "I'll be more'n happy to pick out a coat for ya."

Lark smiled with relief. She hadn't wanted to go to town—not in the company of four men and with the condition of her face. She knew how town gossip was. She could well imagine how the tongues would start wagging at the sight of a lone and obviously beaten woman escorting four men—no matter what the truth was.

"I would greatly appreciate that, Slater . . . if you wouldn't mind," she answered.

He winked at her and nodded, causing her smile to broaden. "By the way, Tom," he began as he reached into the front pocket of his trousers and withdrew a wadded-up, worn bandana, "you owe this girl wages."

Taking Lark's hand, Slater dumped a pile of silver dollars into her palm. Lark's mouth gaped as he then reached into his back pocket, pulled out a roll of paper money, and counted out eight two-dollar bills.

"There ya go," he said, folding the paper money and stuffing it into one of her apron pockets. "That's thirty-two dollars for my half . . . so ante up, little brother."

"You sayin' I won't?" Tom chuckled as he reached around to his back pocket.

"You haven't so far," Slater chuckled.

"Well, neither have you," Tom said.

"No, no, no . . . this is too much," Lark argued, offering the silver coins in her hand to Slater.

"No, it ain't," Slater said, shaking his head. He pointed a warning index finger at her, adding, "And don't you let us go another week without payin' you. Our boys get paid every week. It ain't no different with you."

"Here ya go, honey," Tom said as he unrolled a wad of bills, licked his thumb, and began to count out an amount. "Thirty-two dollars . . . and you've been here a might longer than a month, so I'll toss in another ten just to show I'm more generous than Slater here."

"No, no, no!" Lark argued as Tom slipped the money into her opposing apron pocket. Withdrawing all the money, she laid it on the table, shook her head, and said, "I can't possibly accept this."

"You know what," Tom said, "you're right." Reaching over, he quickly plucked a ten dollar bill from the remaining bills in Slater's hand. "Slater's throwin' in another ten for helpin' us brand Sue."

"That's right," Slater said, snatching the bill back. "And I'll use it to buy you a right nice coat today, baby . . . if that's all right."

Tom laughed, and Slater chuckled.

"Well . . . well, yes . . . that's fine. But it's all too much," Lark argued once more. "Really . . . why would I ever need so much money all at once?"

"That ain't our concern," Slater said, finishing the last bite of ham on his plate. "You earned it, and we just pay you yer wages. It ain't our business what you use it for."

"B-but . . . but I . . ." Lark stammered.

"Next time one of us goes to town, yer face oughta be all healed up. Then you can come with us and buy somethin' nice for yourself at the general store," Slater said. "I'm afraid if ya go this time, folks might think I'm as mean as my reputation tells me to be."

Lark smiled at him. "I still can't accept this sum. It's too much."

Slater sighed with exasperation. Shaking his head, he pushed his chair back from the table and stood up. "I gotta round the boys up and get into town, Tom," he mumbled. "You can stay home and argue with the woman over money . . . but don't let her near any stock that ain't branded yet." He smiled. It was a playful, teasing smile—very close to the smile he always wore in her dreams.

Lark arched one eyebrow as she returned his playful smile. She scooped up the money and deposited all of it into her skirt pocket. "You're right. I did earn this."

"Yes, you did . . . you little bull-brander," Slater chuckled as he strode from the room.

Lark watched as he pulled his slicker off the coat rack by the front door.

"I'll see you girls later," he teased with a wink.

"Well, you best take a hat, sunshine," Tom said. "Summer's over."

Slater nodded, took his hat from the hat rack, and pushed it onto his head. "That it is, girls . . . that it is," he said as he closed the door behind him.

Tom chuckled as he took a bite of ham and

biscuits. "Mama always had to pester Slater about wearing a hat in summer," he mumbled. "Matilda too. I don't know how he works out in the heat without one, and it turns his hair a whole different color entirely. But winter's comin' on, and we don't want him catchin' his death . . . now do we?"

"No . . . we don't," Lark giggled.

"You might need to take up pesterin' him a might too," Tom added. "He goes all summer without a hat . . . then forgets to keep his head warm in winter."

"But he almost always leaves the house with one," Lark noted. "Even when I first came here . . . and it was still summer then."

Tom smiled. "Oh, he just does that because he was used to everyone naggin' him. He mostly tosses it in the barn once he leaves the house." He shook his head. "I can't believe he ain't dropped dead of the heat yet."

Lark sighed, lifted Slater's empty plate from the table, and walked to the sink. Oh, how she loved the mornings at the Evans ranch! Oh, how she loved feeling needed, safe, and warm—and how she loved the two men that were taking such care of her. She thought of the first day she'd met them—of Tom's smile and kindness, of Slater's mask of indifference and feigned bad temper. She could never have imagined knowing such happiness in working for them—in simply knowing them. Furthermore, she could never have imagined falling in love with Slater as she had. That she would ever cross the path of such a man as Slater Evans had been beyond her thinking before she'd come to them—but to have fallen in love with him? She wondered if perhaps she'd put too heavy a price on her heart, if perhaps loving Slater would lead her to an untimely end somehow, for she had begun to think she might die if she were ever driven away from him.

"I'll be out splittin' wood if ya need me, honey," Tom said, startling her as he stepped up next to her to hand her his now empty plate.

"Oh! Thank you," she said, smiling at him.

Tom winked at her as he retrieved his hat and coat from the rack standing by the front door. He smiled and nodded at her, began to whistle a lively tune, and left the house.

Lark was alone once more, alone with her thoughts—her thoughts of happiness, of contentment—her thoughts of Slater and how handsome he'd looked as he'd left the house. She smiled—sighed as she thought of him—lingered in remembrances of her dreams of him.

"Little Lucy Sparrow, perching on a limb so narrow," she sang as she washed the breakfast plates and utensils, *"oh, won't you trill a love song for me? A handsome caballero that wears a wide sombrero . . . is only what I wish for, you see."*

"Well, we're pretty well-stocked," Slater said as he hung his slicker on the coat rack. "So I guess the weather can turn now." He smiled and shivered as if a sudden chill had overtaken him. "Brrr! It's pretty chilly right now as it is. What's for supper?"

"Fried chicken," Tom said, patting his stomach from where he sat in the large chair by the parlor fire. "And it is good!" He frowned a moment and asked, "But what about Eldon and the boys? They didn't have time to cook nothin' up."

"They had supper in town while I was findin' a coat for our little bull-brander here," Slater said. "Look here. I got ya two." He reached into a large burlap bag he'd brought into the house with him, drawing out two brown paper–wrapped packages.

"There's one for ridin' and workin'. But then I thought you might be needin' one for Sunday meetin's and such . . . if you can ever drag our sorry rear ends to 'em."

He held one package out to Lark, and she accepted with a polite, "Thank you, Slater." She was uncomfortable, however, for as he stood watching her unwrap the brown paper—as Tom rose from his chair and sauntered nearer for a better view—she realized she didn't quite know what to expect at having a man purchase clothing for her.

Lark gasped with surprise and delight as she

drew away the brown paper to find a beautiful lavender wool coat. She'd never owned anything so lovely—never even known anyone who had! Well, perhaps a seamstress she'd worked for once. The coat was beautiful—and warm.

Lark held it to her face, marveling at its softness. "It's perfect!" she breathed. "It's beautiful!"

Slater smiled and nodded to Tom. "You see . . . I can know what a woman wants if I have a mind to."

Tom nodded. "Let me see that, honey."

Rather unwillingly, Lark handed the beautiful coat to Tom. He looked at it and inspected one of the inside seams. "Did Mrs. Jenkins wonder what you were needin' with a coat like this?"

"She didn't ask," Slater said, shrugging broad shoulders. "She's scared of me, so she didn't say much to me."

Tom chuckled. "Oh, this oughta set her mind to wanderin'," he said. "It's a fine coat, Slater. I'll give you that."

Slater nodded and handed Lark the second package he'd pulled from the burlap bag. "Here now . . . what do you think of this one then, baby?"

Lark giggled and bit her lip with delight when she drew away the brown paper to see a buckskin slicker had been wrapped in it—a slicker very similar to Slater's, only buckskin-colored and much smaller.

155

She couldn't stop the delighted squeal that trilled in her throat at the sight of the Slater-like coat. "It's perfect too!" she giggled. "Just perfect." She looked up to see him smiling at her—proudly smiling at her. It was obvious he was quite pleased with his purchase.

"Try it on now," he demanded. "Let's make sure it fits. Mrs. Jenkins assured me on the other one . . . but I had to guess on this one by myself in the general store," he asked.

Tom smiled as he watched Slater help Lark put on the slicker. Oh, his big brother had it bad! He shook his head, wondering why Slater didn't just lift the girl in his arms and haul her off to his bed. Well now, he knew Slater would never do such a thing—not without marrying her first. Still, he knew his brother—stood in awe at how he was managing to appear so calm and unruffled all the time. Two coats! Two! And one he knew cost a pretty penny. Tom had purchased a coat from Mrs. Jenkins the winter before; he knew how much old Mrs. Jenkins asked for such a thing. Yep, old Slater Evans was in love. Tom chuckled as he thought, *And he don't even know it.*

"Now let me see," Slater said, taking Lark by the shoulders and studying her from head to toe. He nodded with approval. "Yep . . . yep. That'll do just fine." He frowned a moment, cocking his head to one side thoughtfully. "Hmmm. Still, we don't want yer head to be cold."

Lark smiled as he promptly took the hat from his head, plopping it onto hers. She giggled as it slipped down over her eyebrows. Pushing at the brim, she tipped her head back and looked at Slater from under it. "Do you think this will make a better cowboy out of me?" she asked. "Will I do a better job at branding next time?"

Slater laughed and reached out to position his hat so that it sat tipped and farther back on Lark's head. "I'm sure of it," he said.

Lark allowed herself to gaze a moment into his eyes—his eyes that were fairly twinkling with some sort of unspoken joy. For an instant, she considered that maybe she was the cause of the glistening in them—that perhaps his delight in outfitting her had caused him some sort of unique glee. Still, she swallowed such ridiculous notions, especially when her attention was drawn to his hair.

"You . . . you cut your hair," Lark noted aloud.

Slater nodded and ran one hand through his shortened hair. "Yes, ma'am, I did," he admitted. "I was startin' to look mighty scroungy."

Lark couldn't decide whether she was delighted by the change in his hair or disappointed. The fact that most of the sun-bleached portions of it had been cut away, combined with the shorter cropping of it, gave him a more dominating, almost intimidating appearance. His hair was now mostly its true dark brown—no longer fell over his forehead the way a mischievous boy's may have. In that moment, though it would have seemed impossible an hour before, Slater Evans was even more striking—more handsome—more hypnotically attractive.

"Had me a proper shave too," he added, gripping his chin in one hand and rubbing his cheek. "Have a feel of that, baby," he said, unexpectedly taking hold of both Lark's hands and placing her palms to his cheeks. "What do you think of that? Ain't it nice?" he asked, brushing his face with her hands over and over again.

"Mm-hmmm," was all Lark could manage. Her entire body was covered in goose bumps—her heart pounding like a hammer driving a fence post.

"Ain't prickly at all," Slater said. "Smooth enough to hold baby skin to. Right?"

"Mm-hmmm."

"Even smooth enough to . . ."

Lark held her breath as Slater released her hands and bent forward, softly caressing her left cheek with his right one.

"That soft enough for ya?" he whispered against her neck.

"Mm-hmmm," Lark squeaked.

Again he caressed her cheek with his own, this time slowly brushing her lips with first his cheek and then his chin. His touch was exhilarating beyond anything Lark had ever experienced—the windswept scent of his skin intoxicating!

Lark felt her hands curl into fists at her sides, for she wanted to touch him in return—bury her hands in the dark silk of his hair—throw herself into his arms. Yet she held her breath, determined not to faint, not to reveal any hint of her delight—or desire.

"Yep . . . soft enough to hold baby skin to," he mumbled. "Or even . . ."

Lark's eyes widened at what she felt next—at the sense of Slater's lips only just brushing hers—as she felt him place the tenderest kiss possible to her lower lip.

"Oops," he said, suddenly rising to his full stature. He winked at Lark and said, "See there . . . it's so smooth I slipped."

"Mm-hmmm," Lark breathed, her entire body trembling with rapturous bliss.

He winked again, patting her head and causing his hat to fall down over her eyebrows once more.

Tom chuckled and clicked his tongue, shaking his head. "Why, Slater Evans . . . you devil, you. Now, what's findin' you with such a good disposition tonight?"

Slater shrugged and shook his head. "I guess a good shave and a hair trim can do wonders for a man. Besides, we're stocked up for winter, there's fried chicken waitin' . . . oh! And I dang near forgot!"

Lark watched as Slater turned back to the coat rack, rummaged around in the inner pocket of his slicker, and produced a letter.

"We got us a letter from Katie!" he exclaimed.

"Katie?" Tom chuckled, a broad smile spreading across his face—broad enough nearly to match the one on Slater's.

A nervous sort of unsettling anxiety flickered in Lark's bosom. Katie? A girl? Or a woman? Judging from the delight on the faces of both men, a woman. But who? Lark silently told herself that perhaps this Katie was simply Tom and Slater's sister. Perhaps she'd married long ago and moved away.

"What's she got to say?" Tom asked.

Slater shrugged and began to open the envelope he held. "I ain't read it yet. I figured I'd wait to get home first."

"Who's Katie?" She couldn't stop the question from passing through her lips. She had to know who Katie was.

"Our cousin," Tom answered. "Well, our cousin's daughter. That still makes her our cousin . . . right?" He looked to Slater questioningly.

"Yes . . . I think," Slater said. "I never did understand the cousin mess . . . first, second . . . twice removed. It's nonsense."

Tom smiled and lowered his voice as he looked to Lark and said, "Slater's a little tender about

160

where him and Katie stand as cousins or not . . . on account of him and her was so sweet on each other for so long."

"That ain't true, Tom," Slater corrected. He looked to Lark and said, "I was sweet on her . . . but I didn't pay no mind to whether or not she was my cousin."

Slater looked to the letter and began reading.

Tom winked at Lark. "Daddy always told us that keepin' track of cousins was just like keepin' track of cattle breedin' . . . sires and dames and such," Tom told Lark.

"Oh hell, Tom," Slater grumbled, looking up from the letter and frowning. "Did you ever know one cow who knew whether or not another cow was her cousin?" Slater rolled his eyes with disgusted exasperation.

Lark could've almost giggled at the course of the conversation—if it hadn't been for the fact that the letter from the woman named Katie seemed to hold Slater's attention like nothing she'd ever seen before.

"Oh no," Slater breathed as he read over the letter.

Tom frowned. "What's the matter?"

"John's dead," Slater muttered.

"What?" Tom exclaimed.

"It's true. She says it right here." Slater paused to silently read further into the letter. "He died . . . looks to be about two weeks back."

"Of what?" Tom asked. "He weren't much older than you."

Slater's eyebrows arched, in morbid agreement, as he nodded. "He's dead though," he mumbled as he continued to read the letter.

"What? Did someone shoot him?"

Slater shook his head. "Nope. He was out helpin' to bring in his herd. One of his boys saw him clutch at his chest . . . then he just fell off his horse." Slater looked up, handing the letter to Tom. "She says he was dead before he hit the ground."

"Slater, no," Tom breathed, frowning as he accepted the letter.

Lark watched as Tom began to read the letter. She didn't know what to do—how to react. Should she offer her apologies? Should she leave them alone? She felt she was the intruder—as if she didn't belong there with them.

Slater forced a smile, however, grinning at her as he removed his hat from her head and tossed it at the hat rack. It rung a hook and stayed.

"How about some supper?" he asked, still smiling—though she could see the excess moisture gathering in his eyes.

"I-I'm so sorry," she heard herself whisper.

He nodded, turned, and strode into the kitchen.

Lark looked to Tom for direction. She felt somehow disoriented—uncertain as to what action to take.

Tom looked up from reading the letter. The tear in the outer corner of his eyes made Lark's eyes water.

"Go on and feed him," he mumbled. "It'll help."

Lark nodded, quickly hung her slicker on the coat rack with Slater's, and hurried to the kitchen.

Slater was already sitting at the table. He was rubbing his freshly shaved chin with one hand and seemed lost in deep thinking. Lark said nothing and simply prepared him a plate of food and set it on the table in front of him.

Tom entered the kitchen and took a seat across the table from Slater. He nodded to Lark—a gesture that she should join them. She sat down, noticed the way her hands trembled as she rested them on the table, and moved them to her lap instead.

"John? I can't hardly believe it," Tom muttered as he folded the letter and returned it to its envelope.

"I know it," Slater sighed.

"She's right to come here with us though," Tom said, nodding.

Instantly, fear washed over Lark. Come here? Another woman? A woman that Slater once cared for—obviously still cared for? What use would the Evans brothers have for Lark if their beloved Katie was coming?

"Yep," Slater said, mashing his already mashed potatoes with his fork. "Where else would she go? We got the room, and she knows we love her . . . and the kids. I do know Katherine though. She'll be wantin' to find a place of her own . . . maybe in town . . . but she needs to stay here awhile."

Tom sighed. "It'll be fun havin' the little ones runnin' around," he said.

Slater nodded and said, "I suppose they ain't so little anymore though." He was quiet a moment, still picking at his meal with a fork instead of eating it. "I just can't believe it . . . John." He looked up to Tom, shaking his head in lingering disbelief. "Could have as easy been me. After all . . . I rode a lot harder life than he did."

"He was never as tough as you though, Slater," Tom said. "I couldn't quite ever figure why Katie married him instead of waitin' for you to come back."

There it was—evidence that Slater had been in love with the woman—evidence that he possibly still was. Lark's stomach churned. She thought for a moment that she might lose the contents of it, for she indeed felt ill.

Slater glanced up to Lark, and she instantly dropped her gaze to her lap. This was a private conversation between brothers. She shouldn't be there.

"You think you can handle cookin' and cleanin' up after a grievin' widow and her three young children?" Slater asked.

"Me?" Lark squeaked, disbelieving that she'd heard him correctly. "Y-you want me to stay?"

Slater glanced to Tom and then back to Lark. He frowned, grumbling, "Of course. What? Do you expect us to take care of her and her babies . . . by ourselves?"

"We'll have to get to cleanin' out those rooms in the back of the house, I s'pose. And dig out all Mama's old quilts from the attic," Tom suggested.

"Yeah," Slater said. "And I probably oughta head to town tomorrow and lay in a few more supplies."

Unexpectedly then, Slater reached across the table, gently gripping Lark's shoulder with one strong hand. "Now understand, baby . . . we'll help you," he said. "Don't you worry none about it. We don't expect you to do all this by yourself. Still, you know we've kind of closed up the back part of the house, and even if Tom and I clean them rooms out . . ." He paused and sighed. "Well, we ain't too good at makin' things look warm and pretty. I want Katie and her kids to feel at home . . . safe. We want 'em to know they have a place where they're welcome to stay . . . for as long as they need to," Slater added.

Lark nodded as hope began to beat down the fear in her—beat down part of it, at least. It seemed as though she would stay on through the winter—but it was obvious Slater still cared for this Katie. Silently, Lark prayed that her dreams of Slater Evans would stop—sleeping dreams and waking ones.

"How old are her children?" she managed to inquire.

"Oh, I don't know," Tom answered. "She's got a boy, 'bout twelve, I guess. And there's a girl 'bout six and another boy 'bout . . . what . . . four? Darlin' little babies . . . just darlin'."

Slater rested one elbow on the table—rested his forehead in his hand a moment as he mumbled, "I just can't believe John's gone. Them poor kids."

Lark wanted to touch him—to simply lay her hand on his arm in offering reassurance. In truth, she wanted to wrap her arms around him and promise him that the pain caused by the loss of his friend would subside, that she'd take care of his little cousins, that she'd even take care of the woman he still cared for.

"The three of us used to have such a time together when we was young," Tom began. He looked to Slater and grinned. "Remember, Slater? You and John and me? Remember how we'd go out down by the crick and go swimmin' buck neked. Mama used to get so upset."

Slater chuckled. "Yeah. We had some times, all right. Remember when Katherine caught us swimmin' that one time? She turned as red as an overripe tomata!"

"Poor Katherine," Tom sighed. "Poor little

Katie. Just can't imagine what she's goin' through 'bout now."

Lark's discomfort was increasing. So many thoughts and feelings were battling within her. She wanted to stay—she did! More than anything she wanted to stay on at the Evans ranch. But could she? Could she linger in watching another woman come into the house, a woman both men cared so much for—especially Slater? She thought of a story her mother used to tell her when she was small—about a girl who lived in the cinders and was abused and mistreated by a cruel stepmother and stepsisters. Would her life begin to mirror that of the poor cinder wench? Oh, she knew the Evans brothers would never abuse her, but would they grow to unknowingly ignore her, to put off her company for that of Katie and her darling children? Yet winter was so near—only a breath away. She couldn't leave, even if she'd wanted to, and she didn't. Lark didn't want to leave the Evans ranch. She didn't want to leave jovial, playful Tom Evans—and she couldn't leave Slater. He'd stolen her heart, and she couldn't abandon it—not yet.

"When will they be arriving?" she asked.

"A week before Thanksgivin' . . . so her letter says." Slater mumbled. "I do feel sorry for those kids. They'll have to finish growin' without a daddy now. It's tragic, that's what it is. Plain tragic."

Lark could see that both men were deeply upset. She felt it best to leave them alone. Mourning a friend or loved one was a deeply personal journey, and she was only the housekeeper and cook.

"Well, I-I should . . . I have a few things to finish up," she stammered awkwardly. "Would it be all right with you both if I finished these dishes tomorrow before breakfast?"

Slater and Tom both frowned and looked at her as if she'd just uttered the oddest string of words they'd ever heard.

"Honey," Tom began, "before you come to us . . . well . . . we'd been lettin' the dishes sit dirty for near a week before warshin' 'em."

Slater nodded as he finally started eating his meal. "Most times we didn't even use plates . . . just stood at the stove, eatin' out of the pot. And a man don't need nothin' but his hands for jerky."

"You go on and turn in, if you're wantin' to, honey," Tom told her. "It has been a long day."

Lark nodded. Yet feeling tears of empathy filling her eyes, she bit her lip to keep them from escaping and said, "I am sorry . . . about your friend John."

Tom smiled gratefully, and Slater nodded.

Lark left the kitchen and started toward her room. She paused, however, the beautiful lavender wool coat catching her eye.

Glancing behind her to ensure both men were

still in the kitchen, she hurried to the coat rack, quickly snatching the coat.

Once in her bedroom, she closed the door, exhaling a heavy sigh. The room was dim. She hadn't built a fire in the hearth, for she didn't want to waste wood that might be better burned in winter. Still, she had lit a lamp and now turned up the flame as she sat on the bed to examine the coat.

She smiled as she buried her face against the soft wool. Oh, it felt heavenly! Lark was certain the wool coat even smelled warm. Quickly, she stood, slipping her arms into the long sleeves. It fit her as if it had been made for her! It was warm indeed, and she was soothed, thinking that even if winter proved to be merciless in its low temperatures, she would be safe. Her smile broadened as she thought of Slater's having purchased it for her. She wondered what Mrs. Jenkins thought—wondered what he'd paid for it. Surely the ten dollars Slater had taken from Tom as payment toward a coat could not have afforded both the lovely lavender coat and the leather slicker. Her heart leapt at imagining Slater thinking of her while he was in town not once but twice.

As Lark removed the coat and hung it on a hook beside the bedroom door, she realized how truly chilled the room was. She studied the small pile of wood near the hearth a moment—the wood Slater had brought in the night before when he'd built a fire for her. Oh, it was tempting—to build a fire, open the window just a few inches, and sleep warm. Still, she must not be greedy—or weak. She would be warm enough once she was in bed.

Lark startled as a soft knock echoed from her door.

"Yes?" she called.

"It's me," Slater said from the other side. "I'm comin' in."

She smiled, somehow delighted by the fact that he did not ask her permission to enter—simply informed her he would.

The door opened, and Slater Evans stepped into Lark's bedroom. She hoped her eyes hadn't widened too noticeably as she took in his state of undress. He wore only a rather ragged pair of trouser underwear.

"I almost forgot to start you a little fire in here," he mumbled as he crossed the room in his bare feet and hunkered down before the hearth.

"Oh . . . I-I'm fine. Really I am," Lark stammered, watching the muscles in his arms and back ripple as he worked. "We shouldn't waste the firewood."

"It ain't a waste," he mumbled. "We need to keep you warm."

Lark felt her brows pucker in a slight frown as she noticed the scar on his back just below his left shoulder. It was a strange-looking scar—almost star-shaped—as if a wound had been roughly stitched together once.

"It'll be all right, you know," he said, glancing over one broad shoulder to her, nodding.

"What will?" she asked. In truth, the fact that Slater Evans had appeared in her room so entirely unclothed had entirely rattled her thoughts.

He frowned a little. "Katie and the children," he explained. "It'll be all right. You won't have to do much more than ya do now . . . except cook bigger meals, I guess. I'm sure Katie will see to their mendin' and warshin' and such." He looked back to his task. "I just didn't want ya worryin' about it."

"I'll be glad to help," Lark told him.

She watched as he leaned forward and blew on the kindling. The flame took, and Slater added two small logs. He stood, dusting his hands together and turning toward her.

Instantly, visions of her rather sensual dreams of Slater began to repeat in her mind. She even felt goose bumps rippling over her arms when she realized that, in her dreams, he'd been dressed exactly as he stood before her now—or rather, undressed exactly as he stood.

"You'll like Katie," he told her. "She's a fine woman."

"I'm sure she is," she managed, though a fiery, painful jealousy broke over her at Slater's praises of Katie.

His eyes narrowed a moment, and she feared he might somehow sense her unhappiness. Slater rubbed his chin with one hand and seemed to study her a moment.

"It ain't too often that I get me a shave in town," he said. "But I sure like the way that barber pampers up my face. He puts a warm towel on me after he's finished shavin' me. It sure feels good. Don't you think?"

"I'm sure it does," Lark answered, her heart suddenly hammering so viciously she wondered if it had somehow leapt into her throat. Oh, he was attractive! Everything about him was attractive. She studied his dark hair a moment, mussed as if someone had just tousled it. His eyes smoldered in the fire- and lamplight, the shadows cast by the flames in the hearth dancing across the broad contours of his chest. His trouser underwear sat low on his hips. Lark had the sudden hope that the tattered drawstring was robust enough to keep the article of clothing in place.

"M-my mother used to warm a towel by the fire . . . wrap it around my feet when she tucked me into bed to warm me," she babbled, suddenly quite overwhelmed with nervous excitement. "So . . . so I almost imagine what a warm towel would feel like after a shave."

Slater grinned. "The towel did feel good," he said, taking a step toward her. "But I was meanin' my face. Don't ya think my face feels good after that barber shave?"

He reached out, taking her hand and placing her palm to one cheek. The instant memory of the moments before Slater had remembered the letter from Katie—of touching him—of his touching her, kissing her—caused Lark's body to experience a blissful quiver.

"Y-yes," she stammered in a whisper. "It's very smooth."

"Of course, it ain't as soft as yours," he said, bending to caress her cheek with his own as he'd done earlier. "But it's nice all the same."

Lark's senses were reporting like fireworks! She felt one of Slater's hands come to rest on her waist—felt breathless and near faint.

"I-I . . . I think I forgot t-to . . . to thank you for . . . for the coats," she stammered.

"Then thank me," he mumbled against the corner of her mouth.

"Thank you for . . ."

Her words were lost—lost along with her breath as she felt him press a light yet lingering kiss to her lips.

"What was that?" he breathed. His breath tickled her mouth.

"Thank you for the . . . for the coats," she managed.

"You're welcome," he whispered. He wasn't kissing her, yet his lips lingered in lightly brushing hers. She could feel him smiling. He knew she was unsettled; she knew Slater Evans knew that she was profoundly unsettled!

"Thank you . . . for that fine supper," he breathed against her lips.

"Y-you're welcome," Lark managed.

He straightened then, and Lark found she could not meet his gaze at first. When at last she did look up at him, it was to see him frowning—studying the bruises on her cheek.

"It's lookin' better," he said, lightly caressing her cheek with the back of his hand. Still frowning, he gently pressed his index finger to her lower lip. "We just gotta get that lip healed up," he added. His face softened, a slight grin curving one corner of his mouth. "Before my next barber shave anyway."

Lark gasped slightly, entirely elated by his flirting.

"Good night, baby," he said, winking at her.

"Good night," she managed.

Grinning, Slater turned to leave her room.

Lark gasped once more as one of the two buttons securing the trapdoor flap to Slater's underwear suddenly popped off. She averted her gaze only just in time to keep her innocence intact.

"Oops," he said, turning around and bending over to pick up the rogue button.

He offered the button to her, and—keeping her

gaze on his face—Lark offered him an upturned palm in return. "There ya go," Slater said, dropping the button into her hand. He made no effort to protect his modesty—simply smiled at her, turned once more, and left the room.

Lark gazed at the button in her hand. Had he really kissed her? Really? Perhaps she was only dreaming again. She reached up, pinching her own arm—and it hurt. No, she had not been dreaming.

Slater chuckled as he closed Lark's bedroom door behind him. She'd near fainted when he'd lost his trapdoor button, he was sure of it. She'd near fainted when he'd kissed her too. He closed his eyes a moment, willing himself to move forward and up the stairs—instead of turning around and returning to Lark's bedroom for one more flirtatious kiss.

As he climbed the stairs, he yawned, hoping his visit to her room had reassured her that her place with him and Tom was secure. It had frightened Lark, when he and Tom had revealed that Katie and the children would be coming to stay with them. He'd seen the fear take control of her—visibly seen the fear in her. No doubt she was afraid she'd have to find another place to wait out the winter. But she wouldn't—and he'd wanted to make certain she understood it.

Slater sat down on the side of his bed, stretched

his long arms, and yawned again. He thought of the smile that had crossed her face after he'd started the fire in her room. It wasn't too long after Lark had come to them that he'd realized she had a fear of being cold. He wouldn't have her fearing the cold any longer. He'd make sure she was kept warm. He chuckled as he crawled into his bed. Yep. He'd make sure Lark was kept warm through the winter—one way or the other.

Slater tucked his hands beneath his head and stared at the ceiling. The moon was full and lit the room well. He glanced at his gun belt slung over the back of the nearby chair. As always, the sight of his weapon succeeded in drawing his mind away from frivolous fancies—back to a more sensible point of view.

In that instant, the joy Slater had gleaned from teasing Lark vanished. He scowled, having suddenly remembered his age—the weathered state of his mind and body. Who the hell did he think he was? Did he really think a fresh young sparrow would find any interest in a battered old buzzard? And even if she did— should she? He thought of the day Lark had arrived—arrived with Hadley Jacobson. Hadley was a good man—a young man. Hadley was the sort of man Lark deserved—not beat-up old Slater Evans.

Growling, Slater closed his eyes, determined to get some sleep. Still, as the memory of Lark's sweet breath on his cheek, of the soft pleasure of her tender lips, gripped his mind, he knew sleep was not about to come easy.

He thought of John then—forced himself to think of his childhood friend—his now-dead childhood friend. It was an unpleasant, heart-breaking thought—John gone and Katie a widow, their children now without a father. Yep, a sad and unhappy thought indeed. But Slater always did have an easier time going to sleep while entertaining gloomy thoughts as opposed to glad thoughts. So he tried to think of Katie's misery—tried to envision ways to help her and her children—instead of envisioning Lark's youthful sparkle, her pretty eyes and silken hair, her sparrow's voice, her soft, pastry-sweet lips.

Cussing under his breath, Slater rolled onto his side and closed his eyes. "Go to sleep, you ol' buzzard," he grumbled. "And from now on . . . leave that sparrow alone."

Chapter Eight

Lark couldn't help but smile as she watched Mrs. Gunderson wrap the pretty pink calico in brown paper. She hadn't had a new dress, skirt, or shirtwaist in so long! Already her fingers were tingling, desperate to begin sewing.

She glanced over her shoulder to see Slater

and Tom still standing on the boardwalk outside the general store. The stage still hadn't arrived, and she knew they were both beginning to worry.

"That'll make a right purty dress, Miss Lawrence," Mrs. Gunderson said. "And I'm so glad to finally meet you. I've just heard so very much about you from them Evans boys . . . and it's nice to finally have a face to go with their stories. Why, Tom tells me you're a better cook than Matilda Simpson was."

Lark blushed, simultaneously pleased and suspicious. Tom had often told her she was a better cook than Mrs. Simpson had been, so she didn't doubt he'd also mentioned it to Mrs. Gunderson. What she did doubt was that the stories Mrs. Gunderson had heard—well, she did doubt they were all told by Slater and Tom alone. No doubt Mrs. Jenkins had mentioned selling the lavender dress coat to Slater. No doubt everyone had whispered here and there about the young, unmarried woman keeping house for the unmarried Evans brothers.

Still, it was nice to be in town at last. When Slater and Tom had suggested she accompany them to town to meet the stage bringing Katherine and her children, she'd paused. Lark knew there was bound to be gossip. Yet her desire to visit the general store, to spend some of her collected wages to perhaps procure some fabrics and notions for a few new pieces of clothing for herself—well, she'd decided she could endure the gossip. She'd endured worse, after all.

"Are . . . are those for sale?" Lark asked as her gaze suddenly fell to a shelf of books nestled next to a large pickle barrel.

"The books?" Mrs. Gunderson asked, following Lark's gaze.

"Yes."

Mrs. Gunderson smiled. "Why, yes, they are!" the cheery proprietress exclaimed.

She was a tall, slender woman, older, with gray eyes and hair the color of dried leaves. Lark thought Mrs. Gunderson looked just like she belonged in autumn—as if her appearance matched the weather outside the store.

"We've got several books here that I hear are very interestin' . . . though I haven't read them, of course," Mrs. Gunderson said, leaving the counter and walking toward the shelf. Lark watched as Mrs. Gunderson stooped to look at the books. "Here's one . . . *The Countess of Vista Verde* . . . and here's one called *Two Moths and the Moon*."

Lark frowned, disappointed in the titles the woman had mentioned. "Are there any others . . . perhaps adventure tales . . . or maybe something by Mr. Twain?" she asked.

Mrs. Gunderson looked again. "Hmm. Not that I see right off."

"Maybe some poetry? I read a small book by

Longfellow once . . . and I do like Lord Tennyson," Lark said.

"I know I've got a little book of poems here somewhere," Mrs. Gunderson mumbled. "Ah, yes . . . here it is!" Lark watched as the woman pulled a small book from the shelf. Handing the book to Lark, she said, "*Favorite Poems*. Will that do ya for a spell, do ya think? I can order in anything ya like . . . but this looks like a sweet little book for today."

Lark accepted the book, somewhat disappointed at first. She'd hoped for some grand adventure to read—or at least a collection from a poet she knew. Still, as she let her fingers travel over the pretty little book, its lovely white cover embellished with gold lettering and a pretty rendering of a sprig of lilacs, she smiled. Carefully, she leafed through the small book, pausing to glance over the list of poems in the contents. For all the books the Evans brothers had in their parlor (rather, for all the books in the parlor that had once belonged to Slater and Tom's mother), there wasn't one poetry book. Thus, Lark put the book on top of the stack of paper-wrapped parcels of fabric and notions.

"I'll love it!" she told Mrs. Gunderson. And she would, for Lark had not owned a book since she was a small child.

"Wonderful!" Mrs. Gunderson exclaimed.

Mrs. Gunderson figured the cost of the fabrics, the notions, and the book, and Lark paid her.

"You sure ya don't need me to help ya out with all that?" Mrs. Gunderson asked.

Lark smiled and shook her head. "I can manage . . . but thank you."

"Well, I'll just see ya next time ya come to town then, sweetie. You keep warm this winter."

"Oh, I will."

Mrs. Gunderson tossed a friendly wave, and Lark stepped out of the general store and onto the boardwalk.

"Most likely just runnin' slow," she heard Slater mumble. "Right?" he asked Tom.

"Most likely," Tom agreed.

Lark frowned, however. She could see both men were worried. "How late is it?" she asked.

Slater and Tom turned, and Tom forced a smile. "Oh, near to an hour," he said.

"Have I been in there that long?" she asked, looking back to the general store. Mrs. Gunderson smiled through the large window—tossed another wave.

"Mmm-hmm," Tom said. "And it looks like Mrs. Gunderson had a good day in the general store too."

Slater studied the stack of packages in her arms. "Elvira Gunderson don't let nobody leave without emptyin' their pockets first," he said, grinning. Without asking, he took the parcels from Lark's arms. "Here . . . I'll run put these in the wagon for ya."

"You don't have to do that," Lark began to argue. "I can just—"

"I'll be right back," Slater interrupted, however. "And don't worry. I'll see they're stored safe."

Lark watched him stride across the street to where Dolly and Coaly waited in the alley with the wagon. Eldon, Grady, and Ralston had already headed back to the ranch with the other wagon of supplies. Slater and Tom were determined Katherine and her children would want for nothing while spending the winter at the ranch. Thus, they'd sent the cowboys home to unload before Katherine and her children arrived, explaining that they didn't want Katherine to know they'd laid in extra stores. She'd worry herself sick with guilt.

"He's worried 'cause the weather's lookin' a might threatenin'," Tom explained. "We wanna be sure we get those children home and settled before any snow flies."

"Snow?" Lark exclaimed. Instantly she felt chilled and worried. Lark didn't like snow—not one bit. To her, snow meant hardship—deep, biting cold—fear and anxiety.

Tom nodded, looking up into the sky. "It don't feel cold enough yet, but it's chilled . . . and the air is calm."

"I don't like snow," she whispered.

"You don't?" Tom asked. "Not at all? Not even at Christmas?"

Lark shrugged. "Maybe at Christmas . . . if everyone is safe inside and there's plenty of wood."

She watched as Slater returned from the wagon. Unaware a delighted smile was spreading across her face (for she loved the rhythm of his swagger), she thought how nice a winter might be—how she might grow to like the snow—if it kept Slater in the house and nearer to her.

Oh, he hadn't kissed her again—hadn't even flirted with her too often since the day after Katherine's letter had arrived. He'd returned to the Slater Evans he'd been before—rather brooding, sometimes laughing, most times working himself into a deep fatigue. Lark was disappointed, of course. Yet she'd almost instantly come to understand that his flirting with her, his kissing her, was merely because an unusually good mood had overcome him that day. Pete Walker had only just agreed to sell him five or six Angus heifers come spring. Furthermore, he'd had his hair trimmed and a comfortable shave while he'd been in town. Lark understood these things had simply combined to put him in a more jovial disposition than usual. That was all. Moreover, she'd made up her mind not to linger in melancholy and unhappiness over the fact that he never kissed her again—never appeared unexpectedly in her bedroom intent on building a fire and wearing only his under-trousers. No.

Instead, she'd made up her mind to savor the fact that he had kissed her at all! Yes. The entirety of the day following Slater's flirtatious kisses, Lark had pondered her life—her situation. She was safe at the Evans ranch, after all; even if her heart wasn't, she was. She was safe and warm and earning a hefty wage. It was true that, though she was in love with him, Slater wasn't in love with her. Yet to be near him, to linger in his company, it was the only place she longed to be.

Thus, having thought and pondered, having reevaluated her life and circumstances, Lark had chosen to find happiness instead of disappointment. If the arrival of Katherine and her children meant change, then she would have to endure it. She'd endured worse. Still, the worst she'd endured didn't have the potential to break her heart the way her current situation did. But she was not deterred. She would stay at the Evans ranch for as long as Slater and Tom would have her there. And she would secrete away her love for Slater as if it were the most valuable treasure on earth and she had been called upon to protect it.

Therefore, as she watched Slater approach—as she watched his broad shoulders sway back and forth with the striking rhythm of his saunter—she forced a calmness to her expression and ignored the gripping pain of regret and longing in her heart.

"I hear it," Tom said as Slater stepped up onto the boardwalk.

"Thank you," Lark said.

He nodded and smiled at her a little.

"Listen," Tom said as he leaned over and looked down the street. "Here it comes."

"Finally," Slater mumbled, also leaning over to look down the street.

Lark didn't look in the direction of the approaching stage. She simply tried to steady her breathing and convince herself that all would be well. Pulling the collar of her slicker more snuggly around her neck, she waited and listened to the approaching rumble of the horses and stage, her heart hammering louder and louder, her anxieties growing as quickly as the stage approached.

In a matter of seconds, the stage driver pulled the lines, halting the team of horses directly in front of the general store. Lark held her breath as the shotgun driver climbed down from the stage and opened the door. She saw young faces at the window—the faces of children—wearing expressions of excitement mingled with fear. Instantly, her heart ached for them. They'd lost their father; they'd been stripped from their home and everything familiar.

Lark forced a friendly smile and waved to a little boy who had his nose pressed up against the window as he stared out at her.

Katherine Thornquist was a beautiful woman! Lark felt her mouth drop slightly agape as the stage driver offered her a hand to help her out of the stage. She was small, like Lark, but had hair as bright as the sun and the bluest eyes Lark had ever seen. Lark noted the red, puffy state of her nose and eyes. She'd been crying. Lark thought that she'd probably been crying since the death of her husband. As Katherine stepped gracefully down from the stagecoach, new tears sprung to her eyes. Lark thought it incredible that a woman could still look so beautiful in such a state of agonizing emotion.

"Slater! Tom!" Katherine cried, collapsing into Slater's alluring embrace.

Lark bit her lip as jealousy mingled with empathy. The sight of another woman being held in Slater's arms caused a scream of heartbreak to rise in her throat. She gritted her teeth to keep it silent, however, as her own eyes filled with tears as Katherine began to sob mournfully.

"I can't believe this, Slater! I just can't believe this!" she cried.

"I know, darlin'. I know," Slater said, his voice low and comforting. "But you done right comin' to us," he whispered softly into her hair. He kissed the top of Katherine's head and held her as she continued to sob.

Unable to endure the jealousy or sadness washing over her, Lark looked to see the children alighting from the coach. They rather spilled out—tumbled over the stairs and up onto the boardwalk. A little girl, the image of her mother, immediately clasped the hand of a small, delightfully impish-looking boy. An older boy positioned himself behind them—protectively. No doubt this elder brother had taken on the role of protector in his father's absence. He was tall, yet his youthful good looks revealed his tender age. Lark remembered having been told he was about twelve, and he looked it—save the worry and sadness around his eyes.

Tom hunkered down in front of the little girl and boy.

"My goodness!" he exclaimed. "This ain't little Charlie, is it? Why, it can't be! You're darn near as big as me!"

The toddler giggled with pride and threw his arms around Tom's neck. Tom stood, chuckling and tousling the tike's hair. He glanced down to the girl then. "And this can't be Lizzy, can it?" He let out a long whistle. "My, my, my! You're the spittin' image of yer mama when she was little, sweetheart! Yer a beauty, darlin'."

Little Lizzy blushed and threw her arms around Tom's waist. He patted her back lovingly and then offered a hand to the older boy. "Johnny. You've plum grown up, boy. Didn't hardly know you. Bet you got all the girly hearts a-beatin' like crazy in Sunday school class, don't ya?"

"Naw," the boy muttered shyly, taking his cousin's hand and giving it a firm, manly shake.

Lark's thoughts were that of discomfort and anxiety. She didn't belong here. This was family. She didn't belong. Still, she remembered her resolve to remain brave and determined. Thus, she glanced away from Tom and the children a moment—to Slater and Katherine.

Slater still held Katherine, smoothing her hair and kissing the top of her head repeatedly as she cried. Lark felt a moan of agony threatening to leave her throat, for she'd never known anything so painful as watching another woman linger in the arms of the man she loved. Still, she gritted her teeth once more, straightening her posture in an endeavor to endure.

Slater glanced over at her then, winking at her with reassurance—but reassurance of what? That Katherine would recover and they'd soon be on their way back to the ranch? That he understood she was uncomfortable and wished her to know that she had no need to worry? Whatever his reassuring wink was meant to convey, it did not change the fact that Katherine Thornquist was wrapped in Slater's arms—and Lark was not.

"I'm sorry, darlin'. I wish I could bring him back for you," Slater said. Lark was further moved to her own tears as she saw the moisture heavy in Slater's eyes. "I'm so sorry."

Katherine's sobs only increased, and she tightened her embrace.

"This here's my pretty friend," Lark heard Tom announce to the children. She turned once more, forcing a friendly smile to her face when she saw the three children staring at her.

"Hello," she greeted.

The children stared—Johnny and Lizzy from where they stood and Charlie from his place in Tom's arms. She almost smiled when she saw Charlie's small fingers travel to the back of Tom's neck to begin nervously fiddling with his hair.

"Who're you?" Charlie asked.

"I-I'm Lark," Lark stammered. "I cook and keep house for Slater and Tom."

Charlie smiled. "I think you're pretty," he said.

"Me too," Lizzy agreed. Lark glanced down to see Lizzy smiling at her. The girl stepped forward, taking Lark's hand in her own. "Do you live at the ranch house too?" she asked.

"Yes . . . I do."

"Our pa died," Lizzy bluntly offered.

Lark's heart was tearing in two. The poor babies! How frightened they must be—how terribly frightened!

Instantly, she knelt down before the girl. "I know . . . and I'm so sorry. My daddy died too . . . a long time ago."

Lizzy nodded and smiled at Lark again.

Lark reached up, brushing a strand of hair from the little girl's face. "So we'll be good friends."

"Because we understand?" Lizzy offered.

"Yes . . . because we understand," Lark assured her.

"I'm Johnny," the older boy said, offering a hand to Lark.

Lark smiled, standing and accepting his hand.

He shook hers firmly and announced, "I'm the oldest and plum capable of takin' care of things."

Lark nodded. "I can see that. I'm sure you've been a great comfort to your mother. I'm certain she's very grateful for your help."

Johnny nodded, and Lark's smile broadened, for there was a bit of his cousin Slater in his demeanor—something self-reliant and somewhat impatient.

At last, Katherine gently pushed herself from Slater's arms. Dabbing at her tears with a handkerchief, she turned and offered a small, gloved hand to Lark.

"Forgive me. I'm just . . . I'm just not myself these days. Katherine Thornquist. I didn't intend to be so impolite," she said.

Lark accepted the woman's hand and smiled at her. "I'm Lark . . . and please don't concern yourself with proprieties, Mrs. Thornquist. And please know that I'm so very sorry for your loss."

Katherine nodded, dabbing more tears from her eyes, and said, "Thank you, Lark. Thank you

. . . truly." Katherine smiled at Slater and then Tom. Tom set Charlie down, and Katherine threw herself into his comforting embrace, lingering for several long moments—but not as she had with Slater.

"At least I've got these dear ones to come home to," she said, placing a tender, gloved hand to Tom's cheek.

Tom kissed her forehead. "We're plum tickled to have you . . . and you know it, Katie," he said. "We ain't happy about the circumstances . . . but we're glad you've come to us."

The stagecoach drivers had unloaded Katherine's trunks from the top of the coach. Slater slapped Johnny on the back and said, "You look mighty strong, boy. Why don't you help me get these trunks over to that wagon yonder?" He nodded toward the team and wagon waiting in the alley across the street.

"Yes, sir," Johnny said.

"Alrighty then . . . let's get it done."

"Slater's a might concerned about the weather, Katie," Tom explained. "Do you need anything from the general store before we head for home?"

Katherine forced a smile. "Lizzy and I will simply pay a visit to the powder room inside, if that's all right. Otherwise, we have what we need."

"Then we'll get the wagon loaded and ready," Tom said.

Tom reached into his pocket and withdrew a

silver dollar. "Lark, honey," he began, handing the dollar to her, "why don't you distract Mrs. Gunderson a bit . . . buy the children a licorice whip or somethin' so that Kate don't get trapped into too much conversation?"

Lark smiled, delighted by Tom's thoughtfulness. "That is a very wise notion," she told him.

"I'll keep Charlie out here with us, Katie," he said. "You let Lark go on in first."

"I'd be in there for an hour!" Katherine whispered to Lark. "And I don't really feel up to . . . to . . . to talkin' about . . ."

Lark laid a hand on Katherine's arm. "You just freshen up, and we'll get home and settle everyone in."

Katherine smiled, though her eyes were filled with pain and trepidation. "Thank you," she whispered. "Thank you."

Lark nodded. However, inside she was boiling with conflicting emotions. Why did Katherine have to be so kind and vulnerable? Why did her children have to be so adorable? There was no way Slater could not be entirely captivated by them all—especially Katherine. But what could be done now? Nothing. She simply had to endure whatever the situation afforded.

Inhaling a deep breath of resolve, Lark entered the general store, returning Mrs. Gunderson's wave. "What's all this?" Mrs. Gunderson asked. "Is that Katie Thornquist?"

Yes, it looked as if it would be quite a chore to distract Mrs. Gunderson long enough for Katherine and Lizzy to visit the powder room.

"Yes," Lark began, approaching the counter and lowering her voice, "and I'm afraid she'll just melt if you ask her about it now, Mrs. Gunderson. You see . . . she's lost her husband."

Mrs. Gunderson gasped, and Lark laid the silver dollar down on the counter. "I'll explain . . . but I need three licorice whips . . ."

Mrs. Gunderson nodded, listening intently as Lark explained—as she eyed the silver dollar on the counter and wrapped three licorice whips in white paper.

Slater leaned back against the wagon, watching Lark as she exited the general store with Katherine and Lizzy. His mouth watered as he studied her, and he swallowed the excess moisture of desire. No one could say Slater Evans was lacking in self-control. Nope, no one! It had taken near every bit of strength in him to keep from her—to keep from simply throwing his brains to the wind and having her. Still, with every passing day he wondered how long he could keep his desires restrained, his feelings a secret.

He couldn't keep the amused grin from spreading across his face as she approached. She looked so darn adorable in that little slicker he'd bought for her—good enough to lick.

She smiled as she approached him. "Mrs. Gunderson felt so bad about Katherine's husband," she said quietly, "that she gave me seven licorice whips instead of three." She unfolded the length of white paper in her hand, stripped out a long piece of licorice, and offered it to him. "I know how you like them."

Slater's mouth watered—but not for want of the licorice. "Why, thank you, baby," he said, accepting the length of candy.

"Will you sit in the back with me?" Lizzy asked, taking hold of Lark's hand.

Slater wanted Lark on the wagon seat with him. Still, he knew Katherine would want to talk on the way home. Lark would be more comfortable in the wagon bed with Tom and the children— and warmer. It had become profoundly important to Slater that Lark be kept warm.

"Of course," Lark said, though he sensed she was uneasy. Perhaps she was worried about being cold—though he liked to think she was perhaps jealous that Katherine was already climbing up to the wagon seat.

"Here ya go, darlin'," Slater said, putting one end of the licorice whip in his mouth and lifting Lizzy into the back of the wagon. Lizzy giggled, and Slater thought that it would be good to have the laughter of children at the house.

"And here you go, baby," he said, lifting Lark in the cradle of his arms.

She gasped, startled by his picking her up, and he chuckled as he lifted her over the side of the wagon and into the bed.

He bit into the licorice whip, tearing off a piece with his front teeth and stepping up to sit down on the wagon seat next to Katherine.

"Everybody ready?" he asked over his shoulder. The children nodded, and Tom chuckled as Charlie and Lizzy immediately snuggled up on either side of Lark.

He chuckled when he heard Tom say to Johnny, "Looks like a mighty nice place to be, don't it?" Johnny blushed, and Slater chuckled too.

"Here," he said, taking off his hat. Reaching around, he soundly pressed the hat onto Lark's head. "Keep yer head warm."

She smiled up at him, nodding. Truth be told, he nearly bolted back over the wagon seat to kiss her then and there! She always looked so darling wearing his hat. He'd taken to putting it on her head whenever the opportunity was ripe. The way it sat so low over her forehead—he sometimes wondered if she could just curl up into a little ball and have it swallow her up altogether!

"Thank you for this, Slater," Katherine said.

He unwillingly turned his attention from Lark to Katherine. "You're welcome, honey," he said. He put the licorice whip between his teeth and took hold of the lines. "Girls," he said, slapping the lines at the back of the team. Dolly whinnied as she and Coaly began pulling the wagon home.

Things would be different with Katherine and the children there now. He wondered for a moment if it would be easier to resist pulling Lark into his arms every time he saw her with so many other people in the house—or would it be more difficult? Would other people wanting or needing her time—taking her time away from him—spur him on to more self-control or less?

Lark watched as Katherine linked her arms through one of Slater's and rested her head on his broad shoulder. His hat was warm—smelled like him—and she tried to concentrate on the fact that he'd placed it on her head. She imagined the gesture had been more than simply a concern for her being warm enough—that perhaps it was his way of connecting with her somehow. Still, she had never seen Slater so attentive to anyone— not anyone! She watched while his disarming smile stayed on his face as he talked with Katherine—constantly stayed on his face. Several times, Katherine put her small hand to Slater's whiskery cheek and spoke softly—lovingly smiling up at him.

As the wagon rumbled along, Lark felt the odd sensation of wanting to escape begin to spread through her. Her sense of security—of happiness— was beginning to wane.

She looked up to see Tom watching her as she

handed Charlie and Lizzy a licorice whip. She handed one to Johnny and then to Tom.

"What's the matter, honey?" he asked quietly.

Lark shook her head a little and tipped it back to look at Tom from underneath the hat's brim. She shrugged and said, "Oh . . . nothing. Just a little melancholy, I suppose."

Tom smiled. "Now, I don't understand that . . . not when it's so near to Thanksgivin'," he said. "Christmas is just a ways away too . . . and now we'll have young-uns here for both. That makes for a heap more fun, don't you think?"

Lark smiled and nodded. "Yes. Yes, it does." She could well imagine how delightful Thanksgiving and Christmas would be with the children in the house—especially Lizzy and Charlie.

"Does Santa come to your house, mister?" Charlie asked.

"Course he does, boy! Course he does," Tom said, reaching out to tousle the boy's hair. "I bet old Santy Claus will bring somethin' special for ya this year. You too, Lizzy."

"And Johnny too?" Charlie asked.

"Of course!" Tom exclaimed.

Lark smiled as she saw the relief plain on Johnny's face. The death of his father had forced the boy to growing up faster than he was meant to. It was something Lark understood all too well, and her heart ached for him.

"Even Miss Lark?" Lizzy asked.

"Well . . . I'm not sure he—" Lark began.

"Especially Miss Lark," Tom interrupted. "She deserves somethin' from Santy near more than anybody else."

"Why?" Lizzy asked.

Tom chuckled, and Lark smiled at the familiar mischief gleaming in his eyes. "'Cause she's always havin' to mend your cousin Slater's raggedy drawers, that's why," he answered.

The children erupted into giggles. Tom laughed, amused by his own wit and the delight of the children.

"My drawers are nobody's business but mine, Tom," Slater grumbled from the wagon seat.

Tom winked to Lizzy, put one hand to the side of his mouth, and loudly whispered, "You see why Santy will spoil Miss Lark? Slater's drawers are near as raggedy as he is."

The children laughed, and Lark giggled, gasping when Slater reached around and pulled his hat down over her eyes.

"You hush, baby," he teased her, "or else you'll have to reckon with me and my raggedy drawers."

By the time Lark had pushed the hat back on her head, Slater and Katherine were already lost in their own conversation once more. It seemed as if they were each entirely unaware of anything else—of anyone else. Lark's anxiety thickened like cold mud.

"They was close as kids," Tom said in a lowered voice.

"Were they?" Lark muttered, looking away to the horizon again.

"Yep. I used to feel badly that they was—"

"I know, I know. You felt bad that they were cousins. I know," Lark interrupted, annoyed.

Tom suspiciously arched one eyebrow "Now, you don't have nothin' to worry about, honey. They're just good friends, that's all. Just good friends."

Lark looked at him, attempting to feign innocence. "Worry? Why would I be worried about it?"

Tom smiled. He leaned over Charlie and whispered, "I ain't as blind as Slater, darlin'."

She looked to him, horrified—astonished and thoroughly humiliated. Was it so obvious—her secret where Slater was concerned? She thought she'd been concealing it well. If Tom had seen through her feigned indifference, could others be aware of her feelings for Slater too?

"Oh, don't get yer bloomers in a ruffle, Lark," Tom whispered, though still grinning. "Nobody but me could ever see it."

But Lark didn't believe him. Tom was uniquely observant—she knew he was—but it didn't make her feel any less agitated.

"What's in them packages, Miss Lark?" Lizzy asked, pulling Lark's attention from the worrisome course of her thoughts.

"Oh!" Lark said, suddenly remembering her purchases. "Those are mine. Some fabrics, thread . . . some new needles."

"And a book," Charlie said, scrambling over the wagon bed to pick up the small poetry book Lark had purchased.

"Yes," Lark said as he handed the book to her.

"*Favorite Poems*," Lizzy read as she studied the cover. "Oh, it's so pretty, Miss Lark! Will you read to us?"

"Well . . . it's a book of poetry," Lark explained, thinking her explanation sounded ridiculous, considering Lizzy had already read the title. "Are you sure you want me to read it to you? You might not find it interesting."

"Oh, we love books!" Charlie exclaimed. "We don't care what they are."

"Go on, darlin'," Tom encouraged. "It's a ways home yet."

"All right," Lark said. "Where should I begin?"

"With the first poem," Lizzy said.

Lark opened the small book and turned several pages of publication information, finally settling on the first poem.

She cleared her throat and read, " 'The Gardener's Gate' . . . by George Whickets."

"I know this one," Tom said, smiling.

"So do I," Slater unexpectedly offered from the wagon seat.

"Oh, you do not," Katherine said, playfully slapping Slater on the arm.

Slater glanced over his shoulder to Lark. He winked at her and recited, *"And there beneath the meadow dew . . . lay petals which the soft wind blew . . . from roses where her garden grew . . . beneath her window's fragrant view . . . ?"*

Lark skimmed the page, smiled, and said, "Yes . . . toward the end. Here it is."

He winked at her, and molten warmth traveled through her body.

"Oh, read it! Please read it all," Lizzy begged.

Lark smiled as Charlie laid his head on her lap in preparation for the reading. Even Johnny looked interested. Tom—as ever—was smiling.

" 'The Gardener's Gate,' " she began again, "by George Whickets."

Chapter Nine

Slater pulled the team up before the house.

"Oh, Slater!" Katherine exclaimed. "It's just as I remember! You boys haven't changed it a breath."

"Nope," Slater affirmed. "Me and Tom . . . well, we're pretty set in our ways. Ain't that so, Lark?"

Lark was surprised by his addressing her. "Oh . . . um . . . yes. You're very set."

"Not too set to accept a bit of change, I hope," Katherine offered.

"You ain't no change, Kate," Slater told her. He smiled, adding, "Yer more like . . . habit."

Lark couldn't wait to evacuate the wagon. The jealousy gnawing within her bosom was feverish. She didn't care what Tom said; she did have reason to worry. Katherine was Slater's first love—and from what she'd been told, a body never completely recovers from their first. Furthermore, Katherine was in distress—a beautiful, fragile vision of vulnerability. Lark briefly wished she'd worn the pretty lavender wool coat Slater had given her. At least in that she would've looked somewhat feminine. Instead, she sat in the back of the wagon like a child, wearing a plain buckskin slicker and Slater's hat. Why, she must look ridiculous!

Thus, without waiting another moment, Lark stood up in the wagon bed and leapt over the side.

She needed distraction, for she could feel the tears brimming in her eyes as she watched Slater assist Katherine in elegantly descending from the wagon.

"Charlie," she said, taking hold of the small boy's hand, "would you like to go with me to feed the chickens?"

"Oh yes! Yes!" Charlie chirped, clapping his hands together with excitement. "Can I go, Mama? Can I?"

Lark wondered how any mother could ever deny such an adorable boy anything. Katherine smiled at Lark, and Lark immediately felt guilt rising in place of jealousy, for she seemed a warm, sincere woman—a woman any man could little else but love.

"Yes, Charles," Katherine said. "But you do everything she tells you to. Don't you give her any trouble, do you hear?"

Charlie nodded, and Lark smiled when he threw his little arms around her neck. She lifted him out of the wagon, giggling as he hit the ground nearly running already.

"Which way?" he asked. "Which way to the chickens?"

"I mean it, Charles!" Katherine reiterated. "You better mind Miss Lark." She smiled at Lark again, fresh tears brimming in her beautiful blue eyes. "Thank you," she said, dabbing the tears from her cheeks as they spilled over.

"Can we go, Miss Lark?" Lizzy asked. "Me and Johnny?"

"Of course," Lark said. Little Lizzy was as pretty as a fairy child. Again she wondered how Katherine found the fortitude to keep from giving into them at every request.

"I don't wanna go feed the chickens," Johnny mumbled.

"You may go, Lizzy," Katherine consented. "But you mind too, you hear?"

Lizzy squealed and scrambled down from the wagon. Taking Lark's free hand, she smiled. "Are these chickens for eatin'?" she asked. "Or do these just lay eggs?"

Lark giggled. "Both."

"Are we gonna pick one to chop up for supper?" Charlie asked.

Again Lark giggled. "Not tonight, sweetie." She remembered then, remembered that she would need to start supper soon.

"I'll be in to begin supper directly," Lark said, glancing to Slater.

Slater frowned. "Begin supper directly?" Shaking his head, he muttered to Katherine, "Danged if I can figure what she's sayin' half of the time."

Katherine smiled as she took Slater's arm. "She's charming, Slater . . . just lovely. Wherever did you find such a treasure?"

"Slater didn't find her, Katie," Tom chuckled. "I did."

"Oh, now don't start that," Slater grumbled, pulling off his gloves.

"Come on, Miss Lark!" Charlie said, tugging on Lark's hand. "I wanna see the chickens!"

Lark smiled at him and began to walk toward the chicken house. She paused, however, when she felt someone take hold of her arm.

"Here," Slater said, holding out his gloves. "Take these. It's chilly."

Lark smiled and dropped Lizzy's and Charlie's hands long enough to pull on Slater's far too large gloves.

"We'll be in shortly," she told him as the warmth his hands had left in his gloves traveled up her arms and into her bosom.

"You behave, Charles," Katherine said, wagging a warning index finger at her son. "I mean it."

"Are you sure you wouldn't like to come with us, Johnny?" Lark asked. She noticed the way the boy stood watching them. He did want to come. Still, as he shook his head, she knew his tender male ego had gotten the better of him.

"Come on, Miss Lark," Charlie whined, "before Mama changes her mind."

Lark glanced to Slater and forced a nod and a smile even as her heart ached at watching Katherine wrap her arms around one of his strong ones.

Slater had cared for Katherine in their youth—loved her—it was obvious. And now, now that she'd returned—vulnerable, fragile, and beautiful as any stage actress Lark had ever seen photos of—how could he resist loving her again? Lark swallowed the pain and disappointment in her heart. Turning, she led Charlie and Lizzy toward the chicken house. The chill in the air reminded her that winter was only a breath away. She thought of her little room—of the warm days and nights spent in the Evans ranch house. She could endure watching Slater and Katherine together—but only because her safety and comfort depended on it.

• • •

Slater watched Lark as she walked toward the chicken house with Katherine's children. He swallowed the heated desire gathering in his mouth as she glanced over her shoulder to smile at him. Every muscle in his body tensed as he strained to keep from racing after her—from forcing her into his arms—from ravishing her right then and there!

"I just can't wait to get inside!" Katherine chimed. "It's . . . it's just like comin' home."

She released Slater then, taking Johnny's hand and hurrying up the porch steps toward the front door.

Turning to look at him, she asked, "Is it all right if we just . . . just go on in?"

"Of course," Slater mumbled, unable to keep his attention from returning to Lark. He squeezed his eyes tightly shut for a moment—endeavoring to calm his desires.

"What's the matter with you?" Tom asked.

Slater gritted his teeth and shook his head. "What the hell were you thinkin' when you hired that girl?" he growled to his brother.

Irritation flared in him as Tom chuckled.

"Truth be told . . . I was thinkin' it was about time you started livin' again, Slater," Tom said.

Slater turned and glared at Tom. He raised a scolding index finger and gave it a warning wag as he said, "Well, you better hope I don't take to . . . to actin' on some of my thoughts where she's concerned, boy."

Tom still smiled understandingly. "Well, they can't be that bad, brother."

"Some's bad enough to find me thrown in jail," Slater mumbled.

"Not if you were to marry her first," Tom teased.

Slater frowned and growled as he shook his head. "I ain't talkin' to you if you're gonna be ridiculous."

Grumbling to himself, Slater stormed toward the house. What nonsense Tom could talk sometimes! Stomping up onto the porch, he paused a moment before entering the house. He took a deep breath—calmed himself as best he could. Katherine was hurting, alone, and frightened. He didn't want her knowing how torn up he was over Lark. One more deep breath and he entered the house to find Katherine in tears.

"It's like comin' home, Slater!" she cried. "Just like comin' home!"

Lark showed Charlie and Lizzy how to scatter the feed for the chickens. A smile brightened her face as she watched them. They were beautiful children—absolutely delightful! Her heart ached for their loss—for the insecurity and fear they must be feeling. Oh, certainly they didn't feel it the way Katherine was feeling it, for they didn't understand how difficult it was to provide food and shelter for someone—or one's self. But Lark did. She wondered if Katherine's husband had put aside any money—any provisions for his family.

Oh, Lark well knew that Slater and Tom would never allow Katherine or her children to suffer or do without. Still, to do without a father, especially a good father—to do without his love and protection—it was a frightening thing. Lark knew just how frightening. Yet Slater and Tom could provide that as well, couldn't they? If Katherine stayed on, it was sure Slater and Tom would father the children or at least guide them as any good uncle would. In truth, one of them could even marry Katherine—actually become the children's stepfather.

She tried to brush aside these thoughts, for they caused her to tremble. She well knew which Evans brother Katherine Thornquist would choose to marry—which brother she would choose to father her children—to father more children—Slater.

She couldn't think of it—she wouldn't! If she knew anything, it was that she could not linger in watching Slater marry Katherine—or any other woman. She felt a pain begin to sicken her stomach, gasped as the same pain gripped her heart.

"I suppose it might be interesting to live here."

Lark whirled around. Johnny stood just outside the chicken yard fence.

"I know they run cattle . . . but do they have

horses? I mean, besides the Clydesdales?" he asked.

"Yes," Lark managed, hoping the moisture in her eyes would quickly dissipate. "Several."

"I like horses," the boy said.

"Me too."

"I heard Slater tellin' Mama that you have a way with horses."

Lark shrugged. "Sometimes. I seem to be able to soothe them."

"Will you show me?" Johnny asked.

Lark forced a smile and nodded. "I will."

"We're finished!" Lizzy announced. "What can we do now?"

"Well, I need to start supper," Lark told them, ushering them through the gate and latching it behind her. "And besides, it's getting a little too chilly. Let's get you inside and warm you up."

"Can we run back to the house?" Charlie asked. "Can we?"

Lark nodded. "Yes . . . but be careful."

"We will!" Lizzy squealed with excitement.

As Charlie and Lizzy sprinted toward the house, Johnny fell into step beside Lark.

"How old are you, Johnny?" she asked. She knew how hard it was for boys his age to start any conversation—especially with girls or women.

"Almost twelve," Johnny mumbled. "Daddy was gonna get me my own horse on my birthday come March."

Lark winced at the wrench of heartache in her own chest. "Well, I know it isn't the same . . . but Slater and Tom buy and sell horses all the time. Maybe you'll still get one of your own." She silently told herself that she must remember to mention the boy's birthday and desire for a horse to Slater and Tom.

"Did they give you one?" the boy asked.

Lark shook her head. "No . . . but I don't really have need for one. I'm here most all the time."

"Well, I want one," Johnny mumbled. "I want to cowboy too . . . young . . . just like Slater did."

"It's a hard life," Lark offered.

"How many cowboys do you have here?"

Lark smiled, realizing the boy wasn't about to listen to anything discouraging where his dreams were concerned.

"Four—I mean three," Lark said. "We had four . . . but . . . but one left." She grimaced at the memory of Chet Leigh. Somehow the thought caused her to quicken her step, for she wanted only to be back in the safety of the house in that moment. "I'm sure you'll get to meet them . . . maybe even later this evening."

"They don't come to the house for supper?"

Lark shook her head. "No. The Evans brothers do things a bit different. The cowboys keep pretty much to themselves out at the bunkhouse."

"Maybe I could bunk in with them!" Johnny exclaimed. "Do you think they'd let me?"

"Who? The cowboys . . . or Slater and Tom?" she asked, delighted by the sudden sparkle in Johnny's eyes.

"Either one. Should I ask them?" he asked.

"Well, I'd wait a few days," Lark said. "And . . . and you might want to talk to your mother about it first."

Johnny's shoulders sagged as he climbed the back porch steps. "Well, I might as well not even get my hopes up then."

Lark smiled at the boy with understanding. Tenderly placing a hand on his shoulder, she said, "I'm sure if you wait a while . . . it'll all work out."

Johnny shrugged, then nodded, and smiled a little.

As Lark stepped into the house, she was greeted by the delightful prattle of excited children. She hung her coat on the coat rack, carefully hung Slater's hat there too, smoothed her hair, and followed Johnny into the kitchen.

Slater and Tom sat at the table; Katherine did too. But Charlie was skipping around the room as Lizzy sat on Tom's lap.

"Do you have a rooster that crows in the morning?" Lizzy asked.

"Yes, we do," Tom answered. His smile was as broad as a barn door and caused Lark to smile as well.

"Is there a swimming hole around here in the summer?" Charlie asked.

"Yes, sir . . . there is," Slater chuckled.

"Are we allowed to play in the house, or do you like it quiet?" Lizzy asked.

"Will we get to milk a cow?"

"Yes . . . sometimes . . . and yes," Slater answered.

Charlie looked up as Lark and Johnny entered the room.

"I seen our room, Johnny!" Charlie exclaimed. "We have a bed and everything!"

"Well, that's good to know," Johnny said, smiling at his brother.

"And I get to share a bed with Mama," Lizzy chimed. "A big bed! Bigger than yours, Johnny!"

"Well, that's good . . . 'cause you take up a lot of space," Johnny teased her.

"Who do you sleep with, Miss Lark? Uncle Slater or Uncle Tom?" Charlie asked, childlike innocence radiating from his blue eyes.

Lark gasped, as did Katherine. Slater and Tom, however, simply burst into chuckling.

"I-I have my own room, Charlie," Lark stammered. "My own bed too."

"You sleep all by yourself?" Charlie exclaimed, horrified. "Don't you get scared?"

"No," Lark stammered as Slater and Tom tried to rein in their laughter.

Katherine jammed an elbow into Slater's ribs. "Hush, Slater," she scolded. "He's just a little boy."

"So you ain't never been married, Miss Lark?" Johnny asked.

"Well . . . well, no," Lark answered.

"Why not?" Lizzy asked.

Lark cleared her throat. She was uncomfortable—overly warm. "Well . . . I suppose . . . I'm not . . . I'm only nineteen. I . . ."

"Well, our mama was only sixteen when she married our daddy. Isn't that right, Mama?" Johnny asked his mother.

"I was nearly seventeen, Johnny," Katherine told him. "And Lark's got plenty of time."

"You puttin' your bid in early, John?" Tom teased.

Johnny shrugged his shoulders. "I was just wondering."

"I-I better get some supper started," Lark muttered, snatching her apron from a nearby wall hook.

"Oh, please let me help, Lark," Katherine begged, pushing her chair back from the table.

"Oh no!" Lark exclaimed. A wave of panic washed over her. If Katherine proved to be a better cook and housekeeper than Lark was, then Slater and Tom would have no reason to keep her on. "You go ahead and visit. I'll take care of it." She noticed the immediate disappointment on Katherine's face, however—the returning despair. The woman needed a task—needed to keep her mind from lingering on her loss. Lark quickly glanced to Slater. He nodded his affirmation of her own thoughts. "Unless you really want to," she added, though somewhat unwillingly.

Katherine smiled and strode toward Lark. She took an apron down from another hook and asked, "What can I do?"

"Potatoes?" Lark carefully offered.

"Oh yes!" she breathed, obviously relieved that Lark was allowing her to assist. "Just hand me a knife. Oh, I do feel so much better . . . knew I would!" Katherine paused and turned to look to Slater and Tom. "I'm glad we came here," Katherine said. "Thank you, boys."

Slater rose from his chair and strode to Katherine. Jealously burned through Lark like a hot poker as he bent and placed a loving kiss on her cheek.

"Me too, Katie," he said. "Now, maybe Johnny wouldn't mind helping me finish up the chores 'fore supper."

"Not at all," Johnny said.

Slater's gaze fell to Lark. Her heart began to hammer as she recognized the mischief twinkling in his dark eyes. "And if you ever get tired of sleepin' by yourself, baby," he began with a wink, "then you just let me know."

Lark gasped and felt her cheeks turn scarlet— felt her heart begin to pound with wild delight. Slater chuckled and winked again.

"Well, that is so kind, Uncle Slater! Just so kind!"

Lizzy said. Tom and Katherine both chuckled. "Before we decided to come here, Mama told us you were a nice man . . . and she sure was right!"

"And he's got a real big bed too, Miss Lark!" Charlie added.

"Oh, she knows I do, Charlie," Slater chuckled.

"Slater Evans!" Katherine scolded. "You quit teasin' that girl!"

"She's used to it . . . ain't ya?" he asked Lark.

"I-I suppose," Lark stammered. Oh, how she wished her blush would cool! Oh, how she wished he would simply take her in his arms and kiss her!

"Come on, John," Slater said. "Let's get that team put away. Then I'll take ya out to meet the men who cowboy for us. All right?"

Johnny's face lit up like a summer sunrise. "Yes, sir!" he said.

"I do not know how you've put up with him," Katherine said, smiling. She turned to Tom, wagging an index finger at him as he picked up Charlie and began to bounce him on one knee. "And I know you're no better, Thomas Evans."

Tom chuckled and winked understandingly at Lark. Lark sighed, relieved as she felt her blush begin to cool. Her heart, however, continued to beat at feral pace. He'd teased her! He'd teased her in front of Katherine—and about such an insinuative matter! Somehow the knowledge soothed her anxieties a little.

"Oh, it's so good to be back," Katherine sighed

as Lark handed her a potato. She smiled at Lark—a sincere smile of offered friendship. "And I'm so glad you're here too."

"Thank you," Lark said, for it was all she could think to say.

After supper, however, as the cool and darkness of night descended, Katherine's anxieties returned. She wept near constantly—though she tried to enjoy lighthearted conversation in the parlor. Lark watched her, her own heart aching, for she could well imagine the pain she would know if something were to take Slater's life. He would never be her husband, she would never bear his children, yet the imagined pain invoked by the simple thought of losing him—it was excruciating. Thus she felt sorrow for Katherine—pity and great compassion.

The children were tired—so tired they were growing ill-tempered. Yet it was apparent that Katherine did not have the vigor see to them. As Charlie and Lizzy begged their mother to tell them a story, she began—yet was instantly overcome by such weeping that she could not continue.

"Would it be all right if I told you a story tonight?" Lark asked at last. "Then we could let your mother rest a bit. I'm sure she's very tired from traveling."

Katherine smiled gratefully at Lark as Lizzy and Charlie nodded.

"Want to walk a ways, Katie?" Slater asked.

A sense of near panic filled Lark—but what could she do? Katherine nodded and dabbed at her eyes with a handkerchief. Lark watched as Slater helped Katherine with her coat and took her hand as they left the house.

"What's the story about, Lark?" Lizzy asked, startling Lark from her miserable jealousy.

Forcing a smile, she began, "Once upon a time . . ."

"Oh! I love this one!" Lizzy exclaimed.

"You don't even know which one it is," Johnny grumbled. He was sitting next to Tom on the sofa, and Tom chuckled—as ever, amused.

"Be quiet, Johnny!" Lizzy scolded. "Don't you know all good stories start that way? Go on, Lark. Go on and start again."

Lark smiled as Lizzy cuddled up under her arm. Charlie snuggled under the other.

"Very well. Once upon a time . . ." Lark began again.

Mere moments later, both Lizzy and Charlie were sound asleep.

"They're plum tuckered out," Tom chuckled softly.

"That's 'cause they don't hardly draw breath all day," Johnny said. "Did you ever hear such chatterin' on? They're like two squirrels fightin' over an acorn."

"Should we . . . should we just put them to bed?" Lark asked.

Johnny nodded. "Lizzy won't stir at all now," he said. "Charlie might . . . but I'll see to him." Johnny stood, crossed the room, and scooped his little brother into his arms. "Thank you, Miss Lark," he said. He turned and added, "You too, Uncle Tom."

"You're welcome, Johnny," Lark whispered.

Tom strode toward the big chair where Lark still sat with Lizzy. "I'll get her into the bed . . . and you can tuck her in," Tom whispered.

Lark nodded and smiled as she watched Tom carefully lift the little girl into his arms. Lark was glad that Katherine had made the younger children change into their nightdresses before they'd settled in the parlor. She wouldn't have been able to rest easy if she'd had to put Lizzy to bed in her day clothes.

Once she'd snuggly tucked Lizzy into bed, she quietly closed the door behind her and returned to the parlor. Slater and Katherine still hadn't returned, but Lark tried not to think on it. After all, chances were they were talking about Katherine's husband passing on. What could possibly happen between them with such sad conversation?

"I'm not going to any dance, Uncle Tom," Johnny was saying. "Ain't no way! Not me!"

"Ah, now. Come on, boy! We always go to the Christmas social in town," Tom said. Lark recognized Tom's teasing expression, and she felt a little sorrow for Johnny. "We got us some mighty pretty little fillies 'bout your age round here," Tom chuckled.

"I don't know how to dance. I don't have the knack for it, that's all," Johnny grumbled.

Lark had heard about the Christmas social. Mrs. Gunderson had spoken of it while she'd been choosing fabric in town earlier in the day. It had been a long time since Lark had attended such an event. Mrs. Gunderson had told her that the Evans brothers always attended the Christmas social in town, and Lark had found that a growing excitement had begun in her. Naturally, once Katherine and the children had arrived, she'd simply forgotten about it—until now.

"I ain't much of a dancer myself," Tom told Johnny. "I look about like an ol' bull would look if he were tryin' to waltz . . . but it's mighty fun. Nobody out here is much good at dancin', so you'll fit right in."

"I don't go dancing, Uncle Tom."

Tom chuckled and looked up to Lark. The all too familiar Evans mischief was apparent in his expression. She immediately recognized Tom's intention and shook her head. Tom ignored her, however.

"Why . . . I bet our Miss Lark would teach ya all the dancin' ya need to know. You'd sure enough show Johnny waltzin' and such before the Christmas social," he said, "now wouldn't ya?"

Lark couldn't help but smile as Johnny gazed to

her hopefully—almost pleadingly. "Of course!" she exclaimed, feigning delight. "It would be my pleasure. It's not as difficult as you might think, Johnny."

Johnny smiled. "Really? You wouldn't mind teaching me?"

"Of course not," she told him sincerely. "In fact, let's start just now."

Johnny's smile widened. He stood and straightened his shirt collar. He was a tall boy for his age—several inches taller than Lark.

"Here now," she said, directing him to holding her hand in his—in placing his other hand at her waist. "It's fairly simple . . . if you start by counting it out." She began counting out the steps. "One, two, three . . . one, two, three," she counted. "You see? It's not so hard. It just takes some practice."

"One, two, three . . . one, two . . . oops! I'm sorry, Miss Lark," Johnny apologized as he stepped on her foot.

Lark giggled. "It's fine . . . it's fine. You just need practice." She stopped him, smiled, and began again. "One, two, three . . . one, two, three. You see there . . . you're getting it!"

Johnny only nodded, still too intent on counting out his steps.

"You see this, Katie. I leave Tom alone for one dang minute, and he's got them dancin' around like there ain't nothin' to do in the world."

Lark stopped short at the sound of Slater's voice. Slater and Katherine must've entered through the back door, for she hadn't heard them approach. Lark blushed, somehow embarrassed at Slater's having caught her waltzing.

"Lark's teachin' Johnny how to dance so he'll be ready for the town Christmas social," Tom explained.

"Oh! Do they still have the social?" Katherine exclaimed. She looked to Slater, her eyes sparkling with enchantment. "Oh, I did so love the town socials! Remember, Slater? We used to have so much fun. And dance! Oh, how we'd dance! Remember?"

Slater leaned forward, kissing Katherine's forehead. "Course I remember. You were always the prettiest girl there."

Lark watched as then, quite to her utter amazement, Slater began waltzing with Katherine—and humming. She fancied he looked much younger when paired with Katherine—not so much physically but rather as if his soul felt youthful once more. Certainly, he did not look old in the least anyway. Yet whenever his heart was somehow lightened—whenever mischief and mirth were about him—the weathered appearance that normally accompanied him faded.

Lark's thoughts were interrupted when Slater said, "Wipe that look off yer face, baby. Ain't you ever seen nobody waltzin' before?"

"Not you," Lark answered plainly.

Slater immediately stopped dancing. He frowned, nearly glaring at her. "Well, I suppose that's true," he said. Still looking at Lark, he said, "Here, Johnny, you practice with your mama a minute. Looks like I got somethin' to prove."

"Oh no, no, no!" Lark breathed, stepping backward as Slater advanced upon her. His eyes were flashing with naughty indignation.

"You think just 'cause I'm an old, leathery cowhand that I can't dance?" he asked her.

Lark shook her head and forced a pleasant smile. "Oh no! I just mean . . . well, you and Tom don't spend much time dancing around the house. That's all. When would I have ever had the chance to see?"

Slater chuckled. Taking Lark's hand in his, he put his other at her waist. Then, flashing his brilliant smile, he said, "Is that a fact? Well, that shows how much you don't know . . . 'cause the fact of the matter is, late at night, when you're all cozy sound asleep . . . me and old Tom get up and dance around on the table in our drawers . . . trapdoors a-flappin' in the breeze."

Lark blushed and gasped as Slater began leading her in a waltz. Instantly, she began to perspire—to tremble for the excitement rushing through her at being held in his arms.

"I can do reels and everythin' else too. Astonishin', ain't it?" he asked as Lark began to struggle slightly. He was unnerving her greatly. She felt that if she didn't escape him, then Katherine and Johnny might read her feelings—as Tom had so easily done before.

She gasped and was rendered near breathless as he pulled her body flush with his own.

"Now, you don't want to be dancin' this close to a girl at the social, Johnny," Slater said. "If you do . . . you might find her daddy chasin' ya home with his Peacemaker."

"Slater Evans!" Katherine scolded. "Slap him, Lark! He deserves it."

"I-I'm really not up to dancing well this evening, Slater," Lark stammered. "I'm ever so tired. I'm sure everyone is."

Slater winked to Katherine and said, "Let me translate that for ya, Katie. She means she's embarrassed to be dancin' with me and wants to escape to her room."

"That is not what I said," Lark defended herself, planting her feet firmly and stopping their waltz.

Slater didn't loosen his hold on her, nor did he remove his hand from her waist, although he did release her hand he'd been holding. "But that's what you *meant* . . . ain't it?"

"No . . . of course not," Lark stammered. "I simply meant that I've had a very long day, and I'm tired." Though she adored it, his teasing was so entirely unsettling. Silently, she admitted that he'd been right—she did want to escape. Rather, she needed to escape.

"Oh, leave her be, Slater," Katherine giggled, coming to Lark's rescue. "She's worked so hard today, and besides . . . I'm tired too. We should all turn in."

Slater chuckled and released Lark.

"Good night, Johnny . . . Katherine. I hope you both sleep well," Lark said, forcing a friendly smile. She turned to Tom. "Good night, Tom." She paused, blushing as Slater smiled, staring at her expectantly. "Good night, Slater," she managed. His gaze—the way his eyes seemed to study her almost wantonly—caused a delicious quiver to travel through her body.

"Now, you remember," he began, "don't be comin' out in the middle of the night and surprising me and Tom. You might catch us dancin' around in our drawers."

Lark was delighted by his teasing her. Certainly, it made her uncomfortable. Yet it was nearly what she lived for—his teasing, his attention. Smiling, she felt her eyes narrow as she leaned toward him. "It's nothing I haven't seen before . . . your drawers, I mean," she teased. She caught sight of Johnny and Katherine out of the corner of her eye. Thus, she added, "After all, I am the one who does the mendin' around here."

Slater's eyes twinkled with amusement as he gazed at her. "Yes, you are," he mumbled.

Tom playfully slapped Slater on the back. "You need some sleep, boy," he chuckled. "Once you start into waltzin' and pickin' on Lark . . . it's time for you to hit the hay."

Slater's smile broadened, and he nodded. He ran a hand through his hair and said, "Yep. I'm worn through today. I best get myself to bed."

"Thank you for puttin' the children to bed for me, Lark," Katherine said.

"It was a pleasure," Lark told her—and it was the truth.

"Good night," Katherine said. Johnny nodded and headed to the back of the house.

"You keep that fire goin' if it gets cold, Kate," Slater said. "I'll see you all in the mornin'."

He was gone then, taking the stairs two at a time.

Lark closed the door behind her as she entered her room. She was tired—it was true. Yet her mind was alive with thoughts, feelings—her heart still beating erratically, the result of Slater's flirting. She closed her eyes and placed a hand to her forehead as her tired mind whirled.

She knew her face was still fiery with blushing. She wondered if her heart would even resume an even tempo. She was thrilled by Slater's attentions—devastated by the fact that he cared so deeply for Katherine. Unexpectedly, even to herself, she burst into tears. Yet this was not sobbing—merely the quiet tears of fear, fatigue, and even strange delight.

Lark knew she'd grown too comfortable—too pleased with the life she'd come to know at the Evans ranch. She'd fallen too deeply in love with Slater. Furthermore, she sensed the life that she had enjoyed was all too abruptly coming to an end—or, at very least, about to change, dramatically.

Oh, certainly she'd always known a man like Slater Evans would have had many women in his past. Yet she'd somehow convinced herself that he was so single-minded to his work—to his cattle and horses—that no woman would ever breach his attention. Still, a mature, beautiful woman, recently touched by tragedy and looking as alluring as anything on earth, had now returned from Slater's past—returned to be part of his future. Yes, Slater had flirted with Lark, but it could well have been he meant only to entertain Katherine.

Lark felt weary and discouraged. She knew better than to ponder such matters when she was in such a state of exhaustion. Her arms felt heavy as she reached around to work the buttons of her shirtwaist collar.

"Oh!" she gasped, suddenly remembering she'd left the small poetry book she'd purchased in the parlor. She knew reading a few pages before going to sleep would ease her mind into a more restful slumber.

Quietly, she opened the door and peered into the darkness. Across the way she could see the embers of the dying fire yet smoldered, for an inviting orange glow beckoned her. She paused, unable to remember if she'd heard Slater's boots drop overhead. Every night she waited—waited to hear him settle, hear his boots thud to the floor. It was how she knew he was in bed—how she found her own peace in knowing he slept just above her. Had she heard them a moment ago? She thought she had.

Again she peered across the entry toward the parlor. She unlaced her boots and removed them, not wanting to disturb Katherine or the children.

Slipping out of her room, she made her way to the parlor. Lark marveled at how silent the house was, how the absence of voices and light caused the room to seem lonesome—a room that had been filled with life such a short time before. The book of favorite poems was resting on the edge of a small table, just where she'd left it.

As she reached for it, however, Slater's voice from behind startled her. "What're you doin'?" he asked.

Breathless with residual distress, for she had nearly jumped out of her stockings when he'd spoken, she placed a hand to her bosom to settle her madly beating heart. "You frightened me near out of my skin, Slater Evans!" she scolded in a whisper.

"Sorry," he said, striding toward her. He wore only his long underwear, the front of which were unbuttoned and gaping open to his waist. "But what're you doin'?"

"Retrieving my book," she told him. "What're you doing?"

"My shoulder's botherin' me," he said, reaching across his chest to massage the back of his left shoulder.

Lark remembered the scar she'd seen there. It seemed the cooler the weather, the more she caught moments of Slater rubbing his shoulder or rotating his arm as if working out some stiffness. "I came down to fetch the liniment."

"It's in the kitchen," she whispered, starting to move past him. "I'll get it for you."

Lark gasped as Slater took hold of her arm, growling, "No."

"I-I don't mind," she breathed.

She watched as his dark eyes narrowed—as a deep frowning scowl furrowed his handsome brow.

"I need to quit dancin' around this, baby," he said. His voice was deep—somehow rich and alluring like molasses confection.

"Quit d-dancing around what?" Lark stammered.

"You," he mumbled, taking hold of both her arms and maneuvering her body, pressing her back against the parlor wall. Slater leaned toward her, and panic mingled with elation bathed her in a euphoric sort of anticipation.

Frightened by her own rising desires, Lark put out one hand up and pressed firmly against Slater's chest in an effort to keep from melting to him. "Me?" she choked in a whisper.

"I need to quit dancin' around this," he mumbled. She felt him cover her hand pressing against his chest with his own, squeezing it a moment before releasing it. Lark held her breath as he took her face between his powerful hands and moved closer to her. Instinctively, her other hand went to his chest as well, and she gently pushed at him.

"You're shakin' like a leaf," he said, grinning at her—though the narrowing of his eyes told her his intentions were far beyond mere mischief.

"I-I'm cold," she whispered, though she was far from it.

"I'm not," he told her. "Go on. Slip your arms around me . . . and I'll show you how warm I am."

Lark could hardly draw breath! Every inch of her flesh was alive with goose bumps; her stomach felt as if a swarm of birds had just taken flight inside her.

"Let's quit dancin' around it . . . just do it . . . and get it over with," he said. "Then I'm sure we'll both settle down . . . and get right back in the saddle of everyday livin'."

"D-do what?" Lark squeaked. She was breathless—weak—entirely at his mercy.

Slater's grin broadened to a smile. "Kiss," he breathed.

"Oh n-no," Lark whispered, shaking her head. She pushed at his chest more firmly, terrified of what might happen to her heart if she were to succumb to him.

"Oh yes," he breathed. He brushed the tip of her nose with his own, lightly kissing her upper lip. "Let's just quit dancin' around it. Let's just get it over with . . . quit distractin' each other with wantin' it so badly."

"Maybe I don't," she lied.

"Maybe you're a liar," he mumbled against her mouth. "Now slip your arms around me . . . and let me warm you up a minute. I promise you ain't never been warmer."

"Slater—" she began to argue.

"Shhh," he whispered. "I gotta get this outta me, baby . . . else you're gonna drive me to . . ." He kissed her then—directly on the mouth. His lips were warm and soft, and he buried his hands in her hair. "Quit dancin' around it, Lark," he whispered against her lips. "It's one kiss. Take hold and run."

She gasped as his mouth found hers once more—lips parted—warm and moist. Why would he kiss her? she wondered for a brief moment. The question was fleeting, however—for what did it matter why? Slater was kissing her! All her resistance was beaten, and she allowed her arms

230

and hands to slide over his chest, to slip beneath the fabric of his gaping underwear and around to his back. Oh, he was warm! Warmer than anything she'd ever experienced! His skin was smooth and heated; she could feel the strength of the muscles in his back.

Her heart soared as his manner of kissing her intensified. Over and over his mouth commanded hers, coaxing and leading her to return his affectionate endeavors. He paused, pulling her arms from around him and repositioning them around his. Then he drew her against him, his arms banding about her, pulling her flush with his body as he continued to draw pleasure from her mouth —as she continued to draw pleasure from his.

Even in her dreams, Lark had never imagined such desire—such warmth and fascination! His powerful hands tightened at her waist—traveled over her back and shoulders—clutched her hair in his strong fists—and all the while he kissed her, enrapturing her with ravenous wanting. His mouth left hers for a moment, and she sensed his breath was labored as he trailed moist kisses over her neck and throat.

She heard him swear under his breath as he put a hand to the back of her head and drew her mouth to his once more.

Slater had thought one kiss would satisfy him— at least for a time. He thought if he kissed Lark—

if he quit dancing around his yearning for her and simply had her for a moment—then perhaps his blood would cool and he could return to the man he'd been before his brother had put her in his path. Yet he'd been wrong—ignorantly wrong! He wondered now if he'd ever be able to release her. The sweet flavor of her mouth owned him— broke him like a beaten stallion—and he feared he might not be able to stop, to let her go without . . .

"Uncle Slater? I'm scared."

Lark gasped as Slater broke the seal of their kiss and looked down to Charlie.

"Charlie?" Slater panted. "What're you doin' out of bed, puppy?"

Charlie brushed the tears from his cheeks with the backs of his hands, rubbed his eyes, and sniffled. "I'm scared . . . and Johnny just told me to hush," the child answered.

Lark wiped the moisture from her lips as Slater released her and hunkered down before the boy. "Well, how about you and me sit up for a minute until you're feelin' better? All right?" Slater said.

Charlie nodded and smiled.

"And if *you* still like sleepin' by yourself," Slater said, looking up to Lark, "then *you* best get to your bed too."

Lark couldn't speak. She wondered if she'd be able to walk, for her arms and legs felt as weak as a newborn calf's. Still, she managed to nod.

Picking up her book with one trembling hand, she made to move past Slater and Charlie.

But Slater reached out and caught hold of her arm. "We don't need to dance around that no more," he whispered. "It's done . . . and we're good, right?"

Lark nodded.

"Come on, Charlie," Slater said, taking the boy's hand. "Let's watch the fire burn down a bit more."

Charlie followed Slater to the large chair near the hearth. Slater wadded up a small quilt in his lap, and the boy curled up on it, just like a puppy. Lark smiled as she heard Slater begin to hum a soothing melody.

It was hours before Lark found sleep—before her arms and legs quit tingling—before the sense of Slater's mouth against her own lessened enough for slumber to find her. Yet even in sleeping she did not escape him, for in her dreams she lived the moment over and over again. In her dreams, Slater kissed her—all through the night.

Chapter Ten

"Good morning, Lark," Katherine cheerfully greeted as she entered the kitchen the next morning.

Though she'd had little sleep, Lark had been up for some time preparing breakfast. She was surprised to see Katherine enter the kitchen before Slater and Tom. After all, the sun had just begun to peek over the horizon. Somehow, she'd assumed Katherine would have lingered in resting. Lark found she was pleased in knowing Katherine was an early riser also.

"Hello, Katherine," Lark greeted in return. She felt an uncomfortable pinch in her bosom when she saw that, although Katherine's voice was full of happy greeting, her eyes were red and swollen from weeping.

"Oh no," Katherine exclaimed, "please call me Katie! You make me feel older than the hills with Katherine," she said, coming to stand beside Lark. "May I help?"

"Set the table perhaps?" Lark offered.

Katherine clapped her hands together, her smile broadening. "I'd love to! I need work . . . to keep myself busy. We can't just sit down and give up . . . right?"

Lark offered a sympathetic smile. "No," she agreed. "We can't do that."

Katherine nodded. Lark could see she was struggling to withhold her tears. She cleared her throat as she took the plates down from the cupboard.

"Slater tells me you're a wonderful cook," she said, going to the table to distribute the plates.

"Really?" Lark asked. Her arms involuntarily broke into goose bumps as the memory of all the glorious sensations Slater had slathered her with the night before returned. "I would've guessed he'd more likely have told you about what an unaccomplished cattle brander I am."

Katherine giggled, opened the drawer containing the forks and spoons, and began to count out utensils. Nodding, she said, "He did mention it . . . and I can't wait to meet your Black-Eyed Sue."

Lark giggled, thinking not of the bull that would forever own a female name but of Slater and Tom doubled over, eyes moist with mirth. "I can just imagine those two as boys," Lark said. "They must have given their mother fits."

Katherine laughed. "Oh yes! We all did. My mama was their mama's cousin. I lived very near here . . . and we all grew up together. My John was our dear friend as well." She paused, seeming to refortify herself, and then continued. "You should've seen Slater and Tom . . . rambunctious as anything. My mama used to say gettin' them Evans boys in line was like herdin' cats."

Lark giggled at the comparison. She could well imagine it was appropriate.

"They were always runnin' around half-neked, wallerin' in the dirt, and swimmin' in the pond," Katherine continued. "It was wonderful! We were happy children, with no cares or worries. Then Slater left . . . and everything changed."

"I understand he was very young when he first

left home," Lark prodded. Perhaps Katherine would be more forthcoming with information concerning Slater's years away from the ranch. In the nearly four months since she'd arrived at the ranch, Lark found this to be a subject of conversation that was nearly taboo. Her excitement heightened as she began to wonder if Katherine might not find it so unmentionable.

She smiled as Katherine indeed nodded. "He was only fourteen when he left. I couldn't believe it! None of us could . . . but especially me. I suppose it was because I was a girl and couldn't imagine why anyone would ever want to leave home. I thought I might wither up and die without him." She paused. Lark could see the memory caused her pain. Still, she forced a smile and continued, "But that's when my interest turned to John. In the end, he was the perfect man for me." She dabbed a tear from her cheek with her apron.

"Will you tell me about him one day?" Lark asked. She understood mourning and grief all too well. Though she knew Katherine must be ever so tired of weeping—of heartache and pain— it would help her to talk of John and their life together. It would help her children as well.

Katherine smiled and took Lark's hand in her own. "Do you know what I think?" she asked.

"What?" Lark asked in return.

"I think those rambunctious, half-neked Evans

boys have got ahold of a real treasure in you, Miss Lark Lawrence."

Lark smiled at her. Katherine Thornquist was a kind woman—a rare jewel herself—for her soul was as beautiful as her face and figure.

"And of course I'd love to tell you about my John. I think you know that." She lowered her voice as tears sprang to her eyes. "Though . . . let's wait until we have a moment to ourselves."

Lark smiled, for she'd heard the heavy foot-steps descending the stairs as well. Slater and Tom were awake.

Katherine quickly dried her eyes and sniffled back her own tears, just as Tom said, "Well, good mornin', ladies!" He rather lumbered across the kitchen to where Katherine and Lark stood at the stove. Draping one large arm over Katherine's shoulders, the other over Lark's, he chuckled and kissed Katherine on the cheek. "How'd you sleep, honey?" he asked her.

"Better," she said, affectionately patting his cheek.

"And you, darlin'?" he asked Lark.

"Fine," she lied. She smiled when Tom kissed her cheek as well.

"I slept like the dead," he yawned, "though I didn't much feel like crawlin' outta bed."

"Mornin'," Slater mumbled. Lark looked back to see him rather stumble into the kitchen, rubbing his eyes like a sleepy toddler. He plopped down into a chair at the table, covering his mouth as a long, deep yawn swept over him.

"You look like hell, Slater," Tom chuckled.

"Well, thank you, Tom," Slater grumbled.

"What's the matter?" Tom asked.

Slater looked up, his stare locking with Lark's for a moment. Instantly, her heart began to hammer, her insides to tremble. Her mouth watered as she let her gaze linger on his lips a moment—as the memory of his kiss washed over her.

"I didn't sleep too good," he said at last. "Which reminds me . . . Charlie's up in my bed, Kate. I couldn't get him to go back to sleep unless I agreed to let him come with me."

"What?" Katherine exclaimed. "Oh, Slater! I'm so sorry! He's just had an awful time since John . . . since his daddy's been gone. I thought for certain Johnny would take care of him. I'm so sorry."

Slater simply shook his head. "It's all right," he said. "The poor little pup was plum tuckered out." Slater grinned and added, "He sure is a squirmy little feller . . . just like a worm outta dirt."

Lark watched as Slater's gaze lingered on Katherine, as concern caused his handsome brow to pucker into a frown. "How're you doin' this mornin'?" he asked.

Katherine smiled at him—lovingly smiled at him. "Better," she said. "Much better."

"I'm glad to hear that," Slater said, winking at her.

Lark tried to force the jealousy from rising in her throat, but it was difficult. She thought of the night before—of Slater's wanton affections. Surely he cared for her. He was far too disciplined—far too driven where work was concerned to be weakened simply by desire. Surely he cared for her.

Still, he cared for Katherine too. It was obvious in the way he smiled at her now.

Katherine placed a hand to his cheek then, and Lark lost the battle—her jealousy fanned.

"You've got a priceless jewel in this little Lark, Slater," she said, nodding at Lark.

Slater smiled. "I know."

Lark was barely able to contain the gasp in her bosom. She couldn't believe he'd said what he had! Did he truly mean it? Had he only just confessed to Katherine that he valued Lark?

"She makes dang good cookies," he said then, however. Lark's heart ached a little in realizing he was teasing. He chuckled, adding, "And she ain't ever tried to make me eat rabbit."

Tom smiled, and Katherine sighed wistfully.

"Rabbit . . . how awful," she said. "I'd almost forgotten poor little Jenny. You know . . . I've felt bad about that my whole life, Slater. I'm sorry we had that hard winter and you all had to eat her."

Tom choked. He'd been drinking a glass of milk and now spit it from his nose as he began to cough and laugh.

"Thomas Evans!" Katherine scolded. "It isn't one bit funny." Lark noted the way Katherine bit her lip to keep from laughing, however.

"Oh, never mind him, Kate," Slater grumbled. "He ain't never cared a lick for my tender feelings over Jenny." He looked to Lark and winked. "But Lark does . . . don't you, baby?"

Lark nodded and couldn't help but smile at him. After all, she did care. Oh, he and Tom often made light of the rabbit that had been slaughtered to make stew so long ago. Still, deep in her heart, Lark knew it had been very traumatic to Slater—that it still bothered him. She did understand.

"Mama!" Lizzy chirped as she hurried to the table. "It smells so good in here! What's for breakfast?"

"Mornin', Mama," Johnny grumbled as he slunk into the kitchen as well. "Mornin', Uncle Tom, Uncle Slater . . . Miss Lark."

Everyone offered good mornings in return. In the next moment, everyone smiled and stood silent as Charlie's tiny feet could be heard padding down the stairs. Lark bit her lip, delighted as the little boy came stumbling into the kitchen dragging one of Slater's blankets behind him.

"Good mornin', Mama," he mumbled.

"Oh, honey!" Katherine said, rushing to her son and scooping him up into her arms. "What're you doin' up so early? You beat the sun this mornin'."

"I heard talkin'," he mumbled. He laid his head over his mother's shoulder as she struggled to pull the quilt up over him.

Lark smiled as she saw the boy lift a droopy little arm and wave to Slater. Slater chuckled, nodded, and winked at the boy. The affectionate, though silent, interaction between Slater and Charlie caused Lark's heart to leap. She thought of the patience Slater must have had to muster in giving up his sleep and comfort for Charlie's.

"Let's have you lie down for just a while longer, sweetie," Katherine said. "You'll be a bear if I let you stay up now." She looked to Lark and whispered, "I'll be right back."

"It's fine," Lark told her as she spooned eggs from the skillet onto the plates of those already seated at the table.

"You children are up awful early," Tom said as Katherine took Charlie into the other room.

"Mama says we need to earn our keep," Lizzy explained. "She says we can't just stay here like a bunch of squatters."

"I mean to help with the chores and such," Johnny added. "We're good workers."

Lark's heart hurt. She didn't want the children to feel like they had to work to stay at the ranch.

They were children, after all. She watched as Slater and Tom exchanged frowns.

"Well . . . well, I'm sure we can use the help," Tom began.

"But the things you children will be needed to help with . . . well, they won't need doin' until a little later in the mornin' from now on," Slater added.

Lizzy looked somewhat relieved, but Johnny appeared offended.

"I can work as hard as any cowboy you got on this ranch," he grumbled.

"That's true," Slater said. "The boy does have a point, Tom."

"Yes, he does," Tom agreed. "We might should put him out with the boys a couple days a week. Especially since we're short one hand."

Johnny sighed with pride, though he frowned in the next moment. "Why are ya short a hand?" he asked.

Tom shrugged, "Oh, 'cause Slater beat the tar outta him for . . ." He glanced up to Lark. "For bad behavior."

"You beat the tar out of a cowboy for bad behavior, Uncle Slater?" Johnny asked, his eyes widening with admiration and curiosity.

"It weren't just plain bad behavior, boy," Slater mumbled, taking a bite of the bread Lark had placed on his plate. Lark frowned, the memory of Chet Leigh's attack racing into her thoughts.

"Now, Lizzy," Tom began, "Lark won't need you up this early in the mornin' . . . will ya, honey?" He looked to Lark with a conspiratorial wink.

"No," Lark said. "I usually don't get started cleaning house for quite a while."

"Well . . . can I dust the parlor?" Lizzy tentatively asked. "There's so many interestin' things in there. I'd love to dust it. Can that be my job?"

"If you really want it to be," Lark said, tenderly brushing the girl's cheek with the back of her hand. "Do you want jam on your bread?"

Lizzy nodded with delighted anticipation— watched, enthralled, as Lark spread the shiny red strawberry jam over a slice of bread.

"Then, since you're already up today, why don't you start dusting the parlor as soon as the sun's up?" Lark told the little girl.

"I will!" Lizzy chimed, picking up the slice of jam-slathered bread and moaning with delight as she bit into it.

"He's just so tired out," Katherine sighed as she stepped into the kitchen again. She shook her head, placing a hand on Slater's shoulder. "I'm so sorry, Slater. I'm sure he kept you up all night."

"Not at all," Slater lied. He glanced to Lark and grinned. "I was already sleepin' fitful."

"That shoulder botherin' you again, boy?" Tom asked.

"Among other things," Slater said.

Lark felt her eyes widen, however, as Tom looked to her, smiled, and offered a knowing wink.

"When's Thanksgivin', Mama?" Lizzy asked then. "I can't wait for Thanksgivin'!"

"You ask her that every dang mornin', Lizzy," Johnny grumbled. "You know we still got five more days 'til it comes."

Lizzy stuck her tongue out at her brother, and Lark stifled a giggle as Katherine scolded her.

"I love Thanksgivin'!" Lizzy said. "Will we have turkey?"

"Yes, ma'am, we will," Tom said. "Me and your Uncle Slater will fetch it fresh the day before."

"Do the other cowboys come in for Thankgivin' with us?" Johnny asked.

Lark smiled. It was obvious where Johnny's ambitions were.

"They all got their own plans this year, I'm afraid, Johnny," Slater said. "But you'll get to spend plenty of time with them this week anyhow . . . so don't you worry."

"And don't you be encouragin' my boy to run off to cowboyin' like somebody else I know did once," Katherine said, wagging an index finger at Slater.

"Don't you worry, Kate," Slater said, smiling. "Johnny can cowboy right here for me and Tom."

Katherine sighed, obviously relieved.

"Sit down and eat your breakfast, darlin'," Tom

244

said to Lark then. He leaned over to Katherine and added, "She pulls this nonsense every once in a while, and we gotta remind her to sit down and eat with us . . . instead of hoverin' over us like a mama hen."

"Sit down right here, baby," Slater said, patting the seat of the chair next to him. When she paused, he took hold of her arm and pulled her into the chair.

As she served herself some eggs and spread jam over a piece of bread, she listened to the children talking with their mother, Slater, and Tom. A tiny twinge of resentment flickered in her mind, for this was how it would be now—no more intimate conversation between just Slater, Tom, and herself at meal times. And there were more than twice as many people to cook for, to clean up after. Still, she didn't mind so much—for Katherine and her children were wonderful. Furthermore, at least she would be warm this winter.

She felt herself blush as she thought of the warmth her body had known while in the arms of Slater the night before. She couldn't believe she'd allowed herself to embrace him—to be warmed by the smooth heat of his skin, by the delicious pleasure of his kiss.

She was amazed at how unaffected Slater seemed to be. He sat next to her, casually eating his breakfast, as if nothing had ever transpired between them. Apparently her proximity to him did nothing to unsettle his mind and body the way his proximity to her unsettled hers.

Lark glanced to Slater and smiled as he laughed, displaying the tiny wrinkles at the corners of his eyes. She loved this about him—the fact that his face was not so boyish as the faces of some men. His whiskers were thick, his jaw squared and firm. The wrinkles at the corners of his eyes spoke of years of squinting in the sun—and of laughter. There was nothing weak about him, and though his skin was soft, his hands were strong and callused. Slater Evans was a man—a man of experience, weathered with living and working— and she loved him all the more for it.

"Pumpkin pie too?" Lizzy was asking.

"What?" Lark breathed, startled from her daydreams of Slater.

"Will we be having pumpkin pie for Thanksgiving, Miss Lark?" Lizzy asked.

Lark smiled, though Slater's gaze lingering on her caused her to flush crimson once more. "Of course!" she said. "Your Uncle Tom saved the best pumpkins from the garden for our Thanksgiving pies."

"Oh, Mama!" Lizzy squealed, clapping her hands together with delight. "It's gonna be wonderful!"

Lark smiled as Slater chuckled and winked at her.

It was going to be wonderful! Lark glanced to

Slater once more before picking up her fork and starting to eat her eggs—because any day in Slater Evans's company was wonderful! She silently scolded herself at her next thought, however—that any night spent in his arms would be even more so.

Thanksgiving Day dawned snowy and frigid. Long before the sun had even begun to think about rising, Lark had risen to start the kitchen fires. She'd been so thankful that Slater had killed and cleaned the wild turkey the day before, for she'd overslept a little, and it would have put her behind if she'd had to trudge through the task.

Soon the turkey was in the oven, and she set about in preparing other things for the special meal. She smiled as she surveyed the many pies she and Katherine had made over the past few days. She couldn't wait to see the looks on the children's faces when she told them she'd talked their mother into allowing her to serve pumpkin pie for breakfast! Slater even had Johnny save the cream from the milking the day before for the breakfast pies. It would be a lovely day—no matter the weather.

"It's too much for you, isn't it?"

Lark gasped, startled by the sound of Slater's voice. Turning around, she saw him leaning against one wall, watching her. "What?" she asked, instantly uncomfortable.

"Cookin' and carin' for so many," he explained. "We're runnin' you ragged, aren't we?"

But Lark shook her head. "Oh no. No. I'm fine."

"You tell me the truth, Lark. You ain't even dressed." His eyes traveled from her head to her feet and back, and it was only then she remembered she hadn't taken the time to dress. She'd been afraid that, in oversleeping, the turkey wouldn't have the proper time to thoroughly cook if she didn't get it in the oven immediately. Therefore, she'd simply grabbed her shawl and raced into the kitchen, intending to dress properly once the bird was in. Thus, there she stood—her shawl gaping open, revealing her nightdress. Her hair wasn't even braided, and she combed her fingers from her forehead back to smooth it.

"I-I just needed to get the bird in so it will be done on time," she sputtered as she took several steps toward her room.

Slater stepped in front of her, however, barring her way. She swallowed the lump of titillation in her throat as she looked from his chest to his hair. His underwear (unbuttoned as ever it was) gaped open, revealing the smooth contours of his torso—his smooth, warm torso. Lark knew it was smooth and warm, for she'd felt it once before. His hair was tousled, looking not so unlike Charlie's did when first the little boy awoke each morning. She was grateful Slater had taken the time to pull on his trousers, at least.

Quickly, she looked up into his face. He was frowning down at her.

"It's too much for ya, ain't it? You're too young to have to be—" he began.

Yet Lark's fear of the cold, of winter itself, crept to her thoughts. Likewise, her darkest and deepest fear purely gripped her, for if she did not continue to perform her duties well, then winter and cold seemed nothing to the pain and misery having to leave Slater would heap upon her.

"I'm fine," she told him. "I've been taking care of myself, as well as others, for quite some time now. I'm perfectly capable of caring for Katherine and the children as well as you and Tom. And I . . . I rather resent your implication that I'm not up to the task."

Slater's eyebrows arched in astonishment at the strength of her conviction. "Are ya now?"

"Yes," she said, trying to push past him.

But he caught her arm. "Whoa there," he said. "I'm just concerned about yer well-bein'. You're doin' too much, and you know it. It's wearin' ya out. I ain't sayin' you're not capable of doin' it. I'm just tellin' you to slow down a might. The world ain't gonna end if the turkey's a little late gettin' done."

"This is my job, isn't it? That's why you hired me," she told him.

Oh, he was so alluring! She couldn't look at him without her mouth watering for want of his kiss!

She only wanted him to reach out, gather her into his powerful arms, and assure her he wanted her there—that he would keep her.

"I didn't hire you," he growled through clenched teeth. "Tom did."

A sharp pain like a sliver of glass had been plunged into her chest tore through her heart! What was he saying? What did he mean? Did he mean to tell her that he didn't want her there? That to him she was only a burden, a foundling with a need to earn her room and board? Yet she thought of his kindnesses toward her—of his teasing—of his kiss. He meant something else by reminding her that it was Tom who hired her and not him. The smoldering desire in his eyes told her that.

He took a deep breath and continued, "And he didn't hire you to work yourself to death. So wipe that hurt puppy dog look off yer face . . . 'cause you know what I mean." He raked a hand through his hair. "I mean, I'm plum whipped . . . so I know how tired you have to be. I ain't had a good night's sleep since Katherine and the children arrived, and I ain't cookin' and cleanin' up after them."

Lark understood then, and her heart warmed. He was genuinely concerned for her. She still didn't recognize why he was so adamant she understand that it was Tom who hired her and not him, but she did understand why he was so concerned. Slater was tired—worn through with caring for little Charlie through the night.

"You have to make Charlie sleep in his own bed, Slater," she told him.

Slater shook his head. "I can't do it. He's awful fearful at night," he said. "Probably has somethin' to do with his daddy bein' gone. I just can't tell him no."

"Then send him in to me," she suggested. "I'm sure I can settle him down."

He grinned, and she knew mischief was in his mind. "How about he sleeps in my bed, and *I* run on down to yours?" he teased.

Lark couldn't help but smile, delighted by his flirting—inappropriate though it was. "I'm serious," she said.

"So am I," he chuckled.

"You've got to make him stay with Johnny," Lark said. "You work too hard to miss your sleep. Wake me up if he does it again. Wake me up, and I'll help you put him back to bed." She lowered her eyes a moment. "I know you don't want to worry Katie."

"I don't want to worry Kate," he admitted. "But I don't want you havin' one more thing to do neither."

Lark sighed. "Is he in your bed now?" she asked.

"Yep. Sprawled out like a hound on a hot summer day," he yawned, covering his mouth with one hand.

Lark glanced to the clock on the wall.

"Will he wake up if you move him?"

"Oh yeah," he assured her.

"Well, you've got two hours before you and Tom need to be out breaking the ice in the water troughs, right?"

"We ain't doin' it this mornin'," he told her. "The boys are gonna do it before they head into town for their Thanksgiving invitations."

"Well, then . . . you can take my bed," she said.

Slater grinned. "You gonna be in it too?" he teased.

"Of course not," she scolded with a giggle. "I have so many things to get started. Just let me get changed into my dress, and you can sleep in my bed for a few hours." He grinned at her, but she moved past him and toward her room. "You'll be an old bear all day if you don't get some sleep . . . and I won't have you ruining Thanksgiving for the children."

"What kind of a man goes to bed and leaves a woman to doin' all the work?" he asked as he followed her.

Lark stepped into her room and began to close the door.

"A man who's going to let the woman take a nice long nap once the meal is over," she told him. "Now you wait here. I'll only be a minute."

Closing the door behind her, Lark giggled, delighted by Slater's playful attention. Suddenly, the day promised to be even more magical than before.

Dressing quickly, she opened her door to find Slater standing outside it, propped up against one wall. He did look weary—and she loved him all the more for his patience with Charlie.

"Now, you sleep as long as you can," she told him, taking his hand and leading him to her bed. "Remember . . . I don't want you being ornery and spoiling the day for the children."

He grinned and began unfastening his trousers. "You sure you don't want to stay a while?" he teased.

"You sure you don't want me to slap you?" she giggled. "Now go to sleep. I want this to be a wonderful day . . . for everyone."

"Yes, ma'am," he chuckled.

"Rest well, Slater," she told him, hurrying out of the room. As she closed the door behind her, she heard him moan as he lay down in her bed. She smiled as she entered the kitchen to begin the rest of the preparations for the day—for how delicious would it be to sleep in her bed once Slater had been there? She wondered if her pillow might smell of leather and wind. She hoped it would.

Everything about the day was blissful—the meal, the company, the conversation, the delight in knowing Slater and Tom had abandoned any chore that could go with abandoning and that Katherine and her children were not alone. The turkey was moist, the stuffing delicious. There were crisp vegetables and warm bread. In the evening, Lark served more pumpkin pie and fresh whipped cream, and all through the day there was warmth—wonderful, comforting warmth! Lark had never known a Thanksgiving so marvelous. Not only had the food been delicious—with everyone commenting how they'd never had such a good meal—it seemed every soul in the Evanses' ranch house was merry.

Soon the sun was setting, and everyone sat in the parlor in happy conversation and company. Lark was completely fatigued, having not wanted to rest after the meal, for there was too much delight to enjoy. Now she lingered with the others, listening as Slater, Tom, and Katherine reminisced of Thanksgivings past.

The wind blew outside their cozy haven, blowing the flurrying snow into soft drifts. Still, the fire and parlor conversation were comforting, and Lark soon found difficulty in keeping her eyes open. The thick measure of contentment washing over her lulled her like a rocking cradle, and she began to drift in and out of sleep. Katherine was giggling, telling the children about a Thanksgiving past when the turkey had caught flame in the oven. Slater and Tom chuckled at the memory as well, and the sound soothed Lark. She owned very few fond memories of Thanksgiving.

Thus, she enjoyed hearing the tales of family and mischief told by Slater, Tom, and Katherine. Naturally, it was Slater's voice she enjoyed most. The deep, rich flavor of it caused her mouth to water—and visions of being in his arms began to dance in her weary mind.

"She wore herself out," Slater said. It seemed as though he were somewhere in the distance, however. "I told you she would. And she never did lie down for a little rest. Makes me feel like a lazy ol' hound."

Lark felt numb—nearly intoxicated—though she had the slight sensation of being lifted and carried.

"You boys let her work too hard," Katherine said from somewhere. "And at least take her boots off, Slater. For pity's sake!"

"Sleep?" Lark breathed as she forced her eyes to open a moment. It was Slater's face she saw, and she gasped, realizing she was in his arms— that he was setting her gently onto her bed.

"Don't worry," he mumbled, grinning at her as she sat up, suddenly alert. "I ain't stayin' . . . at least not this time."

"Slater Evans!" Katherine scolded. Tom chuckled, however, winking at Lark. "Now, you just get some rest," Katherine said. "It's been a long day . . . and you've worked far too hard since we've been here."

"Oh no! I'm fine! Really!" Lark argued. She was weary—near the edge of collapse—but she could not fail in her responsibilities.

Slater reached out, taking hold of her face with one powerful hand. "Good night," he said. "And don't get out of this bed . . . 'cause I'll just put you right back in it." He released her face, stood, and sighed. "I'm havin' me some more punkin pie," he mumbled, turning to leave the room. Tom chuckled and followed his brother.

Katherine sat down on the side of the bed, however, smiling at Lark. "I don't think I've ever seen anyone work as hard to please everybody as you do, Lark," she said quietly.

"It's my job," Lark answered.

"Oh, now . . . I know it's a whole lot more than that. You're a very extraordinary person . . . and I thank you for all you've done for me and the children. Now, I want you to get some rest. You've been working much too hard since we arrived . . . and probably even before." She smiled and wiped a tear from her cheek. "You get some sleep. I'll tuck everyone in tonight."

Lark nodded, for she was so very tired. She needed to rest—to surrender to sleep. If she didn't, she feared she might collapse.

Katherine stood and walked across the room, closing the door gently behind her.

Lark stripped off her day dress, corset, and stockings. She pulled her nightdress over her head and sank into the soft comfort of her bed. As she turned to her side, however, she smiled. Her pillow did indeed hold a faint aroma of leather and wind—of Slater. Warm beneath sheets and a quilt that had enveloped Slater for a time, Lark drifted off to sleep, her last thought being regret —regret that she'd been carried in Slater's arms and hadn't even been awake to revel in the heaven of it.

Chapter Eleven

Preparing for Christmas took nearly every moment of Lark's spare time. There were so many gifts to make—for she'd made individual gifts not only for Slater, Tom, Katherine, and the children but also for Eldon, Grady, and Ralston. The tips of her fingers were sore from sewing stitches, yet she was glad she had a skill that allowed her the opportunity to make so many gifts. Furthermore, working on her Christmas offerings in such secrecy filled Lark with a wild anticipation and joy. The excitement, constant and plain on Johnny's, Lizzy's, and Charlie's faces, was thoroughly contagious as well. Thus, Lark found herself near constantly giddy—near constantly overcome with an unfamiliar, rather feverish condition of joy. Even the fact that the ground was blanketed by snow—that it seemed it would linger until spring—even this couldn't dampen her spirits.

Two weeks after Thanksgiving, Slater and Tom took Johnny and Charlie out to cut down a pine tree—a Christmas tree. Eldon, Grady, and Ralston joined them, chopping down a smaller tree for use in the bunkhouse. The men were playful, tossing snowballs with the boys and sliding down hills. Lizzy had set herself to pouting, perturbed about not being invited to go with the men and boys to fetch the tree. Lark had comforted her, however, by allowing Lizzy to assist in mixing a batch of gingerbread and then helping her cut them into different shapes before baking. Lizzy was delighted, especially when the men returned to slather her with compliments on how pretty the cookies were—and how delicious.

That evening, everyone set to work decorating the tree. Slater popped corn in a long-handled pan held over the fire in the parlor. When he'd finished, Lark and Katherine strung the white, fluffy corn on thread to use as an embellishment for the tree. Slater had to pop five pans full of popcorn in all, for the children certainly ate it faster than Lark and Katherine could string it. Tom chuckled, commenting that they should plant two rows of the popping corn come spring instead of just one.

Once the popcorn strings were draped around the tree, Slater went to the attic, returning with a small trunk. Lark had joined the children in giggling with delight as Slater opened the trunk to reveal a lovely collection of items meant to adorn the tree. There were small, velvet pouches festooned with tiny white feathers, twenty or thirty pretty prisms hung on dainty green ribbon. There were several glass ornaments and small cornucopias crafted from colorful papers. Slater explained that he and Tom would fill the cornucopias and velvet pouches with sweets and trinkets before the children placed them on the tree. Then, each evening after dinner, the children could each choose one to pluck from the tree to open and enjoy, until they were all empty.

Lark had never known such an occasion! All the while they worked to embellish the tree, she bathed in the wonder of such warmth and friendship. Finally, once Slater and Tom had placed tiny candles on many of the tree boughs and then carefully lit them, Lark felt tears brimming in her eyes, for she'd never seen anything so beautiful—not in all her life! Still, even more beautiful than the tree were the resplendent, beaming faces of the children as they gazed at the finished creation that branded itself forever in her memory.

Tom hung a sprig of mistletoe in the parlor, and it became the obsessive intention of young Johnny to capture Lark unaware beneath it. Lark was sympathetic toward his feelings, yet it was Slater who suggested she allow the boy to catch her once or twice beneath the sprig of kissing plant. She did—twice—both times placing a sisterly kiss on Johnny's blushing cheek.

Evenings were spent in the parlor sitting before the hearth, eating more of Slater's popped corn and listening to the reminiscent tales told by Slater, Tom, and Katherine. The children often played games or worked puzzles. At times, Katherine's spirits were low in missing her husband. Still, Lark tried to distract her—to keep her busy with baking and other preparations. In truth, Lark worked harder than ever she had before. Still, she was happy. Oh, she longed for Slater's touch—for his attention and kiss—that was true enough. Yet again, she convinced herself that she must be glad he had kissed her at all— joyful that she'd known a moment in his arms. After all, it was more than she'd ever hoped for.

Little Charlie had taken to sitting in Lark's lap in the evenings. Slater had brought his mother's old rocker down from the attic, and each evening Lark would settle in it, cradling Charlie as she rocked and softly sang to him. It seemed this helped Charlie to sleep through the night—to keep him in his own bed with Johnny, instead of finding him sprawled in Slater's. Oh, once in a while he still begged Slater to keep him safe—sniffling and telling the big, strong, soft-hearted rancher that he was scared and missed his daddy—and would only go back to sleep if Slater cuddled him up. Slater could never refuse the boy, of course. Still, Lark's lullaby rocking, combined with Katherine's tender kisses and encouragements, found Slater able to obtain a good night's sleep more often than not.

For near to a month, everyone at the Evans ranch had been anxiously anticipating the festivities of the Christmas social in town. There was to be ham and cake, cookies and games, music and dancing. Lark had worked long and hard with Johnny in teaching him to dance. She'd even managed to stitch herself a new dress out of the pink calico she'd purchased from Mrs. Gunderson. Still, as Christmas Eve dawned, a violent snowstorm made attending the social impossible. Everyone was disappointed. Slater and Tom invited the cowboys up from the bunkhouse for an early supper, and Lark thought that perhaps Eldon, Ralston, and Grady were near as disappointed in the weather keeping them from the social as the children were. No doubt they'd had their hearts set on dancing with a pretty girl or two. Still, the meal in the house seemed to soothe them, and they headed back to the bunk-house with "Merry Christmas" on their lips and arms filled with gifts.

As the snow continued to blow, Lark tried not to let her anxieties concerning cold and winter eclipse her delight in the evening. The sun had set, and all was dark and windy outside. Still, it was warm in the house—especially the parlor where everyone had gathered to enjoy the lovely tree.

"Will Santa Claus come?" Lizzy asked. The worry on her face caused Lark's heart to ache. She hadn't forgotten the hope that burned in a child's bosom where dreams of Saint Nicholas were concerned.

"Well, it's a terrible storm, darlin'," Katherine began. "We wouldn't want Santa to put himself in any danger, now would we?"

"Storm?" Tom exclaimed, however. "Ain't a storm ever been brewed that could keep ol' Santy from makin' his rounds. Ain't that right, Slater?"

"Dang right," Slater affirmed. "Why, when me and Tom were little . . . once it snowed so hard it was deeper than the front door was high. We couldn't get out of the house Christmas mornin', but right there under our Christmas tree . . . Santy left me a bright red wagon. And Tom? Well, Tom got hisself a big ol' rockin' pony! Santy always finds a way," Slater said, nodding with assurance. "So don't you worry, Lizzy."

"That's right," Tom added. "And you young-uns best think about gettin' along to bed now so as he can make his visit."

Lizzy and Charlie squealed with delight, their eyes filled with the bright light of excitement.

Charlie hopped down off Lark's lap and ran to his mother. Throwing his arms around her neck, he chirped, "I'll even stay in my bed all night, Mama!"

"Good, honey," Katherine said, smiling.

"Guess I oughta turn in too," Johnny grumbled.

Katherine glanced to Lark, and they both stifled giggles. Johnny was as excited about Christmas as the younger children were. It showed—no matter how hard he tried not to let it. Lark giggled as she listened to Charlie's and Lizzy's small feet racing down the hall toward their beds. Johnny lumbered along after them, attempting to appear indifferent.

"Oh, Slater! Tom!" Katherine unexpectedly scolded then. "I wish you wouldn't have gotten their hopes up so! You know I haven't had a chance to get to town to . . . to talk to Santa Claus. I barely had enough time to make the things I have for them. Now they'll be expectin' Santa to have been here! I oughta paddle both your behinds." Katherine's face showed deep concern.

Slater and Tom exchanged glances with one another, and Lark smiled, for she recognized the Evans mischief when she saw it.

Tom said, "Don't you worry none, Katie. Santy always visits us . . . no matter what the weather. Ain't that right, Slater?"

Slater nodded. "Yep. Santy always comes." He paused, smiling at Katherine. "You know me and Tom better than to think we wouldn't have planned for Santy. Shame on you, girl."

"What do you mean you planned for him?" Katherine asked.

"Don't worry about it, Kate. Me and Tom know what we're doin'."

"But—" Katherine began.

"Remember that one Christmas when me and you was about fifteen, Katie?" Tom interrupted. He looked to Slater. "That one when you was home, Slater. Remember the town social that year?"

Lark grinned knowingly at Tom. He was only trying to distract Katherine from worrying about Santa Claus.

"Yes, I remember it," Slater grumbled. "And you don't need to be bringin' that up."

"Oh yes! The town social!" Katie laughed. "Tell the story, Tom. You're so good at it . . . and I'd bet my bloomers that Lark hasn't ever heard it." Katherine giggled, winking at Lark.

"And she don't need to," Slater said, wagging an index finger at his brother.

"Well, now . . . let me see," Tom began thoughtfully. He stretched his legs in front of him as he leaned back on the sofa. Tucking his hands behind his head, he continued, "Seems like it was one of the few times you was home for Christmas. Ain't that right, Slater?"

"I was home plenty for Christmas," Slater mumbled. Lark watched as he stoked the fire—wondering if his cheeks were red from the heat of the flames or from anticipation of the story Tom was about to tell.

"Yep," Tom sighed. "I believe that Katie and me was about fifteen or so . . . you bein' all growed up and seventeen." Tom chuckled and smiled at Lark. "Seems old Slater . . . he was pretty puffed up in hisself, ya see, honey," he told her. "You know, him bein' so young and cowboyin' so long and all. This was before . . . anyhow, we all went to town for the social. Ol' Slater didn't ride in the wagon with me and Daddy and Mama . . . no, sir. Slater rode his own horse, 'cause he was a man and too old to be ridin' in the back of the wagon."

"I was a man," Slater said. "Mama was still wipin' yer nose then."

Tom chuckled and winked at Lark. Katherine winked at her too, and Lark's curiosity grew. Apparently this was a story that promised to embarrass Slater somewhat, and she was impatient to hear it.

"So, ol' Slater comes a-ridin' into the town social all spiffied up . . . cleanest white shirt I ever did see him wear, before or since. He had hisself a little bow tie at his neck . . . hair slicked back and smellin' like a rose."

"I never once smelled like a rose, Tom," Slater growled.

"Well, smellin' like a lilac then," Tom teased.

Slater shook his head and continued to toy with the logs in the fire.

"Oh yes," Tom chuckled, "he sent them girlies to swoonin' right and left!" He paused to chuckle once more. "Yep, them young female-type hearts just took to beatin' like bird wings; a few of the old ones took to hammerin' too."

Katherine giggled and nodded to Lark in affirming that Tom was not exaggerating.

"Well, there was this mistletoe a-hangin' up over the punch bowl, ya see. Old Slater, he don't never pay attention to what's a-hangin' up over his head . . . so he waltzes over all handsome and manly like to get hisself a cup of punch." Tom chuckled, and Slater inhaled a deep breath, shaking his head with disapproval.

"Quick as Slater gets to that there punch bowl and starts a-spoonin' out a cup, all these young, wild females come a-flockin' over . . . gigglin' and grinnin' like lunatic women."

"You know, you wind a tale up way more than ya need to, Tom," Slater interjected.

Tom ignored him, however. "One of these silly fillies . . . well, she sorta points up, like this." Tom raised an index finger toward the ceiling. "Ol' Slater, he looks up and sees that mistletoe hangin' there . . . figures he's in a real tight predicament. He's still holdin' his punch cup, but he's a-lookin' around at all them pretty young girls a-wantin' to do some smoochin' with him. He don't see ol' Johnny Thornquist sneak up all quiet like and pour hard liquor into his cup of punch."

Lark smiled and glanced to Katherine. Katherine was smiling, nodding in affirmation of

Tom's tale. Lark was mesmerized. She'd heard Slater and Tom tell stories before, but this one was exceptionally interesting. Slater still hunkered before the fire, shaking his head.

"Keep goin', Tom," Katherine prodded. "Don't quit there."

Tom nodded. "Well, ol' Slater . . . he used to get a might nervous when it came to flirtin' and sparkin' and such . . . so he ain't watchin' what Johnny's doin'. He's too busy lookin' around, feelin' a little too warm . . . a little too much like a side a beef that's been throw'd to a pack of starvin' dogs."

"Oh, come on, Tom," Slater growled.

Katherine and Lark giggled as Slater exhaled a heavy sigh.

"So, what he does is . . . he up and empties that whole cup of punch right down his throat." Tom paused, shaking his head with obvious admiration. "To this day I don't know how he gulped down that rotgut without droppin' dead . . . or at least coughin' a bit," he said. "Well, next thing we know, Slater starts into lettin' all them pretty girls kiss all over him. Oh, he was blushin' beet-red all the while . . . don't get me wrong. But all the same . . . they was kissin' all over him. I ain't never seen the like of it since."

Lark looked to Katherine, thinking Tom might be embellishing the story somewhat.

"It's true," Katherine said, however.

267

"And good old Johnny . . . he wasn't one to miss an opportunity," Tom continued. "Johnny was a rotten little prankster as a kid, and ol' Johnny fills up Slater's little punch cup again . . . addin' in his own contents again. So when Slater takes a breath from all that smoochin', he picks up his cup . . . and since he ain't payin' a lick of notice to anything else, he slams down another cup full of hard liquor. Now, Lark, you know me and Slater don't drink as a rule. And bein' so young and not toughened up to the strength of whiskey or nothin' . . . well, that ol' rotgut is startin' in on ol' Slater mighty quick. Before long, Slater starts plain enjoyin' all that smoochin'. I looked over, and there he was . . . wrappin' them girls up in his arms and plantin' big juicy kisses all over their faces . . . kissin' some of 'em square on the mouth!"

"All right, all right," Slater grumbled. He stood, turning his back to the fire. "Now, that's enough of that bull, Tom."

"Oh no, it's not," Katherine giggled. "Finish it, Tom. Oh, Lark . . . it gets better!"

Lark's smile broadened, though jealousy pricked her heart too. She didn't enjoy thinking of Slater kissing anyone else—no matter what the circumstances.

Tom cleared his throat, looking directly at Slater as he said, "Well . . . to cut a long story into pieces . . . some of them girls' daddies had to throw Slater out of the social! He was dang near attackin' everything in a dress he could get his hands on by the time they tossed him out. A couple of fellers tried to ask him to leave, all nice and polite like . . . but Slater just kept kissin' the girls. It was a sight to see!"

"And the girls were just devastated when he left!" Katherine giggled. "Sobbin' and carryin' on . . . beggin' their daddies to let Slater stay at the social. I thought Emma Jean Gunderson was gonna have a lunatic fit! The way she was carryin' on . . . beggin' her daddy to let Slater kiss her just once more."

"I remember that!" Tom laughed then, slapping his knee as mirth overcame him. " 'But, daddy,' she was hollerin'."

" 'It's just mistletoe . . . it's tradition!' " Tom and Katherine exclaimed in unison.

Lark cupped her hands over her mouth as ripples of laughter overtook her. She glanced up to Slater, and he rolled his eyes with exasperation.

"Ooo, boy! Was he sick the next mornin'!" Tom laughed. "Sicker than I ever seen him since!"

Lark's laughter entirely erupted as Tom and Katherine bent over with mirth.

Slater, however, frowned at his brother and grumbled, "You gotta mouth bigger than any I ever seen, Tom." He looked to Lark then, raising one eyebrow rather daringly. "And what are you snickerin' at, baby? It coulda happened to anybody . . . even you."

Lark drew a deep breath and tried to calm her mirthful laughing. She stood up from the rocker and walked a ways from the fire. The warmth of the flames, coupled with her exertive laughter, found her too warm. "Well," she began, trying to stifle her laughter, "I just . . . I just don't see how you fell into such a trap! I can't see anybody being that naive . . . especially you." Lark sighed as her laughter began to subside to a giggle. She wiped the moisture for her eyes and saw Katherine and Tom do the same.

"Is that so?" Slater asked.

Lark looked up to see him grinning at her. "Yes, Slater," she giggled. "Not realizing you were drinking something other than punch? Truly?" She shook her head in disbelief at his apparent innocence. "Not to mention getting caught under the mistletoe. You'd think a man like you would've been aware of the danger of that."

"Really?" Slater asked. "So you don't think you're green enough to stumble into that same mess?" he asked. His eyes narrowed, and his handsome, alluring smile broadened.

"Of course not," Lark said, still smiling. "Why, the only reason little Johnny caught me under twice is because . . ."

Lark's smile instantly faded, for Slater had raised an index finger, pointing toward the ceiling. The delightful humor of the story had distracted Lark. She hadn't realized—not until that very moment—that she stood directly beneath the sprig of mistletoe hanging from the ceiling. She quickly glanced up, hoping the mistletoe had somehow vanished—knowing that hadn't. Indeed, there it hung in all its traditional glory. In truth, she wanted nothing more in the world than to know Slater's kiss once more. Yet with Tom and Katherine looking on, she was entirely unnerved. She looked back to Slater to find he was impishly grinning down at her.

Quickly, she looked to Katherine and Tom. "Oh . . . but surely . . . well, this just doesn't count. It's only for decoration, after all," she said.

Tom chuckled, his eyes bright with amusement. Katherine giggled, biting her lip trying to restrain her own.

Lark looked back to Slater and gasped as he leaned toward her. "No . . . no, no, no," she whispered, already breathless.

"So you think it was pretty funny, huh?" he asked. "Me bein' naive enough to get caught under the mistletoe?" Lark stepped back from him, but he took hold of her arm. "Oh no, ya don't. Don't you try to run away now, you coward. You've been caught, baby. And after all . . . it's tradition. You wouldn't want to be one to break with tradition, now would you?"

"You wouldn't," she whispered. "Not in front of . . ."

"Oh, I would," Slater interrupted.

Still, she doubted him. Would he really kiss her in front of Tom and Katherine—especially Katherine? Their impassioned moments over a month before had been shared in secret. Lark couldn't believe Slater Evans would really kiss her when other people were nearby to witness it.

"Oh, come on, darlin'," Tom chuckled. "It won't hurt none."

"You know he's right. You know it won't hurt," Slater said, mischief and understanding smoldering in his dark eyes.

He was taunting her—teasing her. She was convinced he wouldn't kiss her with Katherine looking on; he wouldn't kiss her as he'd kissed her before anyway. Straightening her posture, Lark allowed an expression of defiance to own her face. She'd test him—see if he were only teasing her for the sake of amusement. Ceremoniously, she turned one cheek upward toward Slater, for she knew he would not kiss her in any manner other than what Johnny had in the least of it.

Slater chuckled. Taking her chin firmly in one hand, he turned her to face him. "I don't think so," he said.

"I think you've been dipping into the punch bowl again," Lark whispered as her mouth began to water for want of his kiss.

"Maybe," he mumbled as his head descended to hers. His kiss was light—the way he'd kissed her the first time when he'd gotten the barber shave in town. She hardly knew whether or not it had actually occurred. But by the warm thrill running through her arms and the goose bumps breaking over her body, she knew he had kissed her—a little.

Disappointment immediately enveloped her. She wanted him to kiss her—so desperately wanted him to. Yet she'd known he wouldn't—not in front of Katherine.

"What in tarnation do you call that, Slater?" Tom exclaimed.

"Well, I'm sure she ain't all that experienced, little brother," Slater said, winking at her. "You don't want me to scare her to death, do ya?"

Lark's heart still ached. He cared too much for Katherine to kiss Lark in front of her—Lark knew he did. Oh, it was fine to fiddle with Lark here and there—to flirt with the cook when a jovial mood overcame him—but it wasn't something he wanted his dear Katherine to own a knowledge of.

Lark's miserable thoughts were interrupted as Tom stood, strode across the room, and pushed Slater's hand from Lark's face. She gasped as Tom gathered her into his arms, forced her body to slightly arching backward, and kissed her square on the mouth. It was not a fleeting kiss either. Though Tom's kiss was not overly forced or impassioned, it was more of a kiss than Slater had taken from her. Furthermore, it did nothing to affect Lark's senses—other than to startle her.

Still, she had the sense that Tom was only taunting his brother. After all, it seemed his favorite pastime—teasing Slater.

Tom released her and straightened his collar. "Now, that is the way to kiss a girl," Tom taunted Slater, returning to the sofa and depositing himself there once more. He smiled and winked at Lark. Katherine giggled, attempting to stifle evidence of amusement when Slater frowned at her.

"Is that so?" Slater asked. "Well, Tom, to tell you the truth of it . . . I was only tryin' to spare you the humiliation of puttin' you to shame. But since Lark ain't makin' much effort to remove herself from where's she standin' anyhow . . ." Lark gasped as Slater bound her in his powerful embrace. "Then let's quit dancin' around this and get down to some real kissin'," he said. He smiled as he gazed at her a moment. "Hold on to your corset strings, baby . . . 'cause I'm about to teach you a lesson for makin' fun of me."

Lark had determined to struggle—to put off his advances. After all, what else could she do with Tom and Katherine looking on? What would they think of her if she allowed Slater to kiss her—if she kissed him in return? Yet the moment his mouth captured hers, all her determination toward pretenses of propriety vanished. Slater Evans owned her—owned her heart, her desire, her every breath—and she could not keep from melting against him. He was irresistible! Entirely irresistible! Even for the fact that Tom and Katherine were there, she could not resist him. His kiss was playful one moment, driven and demanding the next. He seemed careless of others being in the room—taking her mouth with his in kisses that would flame scandal were they administered in any more public a venue. He broke the seal of their lips, tasting her upper lip ever so slightly with his tongue as he did so. Lark fought to keep her knees from buckling as her body weakened—tried to catch the breath that had literally been kissed out of her.

Lark blushed as Tom clapped his hands and whistled. "Now there ya go, Slater!" he chuckled. "That's the way! I knew you still had it in ya."

"Oh, I gotta lot more'n that in me," Slater said, reaching out to take Lark's face between his hands. He smiled, and Lark couldn't help but smile in return. He meant to kiss her again, and she meant to let him.

"Now, you two, stop that teasing!" Katherine scolded, taking hold of Lark's arm and pulling her from Slater's grasp—though his hand caught hold of a loose length of her hair, tugging at it a moment before releasing her entirely. "You just ignore them, sweetie. They don't have one ounce of good sense between the two of them."

"Well, we best all turn in," Tom said, yawning. "No doubt them young-uns will be up before the sun to see what Santy brung 'em."

Slater nodded. "Yep," he said. "Good night, Kate." Lark watched as Slater leaned over and kissed Katherine on the cheek.

"Good night, darlin'," Katherine said. She winked at him and added, "You little devil."

"Good night, Lark," he said to Lark then. She giggled as he quickly took her by the waist, pulled her flush against his strong body, and kissed her hard on the mouth.

"Stop that!" Katherine scolded, slapping him hard on one shoulder. "You're gonna frighten her away."

Slater released Lark, and she playfully pushed at his chest.

"Good night, Katie," Tom said, kissing Katherine's cheek as Slater winked at Lark and turned toward the stairs.

"And good night to you too, honey," Tom said, kissing Lark's cheeks as well. "I apologize for my brother's bad behavior," he chuckled. He leaned toward Lark, whispering, "Though I suspect it ain't been the first time he's been bad with you."

Lark blushed, tucking a strand of hair behind her ear.

Tom chuckled and followed his brother upstairs. "There won't be no red wagon for you this Christmas, Slater Evans," Tom teased. "You've been naughty."

Lark smiled as she heard Slater chuckle. Then they were gone—the mischievous Evans brothers.

"My goodness!" Katherine exclaimed in a whisper. "Aren't you the lucky girl? Smooching under the mistletoe with Slater Evans! He certainly was in a playful mood this evenin'."

Lark blushed. "He's in a naughty mood, if nothing else." She shook her head. "I have the most difficult time trying to figure him."

"I know what you mean," Katherine began. "When we were younger, I could never tell whether he was teasin' me or not. Still, I think I have him pretty well figured out by now." She paused, smiling at Lark for a moment, though the delight in her eyes seemed suddenly dulled by sadness—or regret.

"Do tell me this, Lark," Katherine whispered, "was it just too wonderful for words?"

"What?" Lark asked, though she well knew what Katherine referred to.

"Slater's kiss, silly goose! What did you think I meant?"

Lark blushed—though she was likewise awash with a strange sensation of worry. Slater's kiss was wonderful—just as wonderful as it had been the times before—too wonderful! Yet the fact that Katherine would inquire about it—the fact that it was plain on her face that she wanted to know Slater's kiss—it frightened Lark in that moment.

Katherine sighed, saying, "He's never kissed me . . . not really kissed me . . . not the way he just kissed you," she said. "Oh, believe me, I tried and tried to get him to . . . you know, that Christmas he came home, the same one where he caused such a commotion at the social. But he either didn't want to . . . or was too blind to see me throwin' myself at him. By the time he'd come home again, I was happily married to my Johnny." She smiled rather wistfully. "But I always wondered though . . . you know . . . if kissin' Slater Evans was as thrillin' and delicious as I'd imagined it would."

"I-I'm sure it was," Lark stammered. Her emotions were miserably conflicting inside her—jealousy, pity, and fear—possessiveness, joy, and confusion.

"You mean you're sure it *is,*" Katherine giggled.

Lark smiled and nodded. "Yes . . . I'm sure it is."

Katherine sighed, wrapping her arms around herself, and gazed into the fire a moment. "I hope Charlie sleeps through the night," she said. "He'll be a bear tomorrow if he doesn't." She smiled at Lark and added, "And so will Slater."

Lark giggled and nodded her agreement.

"You gonna turn in?" Katherine asked.

"In a minute," Lark said. "I'll make sure the candles on the tree stay out . . . and watch the fire awhile."

"Well, good night then," Katherine said, leaning over to kiss Lark on one cheek.

Lark returned the affection, thinking that

Christmas brought out the tender, loving feelings in people. "Good night."

After Katherine had retired to her room, Lark did linger in the parlor. The fire still burned warm and comforting in the hearth, and outside the wind had died to a soft breath instead of a harsh howl.

Lark snuggled down into the large rocking chair and smiled as she gazed at the lovely Christmas tree standing sentinel over the gifts tucked beneath its lowest boughs. What a comforting, secure feeling was there in that moment—in that place.

Chapter Twelve

"What are you doin' up at this hour?"

Lark was startled to wakefulness to find Slater standing over her, scowling.

"Oh, I-I . . ." she began. She was chilled and still muzzy.

"Shh. Don't wake Charlie," he mumbled. "I ain't had me a wink of sleep yet tonight . . . and I sure won't get one if that little squirmy worm wakes up."

Lark smiled and rose as she studied him—studied the top of his ever-gaping underwear, the wool socks on his feet.

"I don't know how you keep from catching cold," she whispered.

Slater smiled, "Well, I'm in a hurry . . . and keep yer eyes away from my hind end. These are the drawers you still need to mend."

"Well, why are you wearing them then?" Lark asked, averting her gaze to the ceiling.

"Well, I wasn't expectin' to play Santy Claus with a whole room full of folks, now was I?"

"I'm sorry. I guess I just fell asleep," Lark told him. "I'll leave you to playing Santa Claus." She stood up from the rocking chair, covering her mouth as a yawn escaped her.

"Wait," Slater whispered, taking hold of her arm as she started to leave the room. "Ain't you gonna stay and help me? It'd go a might faster with two of us."

Lark was delighted—not only by his rather vulnerable appearance but by the conspiratorial excitement sparkling in his dark eyes. "What shall I do?" she asked, making sure to look directly at his face—just in case he turned around unexpectedly.

"You can start fillin' them stockin's," he said, handing her an old flour sack. Lark peered into the sack to see it contained nuts, hard candy, and several oranges.

"Oranges?" she exclaimed.

"Hush," he said, clamping a hand over her mouth. He smiled, however. "Santy went to a lot of trouble to get them oranges. Do you think the kids will be surprised?"

"Oh yes!" Lark giggled. "Entirely."

Lark went about filling the stockings with the sweets and treats from the sack Slater had provided. She found the task to be one of the most wonderful delights of her life—kept imagining how excited the children would be when they found the oranges tucked in the toe of the stockings they'd left for Santa to fill.

When she'd finished with the stockings, she watched as Slater positioned a pretty china doll near Lizzy's stocking. He laid Johnny's stocking on a new saddle he'd carried down from upstairs, and she helped him set up four rows of wooden soldiers for Charlie.

"Whenever did you find the time to get out in these storms and purchase these things?" she asked in a whisper as Slater pulled several brown paper–wrapped gifts from a burlap bag and placed them under the tree with the others already waiting there.

"I didn't," he said. He smiled at her. "Santy left 'em for me."

Oh, he was divine—adorable—delicious—utterly irresistible! Lark loved the delight twinkling in his eyes—loved the fact that he was padding around in his stocking feet and underwear, preparing a glorious Christmas morning for the children. She loved him—so desperately loved him—and her heart ached even as it swelled with joy.

"Dang! It's colder than . . . it's mighty cold

down here," he grumbled when he'd finished laying out his treasures. "I'm goin' back to bed. You can stay here and freeze yer britches off if you want to, but I'm turnin' in . . . for good."

"Me too," Lark said, stealing one last glance at the treasures Slater had placed near the hearth and tree.

"Now, cover yer eyes, baby," he whispered. "I'm goin' up." He smiled and leveled an index finger at her. "And no peekin'."

Lark put her hands over her eyes, giggled, and resisted the urge to peek through her fingers as she heard Slater hurry up the stairs.

Once inside her room, she lit her lamp and knelt before the trunk at the foot of her bed. Raising the lid, she slipped a hand between the tattered clothes she'd taken from her carpetbag and placed inside. Carefully, she removed the photograph she'd hidden there—held it nearer the lamp, smiling as she studied it.

"Merry Christmas, Mama," she whispered as she caressed the sweet face in the photograph. "I miss you."

She replaced the photograph, closed the lid to the trunk, and began to unbutton the buttons at the back of her collar. A smile touched her lips as she thought of her reoccurring dream of Slater—of his fumbling with the buttons at her neck. Perhaps she would have the dream again tonight. What more perfect gift could she ask for than to dream of Slater all Christmas Eve? She bit her lip, her arms and legs erupting with goose bumps as she lingered on the memory of Slater capturing her beneath the mistletoe. It had been a wonderful Christmas Eve—the most wonderful she had ever known!

"Miss Lark, Miss Lark! Wake up! It's Christmas morning!"

Lark rather unwillingly pulled herself from her romantic dreams of Slater and into full consciousness. Again she heard a knock on her bedroom door.

"Miss Lark, it's Lizzy! Come have Christmas with us!" Lizzy called from beyond it.

The door opened, and Katherine peeped in. "Gracious, Lark! How are you managin' to sleep with all this noise? The children are ready to beat each other up to get to their gifts!"

Lark sat up in her bed, quickly gathering her hair and twining it into a loose braid. "I'm so sorry," she said. "I guess I was just sleeping so soundly."

"Just throw a shawl over yourself like I did, sweetie," Katherine giggled. "Christmas mornin' isn't a time to worry about modesty . . . not with children in the house."

Lark smiled and climbed out of bed. Snatching her shawl from a hook on the wall, she followed Katherine.

"Well, it's about time," Tom greeted as she and Katherine entered the parlor. He sat on the sofa, hair tousled, wearing only his underwear and a pair of socks. "Must've been a dang good dream to keep you in bed this long," he teased.

"Mornin'," Slater mumbled. Charlie was leading Slater by the hand, tugging mercilessly on him as if Slater were a barge and Charlie a tugboat struggling to bring him upriver.

Katherine clamped a hand over her mouth to stifle a giggle as Slater reached around with his free hand to secure the trapdoor on his underwear.

"Don't you have a decent pair of drawers, Slater?" Tom asked. "It's Christmas, for Pete's sake."

"I'll pin it here in a minute," Slater mumbled, collapsing onto the sofa next to Tom.

Slater frowned at Lark when he saw her studying him with amusement plain on her face. "What're you grinnin' at, baby?" he asked. "I can see clean through that there nightgown you're wearing."

Lark gasped and looked down at her nightdress. She'd been sure it was a heavy fabric when she'd purchased it. Slater's chuckle and Katherine's scolding index finger told her he was only teasing her, however. She smiled as she watched him run his fingers through his hair, rubbing the sleep from his eyes in the exact manner she'd seen Charlie do.

The children had discovered their stockings and gifts from Santa. Lark was delighted by the way Slater and Tom watched them—chuckling and elbowing one another with pride in having made the children so happy. Katherine was near to weeping. No doubt Slater and Tom's efforts had thoroughly touched her heart. Lark put an arm around her shoulders, and Katherine smiled gratefully at her.

Lark went to the tree. Taking a small package wrapped in brown paper from beneath it, she handed it to Katherine. "It's not much, Katie," she said. "Just a little something to let you know that I care for you . . . and that I'm glad you're here."

"Oh, Lark!" Katherine exclaimed. "How thoughtful! You didn't have to do this."

Lark smiled, however, as Katherine carefully untied the ribbon securing the paper. "Oh!" she gasped as she studied the dainty gloves. "Oh, Lark! They're lovely. Oh, they're lovely!'

Lark was relieved that her gift of the white crocheted gloves seemed to please Katherine. They'd taken so many hours—so many late hours sitting by dim lamplight to manage. Yet Katherine's reaction encouraged Lark.

Lizzy squealed as she found the package Lark had left beneath the tree for her. "Oh, Miss Lark!" the little girl chirped, removing the small crocheted gloves from her own gift-wrappings. "Oh, they're just like Mama's! Oh, they're so pretty. I never ever had anything so pretty!" Throwing her tiny arms around Lark's neck, Lizzy hugged her, whispering, "Thank you, thank you, thank you!"

"You're welcome," Lark giggled, delighted with Lizzy's reaction to her gift as well. Lark smiled with reassured contentment. She'd been so worried everyone would think her gifts insignificant or silly.

"Is there one for me?" Johnny asked, rather tentatively.

"Of course," Lark told him. She reached beneath the tree and found her gift for Johnny. "Here . . . though I'm worried as to whether or not you'll like it."

"If it's from you, I know I'll like it," Johnny said.

"Now there ya go," Tom said from the sofa.

Lark looked over to see the two underwear-clad men nodding. Slater looked to Tom and said, "That boy's even smarter than he looks." Tom nodded again and chuckled. Slater changed the tone of his voice and, imitating Johnny, said, "If it's from you, I know I'll like it."

"We best remember that," Tom said.

"Yep," Slater chuckled.

Johnny opened the gift and smiled as he lifted the black bib shirt adorned with brass buttons up to study it more closely. "Oh, thank you, Miss Lark!" the boy exclaimed. "Thank you. It looks just like the ones the cowboys in town wear!"

"You're welcome," Lark giggled. "And I really do hope you like it, Johnny."

Lark saw the moisture fresh in Johnny's eyes. The boy was truly touched by her gift. Yet she didn't want him to let a tear escape over his cheek and feel foolish in front of the men, so she quickly snatched Charlie's gift from under the tree.

"Here you go, Charlie," Lark said. "I-I hope it's not too . . . well, I hope you're not too big a boy to enjoy this."

"I ain't," Charlie said, even though he was still unwrapping the package.

Lark held her breath. Of all the gifts she'd made, she was most worried about Charlie's.

Charlie unfolded the quilt Lark had made. He was silent for a moment, studying it carefully a moment. "I know this!" the little boy exclaimed then. "Mama, I know this!"

Lark still hadn't taken a comfortable breath. Yet as Charlie's face lit up like the sun, she sighed.

"Look, Mama!" Charlie squealed, "It's Daddy!"

"What?" Katherine gasped.

"It's Daddy's blue shirt. I remember him wearin' this shirt, Mama! Oh, it's Daddy!" Charlie turned the quilt around—smoothed it out on the parlor rug. "You see, Mama?" the little boy asked.

"I do see," Katherine breathed. "I do indeed." She looked to Lark a moment before letting her hand travel over the top of the quilt—the quilt with John Thornquist's shirt stitched to it.

Just after she'd arrived, Lark had been helping Katherine unpack her trunks and get settled into the house. Katherine had kept all of her husband's shirts. She said she planned to cut them down for Johnny to wear—or maybe, because he was growing so fast, he'd grow into them before she had the chance to rework them. Then, when it became obvious that little Charlie was having trouble sleeping—and that the reason was most likely insecurities brought on by the loss of his father—Lark had had a moment of inspiration.

"That's why you asked me for the shirt, Lark," Katherine whispered, running her hands over the front of her husband's shirt that was now securely stitched to the top of Charlie's quilt. She looked to Lark, tears brimming in her eyes. "I thought you planned on cuttin' it down for Johnny." Katherine shook her head. "But, oh, Lark . . . what a wonderful gift."

"You see, Charlie," Lark said, taking the quilt from him, "this way your daddy can always hold you in his arms at night when you're worried or afraid." She wrapped the quilt around him so that the sleeves of his father's shirt folded over his arms. "And I made the other side nice and warm too. Isn't it soft?"

"It's the softest thing I ever felt," Charlie told her. "It feels like . . . it feels just like . . ."

"Your Uncle Slater's old drawers?" Lark prodded.

"What?" Slater exclaimed.

"Yes!" Charlie giggled. "That's what it is! It's so warm. It makes me feel happy!" Lark watched as the little boy softly caressed his father's shirt-sleeves, wrapped the quilt tightly around him, and smiled. "It's right cozy, Miss Lark," he giggled, rubbing his face against the underside of the quilt made from Slater's old underwear.

Lizzy giggled. "Oh, Charlie, it's perfect! Now you'll always have Daddy and Uncle Slater to snuggle you at night!"

Charlie's smile broadened, and he nodded with newfound comfort.

"Well, that's why my fanny is always hangin' outta my drawers," Slater mumbled to Tom. "She's stitchin' quilts out of my good pairs."

Katherine brushed the tears from her cheeks, wrapped her arms around Lark's neck, and whispered, "Oh, Lark! What a treasure you are. Thank you. Oh, thank you!"

"I hope it helps comfort him . . . even if it's just a little," Lark whispered as the woman cried against her shoulder for a moment.

Slater bit the inside of his cheek to keep the tears that were welling in his eyes from running down his cheeks. He heard Tom sniffle and had to fight even harder to keep his emotions in line. He gazed at Lark a moment—barely able to keep from going over, picking her up, and carrying her up to his bedroom to have his fill of her. The gifts she'd made for Katherine and the children—especially Charlie—they were true gifts from the heart, gifts made of love and long, long hours of sewing by lamplight. God had dropped an angel off on his and Tom's porch that day a few months back—that was all there was to it.

He studied her for a moment—her soft hair braided so loosely and laying over one shoulder, her pretty white nightgown, beneath which he was certain she hadn't taken time to put a corset. Her cheeks were rosy with joy, her lips as soft and inviting as a summer berry on the vine. He had to have her—had to own her! Suddenly, the thought of Lark leaving—of her being anywhere that was away from him—caused a sort of desperate panic to wash through him. He'd come to depend on her smile as a way of finding beauty in each day, to depend on her voice to soothe his worries and temper. He couldn't do without her, but he couldn't have her either. He wouldn't have her. He thought of the old buzzard he'd seen picking at a dead rabbit a month or two before. A pretty meadow-lark had been sitting on a fencepost nearby and flew away when the buzzard flapped its wings and barked a caw. Lark deserved a young, strong falcon—not a weathered old buzzard.

In those moments, Slater Evans wished he'd never left home to cowboy—wished he'd never spent ten years doing what he'd done after cowboying. In that moment, Slater Evans wished he hadn't lived such a hard life—wished he hadn't been weathered too young.

"Keep a handle on it, Slater," Tom chuckled quietly. "Christmas mornin' with children in the room ain't no place to grab hold of a woman and—"

"I'm fine," Slater growled. "And what're you goin' on about anyway?"

Tom was still smiling, however. "I'm just sayin' . . ."

"Well, you say too much," Slater grumbled.

Tom chuckled, leaned closer to Slater, and whispered, "You're droolin' like a dog lookin' at a hambone, Slater."

"Shut your mouth before I shut it for ya, Tom."

Tom chuckled again, and Slater willed himself to keep from pouncing on the sweet little hambone sitting by the Christmas tree.

"I know it's not much, but I just wanted—" Lark began to explain.

"Oh, Lark! You do too much and take too little praise." Katherine's eyes were still moist with emotion, and Lark felt self-conscious—for she'd realized Slater and Tom were watching the exchange.

"I have something for you," Katherine said then.

"Oh no . . . no, really," Lark said, shaking her

head. She'd never been good at receiving gifts. She only liked to give them. Receiving them always made her far too uncomfortable.

"It isn't as nice as the gloves, but I hope you'll like it."

Glancing to where Slater and Tom sat on the sofa, Lark blushed and accepted the gift Katherine offered to her. "Katie, really," she began, "I-I . . ."

"Oh, go on!" Katherine giggled. "It's Christmas."

Taking a deep breath, Lark untied the ribbon and removed the paper that concealed the gift. Inside lay two pair of silk stockings. Lark had never owned a pair of silk stockings. In fact, the only women she'd ever known to own them before were the saloon girls in the previous town she'd labored in. She knew that silk stockings were a luxury, afforded by few—especially women like herself—cooks, housekeepers, laborers.

"Oh, Katherine!" she breathed. "I can't possibly . . . however did you come by these?"

"Oh, that's my little secret," Katherine said, winking at Tom.

"Try 'em on, baby," Slater teased with a wink. "We don't mind."

"Slater Evans!" Katherine scolded. "Now you just hush. We're having our Christmas!"

Slater chuckled and turned his attention to Charlie, who was still wrapped in his quilt and busily setting up wooden soldiers.

Tom raised himself from the sofa, sauntered over to the tree, and pulled two gifts out from under it. He smiled, handing one gift to Katherine and the other to Lark.

"These are from me," he proudly announced. "Picked 'em out myself."

Lark smiled and began to open her gift from Tom. "Oh, Tom!" Lark exclaimed as she held up the new dress. It was a lovely dress—lavender with white lace. Lark had never owned anything like it! "It's so . . . so beautiful!"

"Tom! How lovely," Katherine exclaimed, holding up a peacock-blue dress as well. "You've spoiled us!"

"Thank you, Tom," Lark said, feeling suddenly very sheepish about her gift to him. "I-I don't know what to say."

"Try it on!" Slater teased from the sofa.

"You best behave," Katherine said to him, pointing a scolding finger in his direction.

"I have something for you, Tom," Lark said, though she was not nearly as excited about giving her gift to him as she had been a moment before. Yet she was completely caught up in the excitement of the morning, taking two gifts from beneath the tree and handing one to Tom.

Tom tore into the package with as much zeal as the children had torn into theirs. "Well, will you look at that," he said, drawing the neatly stitched white shirt and monogrammed handkerchiefs out of the paper. "That there is the whitest shirt I ever seen!" he exclaimed. "And look at that stitchin'! Mrs. Jenkins best not find out you do work this good, honey."

"I know it's not so fancy or nice as the dress . . ." Lark began.

"Look here," Tom said to Slater. "My initials is on the cuffs . . . and the collar . . . on the handkerchiefs too." He shook his head in awe. "Little darlin' . . . you are somethin' else!"

Lark smiled as Tom bent and kissed her on the forehead. "I know you must think it's, well . . . impractical to say the least, but—" Lark began.

"It's wonderful, darlin'," Tom said. "Truly." He held the shirt up to inspect it once more. "I might have to take myself into town soon . . . just to send the ladies to swoonin'."

Lark turned, handing the other package to Slater. "I'm sure you can guess what it is," she said quietly. "At least, part of it, anyway."

"Well, it's too big to be a new button for my trapdoor," he chuckled as she handed him his gift. She smiled and watched as he opened the package.

"The shirt is a different pattern than Tom's," she explained as he held his white shirt up for inspection. "Yours is an offset bib shirt. I hope . . . I hope it's all right."

Slater smiled, but she wasn't sure whether he was pleased. "I monogrammed yours too," she offered. "On the cuff and the collar."

"It's perfect," he said, his eyes narrowing as he looked at her. "I mean it, Lark. It's perfect."

"And I didn't make you any handkerchiefs," she said, reaching into the paper in his lap and withdrawing the rest of her gift to him. "But . . . I did make this for you." Lark offered the thing to him—smiled when his brow puckered.

"Well, thank you, baby," he said, accepting the gift—a long, slender pillow made out of an old flour sack, filled with dry rice and dried lavender and thyme leaves.

Lark giggled. "It's for your shoulder," she explained. "See?" she said, draping it over his shoulder. "You heat it up by the fire on the stove for a while, until the rice kernels inside warm up and hold the heat. The warmth will soothe the ache in your shoulder . . . and the fragrance of the lavender and thyme will soothe *you*."

Slater smiled, and Lark began to feel more confident in her gift.

"I set it by the fire before we started opening our gifts," she told him. "So the rice is still warm, isn't it?"

Slater nodded, pressing the rice-filled pillow more firmly against his shoulder. "You're quite the little Christmas angel, ain't ya?" he asked. His eyes narrowed, and Lark's heart began to beat more quickly, for she recognized the expression on his face—desire!

"Here, Johnny," Slater said, snapping his fingers

to get the boy's attention. "Hand me that gift under the tree . . . the one from me to Lark . . . would ya, please?"

Johnny nodded, handing the awkwardly wrapped gift to Slater.

"Thank ya, boy," Slater said.

Lark glanced over as Tom exclaimed, having opened the new razor Katherine had given him.

"Here ya go," Slater said, handing the gift to Lark.

"I really wasn't expecting gifts," Lark mumbled. "I really only meant to show my appreciation for—"

"I promise . . . it ain't nothin' so nice as a fine shirt or shoulder-soother," he said.

She smiled, delighted by his obvious appreciation of her gifts.

"It ain't even a pretty dress. I almost didn't want to give it to ya after I seen what Kate and Tom had for ya." He shrugged, looking boyish and entirely adorable. "Honest. It ain't much . . . not compared."

But Lark felt differently. Slater Evans could've given her a rock he'd picked up somewhere, and she would've loved it. A gift from Slater? She could hardly believe it. Her hands trembled as she untied the twine securing the paper.

Instantly, she felt her heart begin to race—felt her eyes brimming with tears as she looked at what Slater had given her. There, resting in her lap, were two beautiful and very new books! Beautifully bound in embellished, dark green covers, flourishes of gold for titles and author names—even so fancy as to have gold-gilded pages—a beautiful copy of *Jane Eyre*, perfectly complemented by a copy of *The Complete Works of Tennyson.*

"Slater!" she exclaimed in a whisper.

"Oh," he said, however. "And then there's this." Reaching out to her, he opened the copy of Tennyson's works and removed a silver book-mark. "I figured you needed a way to remember where you were last readin' when ya have to leave off all of a sudden."

Lark accepted the bookmark as he handed it to her—a solid silver bookmark. The bookmark was a thin piece of silver, with a detailed etching of a bird on it—and her name engraved at the bottom.

"Do you like it?" Slater asked.

She glanced up to him—astonished to see that he looked as concerned about his gift to her as she'd felt about hers to him.

"I do," she managed. "Thank you, Slater." She couldn't keep the tears from brimming in her eyes, for she knew then that he must think of her—for this was a gift that took preparation and planning.

He smiled at her, reached out, and brushed a tear from her cheek with the back of his hand. "I still can't believe you used my drawers to make a quilt for that baby boy," he said.

Lark smiled and laughed. "Well, even as raggedy as your underwear is sometimes . . . it's still good for something."

"You think I might could break in this saddle somehow, Uncle Slater?" Johnny asked then.

Slater winked at Lark. "I do think so, Johnny," Slater told him. "If this weather clears up tomorrow, we'll see which horse fits it best. All right?"

"Yes, sir!" Johnny exclaimed.

Katherine squealed with delight then and rushed to Slater, throwing her arms around his neck.

"Oh, Slater!" she cried, brushing tears from her cheeks. "How did you ever . . . I can't . . . oh, darlin', thank you!"

Lark looked to see that Katherine held a large silver locket and chain in one hand. She opened the locket, and for the first time Lark saw the image of John Thornquist. Somehow—somewhere—Slater had found a photograph of John and had it put in the locket under glass.

Leaning forward, Lark quickly kissed Slater on the cheek. "You really are Saint Nicholas, I think," she whispered.

Late that night, after everyone else had retired, Lark propped herself up in bed, turned the flame in the lamp a little higher, and opened her new copy of *The Complete Works of Tennyson*. She put her face near the book, inhaling the wonderful aroma of paper and leather. She turned the cover page and smiled, delicious warmth filling her bosom when she saw an inscription. There, sprawled in Slater's nearly illegible handwriting, was:

Merry Christmas, Lark . . .
Slater

Lark touched the dried ink—the words written by Slater's own hand. She smiled and began reading.

Chapter Thirteen

Though winter was cold and fierce, the vigor with which it shivered and blew proved too exhausting for it to linger long. Yet winter had been merciless, having kept the children inside most every day from Christmas through late February. Lark and Katherine had been quite hard-pressed to find ways to keep them from whining with boredom—especially Charlie. Johnny was old enough to often help Slater and Tom with outdoor chores or to ride out with the cowboys to check fences and repair windbreaks. Lizzy was fairly content to practice her stitching, to draw, or to play with her dolls. Yet Charlie—Charlie was entirely too pent in. Forever racing through the house or finding his way to mischief, it was Charlie who suffered most from the brutal winter—however short-lived it was.

Still, even for all of Charlie's bottled-up liveliness, he had begun to sleep through the night once more. Katherine credited Lark's quilt. Slater did too, often expressing his gratitude to Lark—for he slept through the night again, as well.

Yet by mid-March, as most days were filled with contented rain or warm sunshine, it was Lark who had begun to sleep fitfully. Christmas had been resplendent! The exchange of thoughtful gifts had touched Lark's heart as nothing she'd ever known. Each night she read from one of the books Slater had gifted her. Even after she'd read them both through from front to back, she still read an excerpt or two from one of them before drifting off to sleep. She treasured the books—treasured his signature and inscription to her inside them—treasured the lovely silver book-mark he'd had her name engraved upon. Still, as spring approached, it was Christmas Eve that lingered most vivid in Lark's thoughts—Christmas Eve and Slater's kiss beneath the mistletoe.

Slater had not moved to kiss her since—not once. Oh, he was flirtatious enough, often teasing her about one thing or the other, but it seemed he no longer found her attractive in any regard. Oh, certainly he was friendly—at least he was friendly when he wasn't tired, brooding, or grumbling about the weather. Friendly—but not too friendly.

For a time, Lark had determined it was the discomfort his shoulder afforded him each time the temperature would drop noticeably that caused him to often seem distracted or lost in his own thoughts. When the frigid cold would set in, or when he'd been working out in the wind, his shoulder would begin to ache, thus turning his temperament to a less than jovial venue. Lark found some comfort in knowing that the rice and herb pillow she made did seem to soothe the ache in him. It was several times she had the opportunity to study the scar at his left shoulder. When first she'd seen it, she'd determined it may have been made by a knife or some such similar weapon. However, one morning when he appeared in the kitchen, bare except for his trousers (having found his bureau lacking in underwear—indeed coming upon Lark in the very process of folding his freshly washed and dried drawers), she'd noticed a smaller scar at the front of his shoulder—a small, round-type scar. Normally, Slater's suspender straps would've hidden this scar, but since he wore no suspenders in that moment, the scar was easily visible. Though she did not know a great deal about wounds, Lark knew enough to surmise that the scar on the front of Slater's shoulder had been made by a bullet, while the terrible flesh-tearing scar at the back had been made by the same bullet as it had exited his body. Naturally, this discovery intrigued Lark—though something in her very soul whispered she should not inquire about it. And she didn't.

Yes, friendly, but not too friendly. That was how Lark thought of Slater's treatment of her. He still worked and laughed with Tom—sat in the parlor with everyone in the evenings after supper. He still played soldiers with Charlie, read picture books to Lizzy, and taught Johnny lessons in breeding and caring for cattle. He conversed comfortably with Katherine, reminiscing about John or counseling her on matters of finance. Still, with Lark he seemed almost indifferent at times.

Of course, Lark often wondered if it were merely she who had changed. Did Slater really treat her so differently than he had before? Other than not having kissed her in near to three months, she thought perhaps his behavior was not so altered where she was concerned. She thought it was simply the fact that she loved him—so desperately loved him—that caused her to think him indifferent. Certainly he talked to her as often as he did the others. Certainly he was kind and teasing. Lark even inwardly recognized that he was kinder and friendlier than he had been when she'd first arrived. Yet she'd hoped for more. She'd dreamt of more—especially after having been kissed by him—so deliciously kissed by him.

Often, late at night when Lark found sleep entirely elusive, she would think on his words—on what he'd said the first time he'd kissed her—the first time he'd really kissed her.

Let's quit dancin' around it . . . just do it . . . and get it over with, he'd said. *Then I'm sure we'll both settle down . . . and get right back in the saddle of everyday livin'.*

Could it be that Slater had gotten over it—whatever it was? Could it be that he'd simply been curious—momentarily tempted by her youth and femininity—and that kissing her once or twice had satisfied his interest where Lark was concerned? Or could it be what she'd feared from the moment he and Tom had received Katherine's letter? Could it be Slater still secreted deeper feelings for the sweetheart of his youth than anyone suspected?

In the dark of night, however, it didn't matter what Slater's reasons were for not kissing Lark again; it only mattered that he hadn't. Lark was in love with him! She loved his playful nature—even his brooding one. She loved the dark brown of his eyes, the tiny wrinkles at the corners of them—loved his strong, square jaw, his powerful hands, his rhythmic saunter. Yet more than all that was handsome and attractive about his face and form, she loved his wit, his tender heart where Katherine's children were concerned, his patience, and his intelligence. Sometimes in the dark cold of night, Lark wondered if she could stay at the ranch—for being near to Slater without owning his admiration, affection, and love had begun to be quite painful and haunting.

Yet how could she leave him? How could she find the strength to strip herself from his presence forever? Furthermore, why would she do so? She loved him, and she loved laboring in service to Slater and Tom—Katherine and the children. Her life at the Evans ranch was more like living a life in the company of family than anything she'd ever known. Even when her mother had still been living—even then their lives had not been so comfortable and safe, so warm and happy. Why then would she leave? Why leave comfort and a measure of happiness, a good wage? Why would she leave? Still, every time she found herself staring at Slater—her heart beating brutally inside her at the thought of his attention (or kiss)—she would wonder if she could stay, for she longed for Slater Evans to want her. More than anything she wanted him to want her—to love her.

Even for all her heartache and worry, however, Lark still knew happiness—and hope. As early spring brought fresh air to breathe, yellow sun-shine to warm, crocus and hyacinth to sprouting in the flowerbeds around the house, life on the ranch began to brighten once more. Calving had begun, and Lark delighted in seeing the new calves romping on the horizon as much as the children did. They were warm and sweet and smelled of milk and grass.

Charlie loved the new calves perhaps more than anyone. One morning, he'd gone missing. Lark and Katherine were nearly mad with worry by the time Slater found the boy out in the pasture, sitting in the new grass, talking to a calf he'd come to favor.

Yes, spring was lovely, and Lark could not bring herself to leave the ranch—to leave those she'd come to love—even for the desperate longing to own Slater's favor that sometimes threatened to overwhelm her.

Tom had taken Katherine and the children to town. The weather was beautiful—especially for late March—and Tom had convinced Katherine that it would do the children good to have a change of surroundings for a while. Lark didn't want to go to town. She'd begun hot ironing the parlor curtains and wanted to finish before supper. Slater had chosen to stay behind as well, being that Outlaw had broken through a fence while trying to charge Black-Eyed Sue. It seemed spring had rejuvenated the old Hereford bull, causing him to find the presence of Sue even more maddening than usual. Outlaw didn't bother too much with Little Joe, Slater's other Hereford bull. Slater claimed it was the fact that Sue had matured so quickly over the winter months, and now that he was more than two years old, and big even then, Sue looked far more menacing than he had in late summer. Furthermore, Pete Walker had driven in Slater's Black Angus heifers. Slater figured Outlaw didn't like the fact that there were five new heifers on the ranch now that Black-Eyed Sue had exclusive bids on—that Outlaw didn't. Outlaw was "feeling his age," as Slater put it—adding that he understood how the poor fellow felt.

So it was that Lark was at the house alone. Oddly, she found the quiet and solitude very soothing. With the children so often trapped in the house over the winter, Lark's ears had begun to ring with the sound of their play or whining. Now she was able to think as she ironed the parlor curtains—to think or to hum to herself a bit.

All the morning long she put the hot iron to the curtains. When she had finally finished (thankfully much earlier in the day than she'd anticipated), Lark decided to allow herself a moment of fresh air. Slater hadn't come home for a noon meal, and she assumed he'd chosen to simply eat jerky with Eldon and the others.

Stepping out onto the back porch, Lark smiled. Spring was lovely! She glanced over the side of the porch to see that several tiny crocuses had begun to bloom. The sight of their deep purples and bright yellows cheered her very soul, and she smiled.

She heard a whinny and looked up to see that Dolly and Coaly had been let into the corral for some fresh air and the chance to run and play. Dolly nodded at her, stomping the ground and whinnying once more.

Lark giggled and called, "All right! All right! I'll come for a visit." As she stepped off the porch and started toward the corral, however, she added, "But only for a moment. Those parlor rugs are so dusty I can hardly breathe."

By the time Lark had made her way to the corral, Coaly was at the fence too. Lark smiled as both horses nuzzled their velvet noses into the palms of her offered hands. "I'm sure you girls are drinking in this day, hmmm?" She patted both horses and brushed their necks with her hands, speaking to them in a quiet, loving voice as she did so.

"If Slater catches me, he'll turn me over his knee," she said. "He thinks I spoil you two, you know." Her smile broadened as Dolly stomped the ground with one enormous hoof. "That's right, Dolly," she giggled. "He is a hypocrite . . . for I've seen the way he pampers you when he thinks no one's watching. If he thinks for one minute that I thought he was really eating five apples a day out of the crates in the cellar . . . really!"

Lark lingered with Dolly and Coaly for a time. Yet as she looked up, glancing beyond the corral, she decided that the fresh air near the corral wasn't quite fresh enough. The warm horizon beckoned, and she soon found herself meandering toward the canyon ridge. Oh, the canyon was too far for a simple stroll, yet she'd heard Tom tell Slater just that morning that the river winding through the small canyon was already running high. She wondered if she might be able to hear the water—hear the rush of the mountain's melted snow as it raced down through the canyon.

She found she had to be wary, however. She'd forgotten how many walking stick cactuses grew between the east fence and the canyon. Some were nearly as tall as she was, and though they owned a certain wild beauty, Lark surmised the prick of their needles would be painful to experience.

All was still and peaceful as she walked. Meadowlarks called back and forth, and the breeze was fresh. Lark fancied that the sagebrush and chamisa were already beginning to show a hint of color. Soon everything would begin to green up a bit; soon the wildflowers would begin to sprout. The thought caused Lark to smile.

"Howdy."

She startled—gasped as she turned to see a man standing a short distance behind her. He had dismounted his horse and stood with the bridle reins draped casually over his shoulder. Immediately, the pace of Lark's heartbeat increased—but not for the same reasons that it increased in Slater's presence. This hammering of her heart was all too familiar to Lark. Though it had been months since she'd known fear for the warning in her bosom, Lark recognized it immediately—a sense of menace. How had he managed to come upon her so quietly? She hadn't heard a hint of his approach!

"Hello," she managed, forcing a friendly smile. She sensed malice from the man, but she would not let him know she sensed it.

The man offered a smile. It was meant to be a friendly, calming smile, but it was marred by yellowed and rotting teeth and more portrayed malevolence than innocence. "Good mornin', ma'am," the man said, touching the brim of his hat in greeting.

"It is a good morning," Lark said as she began to walk in the direction of the house.

"I'm . . . uh . . . I'm lookin' for a feller by the name of Slater Evans," the man began. "He's an old friend of mine, and folks in town tell me he lives here about."

Simply the feeling of dread that enveloped Lark the longer she lingered in the man's presence told her that he was no friend of Slater's. The man was tall with long blond hair—braided and hanging down his back nearly to his waist. A broad, livid scar traveled diagonally from his forehead just above one eyebrow, down and over his nose, to disappear beneath a scraggly red beard.

"Yes . . . he does live near here," Lark said. For

she knew the man would not believe her if she entirely lied.

"Might you be Mrs. Evans, ma'am?" the man asked, his smile broadening.

Lark forced an amused laugh. "Me? Oh no, sir. Not me," she told him. "You want the Evans ranch. This is the Thornquist's place. I work for Mrs. Thornquist."

The man's eyes narrowed, his smile fading to a grin. "Then where might I find the Evanses' place?" he asked.

Inwardly, Lark offered a prayer of thanks, for it seemed the man had believed her—at least for the moment. "Well, you're almost there," she said, smiling. Knowing that the man must've come from town, she turned and pointed east. "The Evanses are just about three miles out from us . . . just a little farther east. Beyond them is the Jacobsen place. So if you get to their place, then you've gone too far."

The man slowly studied Lark from head to toe, and the obvious perusal heightened her fear. "Well, I need to get back," Lark said. "I just stepped out for a breath of fresh spring air. It was nice to meet you, Mister . . ."

"Nice to meet you too, ma'am," the man said.

Lark watched as he mounted his horse—noting he wore a large, sheathed knife on one hip, his gun at the opposing thigh.

"Tell those Evans brothers we said hello," she

said, smiling and resuming her walk back toward the house.

"Yes, ma'am," the man said.

"Bye, now," Lark said, smiling and waving as the man rode off—east.

Instantly, a terrifying sense of panic gripped her! Lifting her skirt, she turned and began running back toward the ranch. She had to tell someone —she had to tell Slater! Nothing in her would accept that the stranger was a good man—that he owned only the intention of visiting with an old friend. He'd inquired about Slater. Therefore, whatever his malevolent intentions were, they were directed at Slater.

Lark glanced over her shoulder to ensure the man was still riding east and not following her.

She cried out as a sharp pain exploded at the top of her right arm. In looking over her shoulder, she'd missed seeing the large walking stick cactus in her path. She stumbled, wincing with pain as she looked to see the cactus needles protruding from her upper arm.

"Ow!" she gasped as she pulled one needle from her flesh. But there was not time to remove the remaining needles. She had to warn Slater. The needles could wait until she was back to the ranch house, at least.

Her chest burned with the exertion of running in the cool spring air, but soon the ranch house was in sight.

"Slater!" Lark called as she approached the corrals. Dolly and Coaly raced across the corral when they heard her, nodding happily in anticipation of her returning to offer them attention.

"I'm sorry, girls," Lark said, pausing long enough to stroke each horse's nose a moment. "I have to find our Slater."

Lark glanced down at her arm again, however, for the pain inflicted by the cactus needles was increasing to a near excruciating intensity. She gasped, "Oh no!" when she saw that the needles were no longer visible above the fabric of her sleeve. Whether it was their natural way or because of the exertion of Lark's run for home, the cactus needles had begun to work their way deeper and deeper into her flesh.

"Slater!" Lark cried. Oh, he had to be within the sound of her voice—he had to be! Lark knew she must remove the cactus needles from her arm immediately, before they drove themselves completely into her flesh. The pain the cactus needles were inflicting was monstrous, and Lark could no longer keep from weeping for the sake of it. Still, she was worried for Slater. In less than half an hour, the man she'd met would know she had lied to him. She had to find Slater! Yet the pain in her arm was nearly paralyzing. Lark's body had begun to tremble.

"Slater!" she cried. Still, she had no idea where to look for him. She didn't know where Outlaw had broken through the fence—didn't know if mending the fence was even still his task. She swallowed the lump of fear in her throat and angrily brushed the tears from her cheeks—though more simply streamed from her eyes.

She had to remove the cactus needles, and then she'd be able to saddle a horse and ride out to look for Slater. Until the needles were pulled from her arm, however, she was nearly helpless.

Hurrying into the house and into the kitchen, Lark reached back with her left hand, struggling to unfasten the buttons at her collar.

"Please, please!" she sobbed as her fingers endeavored to work the buttons at the back of her shirtwaist then. At last her shirtwaist was unfastened, and she carefully slipped her arms from her sleeves, wincing and crying out, for each movement caused pain to flame up and down her arm—even through her body.

Once her shoulders and arms were free of her shirtwaist, she studied the place where the cactus needles were wounding her. The needles, which had once merely pricked her flesh—the greater part of their inch length appearing above her skin—now only showed perhaps a quarter inch above it. Lark wondered if she could indeed remove all the needles, still working their way deeper and deeper into her tender arm, before several managed to disappear entirely.

Her hand was trembling so very violently that

she couldn't grip the short end of any cactus needle protruding from her flesh. Wiping the tears from her eyes, she inhaled a deep breath, held it, and tried again. This time she managed to grip a needle with her fingertips, but as she tugged on it, the pain of the resistance it offered caused her to cry out. Angrily, she brushed at her tears. She had to find Slater—had to warn him. She tried again, moaning and weeping as she managed to extract one of the cactus needles. Panting with pain and relief, she looked to her arm. At least twenty more needles were there—twenty! How would she ever remove them all?

"Lark?" Slater called as he opened the front door, stepping into the house.

"Slater!" Lark cried.

Careless of her pain, of the fact that her shirtwaist now hung at her waist, exposing her camisole and corset, she ran to him. Taking hold of his shoulder, she sobbed, "There was a man! H-he was looking for you! I know he's someone bad. I know he is! I lied . . . I lied to him and told him—"

"What in tarnation?" Slater interrupted, his brow puckering into a frown as he studied Lark's state of undress. "Did a man do this to you?" he growled then.

Lark cried out as he reached out, taking hold of her arms. "No . . . no!" she cried. "He didn't touch me, but you have to listen to me. He's looking for you!"

314

"Ouch!" Slater exclaimed, pulling his hand away from her right arm. "Lark!" he breathed, taking hold of her arm and studying the cactus needles protruding from it.

"Listen to me, Slater," she begged him. "He's the ugliest man I've ever seen! I swear he is! He said he was an old friend of yours, that someone in town told him you lived out this way . . . but he can't be your friend. I know he can't."

But Slater's attention was on her arm. Gripping her at the elbow, he tugged at one of the needles.

"Ow!" Lark cried.

Slater sighed with worry. "We gotta get these out, baby," he mumbled.

"But are you listening to me, Slater? About the man?" she asked.

Slater took her face between his strong hands and said, "I am. I am, baby. But that can wait a minute."

"He didn't tell me his name," Lark sniffled as he led her back into the kitchen. Pulling a chair away from the table and positioning it near the window, he guided her to sit down. "I think he intentionally didn't tell me. I lied to him. I told him this was the Thornquist place . . . that the Evans ranch was farther east."

Hunkering down at her side, Slater again took her face between his hands. "Listen to me," he said calmly, forcing her to look at him. "It'll be all right. Whoever that man was . . . it'll be fine.

But we need to get these cactus needles out of your arm." He brushed the tears from her cheeks with his thumbs. "I promise you we'll worry about the man you saw as soon as we get 'em all out. All right?"

"But . . . but . . ." Lark stammered.

"Sshh," he said. His voice was low and rich—as delicious as molasses taffy. "Let me see to your arm, baby. All right?" He leaned forward, placing a soft kiss to her lips. "All right?" he repeated.

Lark nodded, for his kiss—brief as it was—had served to soothe her somewhat. She held her breath, winced, and wept as Slater pulled another needle from her arm.

He paused a moment, seeming to study her arm in choosing which needle he should extract next. "Grit yer teeth, baby," he mumbled, " 'cause this ain't gonna get any better 'til they're all out."

Lark did as Slater suggested. Gritting her teeth, she tried not to cry when he pulled the next needle from her arm, but the tears streamed down her face no matter her efforts at bravery.

"Them walkin' stick cactus are mean little cusses," he mumbled. She jumped as he extracted a particularly painful needle. He cupped her face in one hand briefly and, frowning with sympathy, said, "I'm sorry. I'm tryin' to be careful."

"I know," Lark breathed.

One after the other, Slater managed to extract the cactus needles from Lark's arm. As fewer and fewer needles remained, the pain in Lark's arm began to lessen. Pain was still there—just not quite so merciless as it had been.

She winced a little as Slater gently gripped her upper arm in both hands, smoothing out her flesh—allowing his thumbs to feel for any lingering needles.

"These two are in real deep," he mumbled. "I can't seem to get a hold on 'em with my fingers." He looked up, glancing around the kitchen as if searching for something to aid him. "Hold on," he said as his head descended to her arm.

Lark watched as Slater endeavored to grip the tiny needle head with his teeth. The warm moisture of his mouth against her wounded flesh felt soothing and somehow served to alleviate a quantity of her pain.

Slater raised his head, pulling a blood-stained cactus needle from his teeth and setting it on the windowsill with the others he'd removed. "Just one more," he said, forcing an encouraging smile. He brushed the tears from her cheeks with the back of one hand and then placed his mouth to her arm again. Lark could feel the final cactus needle as it remained imbedded in her flesh. She could feel Slater's tongue on her skin as he endeavored to grip the needle's head with his teeth.

"This last one's a little devil, ain't he?" he asked, lifting his head and gripping her arm as he studied the place where the needle had sunk. "I don't want it breakin' off in there."

Again he placed his mouth to her arm. Again the warm moisture of his touch soothed Lark, and she smiled when she felt him slowly pull the final needle from her.

Smiling, he plucked the cactus needle from between his teeth. "That's him," he said, holding the needle up to study it for a moment. "That's the one that give me the most trouble." He placed the needle on the windowsill and gently gripped Lark's arm once more. He frowned, running his thumbs over the place on her arm where the needles had been. "Looks like we got 'em," he said. He bent, placing a tender yet lingering kiss to the place. "Does it feel a little bit better now that they're out?"

Lark nodded and managed, "Yes."

"It's gonna bruise somethin' awful," he mumbled.

"It doesn't matter," Lark said. "You made it feel so much better." Her heart leapt as his gaze met hers—as he grinned at her.

"I can make it feel even more better if you like," he whispered, his smile of pure naughty mischief broadening.

"You can?" she asked—breathless. Goose bumps erupted over her arms as he leaned forward, pressing a light kiss to her lips.

"Oh yes . . . I surely can," he said.

Lark watched then as Slater pressed a soft kiss

to the place on her arm from which he'd extracted the cactus needles. He kissed her there once more, his lips then gently caressing the smooth round of her shoulder. She couldn't resist the need to touch him and placed a hand to his cheek, allowing her fingers to weave through the smooth darkness of his hair.

Slater's lips found her neck then, pressing moist, lingering kisses to the sensitive flesh below her ear. He was careful of her tender wounds as he placed his strong hands under her arms, gently— yet forcefully—pulling her from the chair and into his arms as they stood. He paused to direct her arms to his shoulders, and then—then his mouth claimed hers, suddenly voracious, as if her kiss were the only thing that could satisfy some deep and ravenous craving in him.

Pain was dissolved by passion, and Lark was no more aware of the damage to her arm than she was to anything else in all the world! Her desire —her thirst for Slater's kiss—seemed insatiable! Over and over his mouth demanded passion from hers. Over and over she met his demands, bathed in the bliss of his wondrous kiss!

She was lost in the quenching of her desire for him—lost in the delicious jubilation of loving him. He wanted her! He wanted her—at least in some way he did want her—and the knowledge breathed a stronger breath of life and hope into her bosom. Perhaps he did not love her as she did him, but he cared for her in some regard. The impassioned manner of their exchange was proof of his, in the least, desire for her—and Lark was enraptured in the understanding of it.

She gasped, stumbling forward as Slater suddenly stumbled backward, lost his footing, and promptly sat down on his backside. Lark covered her mouth with her hands to stifle a giggle.

"Dang, girl," Slater said, reaching out and taking her hand, pulling her to sit next to him on the floor. "You undone my knees!"

Lark smiled, yet her smile was fleeting—for Slater's mouth captured hers once more, and he maneuvered her to sitting on his lap.

Oh, how she loved him! How frantically—how entirely—how deliciously! He kissed her and kissed her—bathing her in fervent bliss. Lark wished he would never again break the seal of their mouths—that he would hold her forever—that she could somehow meld her very soul with his.

Suddenly, however, he did break the seal of their kiss, took her chin in one hand, and studied her face for a moment.

"Lark," he breathed.

"Yes?" she whispered—though she glanced away—suddenly shy for the passion she'd revealed to him.

"Lark . . . you know I'm old," he began.

"What?" she asked, frowning—puzzled.

"I'm over thirty years . . . and there's a lot you don't know about me . . . about those thirty years," he said.

"There's a lot you don't know about my nineteen years," she offered, hoping to drive the worry from his eyes.

He grinned and breathed a chuckle. "I mean it," he said, looking back to her. "I ain't as fresh as a daffodil no more. I ain't young with my whole life stretched out in front of me the way yours is."

Lark's heart was hammering like a locomotive. Slater cared for her—he did! In that moment, she could see the truth of it in his eyes.

"I know you oughta be with a man more youthful . . . less weathered than me. But . . . but . . ."

"But what?" she prodded. She felt as if her heart were in her throat! Was he—was Slater Evans about to tell her he wanted her?

Suddenly, however, his eyes narrowed. He scowled and said, "This man you saw today . . . the one ya said was lookin' for me . . . you said he was the ugliest man you'd ever seen?"

Lark nodded. "Yes . . . but tell me what you were going to say."

"Tell me what he looked like," he said, however.

Lark felt all the joy she'd been swimming in the moment before rinse away like a dream. "He . . . he was tall . . . with long blond hair," she

321

told him—for what else could she do? "He had a red beard and a scar."

"Here?" Slater asked, moving an index finger across his face to indicate just where the man's scar had been.

"Yes," she affirmed, trepidation suddenly filling her heart.

"And he didn't give ya his name?"

"No."

Slater rubbed at his chin with one trembling hand.

"What's the matter, Slater?" Lark asked. She'd known the ugly stranger was evil; Slater's reaction confirmed it.

Lark's heart leapt as she heard something—the wagon, the voices of the children. Tom and Katherine had returned from town. Slater rose to his feet, taking Lark's hand and helping her to hers. He was still frowning as he studied her for a moment.

"Button this up," he mumbled, lifting her shirtwaist to help her slip her arms through her sleeves. "Otherwise Tom will think I lost my hold on things and had my way with you."

As Lark reached back to button her shirtwaist, the pain in her arm made itself known once more. The ecstasy of Slater's affections had numbed it for a time, but with the end of their passionate exchange, it returned.

"Here," Slater said, turning her away from him and quickly fastening several of the buttons.

Tom burst through the front door, Katherine at his heels. He was pale, and Katherine was weeping.

"Someone's been askin' for you in town, Slater," Tom said. "Someone with long braided hair and one big ugly scar across his face."

"I know," Slater mumbled.

"Oh, Slater!" Katherine cried. "It can't be! It just can't be!"

"Who is he?" Lark begged, suddenly terrified.

Tom was worried, wearing an expression of concern she'd never before seen on his usually smiling face. Katherine's distress was even more obvious.

"It's Samson Kane," Slater said.

"No," Tom breathed, shaking his head.

Lark watched as Slater pulled his pistol from its holster at his thigh. He checked the rounds in the cylinder and holstered it again.

"Slater," Tom began.

"Not a word, Tom. Not one word," Slater growled.

Tom nodded, and Katherine continued to weep.

"I'm goin' to town," Slater said. "Get the children inside. I'll send Eldon and the boys to keepin' watch. Bolt the doors, and don't let nobody in 'til I get back."

"Slater . . . he's one man," Tom said. "We got three cowboys and me and you. Why don't we just wait for him to—"

"No," Slater growled. "He ain't that stupid. If I ain't back by dark, have the boys come inside the house with you. Keep the children and the women away from the windows."

Tom's eyes narrowed. "You're goin' to send a telegram, ain't ya?" Tom growled.

Slater didn't answer—simply turned to Katherine and said, "Lark picked a fight with a cactus, Kate. Clean her up good and put some warm towels to it."

Katherine nodded. Charlie ran into the room then, followed closely by Lizzy and Johnny.

"Keep 'em away from the windows, Tom," Slater growled. Stripping his slicker from the coat rack, he stormed through the front door and over the porch.

"Bolt the door, dammit!" he shouted as he spurred Smokey to a gallop.

Tom closed the door, drawing the large bolt. Lark gazed out the window—watched Slater ride away in a cloud of dust.

"Stay away from the windows, honey," Tom said.

Lark turned to look at him.

"Who's Samson Kane?" she asked.

Chapter Fourteen

"Who is Samson Kane?" Lark repeated. "Tell me, Tom . . . please!"

Whoever Samson Kane was to Slater, he was not a friendly acquaintance. Furthermore, Lark was certain Slater had been about to say something important—something she desperately wanted to hear—but Samson Kane had distracted him from doing so. Lark hated the man in that moment. Samson Kane—whoever he was, she hated him.

Katherine looked to Tom, shaking her head.

Tom inhaled a deep breath. Lark could see his jaw clenching with frustration.

"Tom," Katherine began, her expression that of warning and fear.

"It ain't right, Katie," Tom growled. "She has a right to be told."

"Mama, I'm hungry," Charlie said, tugging on his mother's skirt then.

"Dang it, Charlie!" Johnny scolded. "Can't you see somethin' ain't right with Uncle Slater? Can ya hold on until—"

"But I'm hungry," Charlie whined.

"Me too," Lizzy sniffled.

"It's all right, Johnny," Katherine said, putting a comforting arm around her eldest son's shoulders.

325

"I-I haven't had a chance to start supper yet," Lark said to Charlie. "But . . . but there's bread, and there's still some strawberry jam in the jar in the cupboard."

Charlie smiled at Lark.

"Mama?" he asked, looking up to his mother.

Katherine forced a smile and tousled his hair. "Lizzy, would you get some bread and jam for Charlie and you?"

Lizzy nodded.

"Help them slice the bread please, Johnny," Katherine added.

Johnny sighed with frustration. He was old enough to understand that something was wrong.

"Please, Tom," Lark pleaded in a whisper as the children headed into the kitchen. "Please."

"Slater will have your head, Tom Evans," Katherine said.

"He's had it before, Kate," Tom sighed. He removed his hat—ran his fingers through his hair.

Katherine looked to Lark then. "You have every right to know about Samson Kane, Lark . . . but Slater should be the one to tell you." She glanced out the window, as if she feared Slater might be able to hear her from off in the distance.

"I met him," Lark said then.

"What?" Tom and Katherine exclaimed in unison.

"What do you mean you met him?" Tom asked.

"I met him . . . out beyond the east pasture,"

Lark explained. "He . . . he told me he was looking for an old friend of his . . . Slater Evans."

"Lark!" Katherine exclaimed as tears filled her eyes. It was only in that moment that Lark realized how fortunate she was that the cactus had been the only thing to hurt her.

"He wore his hair in a long braid. He was blond, with a red beard and terrible scar across his face," Lark continued. "He asked me if I knew where he could find the Evans place, and I lied. I told him it was farther east." She paused, and Tom shook his head in astonishment. "I couldn't believe Slater would call such a man his friend. So I lied. I ran back to the house as fast as I could." Lark rubbed at her sore arm. "I bumped into a cactus. Slater removed the needles. I-I knew something wasn't right with that man."

Suddenly, tears sprung to her eyes—tears of fear—fear for Slater's safety.

"Tom, he'll find out soon enough that I lied to him," she sobbed, burying her face in her hands. "He'll figure out that this *is* the Evans place, and he'll . . . he'll come for Slater . . . won't he?"

"It's all right, honey," Tom said, pulling her into the security of his arms. "It's all right. We're here, and he's just one man. Slater won't linger in town . . . just long enough to—"

"Who is Samson Kane, Tom?" Lark pleaded in a tearful whisper. "Why shouldn't I know? If he's dangerous . . . well, then . . . well, then . . . I'm the one who lied to him! He knows where to find me, and that'll lead him straight to Slater . . . and all of you . . . to the children!"

"Samson Kane is a shadow of Slater's past," Tom offered at last.

"Tom! Slater doesn't want her to know. He doesn't want her frightened," Katherine began.

"She's plenty frightened already, Katie," Tom growled.

Taking Lark's face between his hands, he smoothed the tears from her cheeks with his thumbs as he gazed at her, frowning.

"Samson Kane . . . he's bad through and through, Lark—vicious, mighty dangerous," Tom explained. "We was all hopin' he was dead." Tom shook his head. "I can't hardly believe he's alive . . . can't hardly figure why he ain't still in the penitentiary. It's like a bad dream . . . him comin' back like this. I can't believe it."

"But who is he?" Lark asked. "Why is he looking for Slater?"

Tom inhaled a deep breath, slowly exhaling it.

"Slater managed to make hisself a few enemies some years back," Tom answered. "Samson Kane's the worst of 'em." Tom chuckled, though it was a chuckle of sudden understanding, not amusement. "That's how Slater knew it was ol' Samson askin' for him in town," he mumbled. "You seen him yourself."

"But why is Slater going into town?" Lark

asked. She clutched Tom's arms as terror washed over her. "You asked him if he meant to send a telegram. What would a telegram do? Or does he think Samson Kane will go there . . . to town? Does he intend to look for him?"

"No," Tom answered. "Kane's as yeller as they come. And he's scared of Slater . . . no matter what he mighta wanted you to think." He paused. "No, he'll curl up somewhere like a rattler . . . hide in the rocks or the grass until he thinks Slater ain't watchin'."

"I've heard of him," Johnny said. Lark glanced to see Charlie and Lizzy seated at the table eating bread that had been rather sloppily slathered with jam. But Johnny was walking toward them. "I heard of Samson Kane. Daddy told me a story about him once. He used to rob banks and such. And after he'd kill a feller . . . he'd gut 'em like a fish."

"Johnny!" Katherine exclaimed, tears escaping her eyes to trickle over her cheeks. "Don't say such things!"

"But it's true, Mama," Johnny said. "Samson Kane is a murderin' outlaw. Daddy told me the whole country rested easy once he was captured and locked up. Daddy was sure someone would bury a knife in his belly out in Yuma. That's where Daddy said they had him."

"Well, it looks like they don't have him no more," Tom grumbled.

"But . . . but why would he come looking for Slater?" Lark asked. She was utterly frustrated, sensing there was still something she didn't know—something important. "And why would Slater want to send a telegram?"

Tom shrugged. "Slater's gonna want to know why Samson Kane ain't at Yuma prison . . . and the sheriff in town oughta know an outlaw's driftin' close by." Tom paused, and a slight grin of mischief mingled with concern curved his lips. "As far as why Samson Kane's pickin' on Slater . . . well, darlin', let's just say Slater has a way of prickin' at a feller's temper."

Tom had said all he was going to. Lark tried not to be hurt that Katherine and Tom wouldn't tell her more. Yet she was hurt—wounded. She'd been with Slater and Tom for eight months—eight months! She'd been Katherine's friend for more than four. Didn't they care any more for her than this? Didn't they trust her? Or was it truly because they were afraid of Slater's reaction? He'd told them not to say a word, but why?

Lark's eyes widened, trepidation washing over her anew. Only a short time before, Slater had begun to tell Lark something—something about his past. She thought of the way he was forever going on about being old—being weathered. Slater never talked about his life after cowboying—never. He'd started to tell her something. Before Tom and Katherine had arrived home with the children, Slater had started to tell her something. He'd said there was a lot she didn't know about his thirty years. Lark felt a surge of fear tear through her. Samson Kane was an outlaw. Slater was a man who didn't want to talk about his past —didn't want his brother or Katherine talking about it. Could it be that Slater Evans had once run with Samson Kane? Could the reason that Slater never wanted to talk about or even think about his past—could it be because his past was that of an outlaw?

She thought of the fact that Slater rarely left the house without his gun and gun belt. She'd even seen him strap it on to visit the outhouse. On several occasions, she'd seen him from her bedroom window at night, carrying a lantern on his way to the outhouse, dressed in nothing but his boots, his underwear, and his gun belt. She thought of the aging Hereford bull in the south pasture—the bull named Outlaw. She understood then—everything. She understood why Slater was so secretive about his past—understood why he'd danced around his desire for her. Lark understood what he'd begun to tell her in the kitchen, after he'd removed the cactus needles from her arm— after they'd been lost in impassioned kissing. Slater had begun to tell her he'd once been an outlaw!

Lark's mind was blazing with possibilities. Perhaps Slater had helped Samson Kane rob a bank, helped him hide the money. Slater did seem to have a great deal of money. He bought cattle and horses as if it were no kind of burden where cost was concerned. She thought of the coats he'd purchased for her last fall—of the books he'd given her for Christmas. Perhaps Slater had helped Samson Kane rob banks and then given up his outlaw ways. Perhaps Samson Kane had been caught and sent to prison; perhaps he'd spent his time there thinking about Slater and all the money he'd had. Perhaps that was why he was after Slater: he wanted a larger share of their stolen money.

Still, Slater Evans an outlaw? It was inconceivable. Wiping the tears from her cheeks, she thought of Slater's kindness toward the children —toward Katherine and herself. She thought of his good standing with the other ranchers in the county. Surely such a man could never have been an outlaw. Yet Lark knew that outlaws were often the most charming men on earth. Outlaws were often brothers, friends, even husbands and fathers. She knew that certain small towns allowed outlaws to drift through, or even take up residence nearby without ever considering turning them in to the authorities. Some towns—some sheriffs even—considered it a means of protection. If an outlaw was welcome in a town, he was more likely to protect it if trouble came. Lark knew the charm and influence of certain outlaws—and she knew from experience.

Suddenly, her thoughts, her emotions, were too

overwhelming! She loved Slater Evans! She loved him. He couldn't be an outlaw! He couldn't! He was too good, too kind, too wonderful. She had never seen a hint of dishonesty in him, any malice—never! The room began to whirl, to spin, as Lark thought of her mother—of her beautiful mother and the unhappy end she'd met. Lark thought of her mother—thought of her own resemblance to her—wondered if that resemblance were deeper than merely flesh. Yet she'd sworn to herself long ago that she would never fall into tragedy the way her mother had—that she would never fall in love with an outlaw.

"Lark!" Katherine cried as Lark collapsed to the floor.

Everything went dark. For a moment, Lark could hear Katherine speaking to her—could feel Tom's arms about her as he lifted her in them. Yet Lark's faint deepened. Soon there was only dark and silence.

"You told her too much, Tom," Slater was saying. "She'll bolt and run now."

As she drifted into wakefulness, Lark kept her eyes closed. Slater and Tom were speaking in lowered voices. She knew they thought she was still unconscious from the faint that had over-taken her. She had no idea how long she'd slept, yet it must've been a fair piece of time, for Slater had obviously returned from town.

"Well, you shoulda told her a long time ago," Tom growled.

"Probably," Slater mumbled. "But what's done is done now, little brother." He sounded discouraged—somehow hardened—as if his life had entirely disappointed him.

"Was it easy as that?" Tom asked.

"Yep."

"Now what?"

"We wait. That's all," Slater answered. "Samson Kane will show his hand eventually. Might take some time though."

"How long do ya think?" Tom asked.

Slater exhaled a heavy sigh. "Could be days . . . even a couple of weeks. You know how he works . . . like an ornery ol' rattler. He waits until he thinks you ain't payin' a lick of attention. Then he strikes."

There was a pause. Then Tom stated, "You'll have to tell Lark. You oughta tell the children too . . . though I think young Johnny has his suspicions. Seems his daddy told him a few tales here and there . . . about Samson Kane at least."

"What good will it do for them to know everything?" Slater asked.

"Well, yer the one always accusin' folks of hidin' secrets . . . sayin' no good comes from it. Yet you're worse than anybody I know. A danged hypocrite . . . that's what you are."

"I won't deny it," Slater said. "But they don't

need more'n they can chew on . . . just what they need to know to stay safe."

"But you gotta tell Lark, Slater," Tom said. "Who knows what she's thinkin'? She deserves to hear it all."

"I know," Slater mumbled. "I almost told her, you know. In fact, it was right on the tip of my tongue . . . right there in the kitchen. The words were comin' out, but then . . . then I remembered she told me she saw a man. And when I figured who it was . . ." He paused. "It don't matter anyway. I figure the way yer trap flaps at the slightest breeze, you already told her enough."

Tom chuckled. "I did tell her some . . . but you need to tell the whole tale, boy. She's a tough little gal. She ain't gonna bolt on ya, and she sure ain't gonna run."

"She would if she knew what was good for her."

"How's she doin'?" Lark heard Katherine ask.

"She's breathin'," Slater said.

"Well, that cactus didn't do her any good," Katherine said. "And heaven knows you runnin' off to town didn't help either."

Lark felt Katherine's hand on her forehead and used the opportunity to feign sudden awareness.

"What happened?" she asked in a whisper. She turned her head—slowly opened her eyes in pretending to have just come out of the stupor.

"You fainted, darlin'," Katherine said, smiling at her. Katherine stood over her. Slater and

Tom sat in the two chairs opposite the sofa in the parlor.

"I told Tom you'd be more comfortable in your bed," Katherine explained, "but he said he wanted you here on the sofa where we could keep an eye on ya." She smiled. "How's your arm feelin'?"

Lark forced a halfhearted smile in return. "Terrible," she said. Katherine winced and giggled at the same time.

"Those walkin' stick cactus are meaner than the devil," she said.

"We're headin' back to the bunkhouse, boss."

Lark glanced up to see Eldon, Grady, and Ralston striding toward the front door. Eldon nodded to Lark as she looked to him and then looked back to Slater.

"You holler if ya need anything, boss," he said.

"Bolt the door once you boys are in for the night, Eldon," Slater said. "He ain't gonna do nothin' tonight . . . but you keep one eye open anyhow."

"We will," Eldon said.

"Thank you, boys," Slater added. He stood, strode to the cowboys, and offered them each his hand in thanks. "I know you didn't saddle up for this. I appreciate it . . . and I'm sorry."

"We ride for the brand, boss . . . come hell or high water," Eldon said. Ralston and Grady nodded their own affirmations.

"Thanks for supper, Mrs. Thornquist," Eldon said then, touching the brim of his hat as he looked to Katherine.

"Supper?" Lark exclaimed. She'd been unconscious so long Katherine had had to fix supper— and for the cowboys too.

Guilt and worry must've been obvious on Lark's face, for Katherine whispered, "It's all right, Lark," and patted her hand with reassurance. "You're welcome, Mr. Pickering," Katherine said, smiling at Eldon then.

The cowboys left, and Lark watched as Tom strode to the front door, drawing the bolt.

Lark looked to Slater. He sat in a chair across the room from her, staring at her. His eyes were dark, and she sensed a combination of dark emotions boiled in him.

"I put a warm towel on your arm off and on," Katherine said. "But I haven't had a chance to look at it."

"It'll be fine," Lark said, pulling herself to a sitting position. "Are the children in bed already?" she asked.

"Yes," Katherine answered. "They were so tired! I guess the trip to town wore them out today . . . thankfully." Katherine smiled, but it was forced.

"And what of Samson Kane?" Lark asked. She looked to Slater, yet his expression was unchanged.

"Well . . . well . . . I . . . I . . ." Katherine

stammered. She glanced to Slater, who only glared back at her and frowned.

"I'll take care of it," Slater grumbled.

"Well, then I'm headin' to bed," Tom said. "You can keep first watch," he added, nodding to Slater.

"Yep," Slater agreed.

Tom took Lark's hand, squeezing it with reassurance. "You about give me a fit of apoplexy, honey," he said, warmly smiling at her. "You sure you're all right?"

"Yes," Lark told him. "I promise."

"All right then. I'll see you in the mornin'." Tom turned to Katherine. "Good night, Katie. Try to get some sleep. Ain't nothin' gonna get by ol' Slater."

"I know," she said, kissing Tom on one cheek.

"And you," he said to Slater then. "You do what ya need to."

"Yep," Slater said, nodding. "Just what I need to."

Tom sighed and shook his head. Lark sensed there was more meaning in their exchange of words than she understood.

Tom left the parlor and climbed the stairs as Katherine said, "I'll be turnin' in too." She kissed Lark on one cheek. "Good night, sweetie. You wake me if you need anything."

"Good night," Lark responded. "Thank you."

Katherine turned to Slater. "Good night, Slater."

"Good night," Slater mumbled.

Katherine left the parlor as well.

Alone with Slater, Lark's fear and curiosity instantly blended with her desire to be in his arms and caused her insides to quiver. He was still staring at her—simply sitting across the room and staring at her. She thought for a moment that she surely looked a fright. Windblown from her sprint back to the house after meeting Samson Kane, she'd then endured sobbing from the pain of the cactus needles. The blissful moments spent in Slater's arms in the kitchen had no doubt left her further rumpled—and then she'd fainted. No doubt she looked like a tattered vagabond of sorts.

"What're you thinkin'?" Slater asked.

"About . . . about today?" she ventured.

"Yep," he said, still staring at her, unmoving.

"Which part of today?" she asked. "The part where I found myself alone beyond the east pasture with a stranger? The part where I came home and . . . and you were just about to tell me something when you remembered I'd mentioned him? Or the part where you rode off to town without a word of explanation?"

"Yep," was all he said in response.

She was quiet a moment, considering everything. If Slater Evans were an outlaw—retired or not—did she truly want to know? She thought a moment longer. Yet she must know the truth.

"I think . . . I've been wondering . . . thinking,"

she began, "about what you might have been going to say to me there . . . in the kitchen . . . before you remembered I'd told you I saw a man out beyond the pasture."

Slater said nothing, though his eyes narrowed —his frown deepening.

"Samson Kane . . . I understand he's an outlaw," she said.

"Yep," Slater said.

"And . . . and I'm surmising, from what I've been told, that he's escaped from Yuma prison."

"Yep."

"And . . . and he's come looking for you. Probably the first thing he did after escaping was come looking for you."

"Yep."

Lark bit her lip as tears began to well in her eyes. She loved him! Oh, how she loved Slater Evans! Still, in knowing what her mother had endured—how could she have let herself fall in love with an outlaw?

"Did you ride with him before?" she asked. "Has he come looking for you because you betrayed him in some way? The fact that he was imprisoned and you were not . . . did you somehow elude capture or . . . or . . ."

"You think I rode with him?" Slater growled. "You think I'm an outlaw?"

"I-I don't know," Lark stammered as tears escaped her eyes. "I've tried to think of something else to explain it . . . anything else. But with what Johnny said . . . and the very little that Tom would tell me . . . I-I don't know what else to think."

She watched Slater—watched him inhale a deep breath and then exhale it slowly.

He shook his head. His eyebrows arched in thoughtful consideration of what she'd said to him.

"I don't know whether to laugh or be insulted," he said. A slight smile curved his lips, however, and he chuckled. "An outlaw. Well, I certainly didn't think you thought I was that low."

"Oh, but I don't!" Lark exclaimed. "I don't! I can't even imagine it, in truth! But what other explanation could there be, Slater? I . . . I can't think of anything else that might—"

"Samson Kane was in jail because of me," he interrupted. "I saw him kill a man . . . and I testified against him in a court of law. I'm the man who put him in Yuma prison."

All at once, inexplicable relief washed through Lark. Her heart soared with joy and love. Her joy in knowing her own past had tainted her assumptions where Slater's behavior had been concerned—that he was no outlaw but rather a hero—only caused the love she secreted for him to surge to an overwhelming magnitude.

Lark smiled, brushing more tears from her cheeks—tears of happiness and relief. She couldn't speak; she was too beset with joy.

Still, Slater asked, "You thought I was an outlaw?" He shook his head, and Lark did not miss the expression of hurt that crossed his features. Instantly, she was regretful. How could she have ever thought it? She knew Slater was a good man. Suddenly, she was as astonished that she'd ever considered the notion as Slater was. Furthermore, she was disgusted with herself. She'd known outlaws—been able to recognize them her entire life. In that moment, she realized it was even how she knew to lie to Samson Kane when she met him beyond the pasture. Her experience-sharpened instinct had instantly known Samson Kane was an outlaw.

"I-I'm sorry," she began. "I was so frightened . . . and nobody would tell me anything. Tom only said Samson Kane was a shadow from your past . . . that you'd angered him somehow. All I could think was that you'd betrayed him or something. Why didn't Tom tell me you'd testified against him? Why didn't he tell me that Samson Kane has come looking for you for the sake of revenge?"

Slater said nothing at first. "Because I told him not to tell you," he said at last. He shook his head in a manner of self-disgust. "I told him not to. Katie knows I don't like to talk about my past . . . that I don't like other folks talkin' about it. I . . . I can't tell you why it bothers me so . . . 'cause I don't know why myself. It just does. It

342

aggravates me . . . and I don't like to talk about it . . . especially about Samson Kane."

"I understand," Lark said—and truly, she did. She didn't like to talk about her past either. Only she knew why—exactly why.

"It don't make it right though . . . the way I run outta here," he continued. "Especially after you and me was . . . a minute before we were . . ."

"What were you going to say to me in the kitchen, Slater?" Lark inquired. She had to know. Even now, her heart was racing at the memory. She'd been certain he was about to confess to caring for her in those moments before Tom and Katherine had returned with the children—in that moment before he'd remembered to ask her about the man she'd seen.

Slater grinned, though it was accompanied by an expression of defeat somehow. "Fact was, I was gonna tell you about Samson Kane . . . about my past, where I've been, what I done before I finally come home and took to cattle ranchin'."

Lark was disappointed. She'd felt certain he'd meant to tell her more than that. As she'd lingered in his arms in the kitchen, she'd been sure he was going to tell her he cared for her.

"Oh," she breathed. She felt as if the joy she'd known a moment before had been somehow sucked from her body—from her very soul.

"You best get some sleep, baby," he said, rising from his chair. "You've had a long day of it." He strode toward her, hunkering down before the sofa and taking her hand in his. He smiled at her, brushing a strand of hair from her cheek. "I mean . . . lyin' to outlaws, pickin' fights with cactus . . ." His smile broadened as he added, "Kissin' old men."

Lark couldn't help but smile as he winked at her.

"Not to mention thinkin' you worked for a bandit . . . then faintin' and all." Slater nodded. "Yep . . . you put in a full day and then some." He released her hand and stood. "Yep, you best get to yer bed."

"What about you?" she asked.

Slater smiled, and Lark's heart leapt as she saw the mischief in his eyes.

"Are you invitin' me to come with ya?" he teased.

Lark giggled, delighted by his flirting.

"You know what I meant," she said.

"Did I?" he asked.

"Yes, you did," she giggled.

"Well, I've gotta keep watch a while," he told her. "Ol' Samson Kane . . . he's most likely gonna bide his time a while . . . but I ain't positive. So I'll just wait up a while."

"But you're tired," she told him. "You have to be."

Slater shook his head. "Naw. My feathers are too ruffled for settlin' down just now. But I want you to get to yer room and get some sleep."

He took her hand, pulling her to her feet. "Come

on," he said, picking up the lamp from the mantel and carrying it with him as he led her to her bedroom.

Once inside her bedroom, Slater set the lamp on top of the small table just inside.

"I know you're gonna think I'm a devil," he began then, turning her to face away from him as he began to unfasten the buttons on the back of her collar, "but I really do need to take a look at yer arm. Cactus needles don't just hurt. They can cause a nasty infection."

Lark pulled her braid to one shoulder as Slater continue to work the buttons. He'd already unfastened the top two buttons of her collar; two more and the collar would be free. She could feel his fingers brush her skin, and it sent goose bumps blossoming along her arms. Lark couldn't keep the visions of her recurring dream of Slater from playing out in her mind. After all, wasn't it always the same? In her dream, didn't Slater always begin his seduction with the unfastening of her collar buttons?

"My sleeve is damp," Lark said, finding her breathing was uneven. "Katherine must've put a warm compress on it while I was unconscious."

"Yep," he said.

A slight gasp escaped Lark as she felt Slater's hands on her neck. His fingers traveled slowly, caressively, over the exposed flesh at the top of her back—traveled forward and around until—

until she felt him tenderly embrace her neck between his strong hands. She began to tremble as he gently pulled her back against him.

Slater's hands slid beneath the fabric of her shirtwaist at her shoulders. Slowly he pushed the sleeves of her camisole from her shoulders— softly caressing them—sending waves of goose bumps to rippling over her arms. Lark felt as if she would again swoon—this time with delight—as she felt his breath on the back of her neck, and she knew Slater's mouth was close to her skin. He didn't touch her—didn't press his lips to the place, nor even brush his whiskery chin against her. Still, the sensation of delicious anticipation—the deep longing burning through her, her silent pleading with him to kiss her—was nearly unbearable. His warm breath continued to tease her tender flesh —his hovering in not quite touching her as he continued to unfasten the rest of the buttons of her shirtwaist.

Once Slater had unfastened every button, he tucked one hand under her arm, gently pulling her wounded limb from her sleeve.

"It still hurts," he mumbled. It was not a question.

"Yes," she whispered.

Carefully, he ran the palm of his hand over the wounded area of her arm. His touch sent a wave of bliss shivering through her.

"Well, just have to keep an eye on it," he mumbled.

He released her arm then as his arms encircled her waist, pulling her back against the firm contours of his body. His breath tickled her neck just below her ear, and Lark closed her eyes—balled her hands into fists in trying to keep from turning to kiss him. She felt him softly blow on her neck—her shoulder. He was teasing her—taunting her—and it was near torturous! At last, she felt the tender press of his kiss to her neck—felt his whiskers softly scratching her skin.

Another shiver traveled through her, and Slater chuckled.

"Why, you're ticklish, ain't ya, Miss Lark," he whispered.

Lark said nothing, for she couldn't even begin to find her voice to speak.

He caressed the bareness of her shoulder with his whiskery cheek, sending another tremulous quiver through Lark—and she could longer resist him.

Turning in his arms, she sighed when she found he did not pause in pressing his mouth to hers. Slater kissed her—deliciously kissed her—sending warmth and desire coursing through her body—sending love and hope in love being returned burning through her mind and heart.

Slater knew he could not be distracted by passion—by love. Samson Kane was hiding somewhere, lurking in the shadows, waiting for

Slater to lower his defenses. He could not linger in savoring Lark's kiss—the sense of her tender body in his arms. No. The sudden realization that Kane had been close to Lark—that he could have as easily killed her as to believe her lie—pulled Slater's awareness even closer to the danger waiting in the dark. Breaking the seal of their lips, he pulled Lark to him, reveling in the alluring scent of her hair—in the way she fit so perfectly against him.

For the first time in a long time, Slater Evans had something to fight for. He wanted Lark—wanted her more than anything he'd ever wanted in all his life—and he wanted her because he loved her! He could admit it to himself—silently allow himself to hear the words over and over in his mind. He loved Lark, and suddenly, he didn't care that he was older than she was. Suddenly, he knew he had more to offer than he'd thought. He was older than she was, yes—weathered by life—but it didn't matter. For in that moment, something affirmed to him that Lark loved him. In that moment—as all the events of the day and every moment of the past months quickly traveled through his mind—Slater knew that he could make Lark happy. He could! She loved him, and he realized then that her love had repaired a bit of the weathering caused by his past. He loved her—and he would have her! He would! But he'd have to vanquish the threat of harm now threatened by Samson Kane. Thus, he could not be distracted—not for one moment—not even by love.

Lark tightened her embrace of Slater; even for the pain in her arm she held him more tightly. She thought how wonderful it would be to stay in his arms—to sleep in them—and she sighed as her cheek rested against the firmness of his chest.

"Leave your door open tonight," he said. His chin was resting on the top of her head, and she felt him press a kiss there. "Make sure the window is latched, and leave your door open. I need to be able to hear everything in the house."

Lark shuddered as the memory that an outlaw was seeking revenge on Slater returned.

"He'll come for you, won't he?" she asked, already knowing the answer.

"Yep," he said.

Lark smiled, having grown very fond of Slater's short answer of assurance—the one he ever used, even when circumstances might have begged for a longer, more detailed response.

He took her face between his hands—gazed into her eyes. His dark eyes smoldered with emotion, and Lark smiled at him. He cared for her—he did! It was evident in his eyes—in his expression—in his kiss and his touch.

A handsome smile spread across his face as he studied her a moment.

"What is it?" she asked, for she knew something

was in his mind—tripping on his tongue in wanting to be said.

"Nothin'," he said. "I was just thinkin' that the closest I ever come to bein' an outlaw . . . is in moments like this one . . . moments with you, when I'd rather close us in this room and have my way than be a gentleman and leave you to your bed . . . alone."

Lark giggled. "You shouldn't say things like that to me," she scolded—though only because she knew she should.

"I know," he said, releasing her and stepping backward toward the door. "That's what I mean. I gotta be careful or I'll find myself in Yuma prison . . . and all because of you."

He winked and stepped from her room. He started to close the door behind him and then seemed to remember his own instructions and pushed it wide.

"Leave this open," he reminded.

Lark nodded, sighing with mingled delight in lingering pleasure and disappointment as she heard his heavy footsteps echo across the floor, striding him farther away from her.

She should be terrified—only terrified. Yet as she changed her day clothes for her nightdress, the lingering sensation of being held in Slater's arms—the ambrosial flavor of his kiss as it clung to her lips and yet warmed her mouth—caused such a sense of hope and joy to linger in her bosom that even the danger of an outlaw lurking nearby could not dispel the bliss that owned her.

As she lay in bed, sleep was indeed elusive. Still, the comforting sounds of Slater's footsteps in the kitchen and of the warm light that still glowed from the embers of the parlor fire lulled her. At last, Lark drifted to deep slumber, though not with fear and visions of Samson Kane for company but rather with hope and visions of Slater Evans—strong, handsome, desirable Slater Evans—Slater Evans—who was not an outlaw.

Chapter Fifteen

Slater had been right. Samson Kane was hiding. The night had been peaceful. Even Eldon, Grady, and Ralston heard nothing—saw nothing. Lark awoke with hope that perhaps the outlaw had turned coward—decided it was not worth his time to lay in wait for Slater and revenge.

Yet that morning at breakfast, Slater assured everyone that Samson Kane would come—he would not give up. The cowboys were to stay near the house, and the children were to stay inside unless a trip to the outhouse was necessary. Even then, one of the men had to go with them. Lark and Katherine were not to venture out without Slater, Tom, or one of the cowboys to escort them either.

"Samson Kane ain't too good with a pistol or a rifle," Slater explained. "If he's at a distance, he most likely won't get a good shot off. His weapon of choice is a knife."

"That's what Daddy told me," Johnny said, nodding as he finished his eggs.

A cold shiver of fear traveled up Lark's spine, for she'd remembered Johnny's description from the day before—that Samson Kane gutted his victims.

"Well, he's still good enough with a gun to cause damage," Tom said. He looked to Slater, eyebrows arched in a rather reminding expression.

"That's true," Slater said. "So everybody needs to be watchful. All right?"

"All right," Johnny said, nodding.

Charlie and Lizzy nodded too. Lark wasn't at all certain the children understood the danger that was near. She was glad they weren't fearful. She knew what it was to live in fear and insecurity as a child. Katherine's children had already suffered enough anxiety at the loss of their father. Thus, she was happy they did not seem overly concerned.

As Tom and Slater left the house to see to the stock, however, the children were not happy about having to stay indoors. The warm sunshine and fresh breezes of spring beckoned to them like a siren's song, and they were ill-tempered about being forced to stay in. Johnny was impatient, growling and fussing at Charlie and Lizzy like an old bear. Charlie and Lizzy were either quarreling with one another or racing around the house squealing and bumping into furniture.

Finally, Katherine had no other recourse but to separate them in order to settle down her and Lark's already weary nerves. Johnny was sent to his room with a book to read, and Lizzy was put to the task of helping her mother in making bread. Charlie was sent to the parlor. Wooden soldiers in hand, Charlie miserably slunk into the parlor, sat himself in the far corner, and began to set them up in rows.

"I'm so sorry," Katherine apologized as Lark washed several dishes that had been neglected after breakfast. "It's just that, after bein' so pent up all winter, the children can't hardly tolerate another day in the house."

"I wanted to smell the hyacinth today," Lizzy whined, pressing a fist into the smaller mound of bread dough her mother had given her to knead.

"I know, sweetie," Katherine sighed.

Lark smiled, her heart aching with sympathy, for she too had taken every opportunity to enjoy its perfume, knowing the lovely fragrance of early spring hyacinth would soon be spent.

"I just hope Charlie isn't into mischief," Katherine mumbled. "Lark, would you look in on him for me? I swear, when he's anywhere by himself, I'm always worried I'll look up to find he's burned the house down around us."

Katherine continued to knead the dough on the countertop as before, and Lark nodded.

"I'm sure he's fine," Lark said. "But one can never be too sure about little boys." Lark dried her hands on her apron and winked at Lizzy. "Isn't that right, Lizzy?"

"Oh yes, Miss Lark," Lizzy agreed. "Last time Mama sent me to check on Charlie, he was eatin' a bug. He said he'd just always wondered what they'd tasted like."

"Oh dear," Lark said, frowning. She certainly hoped Charlie hadn't decided to see if one bug tasted different than another. Hurrying into the parlor, she was relieved to see the boy had not taken to eating bugs to battle boredom. Rather, he sat in the chair in front of the old desk in the corner.

At once—though Lark was relieved Charlie was not crunching on some multilegged creature—she knew that the desk was rarely touched. Slater and Tom had explained to her that it had belonged to their father—that they somehow liked the idea of it being just the way he'd left it. Just as they'd liked the idea of their mother's knitting basket remaining on the floor near one end of the sofa, just as she'd left it—before the fever had taken them both within three days of one another.

"Charlie?" Lark ventured, hoping the boy hadn't

had time to disturb the desk too much. "What're ya doin', sweetie?"

Charlie turned around, smiling and eyes bright with excitement.

Instantly, Lark's worries increased. It was well she knew the expression plain on Charlie's face in that moment—he'd been into something.

"Look what I found, Miss Lark," he said in a conspiratorial whisper. "Here in this desk drawer."

Lark hurried to Charlie and the desk, hoping what he'd found was something easily replaced or shut away.

"Honey, you know none of us touch Mr. Evans's desk," she said as she approached.

"But look," Charlie said, holding up a key. "This key was in the drawer. I know'd it wasn't there before, so I turned it and pulled . . . and look what I found inside."

Lark did look. As Charlie pulled the drawer open once more, a slight gasp escaped her as she saw what lay in the drawer.

"I know what this is," Charlie said, picking up the silver US marshal's badge and holding it out to her. "I seen these before. I saw one on the sheriff when we was in town yesterday even. This is a lawman's badge!"

Lark was astonished! Had Slater and Tom's father truly been a US marshal? She wondered why she'd never heard either man mention it.

"And look here," Charlie continued. Reaching

into the drawer, he removed a finely crafted wooden box. Lifting the lid, he whispered, "Pearl-handled pistols!"

"Charlie!" Lark breathed. "We shouldn't be—"

"But what does it say?" Charlie interrupted, obviously careless of any ramifications of having discovered such a treasure. "Right here . . . on this gold plate on the inside of the box?"

Lark looked to the place Charlie indicated. There, on the inside of the box lid, was indeed a rectangular gold plate. Lark could see an etching or engraving on the plate and moved closer in order to see it more clearly.

"What does it say?" Charlie asked. "And what does this paper say too?"

Charlie handed Lark a paper—a telegram—yet her attention was still on the gold plate.

"And feel how heavy this badge is, Miss Lark!"

Charlie offered the marshal's badge to Lark, and she accepted it—though her attention was fixed to the gold plate in the box containing the pearl-handled pistols.

"It says," she began, *"Presented to US Marshal William S. Evans with much gratitude and thanks from the people of the great state of Texas."*

"William S. Evans?" Charlie asked. "Who's that? Uncle Slater and Uncle Tom's daddy? Is that who hid these in this drawer? I'm sure glad someone left the key in it! Ain't these pistols a sight?"

But Lark's heart was in her throat. Her stomach churned as understanding began to wash over her.

"And what's on that paper, Miss Lark? What's that say?" Charlie begged.

With a trembling hand, Lark raised the telegram and read aloud, *"By telegraph from Washington D.C. To US Marshal William Slater Evans stop. To certify that you are hereby reinstated as United States Marshal stop. Permission to act as your judgment dictates concerning escaped prisoner Samson Kane or any other fugitive, criminal, or law-breaking citizen stop."*

"William S. Evans!" Charlie exclaimed, pointing to the gold plate in the gun box lid. "William Slater Evans? Uncle Slater's a lawman?"

"William S. Evans?" Lark whispered, tears springing to her eyes. The name echoed through her brain, growing louder and louder until her head began to ache with the pounding.

"What's the matter, Miss Lark?" Charlie asked then. "You feelin' okay? Is yer cactus stings hurtin'?"

"No . . . no, I'm fine, Charlie," Lark managed. Closing the pistol box, she returned it to the drawer, laying the telegram and badge inside as well. "Put the key back where you found it, Charlie . . . please," she whispered. "I . . . I don't think your Uncle Slater wants anyone to know about this . . . at least, not right now. S-so let's keep this our secret, all right. Do you understand?"

Charlie's brow puckered. He seemed thoughtful for a moment. Then, shrugging his shoulders, he said, "All right," and hopped down off the chair.

As Charlie returned to his corner—as he began to mumble under his breath in speaking for his wooden soldiers—Lark's hand clutched her throat.

"William Slater Evans," she breathed. "United States Marshal," she gasped, finding an easy breath elusive. "No! No . . . it can't be!" she whispered.

In a wave of despair, shame, and horror, memories of her past—the truth of who she truly was—flooded her consciousness like a nauseating poison. She heaved once, nearly losing the contents of her stomach.

"No! Please, no!" she cried as tears poured over her cheeks. The pain—the fear she'd known the night before when she'd thought for a time that perhaps Slater Evans was an outlaw—paled in association with the truth she'd only just discovered. William S. Evans—William Slater Evans—United States Marshal—revered and respected lawman. Lark was miserably well acquainted with the legend of US Marshal William S. Evans.

"Are you behavin' for Miss Lark, Charlie?" Katherine asked.

Lark's hand flew to cover her mouth as another wave of anxiety-driven nausea washed over her.

"Yes, Mama," Charlie whined with aggravation.

"I've got the bread in the oven, Lark," Katherine said. "Would you and Charlie like to work a puzzle with Lizzy and I?"

Struggling to speak—to keep from collapsing in a heap of emotional despair—Lark shook her head.

"Y-you go ahead and start without me," she managed. "I'll be along shortly."

"All right," Katherine said. "Come on, Charlie."

"Miss Lark needs some time, Mama," Lark heard Charlie say. "We found a box in that desk with a couple of pearl-handled pistols in it . . . and a badge too. Did you know Uncle Slater was a lawman, Mama?"

Lark winced—nearly broke into hysterics—for if one thing was certain in life, it was that the innocence of a child prevented him from keeping a secret.

"Run on in the kitchen and wait for me, Charlie," Lark heard Katherine tell the boy. "I'll be right there."

Lark stiffened as she felt Katherine take her shoulders. She bit her lip, withholding the sobs begging to escape her.

"So now you know," Katherine said softly. "I swear I don't know why he's kept it from you. It's so obvious the two of you are—"

"He is William S. Evans . . . isn't he, Katie?" Lark asked, though the evidence had already proven the truth. Yet somehow—somehow she still hoped she would wake up and discover it had all been a dream—that there was not a badge in the desk drawer—no guns—no telegram.

"William Slater Evans," Katherine said. "One of the greatest lawmen there ever was. Slater's the one who took Samson Kane in, you see. That's why Samson Kane came here when he escaped . . . why he's come for Slater. Nobody could touch Samson Kane . . . not until Marshal Slater Evans went out after him." Katherine paused—squeezed Lark's shoulders with affectionate reassurance. "I don't know why he keeps the truth so quiet," she said. "I suppose . . . I suppose he doesn't want anyone gushin' praise all over him and such things. Or maybe, maybe the things he saw . . . the men he brought in . . . maybe all of it was just too terrible. Maybe he just doesn't want to think about it anymore."

Lark buried her face in her hands—bitterly wept.

"Why, honey!" Katherine exclaimed. "Whatever is the matter? If you're worried about Samson Kane gettin' to Slater . . . don't! There's not an outlaw ever born that could get the best of Slater!"

Lark was weak—frightened. Everything she loved was about to be stripped from her, but not by Samson Kane—no! Everything she cared for—

Katherine and the children, Tom, her life at the ranch—all of it would be taken from her. All this still didn't break her heart the way thoughts of losing Slater did. And she would lose him—if she'd ever even truly had him at all. She couldn't think of what the expression on his face would be when he found out—wouldn't think of the utter disgust and hatred he would own for her when he did—if he did.

Instantly, she thought of escape. Slater need never know! She could run—run as she'd been doing for years! Spring had come. The warmer weather would enable her to run, and she would! She would rather run from Slater—let her heart take to bleeding, bleed out on the new spring grass. She would rather die a slow, miserable death than to have Slater Evans discover the truth and loathe her for it.

"Samson Kane will not harm Slater, Lark," Katherine said, turning Lark to face her. "I promise you he won't." Katherine wiped the tears from Lark's face, smiled, and said, "Slater will send Samson Kane back to prison or kill him . . . and then the two of you can finally settle into one another."

Lark shook her head, continuing to weep.

"No," she cried in a whisper. "You don't under-stand."

"I understand he's in love with you," Katherine whispered. "That he's havin' a mighty hard time keepin' himself from just takin' you in his arms and—"

"No!" Lark interrupted. "You don't understand! If I stay, he'll find out. He'll discover the truth if I stay. And if he knows the truth . . . oh, Katherine! I couldn't face him if he knew the truth!"

"If you stay? If he finds out what truth?" Katherine asked.

Lark shook her head. "I-I can't tell you, Katie," she cried. "You'll hate me too!"

"What's the matter?" Tom asked, unexpectedly entering the room.

Lark gasped, "Oh no!" Tom would hate her too—despise her! Yet in that moment, Lark knew no one would despise her for the truth as thoroughly as Slater would.

"She's upset, Tom," Katherine said.

"Well, I can see that, Kate," Tom grumbled. "What's the matter, Lark? Aren't you feelin' all right?"

"No . . . no!" Lark cried. "I have to leave. I have to leave before you all—"

"Leave?" Tom exclaimed.

"She found Slater's badge," Katherine explained. "Rather, I think Charlie found Slater's badge . . . in the desk, he said."

Tom sighed. "Darlin'," he began, "is it really so terrible as all this? Bein' in love with a lawman?" He smiled and gathered her into his arms. Lark clung to him for a moment—prayed for the

362

strength to believe Slater would still want her after he discovered the truth. "They ain't such bad fellers . . . a little pouty sometimes maybe. But you know Slater loves you, and just because he's the law—"

"You don't understand!" Lark cried. "You don't understand!"

Tearing herself from his arms, she fled to her bedroom, closed the door, and drew the small bolt.

"Lark! Honey!" Katherine called from the other side.

"Give her a minute here, Katie," Tom said. "We'll give you a minute, darlin'," Tom said. "Then you come out and let us help with whatever is eatin' at ya. All right?"

"Yes," Lark sniffled. "Just give me a moment to collect myself. Just a moment."

"All right then, honey. Take yer time. You just take yer time."

But Lark knew Tom too well. Tom Evans didn't take to waiting. No doubt he was already heading for the front door, intent on summoning Slater.

Quickly, Lark went to the wardrobe, withdrew her old carpetbag, and began stuffing her clothes into it. She opened the trunk at the foot of her bed and removed her mother's photograph. The old clothes in the trunk could stay. The new ones she'd sewn over the past few months and the dress Tom had given her for Christmas were much nicer. Hurriedly she opened the bottom drawer of the small washbasin and pitcher stand. Long ago she'd found some of Mrs. Simpson's things in it—including a small photograph of Slater and Tom inscribed by both men to say, *Our Dear Matilda. Merry Christmas from your boys.* Taking the photograph was stealing; Lark knew it was. Still, Mrs. Simpson could no longer treasure it— and Lark would.

Lark paused to glance around the room. Renewed tears streamed down her face as she thought of the joy she'd known in living there— in sleeping each night knowing Slater was sleeping just above her.

Carefully, she drew the small bolt at the door, opened the door a crack, and peered out. It was as she thought. Tom was nowhere to be seen. Katherine wasn't at the door either. Lark assumed she'd gone to check on Charlie and Lizzy.

Quietly she crept from the room, closing the door behind her so that they would not know she'd left. Making her way to the back of the house, Lark managed to slip past Johnny's room unnoticed. Johnny was sitting on the floor with his back to the door, intent on a book he was holding in his lap. Therefore, he didn't hear Lark open the door and slip through it.

Instantly, she realized that without her slicker or even her lavender wool coat, she would have to find shelter before dark. The sun warmed the spring days, it was true, but the nights were still far too cool to endure comfortably. As she stood on the back porch, trying to find the courage to run, Lark thought of Samson Kane. She knew that if she happened upon him while trying to flee, he would surely kill her—for it was certain he knew that she had lied to him. Still, she wouldn't think of being killed by Samson Kane—or, worse, gutted like a fish by the outlaw. She simply would not cross his path.

There was no more time to plan. Tom may have found Slater by now, and though she was not sure of the depth of his feelings for her, Lark knew Slater cared for her—that he would return to the house once his brother had told him of Charlie's discovery and Lark's reaction to it.

She glanced to the barn—to the corrals. There was no sign of Slater, Tom, or the other Evans ranch cowboys. Lifting her skirt with one hand and holding tight to her carpetbag with the other, Lark stepped down off the porch. She would run—run as fast as her legs would carry her. If she could make it to town, perhaps she could find a room at the inn, for she was not so destitute as she had been when first she'd arrived. Slater and Tom had paid her well to be their cook and housekeeper—even increased her wages once Katherine and the children had arrived. Having spent very little of her collected wages, Lark knew she could easily survive until she found other means of work—even for months if need be.

Creeping toward the barn, Lark slipped to one side of it, inching her way down its length with her back to the outer wall, keeping her attention on the house.

"What you runnin' from, baby?" Slater asked.

Lark gasped—turned to see Slater standing behind her, a furious glare furrowing his brow.

"You," she said, bursting into tears.

"That's what I thought," he said.

She gasped once more as he snatched the carpetbag from her hand. Bending over, he placed one broad shoulder into Lark's midsection, effortlessly lifting her onto one shoulder. Lark had seen him lift grain and flour sacks this way, carrying them to the cellar. But grain and flour sacks didn't wriggle and move.

"Put me down!" she cried, weakly beating on his back with her fists. "You won't care that I'm leaving once I've told you!"

"Oh, I'll put you down all right," he growled, stepping into the barn. "After I've tanned yer fanny!"

Lark yelped with astonishment as Slater rather tossed her off his shoulder to land softly in a pile of straw. Glaring at her a moment, he dropped her carpetbag and folded strong arms against a broad chest.

"Tom tells me that you don't take too kindly to lawmen," he said. "Especially ones who've been keepin' secrets."

"You don't understand," she began.

"I understand that I shoulda told you before," he said. There was pain in his voice—regret in his expression. "I shoulda told you, Lark . . . but now you know why I was afraid to. I'd knew you run from me when—"

"Don't you see?" Lark cried, burying her face in her hands. "It's not you! It's not beautiful, wonderful you, Marshal Evans! It's me!"

"Lark—" he began, taking a step toward her.

"Stop! Stop! Don't come near me!" she cried. "Don't you see? It's not that you're a lawman. What would be the wrong in that? It's . . . it's which lawman you are!"

"Lark," he said, "I don't understand."

"Do you recognize the name Eddie Dean Wakley?" she asked, holding up a hand in a gesture that he should not move closer to her.

Slater paused—frowned—shrugged. "What does that have to do with the shade of General Lee's drawers?" he asked.

"Do you remember him?" she asked, again. "You're the US marshal who tracked him down, aren't you? You're the marshal who took him to the state prison in Texas . . . aren't you?"

Confusion was plain on Slater's face as he nodded. "Yes, it was me . . . maybe eight . . . maybe nine years ago. But I don't understand—"

"Do you remember when you found him?" she asked.

"Well, sure, but—"

"Tell me about it, Slater. Tell me about the day you found the outlaw Eddie Dean Wakley."

"Baby, please—" Slater began.

"Just tell me, Slater!" she cried. "Just tell me!"

Slater took a deep breath—ran a hand through his hair.

"All right. All right. Though I don't see what this has to do with—"

"Just tell me, Slater. Please."

"I was . . . I was down in south Texas, almost to Mexico. He was holed up in El Paso. Eddie Dean Wakley was as bad as they come, and I'd been chasin' him for months. I chased him halfway to Canada and then all the way back to Texas before I finally cornered him." He paused, shaking his head in frustration. "Baby, can't I just kiss you and settle you on down that way? I don't see what this has to do with why you're runnin' from me."

"You chased him to Texas," Lark prodded, however. "And . . ."

"And . . . and what?" he growled.

"And . . . and who was with him when you found him?" Lark asked, biting her lip to try and keep from melting into sobbing once more.

"Baby, I don't know," he said, shaking his head. "I don't know. He was holed up in the upstairs of a saloon. I pistol whipped him and . . ."

He paused, his eyes narrowing. Lark wiped at her tears with her sleeve.

"He had a wife," he said, lowering his voice. Lark's heart began to hammer as she wondered when complete realization would take hold of him. "She was a pretty thing. I remember I felt so guilty somehow takin' him away and leavin' her there . . . but I figured she'd be better off anyhow. He'd been draggin' her all over creation . . . her and the little girl." He paused again, inhaled a deep breath, rubbed at his whiskery chin with one hand. "I hated to think on how he treated that little girl. She looked just like her mama . . . a lovely little thing she was. I remember her mama called her Birdie . . . but that wasn't her real name."

Lark watched as Slater was then rinsed with recognition.

"Her mama called her Lark," he whispered. "That was the name of Eddie Dean Wakley's little girl. Wasn't it?"

Lark nodded. "Lark Medora Wakley," she whispered. "Lawrence was my mother's maiden name."

He was quiet a moment—glanced away from her. She saw him swallow, saw his eyes mist with moisture.

"Are you runnin' from me because you hate me for takin' your daddy to prison . . . for leavin' you and your mama with no man to look after you?" he asked. "Or are you runnin' because you thought I'd give a damn who your daddy was?"

"My mother always thanked God for you in her

369

prayers," Lark whispered. "Every night until she died, she thanked God for bringing you to us . . . for making you a strong enough man to take my father and set us free. I thanked God for you too."

Slater glanced away a moment, and Lark could see his jaw clenching and unclenching to bridle his emotion.

"But that doesn't change the fact that my father was an outlaw . . . even if he is dead. He died in prison, but he was an outlaw . . . no better than Samson Kane," she added.

Slater shook his head. "Eddie Dean Wakley robbed trains and banks, Lark," he said. "He murdered people . . . but he didn't torture 'em first. He wasn't the monster Samson Kane is."

He studied her a moment, and she brushed more tears from her cheeks. He wasn't glaring at her— wasn't looking at her with an expression of revulsion the way she'd expected him to.

"Did you really think I'd care about it . . . about your daddy bein' an outlaw?" he asked. Through her tears, she thought Slater looked almost wounded.

"Don't you?" she asked.

"No," he breathed.

Lark buried her face in her hands, sobbing with relief. It couldn't be true! Surely it couldn't be! This was the man who had hunted her father down, taken him to prison. How could he not care that she was an outlaw's daughter?

Still, as she felt his hands on her shoulders—as she looked up to see him hunkered down before her—the truth did begin to pierce her heart. He didn't care! She could see it in his eyes.

"Do you care that I'm an ol' law dog?" he asked. "I mean, I did put your daddy in the prison that killed him."

Lark shook her head. "I told you," she whispered, "my mama and I thanked God for you . . . every night." She smiled at him as he brushed the tears from her cheeks with the back of one hand. "I guess you're feeling pretty foolish about now," she said.

"Well, I'm always feelin' foolish in one way or the other," he chuckled. "But why do you say it?"

Lark smiled. "Because you were worried over me finding out about *your* past," she said.

Slater sank to his knees, gathering Lark into his arms as he laughed. He chuckled.

"Is that what you were going to tell me yesterday, Slater?" she whispered, letting her forehead rest against his neck as he held her. "You were going to tell me the truth, weren't you? About who you really are?"

"I was gonna tell you the truth about somethin' anyway," he said, kissing the top of her head. He was so warm—so strong. She heard him chuckle again.

"What has you so amused?" she asked.

"It kinda reminds me of some of them tales ya

hear that ya know somebody just made up," he said. "A United States marshal . . . fallin' for the daughter of an outlaw he once rode down? Who's gonna believe that?"

Lark pulled herself from his arms, studied his face a moment. What was he saying? Was he confessing his feelings for her at last? He smiled, cupping her chin in his hand.

"Yes, Lark," he said, grinning at her. "I have fallen for an outlaw's daughter."

"H-how fallen are you?" she asked.

"Well, we'll talk about that later," he said. "If I start talkin' about it now . . . well, let's just say I got an outlaw to be wary of." He smiled, placed a soft kiss to her lips, and whispered, "And so do you . . . 'cause you do bring out the scoundrel in me, Miss Lark."

Lark smiled and whispered, "Y-you really don't care who I am?"

"Of course I care who you are, baby," he whispered against her mouth. "I just don't care who your daddy was."

Oh, his kiss was the flavor of paradise! Heated and driven, Slater's kiss sealed Lark's hopes. He loved her! She recognized it now—recognized the consuming love his kiss conveyed to her soul! He pushed her back in the straw pile as his mouth endeavored to consume the passion of hers.

All at once, however, he pulled away from her, pulling her to her feet in the same motion.

"This ain't safe for you," he mumbled. "And not just because there's an outlaw roamin'," he added. The mischievous smile she so adored accom-panied a playful wink. Kissing her hard on the mouth once more, he picked up her carpetbag, taking hold of her hand and leading her from the barn.

"Will it be tonight?" Johnny asked as everyone sat at the table for supper.

Katherine and Lark had fed a nice supper to Eldon, Grady, and Ralston while Slater and Tom kept watch from the front and back porches of the house. Now the cowboys took their watch while Slater and Tom had a meal.

Slater shrugged as he chewed a bite of his supper.

"I don't know, Johnny," he said. "Ol' Samson . . . he's either hidin' like a rat or strikin' like a snake." He looked at Johnny, adding, "But don't worry. We'll be rid of him soon enough."

"Who is Samson Kane, Uncle Slater?" Charlie asked then. "And why does he want to kill you?"

"Hush now, Charlie. We don't need to talk about it now," Katherine said.

Yet Slater looked up from his meal.

"Secrets . . . it ain't good to keep some of 'em, Charlie," Slater said. "Most of 'em probably." He leaned back in his chair and sighed. "I reckon it's about time I quit ignorin' where I been. After all, it made me who I am." He glanced to Lark and smiled. "And I guess maybe that's a good thing."

Lark smiled. Indeed it was a good thing. Whatever happened to make Slater the man she loved—whether it was birth, experience, or both—it was a good thing.

"Well," Slater began, "me and my daddy didn't get along together most of the time, Charlie. My mama always said it was because we were too much alike."

"Amen," Tom mumbled.

Katherine nudged Tom with one elbow, quietly scolding him.

Slater grinned and continued, "I wanted to be my own man . . . wanted to see the whole of this great country of ours. I wanted to ride free in the open, herd cattle, and sleep out under the stars. So when I was near to Johnny's age . . . a might older . . . I left. I was big for my age and pretty full of myself too. So I hired on to cowboy for a rancher who was drivin' a herd out to Texas." The children were entranced—and so was Lark. She'd wondered about Slater Evans from the moment she'd met him—wondered about his past and why he felt so weathered.

"I cowboyed for near to five years. Then one day, a band of rustlin' outlaws scattered the herd I was helpin' drive. They killed six of my good friends. I won't go into it all now, but I ended up a deputy in a little ol' town in south

Texas. I had me a reputation soon enough, and to cut into the meat, by the time I was twenty-one, I was United States Marshal William S. Evans."

Slater smiled at Lark, his eyes smoldering with emotion.

He loves me, she thought.

The children were completely enthralled, and Slater continued, "I took down a good many outlaws . . . real bad men, some of 'em. The governor of Texas even give me a set of pistols for bringin' in a bad hombre named Samson Kane."

"Samson Kane?" Charlie asked, his eyes as wide as supper plates.

"Yep," Slater said. "Samson Kane was about the worst I ever run into. Killed folks, scalped Indians, robbed banks—you name it . . . he done it. He went by Samson 'cause he never cut his hair. He let it grow all long and straggly . . . then braided it like a woman.

"Well, one time me and old Samson had a go-around. I'd seen him kill a deputy down in El Paso, and when I caught up to him . . . well, we did go around, using fists and feet and whatever else was handy. Now, ol' Samson carried himself a big knife . . . an Arkansas toothpick, they call it. Sailors use 'em a lot . . . wear 'em in a holster on their back. But not Samson Kane . . . nope. He sheathes his at his leg . . . his thigh, opposite his pistol. Anyway, me and Samson was goin' around, and he up and pulls this knife . . . starts pokin' it at me. I can't even recollect how, but somehow, I got hold of the knife and gave him a sting he won't soon forget . . . right across his face like this." Lark watched as Slater indicated the place on his face where Samson was scarred.

"*You* gave him the scar?" Lark asked.

"Yep," Slater said, shaking his head. "I suppose that's another reason he don't care too much for me."

Johnny chuckled—silencing his momentary amusement when his mother glanced at him with disapproval.

"Samson Kane was madder than a hornet . . . but bleedin' and hurt enough he couldn't go 'round with me much after that. So I drug him off to the county jail, and the doc in town stitched him up. I testified in court to what I'd seen him do—to the murder of the deputy. Then I drug his sorry hind end to Yuma. They locked him up, and I went on my way."

"But this ain't the first time Samson Kane's escaped from Yuma, now is it, Slater?" Tom urged, nodding at his brother.

"No," Slater admitted. He inhaled a deep breath, exhaled, and said, "A couple years later, I'm ridin' along mindin' my own . . . and I hear a voice behind me say, 'Yer done fer, Marshal Evans.' I drew my gun and turned, but I heard gunfire before I'd pulled my trigger. The bullet grazed my head just here." Slater turned his head and parted his hair on the left side of his head with his fingers to reveal a thick scar. "The graze to my head dizzied me up a bit, and before I got myself straight, ol' Samson Kane shot me again . . . here . . . in the shoulder."

Slater unbuttoned his shirt and pulled it aside to show the children the scar at the front of his shoulder.

"It's worse at the back," Lizzy said. "I seen it one day when you were bathin'."

"Lizzy!" Katherine exclaimed.

"Did ya now?" Slater chuckled.

"But how did you get him back to Yuma?" Johnny asked.

"Shot him in the leg," Slater said. "And when he fell off his horse, I kicked him the gut and beat the sense out of him . . . tied him up, tossed him over his horse, and took him back."

"Why didn't they hang him?" Johnny asked.

Slater shook his head. "I don't know. They were supposed to." He paused, chuckling to himself. "Now I'm thinkin' I shoulda made sure they did . . . or else hung him myself when I had the chance."

"Well, I think that's just about enough talk of outlaws and shootin'," Katherine said. "It's late, and you children need to be gettin' to bed."

"Aw, Mama," Charlie whined. "I wanna stay up and hear more about cowboys and outlaws and such."

"And that's exactly why you need to get to bed," Katherine sighed, rolling her eyes with exasperation.

"You're not gonna get upset and run off again, are ya, Miss Lark?" Lizzy asked.

Lark blushed. "No, Lizzy," she said. "I'm fine now." She looked to see Slater smiling at her. He winked, and she said, "I'm just fine."

Chapter Sixteen

"It was Chet Leigh's horse we seen out there, Slater," Tom said. "He was pretty far off . . . but there ain't no mistakin' that strawberry roan he rides."

"And ol' Outlaw ain't nowhere to be seen," Eldon added. "Little Joe neither . . . though Chet must naughta had time to let loose the Angus bull. Sue's right where we left him last night."

"Well, it ain't coincidence," Slater grumbled. "Chet Leigh ain't gonna just show up one mornin' to cause trouble . . . not without help. He's too yellow for that. Nope . . . he met up with Samson Kane somewhere. That idiot cowboy is ridin' with that dirty outlaw."

"Chet's from Texas, Slater," Tom reminded his brother. "He knew who you was. He probably heard Samson Kane askin' around about ya somewhere between here and Yuma."

Though the men conversed in lowered voices, the quiet of early morning somehow made their conversation more discernable. The sun was just peeking over the horizon. Lark had risen from her bed, dressed, and was preparing to start breakfast when she heard Slater, Tom, and Eldon's discussion. Now she stood just outside the kitchen, listening as the men sat at the table talking. Tom and Eldon had been out that morning searching for any evidence that Samson Kane might be lingering nearby. From what Lark had heard so far, it sounded as if Samson Kane now had some assistance with his vengeful intentions—Chet Leigh. Lark thought of the last time she'd seen Chet Leigh, and her hand involuntarily moved to her cheek at the memory. The swelling and bruising Chet's attack had left on her face were long gone, but the horrible recollection of his abuse would never leave.

Still, even for the frightening memories she now possessed of both Chet Leigh and Samson Kane, it was Slater she was worried about. No doubt Chet hated Slater for beating him senseless and sending him away. He'd probably relish the chance to beat Slater senseless in return. Furthermore, she already knew what Samson Kane's intentions toward Slater were. After all, the outlaw had tried to kill him before. It was unlikely his plans had changed. The thoughts of what either villain would do to Slater if they caught him off guard sent a tremor of terror shooting through her. Why couldn't Samson Kane have died in prison the way her father had? Why couldn't Chet Leigh just have ridden away and never looked back?

Weary of eavesdropping, for she wanted to know every detail of what the cowboys had discovered, Lark stepped into the kitchen.

Slater looked to her, and her heart leapt as he smiled. Even the danger lurking in the lingering dark hours of morning couldn't dampen the sheer elation she felt at seeing his smile, for it reminded her that he loved her—that he'd *fallen* for her.

"Samson Kane and Chet Leigh . . . what will they do?" she asked.

"Cause trouble," Slater answered.

"Ol' Outlaw is gone . . . and Little Joe too," Eldon offered. "It was Chet who let 'em out. Ain't a doubt in my mind."

"They're tryin' to draw us out," Tom explained. "They know how important them bulls are . . . and they're hopin' some of us will ride out to try and round 'em up."

A sudden vision of Samson Kane's vile, malicious smile crossed Lark's mind, and she winced at the sickened sensation the image left in her stomach.

"Will you ride out to round them up?" Lark asked.

"No," Slater mumbled. "Samson Kane ain't too

380

good with a gun, but Chet Leigh is. And both of 'em are such cowards they'd try to shoot us from a distance instead of facin' us like men." He glanced to Eldon and added, "And any of you boys are fools to think Chet won't pick you off just because he used to ride with ya. Once a man turns to outlawin' . . . he don't usually look back."

"Well, we can't just sit here and do nothin', boss," Eldon grumbled. "We can't just sit on our fannies and wait. Can we?"

"Not for too long, no," Slater said. "But there oughta be a posse of marshals here by tomorrow mornin'. Once I sent that telegram requestin' reinstatement . . . well, they know Kane's here now, and they'll come for him."

Tom chuckled. He shook his head, having been amused by something or someone.

"And what's so funny?" Slater asked, frowning with disapproval.

"I just never thought I'd see the day when you'd be willin' to wait somethin' like this out, that's all," Tom answered.

"We got women and children here now," Slater said. "You know that, Tom. We can't risk a shootout . . . not when they can see us and we can't see them."

Tom nodded. "Oh, I know it. I do know it," he said. "I was just admirin' yer patience . . . since you didn't seem to be born with too much of that particular virtue in the first place."

"I got me plenty of other virtues, little brother," Slater said. He glanced to Lark, winking at her. "Just ask Lark. Ain't I got plenty of virtues, baby?"

Before Lark could answer, however, Tom said, "Bein' good at kissin' ain't a virtue, Slater." Eldon chuckled, and Lark blushed.

Slater nodded and said, "Maybe so . . . but the way I keep from draggin' Lark on upstairs with me every night . . . now that is." He looked to Lark and added, "Ain't that right?"

The rifle report startled everyone. Instantly the men were on their feet, the rifles they'd each had setting on their laps at the ready.

"Grady! Hey there, Grady," Slater called through the kitchen window, standing slightly ajar.

"It ain't me, boss!" Grady answered from his post on the front porch.

Another shot rang out, and Lark heard something fall against the back door.

"It's Ralston," Tom said.

"Eldon . . . watch the front of the house from the window," Slater ordered Eldon. He looked to Lark then, pointed an index finger at her, and said, "You stay here."

Lark nodded, though a wave of terror washed over her.

"Ralston?" Tom called as another gunshot echoed through the still morning air. "You all right, Ralston?"

Slater and Tom hurried toward the back of the house.

"Get the children to the kitchen, Kate," Lark heard Slater order. "Sit 'em down under the table so they don't give as good a target."

"But, Uncle Slater," Charlie began, "Johnny ain't with me. He left a while ago. I saw him climb out the window . . . but he didn't know I saw him."

"What?" Slater exclaimed.

"Johnny!" Katherine cried.

Lark startled as another shot reported, accompanied by the sound of shattering glass.

Katherine and the children screamed and hurried into the kitchen.

"Get under the table!" Katherine told Lark as she and the children dropped to their knees.

Pushing chairs out of the way, Lark and Katherine huddled under the table with Lizzy and Charlie.

"Oh, Johnny!" Katherine cried, shaking her head. "What on earth was he thinkin'?"

Lizzy and Charlie were sobbing. Tears welled in Lark's eyes as well—made even more profuse by the unpleasant memories that came flooding back to her in that moment. Suddenly she saw herself as a child—felt herself wrapped in the protection of her mother's arms—closed her eyes and envisioned a time when she and her mother had huddled under a table for safety as her father exchanged gunfire with a lawman. Her father had gunned down the lawman. Lark could still see the life fading from his eyes as her father stood over him—as he, Eddie Dean Wakley, taunted the old sheriff as the dying lawman drew his last breath.

"Lark . . . Lark!"

Lark opened her eyes to see Slater hunkered down before her.

"Ralston's been shot," he said, drawing her thoughts back to the present. "If we drag him in here, will ya see what you can do for him?"

"O-of course," Lark said. "Of course." She started to crawl out from beneath the table, but Slater shook his head.

"Don't stand up . . . not any more than you have to," he instructed. "Do you hear me?"

Lark nodded, and Slater winked at her.

"It'll be all right," he said.

"I know," she whispered.

Slater looked to the children then—reached out to press an encouraging palm to Lizzy's cheek, then to Charlie's.

"Everything will be fine," he said. "Don't you worry. I'll find Johnny."

"Why would he leave the house?" Katherine cried then. "He knows the danger!"

Slater shook his head. "He come to me last night and asked me if he could ride out with the boys this mornin'," he explained. "I told him no, and I know it hurt his pride . . . but I didn't think he'd try to go off on his own though." Slater reached beneath the table again, slipping a hand to Katherine's neck and moving to kiss her cheek. "But don't you worry. I'll bring him back to ya, Kate."

Lark placed a hand on Slater's arm. "Samson Kane . . . he's using Johnny to draw you out."

Slater nodded. "Yep."

Tom drug Ralston into the kitchen and laid him out on the floor in front of Lark.

Instantly, Charlie and Lizzy began to sob. Lark's heart ached for the children. They'd endured so much loss and hardship. She hated that they now would know a new kind of fear.

"He's got the boy," Ralston panted. The cowboy's right thigh was bleeding, as well as his shoulder. "But it ain't yer outlaw that took him. It was Chet . . . Chet Leigh."

Slater and Tom exchanged glances, and Slater exhaled a heavy sigh.

"The boy didn't come out the back door or I'da seen him. He musta slipped out the window," Ralston panted. "I'm sorry, boss," he said. "I . . . I didn't see him for the dark, I guess. I'm sorry."

"It's all right, Ralston," Slater said. "It ain't none of it yer fault."

"Get to the back door, will ya, Eldon?" Tom asked.

"Yep," Eldon said, leaving his post at the kitchen window and heading for the back door.

"It's Chet, boss," Ralston said. "It's that dang Chet Leigh. I can't hardly believe it. We was saddle pals not so . . . not so long ago." Ralston's speech was slurred, and Lark was certain he would soon lose consciousness.

"I know, boy," Slater said. "You done good. You kept him from gettin' in at the women and children."

"You shoulda beat him a little worse when ya had the chance, boss," Ralston whispered, "that no-good snake in the grass."

Ralston was unconscious then. Slater and Tom quickly inspected his wounds.

"He'll live," Slater said. His brow was puckered with concern and anger.

"If he don't bleed out," Tom added.

"Do what ya can for him, baby," Slater said. "I gotta go for Johnny."

"But it's a trap!" Lark exclaimed as a new terror gripped her then. "They're just trying to draw you out so they can—"

"I know," Slater interrupted, placing a hand to her cheek, caressing her lips with his thumb. "But I'm smarter than both of 'em. You know that's true, don't ya?"

Lark nodded, trying to summon courage.

"I'm better lookin' too," he teased.

Lark couldn't help but return his loving smile.

"And anyway, he ain't goin' by hisself, honey," Tom said, smiling with encouragement. Tom looked to Katherine. "We'll bring that boy home safe, Kate. Don't you worry neither."

Katherine nodded, wiping tears from her cheeks.

"Now give me some sugar and let me go," Slater said.

Placing a strong, warm hand to her cheek, Slater raked his fingers back through her hair. Pulling her to him, he captured her mouth with his in such a driven and impassioned kiss that Lizzy exclaimed, "Shame on you, Uncle Slater!" even for her frightened tears.

"I'll be right back," Slater whispered. "I promise." He released Lark, stood, and strode toward the back door.

"Just sop up the blood as best ya can," Tom said, nodding toward Ralston. "Put some pressure on them bullet holes, and we'll take care of him when we get back with Johnny."

Lark nodded—though she wondered if her courage would fail her. She was trembling so terribly she feared she might not be able to leave the small haven of the table.

"Tom," Kate began. Lark wept as she saw the panic in Katherine's eyes.

"Don't you worry, Kate," Tom said then. "You got one of the greatest United States marshals to ever sit a horse ridin' out after yer boy. Johnny will be fine." Tom paused, chuckling and adding, "Well, he'll be fine once Slater's through chewin' on him for gettin' hisself caught." Tom looked to

Lark then—smiled with reassurance. "Don't you worry neither," he said. "Slater will be fine. He'll be back before you've had time to miss him."

Lark nodded, brushing tears from her cheeks. "Be careful, Tom."

"I always am, honey." He stood, striding after his brother.

Katherine still held tight to her children, endeavoring to offer them some fragment of reassurance. Lark knew she'd have to tend to Ralston alone. The children needed to be tucked in their mother's embrace.

Trembling, she crawled from beneath the table to Ralston. The cowboy's shirt was soaked with blood at his right shoulder. She glanced down to see that the bright red bloodstain on his right trouser leg was expanding—spreading as the sturdy fabric soaked up the blood escaping the bullet wound inflicted there.

"Ralston?" she said, placing her hand on his chest. She sighed with relief when she felt the sturdy beating of his heart and the rise and fall of his chest as he breathed.

Wiping at her tears, Lark tried to concentrate on what must be done to help the wounded cowboy. Her thoughts were, of course, with Slater and Tom and Johnny—for the recklessness of youth had further endangered them. Still, she knew that no one on earth understood Johnny's hasty actions better than Slater—understood the boy's desire

388

and determination to leap into manhood too soon.

"Slater," she breathed as she tore open Ralston's shirt to inspect the severity of the wound at his shoulder. "Please, Slater . . . please," she mumbled as she worked—as she brushed tears from her cheeks with the back of her hand. "When you find Johnny . . . when Samson Kane and Chet Leigh come for you . . . oh, please, please, please come back to me. Slater . . . please come back to me."

"He knows you can track 'em," Tom said, checking his saddle cinch.

"Oh, I'm sure he's countin' on it," Slater mumbled. He shoved a foot in the stirrup and mounted Smokey. Slater rode out of the barn, reined Smokey in, and studied the tracks in the dirt on the ground.

"That fool boy," Tom said as he rode from the barn, reining in beside Slater.

"All boys are fools . . . in one way or the other. Men too," Slater growled. He shook his head as he recognized the horseshoe prints belonging to Chet Leigh's horse. "But I'm still gonna wring his neck when I get my hands on him."

Slater spurred Smokey to a slow walk, carefully studying the footprints and hoofprints on the ground.

"Yep. Looks like Johnny crawled out the window here," he said, pointing to the ground beneath the window of the room where Johnny and Charlie slept. "Then he run off over this way . . . to the side of the house, here," he continued, following the tracks, "and here's where Chet got him." Slater followed the hoofprints as they led east, away from the house. He studied the manner in which the hoofprints then made a deeper impression in the soil. "Johnny's on Chet's horse . . . and Chet took him by hisself," he told Tom. "Samson Kane wasn't with him."

"Maybe Kane don't have nothin' to do with this," Tom offered hopefully.

"And maybe you didn't know Lark would end up twistin' me around her finger when ya hired her," Slater said.

Tom chuckled, and Slater spurred Smokey into a trot.

They had to find Johnny. They had to find him alive, and he had to stay that way. Slater silently cussed the boy up one side and down the other for being so headstrong. He'd told Johnny just the night before that he couldn't ride out with Eldon and the others, and he'd told him why. Oh, he remembered well enough how it felt to be twelve years old and feeling your oats, so he'd told him that his mama and little sister and brother would fret too hard if Slater let him ride out—instead of telling him that a boy of twelve wasn't ready to face outlaws. He'd reminded Johnny that his mama had just lost her lover and husband and that the little ones still weren't feeling safe without their daddy nearby. He'd told the boy that his family needed him—that Tom and the cowboys could help protect the outside of the house but that his mother, brother, sister, and even Lark needed a man to protect them inside it. Slater had assumed the boy had settled his determination to ride off in search of heroism. He sighed, shaking his head at his own ignorant assumptions. He should've tied the boy to the bedpost—because he knew how Johnny thought. Slater had thought the same way when he'd been Johnny's age. He should've known the boy would disobey him and ride out in search of adventure—for in his heart, Slater knew he would've done the same.

As he tracked Chet Leigh's horse, Slater struggled to keep his thoughts on being wary of an ambush. Visions of Lark kept sweeping through his mind—visions of her smile, her alluring form, and her tempting lips. His mouth watered at the thought of her kiss, his arms longed to hold her, and his body ached to know the sense of hers pressed against his once more. He hadn't wanted to leave her. In truth, he'd secretly paused a moment before going after Johnny. For just a moment, he'd considered sending the others out after his reckless nephew.

Still, it was Slater that Samson Kane wanted. He was the reason everyone else was in danger—including young Johnny. Slater wouldn't let the people he loved suffer any longer because of the past that still haunted him. He wanted nothing more than Lark—nothing. Yet he couldn't live with himself if anything happened to Johnny. Experience and a weathering past had proven to Slater that if he wanted to own Lark—wholly own her heart, mind, body, and soul—then he had to be the man he was born to be, the man who fought against evil no matter what. He couldn't live with himself otherwise, and he was sure Lark couldn't either.

He'd have her—he would! He'd beat down Samson Kane and Chet Leigh—hang them if he had to—but he'd have Lark. In that moment, Slater was tired of pussyfooting around. He loved Lark. Oh, he'd tried to fight it, sure enough—but he couldn't, and he loved her. He loved her, and he was suddenly tired of holding back. His past was his past. Nothing could change it. In fact, his past might just be what made he and Lark so well suited for one another.

Enough! Slater growled low in his throat. He'd take care of Samson Kane and Chet Leigh, and then—then he'd marry Lark. He'd tie her up and drag her to the preacher's house if he had to. Time was too precious to be wasted—and he'd wasted plenty.

"He's ridin' fast," Slater said to Tom. "He ain't far ahead though. I think he's headed for the canyon ridge. I don't want him gettin' that far. Come on, Tom. Let's get that boy and bring him home."

"We're most likely ridin' straight for a shootout," Tom said.

"Yep," Slater mumbled.

Tom smiled. "I ain't never had the pleasure yet, big brother," he chuckled. "Oughta be mighty interestin'."

Slater smiled. "Oh, by the way . . . I'm deputizin' you, little brother. It's only temporary, of course."

"Of course," Tom said, smiling.

"Get on, Smoke!" Slater shouted then.

As Smokey broke into a gallop, Slater leaned forward in the saddle, keeping low in case Chet Leigh had already set up to fire on him and Tom. He felt his eyes narrow—felt his attention finally begin to focus on bringing Johnny home.

As Slater rode toward certain danger—rode with his reins in one hand, his rifle in the other, and his brother at his side—he knew he'd do whatever he had to do to get back to the house—to get back to the woman he loved—to get back to Lark.

Lark wadded up her apron, pressing it to the wound at Ralston's leg. The wound was bleeding more profusely than the wound at his shoulder. She pressed harder, wincing as Ralston moaned.

"Do you think it would be safe to fetch some water for him?" Lark asked, looking over her shoulder to Katherine.

Katherine shook her head, however. "I don't

know. Just . . . just keep your head low maybe," she answered.

"I think the bullet went through his shoulder . . . but I'm not sure about his leg," Lark said. "I think it's still in there."

"Well, we certainly can't dig it out now," Katherine said. "Not until—"

Lark cried out, and the children screamed as the front door burst open. Samson Kane stepped into the house, wielding a large bloodstained knife in one hand and a pistol in the other. He smiled— the same heinous, malevolent smile Lark had seen in her waking nightmare beyond the east pasture.

A low chuckle resonated in his throat as he studied Lark, Katherine, and the children.

"Well, lookie here," he said, slowly striding toward them, wiping the blood from his knife on his pant leg. "Is this where Marshal Evans keeps his women, under the table in the kitchen? I knew that self-righteous lawman wasn't the lily-white angel he makes hisself out to be." The outlaw hunkered down and pushed his hat back on his head, glaring at them. "So he's got hisself a couple a babies too, is it?" He chuckled again. "Well, ain't he been the busy bee?"

For a moment, Lark couldn't speak. Terror had numbed her tongue. She could only stare at Samson Kane—unable to believe he was in the house with them. She wondered where Slater was. Had Samson Kane killed him? Was he lying dead somewhere? Was it Slater's blood staining Samson Kane's knife? No! No! She wouldn't believe it. Slater and Tom hadn't been gone long enough for Samson Kane to have murdered them, whether or not Chet Leigh was helping him. No. Slater and Tom had ridden out after Johnny—and Lark understood then. Samson Kane hadn't lured Slater out of the house to ambush him in the open. He'd lured him out of the house in order to ambush him when he returned! It made perfect sense, from an outlaw's point of view—especially one who was outnumbered. With Slater and Tom gone, and Ralston wounded and unconscious, Samson Kane had only two men to take down before he could gain entrance to the house— instead of five.

Lark's eyes filled with tears as she wondered what the fates of Eldon and Grady had been. Were they dead? Her gaze lingered on the blade of Samson Kane's large knife as she remembered what Johnny had told her—that his father had told him Samson Kane often gutted his victims like fish. Horrible images flashed through her mind as she thought of Grady and Eldon—as she thought that Ralston was no doubt the luckiest of the three.

The true danger Katherine and the children were in began to sink into Lark's consciousness. Then, as Samson Kane's attention began to linger on her—as a smile of both anger and triumph spread across his ugly face—Lark realized the danger she was in as well.

She was panicked, yes. Yet even as panic and ultimate fear washed over her, hope gave her courage—hope that Slater was still alive, that he was unharmed, that he would still vanquish Samson Kane and survive.

"Marshal Evans isn't here," Lark said as her senses began to return.

Samson Kane nodded. His eyes narrowed as he growled, "Ain't you learned yet that lyin' is a sin, woman?" He studied her for a moment. "You lied to me the other day . . . even though you knew I'd find out, didn't ya? That was brave—ignorant, but brave. I'll give ya that. Are you still tryin' to protect that filthy Slater Evans?"

"He's gone," she told the outlaw. "He's gone to hunt you."

Samson Kane chuckled, laughed, and shook his head.

"He's gone after that fool boy, woman," he said. "I knew he would. I can't tell ya how happy I was to see that boy climb out that winda this mornin'. Why, me and Chet . . . we just been waitin' for somebody in this house to do somethin' stupid. I was hopin' it'd be Marshal Evans that let his guard down . . . though I shoulda know'd better than to hope for it. But then that boy crawled out the winda. It couldn'ta worked out better if I'd planned it that way."

"He'll be back soon enough," Lark told him. She wanted to scream—to scream and burst into tears. Still, she knew that's what Samson Kane wanted her to do. Therefore, she wouldn't.

"Oh, I'm countin' on it," Samson Kane said. "I'm just hopin' Chet Leigh's as good a shot as he claims to be. If he can take care of Slater Evans's brother, then that leaves the marshal for me to deal with . . . just me and Marshal Evans. I been waitin' for that for a long, long time."

Tears filled Lark's eyes, even for her efforts to appear brave. She could see Samson Kane's plan all too clearly in that moment. He'd been methodical—planned to eliminate all the men at the ranch so that Slater wouldn't have any assistance in fighting him. Once the other men were neutralized—or dead—Samson Kane and Chet Leigh could face Slater alone. Slater would be outnumbered.

"You're a coward," Lark growled.

Lark gasped as the back of Samson Kane's hand met with her cheek. The children cried out—whimpered with fear.

"I ain't no coward, woman," Samson Kane growled. "I just ain't stupid enough to let Marshal Evans get the better of me again." Kane's eyes narrowed. He studied Lark, his gaze lingering on her in a lecherous manner. "Yer the one, ain't ya?" he asked. "Yer the woman that's got ol' Marshal Evans so wound up that he beat the tar outta Chet."

"He would've beat him for treating any woman the way he treated me," Lark countered.

Samson Kane smiled his wicked smile—nodded. "You're what's gonna get me that arrogant lawman right to where I want him," he said. "Oh yes, indeed. You are what's gonna finally get Marshal William S. Evans killed, woman."

Lark winced and couldn't keep the tears from spilling from her eyes. Was it true? Would she be the means to Slater's murder?

Samson Kane reached beneath the table, taking hold of Lizzy's arm.

"Come on, now, girl," he said as he struggled to remove the sobbing child from her mother's embrace. "Come on now. Let's me and you wait for Marshal Evans to ride on back to the house."

Katherine, however, held tightly to Lizzy.

Lark gasped as Samson Kane pressed the blade of his large knife to Lizzy's throat.

"Give her over to me, woman," he told Katherine. "Unless you wanna see her carved up right before yer eyes . . . you give her over to me. I won't hurt her. I don't mean to harm children. I just don't want the marshal's woman tryin' anything stupid. And I figure if the little one is waitin' with me . . . she won't."

Lizzy sobbed as her mother released her—as Samson Kane picked her up with one arm and carried her with him as he stepped back from the table.

"We'll just wait here," he said. "It won't take the marshal long to kill ol' Chet and bring that boy back. Let's all just sit here and wait for him."

"He'll kill you," Lark said.

Samson Kane chuckled. "Naw. Maybe in the past, but not now . . . not with lovin' a woman. Women weaken men, distract 'em, get 'em killed. This time Marshal Evans is gonna find his guts spillin' out on the ground before he even knows what hit him." He smiled and winked at Lark. "And you got yerself to thank for that."

Lark brushed the tears from her cheeks. Was Samson Kane right? Would the fact that Slater loved Lark weaken him somehow? No! No, she wouldn't believe it. Love made people stronger —not weaker. Slater would return, and when he did, it would be Samson Kane who would die.

Chapter Seventeen

Slater growled as he felt the bullet whiz past his head.

"He's in that cluster of rocks yonder," Slater shouted to Tom. "Get around behind him."

"No," Tom shouted. "I'll draw his fire. You get to his back. You're a better shot than me."

"Tom!" Slater called. It was too late, however. Tom spurred his horse to a faster gallop. Drawing his pistol in favor of his rifle, he squeezed off several rounds toward the cluster of rocks ahead of them.

"Aim high. You don't want to hit Johnny by mistake," Slater growled.

Gritting his teeth, Slater reined Smokey to run in opposition to Tom's horse. Either he or Tom would take a bullet—he was near sure of it. Chet was a good shot and had a perfect defensive position. Still, if Chet was shooting at Slater or Tom, he couldn't be holding a gun to Johnny.

Slater felt the bullet graze his arm, but he didn't flinch. Tom fired over the rocks, and Slater rounded the cluster of large boulders. He saw them—Johnny and Chet. Johnny was tied up and sitting on the ground nearby.

Slater pulled Smokey to a hard halt and dismounted.

"I'll shoot the boy!" Chet hollered, leveling his rifle at Slater.

"Samson Kane's usin' you for a fool, Chet Leigh," Slater growled, striding toward them.

"You stay there, boss," Chet growled, taking aim.

"He wants me to kill you . . . else he wouldn't have sent you out to do such a thing as takin' this boy," Slater said, though he did stop in his tracks.

"You made a fool of me, Slater Evans!" Chet shouted. "You made a fool of me. And after you sent me off . . . I run into Samson Kane. He and me robbed a stage . . . and I shot a man. You did that to me, Slater Evans."

"You did that yerself, Chet . . . and you know it," Slater said. "Now put that gun down, and let the boy go. Don't make me shoot you."

Tom rode up behind Chet then, reined in, and dismounted. Chet glanced behind him.

"Now, Tom . . . don't you go doin' nothin' here," Chet warned. Chet leveled the rifle at Johnny.

"Chet Leigh," Tom began, "now . . . you ain't no child murderer, boy. You ain't. Don't let this outlaw turn you into one."

Chet was nervous—hesitant. Maybe he'd killed a man in robbing a stage, but killing a child was different. He knew Chet didn't want to hurt Johnny. Oh, he'd kill Slater if given half a chance maybe, but that was different than killing a boy.

"Don't you point that rifle at that boy!" Slater growled. "You point that rifle at me . . . if yer man enough to do it."

Chet's temper was piqued, and he leveled the rifle at Slater.

"I'd kill you, Slater Evans," Chet growled. "But that ain't the plan now, is it?"

Slater felt his eyes narrow. "What're you talkin' about, Chet?" Still, Slater's instincts leapt with sudden understanding. "Where's Kane?" he asked. It was a trap—sure enough it was. Yet in that moment, Slater realized that Chet luring Slater and Tom away with Johnny for bait wasn't

401

so Samson and Chet could ambush them. It was so they'd be away from the house—so that the women and children would only have two men guarding them instead of the five there had been before Ralston had been shot and Slater and Tom had gone for Johnny.

Panic the like he'd never known gripped Marshal William S. Evans. Lark! Samson Kane was out for revenge. What better way to hurt a man than to hurt the woman he loved? Losing Lark—it would be worse than death. Slater would rather die than see her harmed.

"I said, where's Samson Kane?" Slater shouted.

Chet smiled, chuckled, and said, "Where do you think he is, marshal?"

"He's back at the house," Tom said.

Slater inhaled a deep breath. Fear was fast overtaking him, and he had to fight it. He had to think clearly.

"Is that true?" Slater asked.

Chet chuckled. "That girl's gonna pay for what you done to me," he said. "And so are you."

As Chet leveled his rifle—as he took aim at Slater—Slater said, "If that's true, Chet Leigh . . . then I don't have time to deal with the murderin' likes of you."

An instant later, a shot rang out.

Slater spun his pistol and shoved it in the holster at his thigh as Chet Leigh crumpled to the ground—a bullet hole between his eyes.

Tom shook his head as he lowered his rifle and strode to Johnny.

"Ain't one to waste words, are ya, brother?" he asked as he hunkered down to untie his nephew.

"Nope," Slater said. He turned and mounted Smokey. "You all right, Johnny?" he asked.

Johnny nodded, obviously ashamed of having enabled Chet Leigh to help Samson Kane with his vengeful plans.

"You're gonna have to walk back then," Slater said. "I need Tom right at my heels."

"Yes, sir," Johnny said.

Slater didn't wait for Tom to finish untying Johnny. He didn't wait to draw even one more breath.

"Smoke!" he growled, spurring his horse into a gallop toward home.

Terrifying thoughts ricocheted in Slater's mind as he rode. What would Samson Kane do to Lark—to Katherine and the children? He couldn't let his experience with outlaws devour his mind now. He had to get back; he had to end the nightmare.

Slater ground his teeth as he rode. His heart was hammering hard—felt like it had leapt into his throat somehow. He'd never told Lark he loved her—never actually spoken the words anyway. In the barn, he'd confessed having fallen for her, but he'd never breathed the three words a woman needed to hear from the man she loved—the three words a man needed to speak to the woman he loved. What if he died fighting Samson Kane, never having told her that he loved her? Why hadn't he just said it to her the day before, even that morning? Slater Evans swore to himself that, if he made it through facing Samson Kane without dying, the first words out of his mouth to Lark would be . . .

"I love you," he growled as he rode.

Lark stared at Lizzy, brushed the tears from her own cheeks, and tried to think. Slater would return for them; she knew he would. But he'd be returning to an ambush. How could she warn him? How could she get Lizzy out of Samson Kane's vile grasp?

She thought of Slater—of his kiss and powerful embrace. She thought of her mother—of her loving heart and sad end. So many things bounced about in Lark's mind that she could hardly hold a single thought for more than a moment. And then—then it came to her. As she thought of her mother—of her mother's photograph hidden in the trunk at the foot of her bed—she thought of something her mother had once told her.

All outlaws have tender egos, her mother had said. They'd been talking of her father. It was a time long after her father was gone, and her mother had been explaining that one of the reasons he was captured was because someone had called him yellow—called him a coward for not having the guts to kill another lawman. *It's their weakness,* she could hear her mother's voice whispering in her mind. *It's their Achilles' heel. Every outlaw meets his end because of his own arrogance and pride.*

"I see you for what you really are now, Mr. Kane," Lark said. She was astonished in hearing the words coming from her own mouth. Yet she couldn't allow Lizzy to linger in the monster's grasp; she couldn't allow Slater to return to an outlaw's well-laid trap.

"And what's that?" Samson Kane chuckled.

"A coward."

Samson Kane's smile broadened. "You plannin' on gettin' my dander up so I'll be distracted when yer lover comes ridin' in?"

Lark shook her head. "No. I'm just telling you the truth of what I see. What kind of outlaw hides behind children? I know my father never did. He never put me between himself and danger. He put me in danger maybe . . . but never between himself and danger the way you're doing."

"Yer father?" Samson Kane asked.

"Yes," Lark said. "Eddie Dean Wakley . . . he was my father. Perhaps you knew him. He died in Yuma prison."

Samson Kane smiled and began to chuckle.

"Yer Eddie Dean's girl?" he asked. Lark's stomach churned with nausea, for Samson

Kane's obvious delight in finding out her father was Eddie Dean Wakley seemed proof enough that the two outlaws had known each other. Samson Kane chuckled. "Why, I know'd Eddie Dean. I killed him for beatin' me at a game of cards. He weren't cheatin' or nothin' . . . but it made me mighty angry. So I killed him. It weren't no easy task neither. Eddie Dean Wakley was one tough ol' hombre."

Lark tried not to allow her emotions to show in her expression. It bothered her to know her father, even for the bad outlaw he had been, had died over such a small thing as a game of cards. Furthermore, she loathed Samson Kane all the more for being the one who had killed him. Still, she remained, for all outward appearances, unmoved.

"Well, whether you killed him or not, he was a better man than you . . . a better outlaw too," Lark said. "My father would never have hidden behind a little girl."

Samson Kane chuckled, but his eyes narrowed. "You cause a lot of trouble for ol' Marshal Evans," he said. "Leastways, that's what Chet Leigh said."

"Chet Leigh is a coward too," Lark told him. "It's no wonder the two of you partnered up— two cowards . . . hiding behind children."

Lizzy cried out as Samson Kane flung her aside to take hold of Lark by the throat.

The stench of his breath nearly caused Lark to lose the contents of her stomach. She rather wished she would—rather liked the idea of vomiting on Samson Kane.

"Now . . . don't you go provokin' me too far there, woman," Samson Kane growled into her face. "It'll hurt Slater Evans to see you layin' on this floor with your throat slit . . . as much as it will to see me cut yer gullet while he's watchin' me do it. So even though I want to see his face when I kill you . . . I won't wait to do it if you keep peckin' at me like you're doin'.

"Now," Samson Kane said, maneuvering Lark's body until she sat with her back against his chest, his hand at her throat and his knife held at her bosom. "Let's you and me get comfortable. It won't take long for Marshal Evans to ride on back after he's saved that fool boy's skin."

"He's in the house, boss," Eldon whispered as Slater bent over him. "I-I think he near clean cut my arm off here."

Slater looked at the massive knife wound at Eldon's shoulder. In truth, he wondered if the cowboy would survive the wound. Still, there was hope—more hope than there had been for Grady. Grady's throat had been cut ear-to-ear.

"I'm sorry, Eldon," Slater whispered. "All this is comin' down because of me."

"All this is comin' down because there's outlaws like Samson Kane, boss," Eldon said. "Men like you . . . they're the only reason we ain't overrun with 'em."

Slater nodded, trying to believe what Eldon was saying.

"I'm goin' in through the window Johnny come out of," he whispered to Tom. "You get 'round under the kitchen window and wait for me."

"He's got a gun or a knife to somebody's head, Slater. You know he does," Tom whispered.

"I know," Slater said. "But in the end . . . he wants to kill me. He don't wanna hurt one of them and risk gettin' my temper riled."

"I hope you're right," Tom said.

"Me too," Slater whispered. He knew Samson Kane—at least he thought he did. Samson Kane might think about hurting Lark, Katherine, or the children in order to provoke Slater, but he'd think better of it, knowing anger would only make Slater stronger instead of rendering him debilitated.

Quietly, Slater climbed in through the window of Johnny and Charlie's room. He could hear voices—Samson Kane's and Lark's. Though he wanted nothing more than to bolt into the kitchen, shoot Samson Kane, and take Lark in his arms, he knew he had to be careful—to listen.

"I could stab this boy and put him clean out of his misery," Samson Kane said, taking his knife

408

from Lark's bosom and holding it over Ralston's body. "He's gonna die anyway . . . one way or the other. I might as well stick this blade through his heart and make it quick."

"No!" Katherine cried, hugging her children. "You let him be!"

But Samson Kane chuckled, pressing the tip of the knife to Ralston's shirt over his heart.

As Samson Kane's grip lessened at her throat, Lark didn't pause but snatched the opportunity to quickly leap from his grasp.

"Get back here, woman!" Samson Kane shouted, rising to his feet.

Lark didn't pause, however, and raced to the opposite side of the kitchen. Samson Kane made to follow her, but Katherine reached from under the table and took hold of his ankle, tripping him.

"I'll deal with you later," the outlaw growled, pointing to Katherine with the long blade of his knife.

Katherine's intervention allowed Lark time to reach into one of the kitchen drawers, however— the drawer housing the kitchen knives. She picked up the largest knife in the drawer and turned to see Samson Kane striding toward her. The outlaw was furious, lumbering toward her and wielding his deadly blade. Inhaling a deep breath, Lark took hold of the blade of the knife she held, hurling it at the outlaw. Samson Kane hollered as the knife hit him square in the chest. It hadn't killed him, but it surprised him, and he stumbled backward.

"Why, you little . . ." Samson Kane mumbled as he reeled toward Lark.

"Slater!" Lark cried as she saw Slater burst into the room, his rifle leveled at the outlaw.

Samson Kane whirled around, simultaneously throwing his own knife. Though Slater had had his rifle leveled at the outlaw, he raised his arm to shield his body from the knife. Samson Kane's blade buried itself into Slater's forearm as Samson Kane drew his pistol. But before he could trigger his gun, however, Slater pulled the knife from his forearm, throwing it at the outlaw as Tom burst through the front door.

The blade of Samson Kane's deadly Arkansas toothpick buried itself into its owner's chest next to the kitchen knife Lark had thrown—buried itself in Samson Kane's heart.

Samson Kane gasped—stumbled backward. As he lost his grip on the pistol, it clattered to the floor.

"Marshal Evans," Samson Kane breathed, pulling the knife from his chest, "I ain't goin' back to Yuma prison."

As Samson Kane lunged, Slater drew his pistol, shooting the charging outlaw between the eyes as Tom leveled his rifle at his back.

As Samson Kane fell dead to the floor, Slater spun his pistol back into the holster at his thigh.

"You got that right, outlaw," he said. "You sure enough got that right."

Lark stood frozen, unable to move. Lizzy and Charlie scrambled from beneath the table and into Tom's arms. Katherine too left the safety of the table, gasping and sobbing as Eldon Pickering stumbled into the room then.

Lark remained stunned by what had transpired—stunned by the amount of blood on Eldon, Ralston, and Slater.

Slater was there then—there and holding her in his arms.

"I love you," he whispered against her ear. "I love you, Lark."

Lark burst into tears of residual terror, of relief, of unmeasured joy.

"I love you," she cried as he took her face in his hands.

He kissed her—kissed her hard and passionately. The warm moisture of his mouth served to revive her—to breathe hope and wonderment into her once more.

"It's all right, babies," Lark heard Tom saying. "It's all right."

"Where's Johnny?" Katherine asked.

Unwillingly, Lark allowed Slater to break the seal of their lips.

His eyes never left hers, however, as he said, "He's fine, Kate. Though I suppose one of us oughta go back and give him a ride home."

A thundering that had begun in the distance now moved closer. Eldon looked out the kitchen window.

"Riders," he said. "About five of 'em."

Lark's heart leapt with returning fear for a moment until Eldon added, "They got badges, and Johnny's ridin' with one of 'em."

A moment later, five United States marshals stepped into the house, guns drawn.

The lead marshal looked to the dead outlaw on the floor. "Would that be Samson Kane then?" he asked.

"Yep," Slater said.

The marshal looked to Slater, smiled, and offered a hand.

"Are you Marshal Evans?" he asked.

"Yep."

"I'm mighty honored to meet you," the man said. "Legends ain't easy to come by."

"Thank you," Slater said. The other marshals mumbled their admiration as well, shaking Slater's hand before going to inspect the dead outlaw. Yet Slater never let go of Lark, keeping one arm at her waist, even for the blood from the wound at his arm.

"Johnny!" Katherine exclaimed as Johnny burst into the room then.

Lark wept as she watched Johnny embrace his mother, his sister, and his brother.

"I oughta skin you alive for runnin' off like

that!" Katherine scolded even as she kissed her boy over and over again.

"Looks like the world is finally rid of Samson Kane," the lead marshal said, smiling at Slater. "The boy says you shot his partner too?"

Slater nodded. "I'll point ya to him . . . but I got me a couple of cowboys here that need some doctorin'. I'll see to my friends, or the boy can take one of you out to collect Chet Leigh."

The marshal glanced to Ralston and then Eldon.

"We'll help ya haul these boys to town," the man said.

"I'd appreciate it."

Tom chuckled, shaking his head as he studied the dead outlaw. "Ol' Matilda would have a fit if she seen the mess you made in here today, Slater," he said.

Slater smiled and nodded. "I don't doubt it. She's probably rollin' in her grave right this minute."

Lark watched as the marshals dragged Samson Kane's body out of the house—as they carried Ralston outside—as Katherine wrapped Eldon's arm with her apron.

Slater reached up, ripping the sleeve from his shirt and using it to roughly bind his own wound. Johnny sat on the floor, hugging Lizzy and Charlie.

Lark was astonished by the resilience of youth —by how quickly terror could be squelched

413

when safety had returned. Once the bodies of Samson Kane and Grady were moved, once Eldon and Ralston were bandaged and loaded in the wagon to head for town, Charlie and Lizzy and even Johnny lingered in sitting at the table with their mother. They still trembled now and again —still needed Katherine's reassuring touch—yet their eyes were bright once more. It seemed that the fear that had hung heavy over them for the past few days had vanished. Slater had vanquished it by killing Samson Kane. Brutal as the morning had been, the sun was bright, and fear was gone.

Lark glanced from where Katherine and the children sat at the table to where Slater and Tom stood talking to the posse of marshals. She smiled when she saw that Slater was staring at her—his eyes smoldering with admiration and desire.

"You coulda got yerself killed, provokin' Samson Kane like that," he told her. Lark smiled as she saw the residual fear in his eyes—the true and boundless love there. "You knew I'd come for you. I was in the other room and heard you provokin' Kane. Why did you take such a risk when ya knew I'd come for ya?"

Lark reached up and placed a hand to his cheek. He was so handsome. Oh, how she loved him! How thoroughly, wholly, and desperately she loved him!

"Because I did know you'd come for me . . . and that he'd try to kill you when you did," she told him.

A deep moan sounded in Slater's throat as he pulled Lark into his arms and kissed her. Lark heard the understanding chuckles of Tom and the posse of United States marshals that were looking on, but she didn't care. She wasn't shy or embarrassed. In fact, she continued to return Slater's delicious, impassioned kiss—returned it with fully as much driven desire and vigor as Slater used in administering it.

It wasn't until Lizzy scolded, "Shame on you, Uncle Slater!" that Lark smiled as Slater chuckled and pulled his mouth from hers.

"Let's get these cowboys patched up and see to poor Grady," he said. He grimaced as he brushed Lark's cheek with the back of his hand. "That boy gave his life for all of us." He looked to Tom. "I think he deserves a place in the family cemetery . . . next to Matilda."

"Yes, he does," Tom said. "Yes, he does."

"In the meantime," Slater began.

Lark's body erupted with goose bumps as he put his lips to her ear and whispered, "Are you gonna marry me today so I can keep you in my bed tonight?"

Lark felt the blush rise to her cheeks—felt a mad rush of delight and desire fill her bosom.

"Uncle Slater!" Lizzy scolded again. "What're

you sayin' to make Miss Lark blush so? She's as red as a tomata!"

Slater chuckled and looked to Lizzy.

"I'm just askin' her if she'll marry me today so that I can keep her in my—" he began.

Lark's hand over his mouth silenced him, however, and he chuckled.

"Oh!" Lizzy squealed, clapping her hands together. "Are you gonna marry him, Miss Lark? Oh, please do! I know it's been an awful mornin'—I'm still shakin'—but, oh, do please marry him."

Lark blushed, entirely aware of the five United States marshals looking on, of Eldon Pickering, of Tom and Katherine and the children.

"Of course she'll marry him," Tom said, smiling. "After all, it's why she came here . . . ain't it?"

Lark blushed redder still yet sighed with joy as Slater kissed her once more.

"Well?" he asked.

"Of course I'll marry you," she managed to answer. "After all . . . it is why I came here, isn't it?"

Slater laughed and gathered her into his arms. "Yes, it is, baby. Yes, it is."

Lark smiled—sighed with perfect joy and contentment as Slater kissed the back of her neck as she lay in his arms.

Running her hand gently over his bandaged arm, she asked, "How does it feel?"

"What?" he asked, pulling her body tightly against his and kissing the back of her neck once more.

"Your arm, silly," she explained. Slater was warm—oh, so warm—and in his arms, Lark felt more secure than she ever had in her entire life.

"Oh, that," he said. "I plum forgot about it. It's fine."

Lark giggled and squirmed in his embrace until she lay facing him.

"You forgot about it?" she asked. "How could you forget about it?"

Slater shrugged his broad shoulders and buried a hand in her soft, loose hair.

"You make me forget everything painful or unhappy," he said. He smiled. "Right now . . . I could even forget that I'm a beat-up ol' lawman and you're just a spring daffodil."

"You're a handsome lawman, and I'm plenty weathered to keep up with you," she whispered, breaking into goose bumps as his hand caressed her shoulder.

"Oh, are ya now?" he teased.

"Yes," she giggled.

His smile broadened. "Well, then . . . how about you and me round up our own herd and move up north a ways . . . leave Tom, Katherine, and the children to runnin' this place?"

Lark smiled—yet simultaneously frowned. Although she liked the idea of being alone with Slater—of being entirely secluded with her husband—she was worried about the others. Slater was their leader, the rope that tied them all together. If she selfishly stripped him away, how would they manage?

"You're not worried about everyone else?" she asked.

"I do . . . some," he admitted. "But Tom's capable of runnin' the ranch. He can hire on more cowboys if he needs to. All I know is I want you to myself . . . all to myself. I'm tired of sharin' your attention. I want you all to myself."

"I want you all to myself too," Lark confessed as he kissed her.

"Then you'll run away with me . . . up north to a place of our own, Mrs. Evans?" he asked. His voice was low, alluring—entirely bewitching. He owned her will, and Lark suspected he knew it.

"Of course," she breathed against his mouth. "After all . . . it is why I came here, isn't it?"

Slater pulled her snugly against the powerful warmth of his body. "Yes, it is, baby," he mumbled as he kissed her. "Yes, it is."

Author's Note

Fifteen years ago I wanted to send something special to one of my closest friends (Sandy) for her upcoming birthday. Unable to think of any sort of original or clever gift to give, I decided to write a story—a story specifically written for Sandy. I had been writing here and there for a while—one or two short stories a year, which I would then copy to give as Christmas presents to a very few close friends and family members. Yet Sandy had always been at the top of my list to receive new stories—as well as being my most encouraging friend when it came to writing. Therefore, I hoped she would enjoy a story written just for her.

However, in true "Marcia" form, I had waited until the last minute to be hit by both the inspiration to write a story for Sandy as well as the actual idea for a story. I had three small children, was in that crazy (but most beloved and cherished) "young mother with too many things to do" phase of my life, and couldn't see how I could possibly manage to write a story for Sandy's birthday. Her birthday is March 7, you see—and I was hit with the inspiration approximately March 1. I'm not exaggerating.

There was only one thing to do—beg for

Kevin's help! Thus, I asked Kevin if he thought he could entertain the kids for an entire day while I wrote a story for Sandy. Being the kind and heroic hunk of burnin' love that he is, he agreed —and I was excited to know that I was going to have an entire day to write! At the time, an entire day dedicated to writing was an inconceivable concept to me. Usually I had to steal ten minutes here, half an hour there, or get up at four AM to have maybe a solid hour or so to write. So the concept of having an entire day was fairly unfathomable.

Yes, Kevin had gifted me an entire day so that I might write a gift to Sandy (whom he loves too— after all, our only daughter is named after her). Thus, early in the morning, a few days before Sandy's birthday in March of 1995, I grabbed the big white flour bucket I used for a desk chair, sat myself down at the computer, and began to write a story entitled *Weathered Too Young*. Twelve hours later, I'd finished. The inscription read: "To My Bosom Friend, Sandy, In Honor of Your 30th Birthday." For a cover, the book (rather manuscript) boasted a picture from the front of a card Sandy and I had each purchased for one another in college—the picture of a dark-haired, blue-eyed, gorgeous man that we'd gasped and giggled over when we'd found him in the card store in downtown Rexburg, Idaho, eleven years before. I scrawled *Weathered Too Young* across the Xerox of the hot-guy card, gift wrapped the manuscript, slid it into an envelope, and mailed it the next morning. Sandy loved the story (at least she claimed to at the time—she still claims to). I let several friends read it over the years, but *Weathered Too Young* remained fairly exclusive until eight years later, when it was released to the public as an e-book.

Just before *Weathered Too Young* was released in e-book form, I did take the opportunity to make some subtle changes. When I began writing, I couldn't always think of character names I liked at first. Now the names are usually synonymous with the birth of the character, but it didn't used to happen that way for me in the beginning. Therefore, I would often simply plug in any old name—just to get me through until the character whispered their real name to me. This was definitely the case with *Weathered Too Young*. Short on time, I'd originally named Lark Lawrence "Lori." Slater was actually Billy (William Slater), and Tom was Sammy. Being that I had to send the book immediately after writing it, I never had the chance to change the names as I'd wanted to. Therefore, just before the e-book version of *Weathered Too Young* was released, I did change some names. Now, as you may have noticed (if you read the original e-book version), I also made some name changes along the way while rewriting *Weathered Too Young* into a novel. Jack became Hadley, and Katherine's last name was changed from Thatcher to Thornquist (because she's not at all related to Reese Thatcher from *An Old-Fashioned Romance,* and I didn't want anyone to be confused).

I'm going to pause here and share an absolutely unnecessary tidbit. As I was rewriting *Weathered Too Young,* I became curious as to whether Samson Kane's name had actually been Samson Kane in that original manuscript. I thought it had been but wasn't sure since I don't even have a copy of that original story. (You know how you make something for somebody but never make one for yourself? That's what happened here. I found the same thing to be true of cross-stitching many years ago—though, for me, it never seems to be true where cookies and cake is concerned.) Therefore, I picked up the phone and called the person who I knew did have the only original manuscript—my best friend, college roommate, and inspiration in so many ways—Sandy.

"Was Samson Kane's name really Samson Kane in that original book I wrote for you?" I asked.

"Well, let me grab it and see. I have it right here!" Sandy exclaimed. Sandy began to thumb through the old manuscript—the one I'd written so long ago—the one I'd signed "Lolita Ce de Baca," which is still my pseudonym of choice (I plan to write under it again someday).

"Hmmm," she said. "Let me see. Oh, here it is!"

(Now this is the funny part. I'm going to type Sandy's exact words here because she made a verbal typo—not unlike many typos I'm well-known for—only this one cracked me up!)

"Ah, yes," she began, "Here we go. It says, 'Lori turned to see Samson Kane running lamely yet intently toward them, wielding his enormous wife.'"

Instantly, I was undone! I laughed so hard my back hurt, and I couldn't catch my breath.

"Oh!" she giggled. "Wait, I mean . . . wielding his enormous *knife!*" she corrected. Too late. We were roaring—really busting a gut.

(Which reminds me of the time my little six-year-old nephew was sitting in the backseat of my sister's van watching *Jumanji*. My sister and her kids had just picked me up from the Atlanta airport, and I had brought *Jumanji* for them to watch on the two-hour trip home. The scene with all the rhinoceroses running through town came on, and my little nephew (who then had trouble saying his Rs) exclaims, "Oh no, Auntie! A herd of stampeding winos!" I had a sudden vision of a crowd of inebriated men racing through the streets and nearly laughed myself into a visit to the hospital! Next time you're feeling a little blue, just visualize herds of stampeding winos and villains wielding their enormous wives. It's good for the soul, ain't it?)

Anyway, back to my original venue of useless

babble—the novel version of *Weathered Too Young*. I became curious awhile back, being that I could hardly remember the story of *Weathered Too Young*—as to exactly how it played out. So I printed a copy, sat down, and read it. Instantly, I was agitated. I felt like I'd read a condensed version of something! I mean, the characters had so much more to say. More importantly, Slater and Lark had so much more kissing to do! Sure, the e-book was fun—a quick and easy read, a zippy little escape into romance—but there was so much more! I couldn't sleep that night. I knew I had to rewrite it—tell more of the story. Furthermore, certain events had been somewhat misrepresented in the original book, being that'd I'd written it so fast. Thus they too were corrected.

As you may or may not know, an e-book is usually a story that is haunting me, begging to be told, keeping me awake at night. Yet often I'm in the midst of one story or novel when inspiration for another story hits. Thus, I'll pause—take the time to write the e-book so that my mind can let it go and my friends can have a "quick fix" to read. Readers really enjoy e-books, and I like knowing that a story won't be lost while it waits its turn to be told. However, once in awhile, an e-book will begin to haunt me after a while— begging for attention once more, demanding to be lengthened into a novel. This is exactly what happened with *Weathered Too Young*. I couldn't focus on anything else. I was driven to "flesh out" the story—to let the reader linger in watching Slater and Lark's relationship develop—to lengthen their passionate moments. And so I silently screamed, "Stop the presses!" I pushed aside the project I had been working on, for *Weathered Too Young* needed a broader voice.

(Blah, blah, blah! Are you thinking, "Sheesh, Marcia! Is there ever one organized, concise thought in your brain?")

Of course, the novel *Weathered Too Young* belongs to Sandy just as the e-book did—just as that original manuscript did. So does the sequel to *Weathered Too Young*—*The Windswept Flame* —as well as another little story you may have read entitled *Daydreams*. Twenty-six years after meeting, Sandy is still the first person I send a story to or send the individual chapters to as I'm writing. I still depend on her affirmation of a story—her approval of it. Sandy—the truest friend—a cherished friendship. In truth, I can't imagine what my life would have been like without her.

As one final little ditty into my weirdness, I did call and ask Sandy to tell me everything about the original title pages on that old manuscript.

She said, "You did! You wrote 'Weathered Too Young' in your handwriting, and then you put the picture of that totally hot hairy-chest guy we had hanging in our dorm at Ricks. And then in tiny handwriting, you signed it 'Lolita Ce de Baca'!"

I thought you might get a kick out of it, knowing me as you do. So I further imposed on Sandy and asked her to e-mail me the exact text of the original title pages. In Sandy's own words, here's how the first few pages of the original manuscript read:

"Title Page—Handsome guy with too much chest hair up to his chin and incredibly blue eyes is the picture on the cover. In your handwriting it says 'Weathered Too Young' above the picture and at the bottom it says 'By: Lolita Ce de Baca.' Turn the page and it says . . . 'Weathered Too Young.' Turn the page and it says, at the bottom, 'Copyright 1995 by Marcia . . . /Lolita Ce de Baca (and then in italics) Weathered Too Young is one volume of the (italics here again) Ridiculous Romance Rubbish series by Lolita Ce de Baca.' Turn the page and it says . . .

'To My Bosom Friend, Sandy, In Honor of Your 30th Birthday'

Turn the page and Chapter 1 starts . . ."

Every story I write holds a special place in my heart, but *Weathered Too Young* is unique because of the meandering path it wandered in becoming a novel. Oh, I know I tend to babble on nonsensically, but I hope you enjoyed this little insight into the history of *Weathered Too Young*. I hope you enjoy knowing that twenty-six years ago two silly girls found true and everlasting friendship as they danced and sang and laughed their way through college—that anytime they're together, they still dance and sing and laugh . . .

Weathered Too Young Trivia Snippets

Snippet #1—Shortly before I wrote *Weathered Too Young*, I was expecting a rare visit from Sandy. She lived in Farmington, New Mexico, at the time and was coming down for a couple of days. I was so excited—so I made a sign to put at the end of our street to greet her. With my sign and duct tape in hand, I walked down to the end of the street to attach the sign to the street sign at the corner. A huge walking stick cactus was growing very near the street sign, and although I was aware of it initially, I sort of forgot about it. As I stepped back from attaching the welcome sign to the street sign, my right thigh brushed up against the cactus. Oh my heck! I could never have imagined the pain! The house was maybe a block or two away, and by the time I got home and stripped off my jeans, only about a quarter of an inch of the cactus needles were still visible above my flesh! The other three-quarters of an inch of each needle had worked their way deep into my muscle (or fat—whichever way you want to look at it—probably muscle back then though). I had to use the pliers to pull the cactus needles out, and the bruising and soreness they left—unbelievable! Thus, real life inspires fiction—and poor Lark!

Snippet #2—My mother once told me a story about a team of draft horses her father owned—Dolly and Coaly. They weren't Clydesdales, but they were a team nearly their entire lives. One day my grandpa took Coaly (and only Coaly) out to do something. Dolly was beside herself at being left behind! She was so upset, she bolted into a barbed wire fence, seriously wounding herself. Her legs and chest were severely lacerated. My mom remembers my grandpa using clothespins to hold her wounds closed until they started to heal. Dolly did heal, and she and Coaly worked as a team for many more years. I don't know which is which, but just for fun, here's a photo of Dolly and Coaly taken in approximately 1943. That's my grandpa with the lines and my mom and her baby sister beside him.

About the Author

Marcia Lynn McClure's intoxicating succession of novels, novellas, and e-books—including *The Visions of Ransom Lake*, *A Crimson Frost*, *The Pirate Ruse*, and *The Bewitching of Amoretta Ipswich*—has established her as one of the most favored and engaging authors of true romance. Her unprecedented forte in weaving captivating stories of western, medieval, regency, and contemporary amour void of brusque intimacy has earned her the title "The Queen of Kissing."

Marcia, who was born in Albuquerque, New Mexico, has spent her life intrigued with people, history, love, and romance. A wife, mother, grandmother, family historian, poet, and author, Marcia Lynn McClure spins her tales of splendor for the sake of offering respite through the beauty, mirth, and delight of a worthwhile and wonderful story.

Center Point Large Print
600 Brooks Road / PO Box 1
Thorndike, ME 04986-0001 USA

(207) 568-3717

US & Canada:
1 800 929-9108
www.centerpointlargeprint.com